OBSESSION

OBSESSION

A NOVEL

KATHI MILLS-MACIAS

BROADMAN
& HOLMAN
PUBLISHERS

Nashville, Tennessee

Published by Broadman & Holman Publishers, Nashville, Tennessee

0-8054-2149-1

Dewey Decimal Classification: 813
Subject Heading: MYSTERY—FICTION
Library of Congress Card Catalog Number: 00-060822

Unless otherwise stated all Scripture citation is from the New King
James Version, copyright © 1979, 1980, 1982,
Thomas Nelson, Inc., Publishers.

Library of Congress Cataloging-in-Publication Data
Mills-Macias, Kathi, 1948–
    Obsession : a novel / Kathi Mills-Macias.
        p. cm.
        ISBN 0-8054-2149-1
        1. Young women—Fiction. 2. Fathers—Death—Fiction.
3. Accident victims—Fiction. 4. Police—Fiction. I. Title.
    PS3563.I42319 O27 2001
    813'.54—dc21

00-060822

CIP

4 5 6 7 8 9 10 05 04 03 02

DEDICATION

To Yeshua,
the faithful Lover of my soul,
and to my husband, Al,
the love of my life. . . .

ACKNOWLEDGMENTS

A note of thanks to the many people who worked with me, prayed for me, and inspired me during the unfolding of this book:

To Dave and Becky Bellis, who generously gave of their time and expertise in the development of *Obsession*'s proposal.

To my agent and friend, Lawrence Jordan, who continues to impress upon me that God's purposes will be accomplished "in the fullness of time."

To my "eagle-eye" proofreaders: Detective Doug Lane, Laurel West, and Jane Hall.

And, finally, to the wonderful people at Broadman & Holman, particularly editorial staff members Vicki Crumpton and Kim Overcash. (I hope you got a finder's fee, Kim!)

Many blessings to you all.

CHAPTER 1

The ringing phone was no surprise to Toni Matthews. It was, in fact, just one more interruption to an already long and frustrating day. Yet, in some ways, Toni welcomed the distraction. Having thrown herself into the business at hand in an effort to forget the aching in her heart, she wondered if she would ever make sense out of the mountains of paperwork staring her in the face. *And what if I do?* she asked herself as she reached for the phone. *Even if I finally manage to figure out what to do with all this . . . mess . . . then what?*

She took a deep breath and tried to focus. "Matthews and Matthews Detective Agency, Toni Matthews speaking. May I help you?"

The brief pause was followed by a soft, hesitant voice, obviously that of an elderly woman. "Matthews Detective Agency? Matthews and Matthews?"

Toni suppressed an impatient sigh as she ran her fingers through her short blonde curls. "Yes," she answered. "This is Toni Matthews. How can I help you?"

Another pause. "I . . . I'm calling about Julie Greene, my . . . granddaughter. Is . . . Mr. Matthews available? He knows all about her case."

Hot tears stung her eyes as Toni swallowed the unwelcome lump in her throat. "No," she managed to choke out. "Mr. Matthews is not available. He's . . . deceased. This is his daughter, and I'm taking care of his affairs. I'll be happy to help you if I can, Mrs. . . ."

"Lippincott. April Lippincott. Oh, my dear, I'm so sorry! I had no idea. How did it happen? When?"

Toni sighed. One more client who hadn't read the local obituary columns in the last few weeks. One more explanation to give. One more contract to refer to another agency. She cradled the phone against her shoulder and rubbed her pounding temples. "I'm sorry, Mrs. Lippincott. Let me take your address and mail you a letter explaining the situation. I'm in the process of doing that with all my father's clients. It may take a week or so because Lorraine—my father's secretary—quit about a month ago, just before he . . . just before his heart attack. So I'm filling in. I'll get those letters out in the next few days. Would that be all right?"

"Oh, certainly, my dear. Of course. But . . ." There was that annoying pause again. "It's just that your father was . . . so close to finding my Julie. He was supposed to get back to me a couple of weeks ago and he . . . he seemed so sure of having news for me by then."

Stifling another sigh, Toni grabbed a pen. "I'm sure he was, Mrs. Lippincott. And I'm sure that whatever information he may have found out about your granddaughter is in her file. Let me get that letter off to you with some agency referrals and an explanation of how to obtain the necessary files from my father's office. Now, is that Lippincott with one t or two?"

Finished at last, Toni hung up the phone and looked around at the small but comfortable office. Paul Matthews was never one for decorating. In fact, since his wife, Marilyn, had died of cancer twelve years earlier, little about the familiar two-room business had changed. It was as if Toni's mother were still here, working alongside her husband in the detective agency they had started together soon after they were married. Paul had set up his desk and files in this back room and had done all the agency's field work. Marilyn had her desk in the front office and had served as bookkeeper, secretary, and receptionist. Together they poured over cases, searching for over-looked clues, sometimes late into the night. When Marilyn died, leaving Paul to care for two-year-old Melissa as well as fourteen-year-old Toni, he had resolved to keep the agency going and to retain the name of Matthews and Matthews, hoping that one or both of his daughters would one day join him in the business.

Now, twelve years later, Paul was gone too, having died of a heart attack while on a fishing trip just three weeks earlier. Suddenly Toni, the older of the two remaining Matthews family members, was forced to face the decision she had wrestled with for years. With graduation less than a month behind her and a fresh master's degree in literature under her belt, should she fulfill her father's dream of keeping the detective agency going? She had, after all— strictly in an effort to please him—obtained the necessary license to do so. But now, with her father gone, should she put the agency up for sale and pursue her own dreams of settling down and marrying her fiancé, Brad Anderson; teaching part-time at the local college while she attempted to develop the writing career she had longed for since she was a little girl? Thanks to her dad's prudent financial planning, Toni had the financial means to take her time in making that decision.

She shook her head. *Enough of this daydreaming and feeling sorry for yourself,* she scolded silently. *There's work to do—and lots of it. The first thing is to take care of that client before she shows up on the doorstep wanting to know what's taking so long. What was her name again? Lippincott, April Lippincott, asking about her missing granddaughter,*

Julie Greene, and wanting to see her file. Guess I'd better see what I can find out about this girl before I start on anything else.

The phone rang again. Toni looked at it and decided to let the call go on the answering machine. If it was Brad, she'd hear his voice and pick up. Anyone else could wait. Rising from her chair, she walked over to the gray metal filing cabinet, ignoring the slightly agitated male voice on the answering machine wanting to know who would be taking over the agency's current cases. As Toni pulled out the top drawer marked "Active Cases," the machine beeped, signaling the end of the message. Even as her fingers walked through the files looking for Julie Greene's name, a smile tugged at her lips. *Only my dad would insist on keeping his files in this antiquated metal cabinet. No matter how hard I tried, I could never get him to even consider a computer.* "Your mother and I bought this office furniture together," he had explained to her many times. "And she set up the filing system. It worked just fine for us then, and it'll work just fine as long as I'm here to keep this office going."

Toni's smile disappeared, and the ache in her heart, as well as the pounding in her head, returned at the reminder of her father's sudden death. Pulling up Julie Greene's file, she shuffled back to the desk and plunked down in the worn leather chair. Reaching into the top right drawer, she rummaged around for a bottle of aspirin, gave up, and then opened the file. Toni gasped at the picture of the pretty young girl staring back at her. The long, curly blonde hair, the wide blue eyes, the tentative smile . . . she knew she was looking at a recent picture of Julie Greene, and yet it could almost have been a picture of herself ten years earlier. Toni wondered what her father must have thought when he first saw the picture of this runaway teenager from Colorado.

Taking a deep breath, she began to turn the pages. Suddenly the words on a piece of scrap paper, written in bright red ink—obviously her father's handwriting—jumped out at her: "Eagle Lake, 6 A.M., Wednesday."

Toni's headache was forgotten. *Eagle Lake? But that's where Dad was when . . . Why would he have put a note about Eagle Lake in Julie Greene's file? And Wednesday? That was the day of his heart attack. Could it have been the same Wednesday? What was supposed to happen at six o'clock on Wednesday morning at Eagle Lake that could possibly have involved both Julie Greene and my dad?* Frowning, she began to read through the file. Just who was this Julie Greene anyway? Was there a connection between Julie and Paul Matthews's trip to the lake? If so, did it have something to do with Mrs. Lippincott's assertions that Toni's father was about to close in on Julie's whereabouts?

"Miss Matthews? Excuse me, are you Toni Matthews?"

Toni jumped as the voice penetrated her concentration. Snapping her head up, her blue eyes opened wide at the sight of the tall, broad-shouldered man standing beside her desk, his gray sport shirt open at the collar. From the expression on his face, he appeared almost as startled as Toni.

The young man with the dark eyes and dark, wavy hair cleared his throat. "Are you Toni Matthews?"

Toni found her voice. "Yes, I am. How can I help you?"

"I'm Abe . . . Abe Matthews." He smiled. "No relation, of course."

Toni frowned, ignoring his attempt at humor. "Abe Matthews?" She shook her head. "I'm sorry, but . . . should I know you?"

The concern on his face was obvious. "No, not at all. It's just that I knew your father—not well, of course. . . . Actually, I'm a detective with the River View Police Department, and your father and I met when a couple of our investigations crossed paths, and . . . I was shocked when I heard about his death. In fact, I was at his funeral—not that I'd expect you to remember that, with all those people there and all that was going on, and also with the way you must have been feeling, but—"

"You knew my father?"

He nodded. "Yes. Of course, as I said, I didn't know him well, but we had talked a few times, and . . . anyway, that doesn't matter right now. I was just driving by and thought I'd take a chance and see if your father's secretary was in. I have something of his that I wanted to return, but I didn't feel right bothering you at home so soon after . . ."

His voice trailed off as Toni noticed the book in his hand. "You have something that belonged to my father?"

He held out the book. "It . . . might sound silly, but it's a book on fly fishing. Your dad and I both have—*had*—a passion for fishing, as you know. . . . Well, as you know about *him*. Anyway, we got to talking about fishing one day and he lent me this book just before he went on his vacation. I was going to return it to him when he got back, but . . ."

Toni stood up and reached out to take the book. "Thank you, Detective Matthews. I appreciate your bringing it by."

"Abe," he said, placing the book in her outstretched hand. "Please . . . call me Abe, especially when I'm not on duty."

She was annoyed with herself for the flush she felt creeping up her neck and cheeks at the touch of his hand. "Yes, well, thank you again . . . Abe."

They stood silently for a moment until Abe cleared his throat and looked around. "So, where's the secretary? Irene, was it?"

"Lorraine. She quit suddenly, about a month ago. She hadn't been here very long, and she didn't really give any reason for leaving. My dad didn't have time to find anyone to take her place, so I filled in for him while he looked for someone, but then . . . he died. That's why I'm here now, trying to figure out what needs to be taken care of immediately, answering calls, referring contracts, things like that."

"Oh. Sure. There must be a lot of details to take care of and . . ." He cleared his throat again. "Have you . . . decided what you'll do with the agency? I mean, I assume you're going to sell it or . . .?"

Toni shrugged, suddenly feeling very tired. "I don't know," she said, her voice breaking as she fought tears. "I . . . really don't know . . . I . . ."

"I'm sorry. I shouldn't have asked. It's none of my business. It's just that your dad had mentioned how happy he was that you'd gotten your license and how he hoped you'd follow in his footsteps someday, so . . ."

The tears spilled over then as Toni's headache returned with a vengeance. She put her hand on the desk and leaned against it, still clutching the book in her other hand. "No. It's not your fault. Really. It's . . ."

Just as she wondered if her legs would give way, she felt his hands grasping her arms and helping her back to the chair. She collapsed into it and laid her head back with her eyes closed, tears slowly trickling down her cheeks. She was too weary even to be embarrassed by her uncharacteristic show of weakness.

"What can I do?" Abe asked, handing her a tissue from the box on the desk. "Can I call someone or get you something?"

"An aspirin. Please. My head is pounding."

In the couple of minutes it took Abe to retrieve some aspirin from his car, Toni had taken some deep breaths and managed to stop the tears. She gladly accepted the aspirin and the cup of water he brought her from the cooler in the front office.

As she swallowed the aspirin, Abe knelt beside her, his hand on the arm of her chair. "Is there anything else I can do? Someone you'd like me to call or . . ."

Toni shook her head. "No. I'll be fine. Really. I'm just a little tired. There's been so much . . ."

"I can imagine," Abe answered, his voice low. "I'm sorry if my coming here made it worse."

Impulsively, Toni laid her hand on his. "Not at all. I appreciate your bringing the book and—"

They both jumped when they heard the voice and realized they were not alone.

"Toni? What's going on here? Are you all right?"

Toni and Abe looked up at the figure framed in the doorway.

"Brad," Toni exclaimed as she and Abe rose to their feet. "I didn't hear you come in."

Brad raised his eyebrows. "I'm not surprised." He turned toward Abe. "I'm Brad Anderson, Toni's fiancé. And you are . . .?"

Abe stuck out his hand. "Abe Matthews," he said. "I was just—"

"Mr. Matthews is a police detective, and he was a friend of my dad's," Toni interrupted. "He was returning one of Dad's books."

"I see," said Brad, shaking Abe's hand. "That explains why you look familiar. I'm a lawyer, and I'm sure that in a town the size of River View we're bound to have run into each other a few times over the years. It's nice to meet you, Mr. Matthews."

"Yes, well, it's nice to meet you, too, Mr. Anderson." Abe looked at Toni. "Well, Miss . . . Matthews, I've got to run. I'm sorry if I disturbed you. . . ." Nodding his goodbye, he didn't wait for Toni to answer but stepped around Brad and hurried through the door into the outer office. Brad and Toni stared after him until they heard the front door close.

"What was that all about?"

Toni turned toward Brad. Dressed impeccably as always, his off-white summer suit complemented his pale blue shirt and navy tie. She was glad to see him. His familiarity comforted her. But the slight irritation on his face reminded her of how tired she was. She sat back down in her chair.

"He just stopped by to return that," she said, pointing to the book.

Brad picked it up. "Fly fishing?" He turned it over, examining it as if expecting to find some explanation. "I don't get it. He came to return a book about fly fishing?"

Toni nodded, running her fingers through her hair as she tried to pull herself together. "Yes. I guess he borrowed it from Dad."

"So this . . . detective . . . he and your dad were good friends?"

"They knew each other. How close they were, I don't know. He did mention that he'd been at Dad's funeral, but I can't say that I remember seeing him."

Brad raised his eyebrows. "Hmm. Another reason he looked familiar." He paused. "So I gather you two have never met before?"

"I don't believe so. Why?"

"No reason." Brad shrugged. "I thought maybe . . . I don't know; it just seemed as if you two knew each other."

Toni sighed. "No. Don't know him. Just met him today. Look, can we change the subject? I'm really tired. I think maybe I need to get out of here and go get something to eat."

Brad's face brightened. "Great idea. In fact, that's exactly why I'm here. How about an early dinner somewhere? A good steak might be just what you need."

"Oh no, I can't go out looking like this," Toni protested, looking down at her jeans and oversized pink shirt. "You're dressed for it, but I—"

"You look great," Brad insisted. "You always look great. Come on, let's go somewhere really nice. We can go by your place so you can change first if you want."

Toni shook her head. "Seriously, Brad, I really can't. I'm just too tired. Besides, Melissa will be home soon. She spent the night with Carrie last night, but she said she'd be home in time for dinner. Why don't you just come and eat with us? It'll be potluck, I'm afraid, but—"

Brad interrupted her. "I've got a better idea. Why don't we pick up some Chinese food on the way home? Melissa loves it, and that way nobody will have to cook or wash dishes."

Toni smiled, grateful for Brad's thoughtfulness. It was one of the many things she loved about him. "You've got a date. Just let me clear a few things off my desk. It won't take long."

As Toni stood and reached out to pick up the files and notes from her desk, she spotted the open file on top and remembered what it was that she had been so engrossed in reading when Abe Matthews had interrupted her.

"Julie Greene," she said, picking up the file. "Something's just not right about this."

"What's not right? Who's Judy Greene?"

"*Julie* Greene," she answered, pointing to the scrap of paper with the bright red notation. "Look at this."

Brad leaned over Toni's shoulder and read the note out loud. "Eagle Lake, 6 A.M., Wednesday." He straightened up and shrugged. "What's that supposed to mean?"

"I'm not sure," she said absently, still staring at the file. "But . . . that's where my dad was when he had his heart attack. Doesn't it seem a bit strange that this would be in one of Dad's client's files?"

Brad shrugged again. "Not necessarily. Just because that's where your dad was when . . ." His voice caught and Toni felt his hand on her shoulder. "Honey, there are all sorts of reasons why that notation could be in the file. Eagle Lake is a very popular place around here, you know."

Toni nodded and looked up at her fiancé. "I know," she said, her voice soft as she saw the compassion in his hazel eyes. A shock of sandy blond hair fell across his forehead, giving him a vulnerable look that belied the disciplined lawyer's mind that Toni so respected. In spite of herself, she smiled.

Brad's response was immediate. Leaning down, he kissed her gently. "You look exhausted. Come on, let's go get that Chinese food and head over to your place." He took the file from her hands and laid it on the desk, then lifted her to her feet and pulled her close, nuzzling her hair. His voice was husky. "There's nothing here that can't wait until tomorrow."

"Maybe," she murmured. "I suppose. But . . . there's still something strange about this Julie Greene case. A missing teenage girl from Colorado . . ." She lifted her head and looked up at Brad. "How did her case end up in my dad's office, way out here in the Northwest? And why was this girl's grandmother so sure that Dad was about to solve this thing? How does all that tie in with Eagle Lake? I thought Dad's cases were all pretty tame. You know, simple civil cases. He never got involved with anything criminal or dangerous. I just don't get it—"

Brad interrupted her with another kiss, then pulled back and gazed down at her. "You aren't supposed to get it," he said. "Just because you have a license doesn't mean you're a detective, remember? Your dad was the detective. These were his cases, not yours. All you're supposed to do is tie together some loose ends and refer his clients to other agencies so we can get on with our plans. I know it's too soon after losing your dad to set a wedding date, but you know I don't want to wait any longer than we have to. I'd been hoping for a summer wedding, but obviously that's not going to work. Maybe late fall or winter . . .?"

Toni opened her mouth to protest, but Brad placed a finger against her lips. "I know what you're going to say. I've heard the arguments before, and like I said, with what's just happened with your dad, we need to wait a while longer. But, Toni, I've already waited almost ten years!"

She took his wrist, raised his hand to her lips, and gently kissed his palm. "I know," she said. "I know you've waited a long time. You've been telling me since high school that you want to marry me. But there was college and graduate school for me, college and law school for you, and now there's Melissa to think of, besides taking care of Dad's affairs. There's just no time to plan a wedding right now."

"Toni, I've told you a million times. When we're married, I'll be thrilled to have Melissa living with us. She's almost as much of a kid sister to me as she is to you! And besides, we've both agreed we don't want a huge wedding—just something simple, with Pastor Michael officiating, some family and friends. . . . Toni, I don't want to downplay the importance of settling your dad's affairs and dealing with your own emotions, but . . . sooner or later, we've got to pin down a date, don't you think? And as much as I love Melissa, I'd really like to tie the knot before we're too old to think about having kids of our own."

Toni smiled. "So would I. You know I want that too. But—"

"But this is not the time to talk about it. OK, we'll discuss it later." He pulled back and glanced over at the desk. "For now, let's close that file and lock this place up for the night. It'll all be here waiting for you in the morning." Brad let her go and reached over to close Julie Greene's file. "There," he said. "You see how easy that was?" He took her arm and began to walk her toward the door. "Come on, my

stomach's growling. And knowing you, I'll bet you haven't eaten anything all day."

"Wait," Toni said, pulling away and returning to the desk. She
opened the bottom left-hand drawer and grabbed her purse. "Can't
leave without this." She took a step, then turned back once more.
"Think I'll just take this along for drill," she added, picking up the
Greene file and tucking it under her arm. When Brad rolled his eyes
at her, she grinned. "Well, Mr. Anderson, what are we waiting for?
Let's go. I'm starved!"

∾∾∾

Melissa was curled up on the worn floral-print couch, writing in
her journal, when they walked in. She looked up and brushed her long
auburn hair back from her face, a faint smile touching her lips when
she saw them. "Hi, guys," she said, her voice soft with a sadness that
broke Toni's heart. The loss of their father had taken a heavy toll on
the once bubbly teenager. Seeing the change in her little sister only
added to Toni's pain.

"Hi yourself," she said, forcing a cheerfulness into her voice and
hoping it was reflected in her face. "Glad you're back. Did you have a
good time at Carrie's?"

Melissa shrugged. "Sure. I guess so."

Brad walked over to the couch and bent over to kiss Melissa's
cheek. "Hey, kid," he said, holding up the bag of Chinese food.
"Brought you some almond chicken."

Her smile widened slightly. "My favorite. Thanks, Bro. You're the
best."

"That's what I've been trying to tell your sister," he said, turning to
walk toward the kitchen. "Maybe you can help me convince her of
that so she'll marry me!"

Melissa laughed and got up to follow Brad. "If she doesn't, I will,"
she assured him.

Toni couldn't help but notice that, even in jeans and a T-shirt, Melissa was beginning to look more like a young woman than a little girl. She breathed a prayer of thanks for Brad's ability to draw Melissa out of her shell. As she entered the bright, pleasant kitchen where she had spent so many hours of her life, the aroma of Chinese food began drifting up from the cartons Brad and Melissa were opening. "How about paper plates tonight?" she asked.

"Sounds good to me," said Brad.

"Absolutely," Melissa agreed. "And plastic forks too. Why wash dishes when we can just throw them away?"

Brad laughed. "A girl after my own heart. Maybe I should just go ahead and marry you instead of your sister."

"Maybe you should," said Toni, coming up behind them. "But I'm afraid you'd have to wait even longer for a wedding with Melissa than with me."

Brad turned and took the plates and forks from Toni, shaking his head. "I just can't win around here, can I?" He sighed loudly. "OK, OK. No more discussions about weddings. Let's eat this stuff before it gets cold."

They sat down around the old oak table that had been in their kitchen for as long as Toni could remember, then joined hands and bowed their heads.

"Thank you, Father," Brad prayed, "for your loving care and your provision for us. We ask you to bless this food, in Jesus' name. Amen."

Melissa grabbed the carton containing the almond chicken, while Toni and Brad pretended to fight each other over the sweet and sour pork. "Oh no, please, go ahead," Brad said, his voice dripping with martyrdom. "I'll wait. After all, I'm very good at waiting, you know."

Toni ignored him and scooped the food onto her plate, then passed the carton to Brad. "I saved you a little," she said, "just because you're *soooo* patient."

They continued to tease each other as they ate, keeping the conversation light and the mood playful. By the time they were finished, Toni was beginning to feel her strength returning.

"That was great," she said, reaching over to lay her hand on Brad's arm. "Thanks."

Brad smiled and winked at her. "You're welcome . . . as always."

"Yeah, thanks," Melissa added. "You're all right, Bro. I don't care what anybody says."

Brad raised his eyebrows. "Oh yeah? And just what do they say about me, anyway?"

"I'll never tell," said Melissa, standing up and beginning to clear the table. "I've been sworn to secrecy."

"Oh, great," said Brad, getting up to help her. "Not only do my proposals get turned down around here, I can't even defend myself because no one will tell me what 'they' are saying about me."

Toni watched her fiancé and her little sister working and joking around together, and she wondered how she and Melissa would have ever made it through all of this without Brad. She knew what a vulnerable time this was for Melissa, who was the same age now that Toni had been when they had lost their mother. Melissa, of course, didn't remember Marilyn Matthews, although she had certainly cried for her when she died. But Toni remembered her, and their father's death only intensified those painful memories.

"So, Melissa," she said, trying to refocus her thoughts, "have you thought about what you might want to do this summer? I know school just got out yesterday, but we probably should talk about your plans soon."

Melissa hesitated as she placed the almost empty food cartons in the refrigerator, then came and rejoined Toni at the table. "Actually, I have thought about it. To tell you the truth, I really wasn't looking forward to almost three months with nothing to do, especially now that . . . Well, you know, I won't have Dad to go fishing with or . . ." She stopped, and Toni knew she was fighting hard to maintain her composure. Then she took a deep breath and continued. "When I was at Carrie's last night, her mom's friend stopped by. You know, Beth Johnson, the receptionist at the dentist's office? She's looking for someone to take care of her little boy, Tyler, for the summer. He's almost seven. They just live two streets over from us, and she works Monday through Friday from eight to five. Mrs. Johnson's mother has been watching Tyler after school but would rather not be tied down all day during the summer, so they need someone as soon as possible. Anyway, she was wondering if Carrie could do it, but the Johnsons have a cat, and Carrie's allergic. So I thought, maybe . . ."

Toni pursed her lips. "Full time? Are you sure you want to make that much of a commitment? I know you're great with kids and you've done some babysitting in the evenings for a few people, but all day, five days a week? That's a lot."

Melissa nodded, her green eyes intense. "I know. And that's one of the reasons I want to do it. I need something to keep me from thinking about . . ." The tears came then, and she dropped her eyes. "Something to keep me busy."

Brad walked over and put his hand on Melissa's shoulder. "I think it's a good idea," he said, looking over at Toni.

Toni nodded. "I suppose you're right. Both of you. But I'll have to talk to Mrs. Johnson before you start and make sure about all the details."

Melissa looked up. Tears still glistened on her long lashes, but the relief was evident on her face. "Thanks," she whispered. Then she reached up and put her hand on Brad's, which still rested on her shoulder. "And thank you, Bro."

"Yeah, I know," said Brad, lightening the mood as he sat down next to her. "I'm the best—no matter what anybody says!"

Melissa managed a giggle and slugged him playfully in the arm. "Just don't let it go to your head."

Brad grimaced. "Fat chance of that around here. The last time I got any respect around this place was back in April when you all invited me over for a birthday dinner. And then, of course, I only got the respect because of my ancient age."

"Ancient, that's for sure. You're even older than Toni."

"Only by two years," Brad answered defensively. "And it'll be another two years before I hit the dreaded 3-0. What kind of a birthday celebration will we have then?"

"That depends," said Melissa, "on how much excitement they allow at the nursing home."

Brad appealed to Toni for help. "Aren't you going to defend me? Do you hear how your baby sister is picking on me here?"

Toni didn't answer. Brad's mention of the word "April" had sent her thoughts in another direction. *April Lippincott and Julie Greene. Wednesday morning at Eagle Lake. I need to look at that file again.*

"Toni. Hey!" Melissa snapped her fingers in front of Toni's face. "*Hellooo.* Where are you? Come back, we're talking to you."

Toni shook her head. "Sorry. I was just . . . thinking."

"No kidding," said Melissa. "About what?"

"Oh, nothing, really. It's just . . . one of Dad's clients. A missing girl and her grandmother and Eagle Lake . . ."

Melissa frowned. "Eagle Lake? That's where Dad . . ."

"I know." Toni forced a smile. "Sorry. I shouldn't have mentioned it. Really. It's not important."

"If it's not important," Melissa asked, "why were you thinking about it?"

Before Toni could answer, Brad intervened. "Hey, I've got an idea. Let's go for a walk and burn off some of these calories we just inhaled. Come on, you two. It won't be dark till almost ten, and it's not raining outside. Around here we have to take advantage of evenings like this. They're few and far between."

"True," said Toni, glad for the change in conversation. "Just let me grab a light sweater. You should too, Melissa. It may not be raining, but it's not what I would call shorts weather either."

"Is it ever in Washington?" asked Melissa.

"Hey," Brad teased, standing up and walking toward the door. "I've seen you wear shorts before."

"Two or three times, maybe," Melissa agreed, getting up from the table, "in the middle of August."

"OK, OK," Brad conceded. "So we don't exactly live in the Sunbelt."

"Now that's an understatement if I ever heard one," said Toni, following them into the living room. As she headed for the hall closet to grab a sweater, she spotted the Julie Greene file lying on the antique cherry coffee table in front of the couch. She stopped, but before she could reach out to pick it up, Brad stepped in front of her.

"Hey there, Miss Workaholic," he teased, "we're going for a walk, remember? That can wait till we get back. Better yet, it can wait till tomorrow."

"But I just wanted to—"

"Later," Brad insisted, taking her by the arm and turning her toward the front door. "Walk first, read the file later." He shook his head and sighed as she pulled her arm away and looked longingly back toward the file. "I knew we should have left that file on your desk with that fishing book."

"Fishing book?" asked Melissa, sliding her arms into her sweater as she waited for them in the doorway. She reached back and scooped her long hair out from underneath the sweater. "What fishing book?"

"Fly fishing," Toni said. "It's a book about fly fishing. It was . . . Dad's."

"Oh." Melissa's chin trembled slightly as she looked at Toni questioningly. "You were reading it?"

Toni shook her head. "No, I—"

"Because if you're not, I'd like to. Dad only took me fly fishing a couple of times, but . . . I'd like to read the book." She paused. "Actually, I'd really rather have it if . . . if you don't want it, that is."

"Of course you can have it," Toni said. "You know me—not much on fishing, I'm afraid. That was Dad's thing—and yours. It's only right that you should have it. I'll bring it home to you tomorrow."

Melissa smiled. "Thanks. I'd like that." She looked at Brad. "So, are we going for a walk, or not?"

"If you can help me tear your sister away from that file."

Grinning, Brad and Melissa each took Toni by an arm and propelled her away from the coffee table. "Come on, Sis, let's get out of here before it gets dark," Melissa said. "Grab a sweater and let's go."

"OK, OK," Toni said with a laugh. "You win. I know when I'm outnumbered."

As Toni pulled a white sweater from a hanger in the closet, Melissa pushed the screen door open, then turned back. "So why did you have Dad's fly fishing book out anyway?" she asked.

"I didn't. Abe . . . Detective Matthews from the River View police stopped by to return it. I guess he borrowed it from Dad."

Melissa's face brightened. "Abe was there?"

Toni was puzzled. "You know Abe Matthews?"

"I sure do. I met him at Dad's office a couple of times. I saw him at the funeral too, but I didn't get a chance to talk to him." She smiled her dreamiest smile. "He is *soooo* good-looking, don't you think?"

Toni glanced at Brad, who raised his eyebrows as if to say, "Well?"

"I didn't notice," said Toni, pushing past the two of them and stepping out onto the front porch.

"Didn't notice!" exclaimed Melissa, following close behind her. "Give me a break! How could you not notice? I mean, he's gorgeous! Carrie thinks so too. She was with me once when he stopped by the office, and she says he's a real hunk. I don't see how you could not notice a guy like that."

"Well, I didn't," Toni said quickly, shoving her arm into a sleeve. "So, what about this walk you two talked me into? Are we going, or not?"

She hurried down the steps and out the walkway to the sidewalk, avoiding the questioning look she was sure was in Brad's eyes. So what if Abe Matthews was good-looking? Why should that matter to her? She would probably never even see him again.

CHAPTER 2

The mid-morning sun was a welcome change from the long months of rain that seemed to dominate the Pacific Northwest between October and May. The temperature didn't constitute a heat wave, by any means, but it warmed Toni's back and shoulders. With the Julie Greene file tucked under her arm, she strode purposefully toward the police station, barely noticing the glorious profusion of flowers that lined the streets and decorated lawns, heralding the long-awaited arrival of summer.

It had been a late night. After returning from their walk, Brad had stayed briefly, then gone home leaving Toni and Melissa to retire to their respective bedrooms—Melissa with her ever-present journal and Toni with the intriguing Julie Greene file. As she propped herself up in bed against a comfortable stack of pillows, she had studied the pages until long past midnight. The more she read, the more certain she became that this nagging suspicion about a possible connection between the Julie Greene case and her dad's death was worth pursuing. By the time her eyes began to droop and she could read no more, she had made up her mind to take the file to the police first thing in the morning.

It was the phone, rather than the alarm, that woke her. She opened her eyes, startled, then squinted at the clock on the bed stand next to the ringing phone. Seven-thirty! It couldn't be. She never slept that late, especially this time of year when the morning light peeked through her window soon after four o'clock. Even if she forgot to set her alarm, Melissa should have been up by now, getting ready for school.

Then she remembered. School was out for the summer. Melissa, with nowhere in particular to go, was sleeping in. Toni, on the other hand, did have somewhere to go, and she had fully meant to be up and around long before this.

She grabbed the receiver. "Hello?"

"Toni? You sound surprised—or sleepy, or something. Did I wake you?"

Toni smiled. Even when her alarm clock let her down, Brad never did. He was as dependable and predictable as the evergreen state's annual rainfall.

"I'm afraid so," she admitted. "But I'm really glad you did. I guess I forgot to set my alarm, and I overslept."

She could hear the smile in his voice as he answered. "Good for you. You deserve it. Besides, you don't have a time clock to punch. Technically, your dad's office is closed, so you can get there when you get there, right?"

"Well . . . true. The office is closed, but . . ." She spotted the file lying on the floor beside the bed. "Brad, I was up late reading that file and—"

"I knew it," he interrupted. "I knew as soon as I left last night you'd start digging into it. I think there's more of your dad's detective blood in your veins than you realize. Sweetheart, what is this obsession you have with this Julie person?"

"Greene. Julie Greene. And it's not an obsession. It's just . . . well, a hunch, something I need to check out. I really think there's some sort of connection with this girl's case and my dad's death. I think Dad was getting close to finding out where Julie is, what happened to her, and . . ." Her voice trailed off as she realized she wasn't yet ready to voice her suspicions about what might have happened to her father.

There was a brief silence on the other end of the phone. "You don't think . . . surely you don't think that . . . Toni, your dad had a heart attack, plain and simple. He had a heart problem for several years and was on medication for it. You always knew something like this could happen. So why would you think—"

"I don't know what I think," she interrupted, "but I know what I've got to do. I'm going to take this file down to the police station this morning and see what they say about it."

"What?" Brad sounded incredulous. "You can't do that! Have you thought through any of this? What are you going to say? What are you going to tell them? Who are you going to talk to?"

"Of course I've thought it through," she said. "Well, sort of. After all, Dad was a detective in this town for many years. He has a few colleagues and acquaintances at the station. No one really close, but I'm sure at least one of them will be willing to hear me out."

There was another pause, and when Brad began to speak, his tone was more conciliatory, as if he were trying to soothe an overwrought child. "Toni," he said, "sweetheart, listen to me. You've been under a tremendous amount of strain these last few weeks, not to mention the grief. Don't you think you're letting all those emotions cloud your judgment? I think you're reading something into this that just isn't there. I think you need to let it go, to concentrate on clearing out what needs to be done at your dad's office and then focus on getting your life back together. We have plans to make, a wedding, your teaching job, and—"

She interrupted him again. "I'm not interested in making plans, Brad. I know that sounds coldhearted, but it's a fact. Right now the only thing I can think of is that my dad is gone. He's dead, and if there's something more to his death than what we've been told, I want to know about it. Until that's settled, I really can't think or talk about anything else. If my emotions are clouding my judgment, well then, that's the way it is. I really can't set my emotions aside just because you think I should. They're a part of me right now—a big part! And you're just going to have to accept that."

She heard him sigh, and she realized he was resigned to letting her do what she felt she must do. They had known each other for a long time, and she was confident that Brad knew what to expect when she set her mind to something. In that way, as much as in looks and coloring, she was just like her father. Both were single-minded, with bulldog tenacity once they sank their teeth into something. The problem had been when they dug in at opposite ends of a situation. The impasse could go on indefinitely.

"Do you want me to go with you?" His voice was tentative. "I have a couple of early morning appointments, but I'm sure I could reschedule them."

She shook her head, as if he could see her. "No. I think this is something I need to do by myself. Thanks anyway."

"Sure." Another pause. "So what about an early lunch, since I know you won't take time for breakfast? I can come by your dad's office and pick you up."

She smiled again. "I'd like that. In fact, with the sunshine streaming through my window, I'm tempted to suggest a nice leisurely picnic at the park."

"You're on. I'll pick up the sandwiches. See you at eleven o'clock."

After a quick shower, a glass of juice, and a scribbled note to Melissa, Toni set off clutching the file and opting for a brisk morning walk rather than driving the short distance to the station. As she mounted the steps and reached for the glass door under the "River View Police

Department" sign, the door suddenly swung open toward her, and she found herself staring up into the face of Detective Abe Matthews.

Toni couldn't tell which of them was more surprised. She found her voice first. "Detective Matthews. Good morning."

He hesitated. "Good morning to you, Miss . . . Matthews." He frowned, his dark eyes puzzled. "What are you doing here? I mean, what brings you . . .?"

He seemed to run out of words just as his forehead smoothed out and his eyes widened. Toni swallowed a smile, determined to maintain a businesslike demeanor.

"I'm here to talk to someone about . . . my father."

He raised his eyebrows, and Toni found herself wondering if his eyes were always so expressive. "Your father? What about him? I mean, is there something I can help you with, or . . .?"

Toni shook her head. "No, it's just that . . . well, I need to talk to someone who knew Dad, someone who—" She caught herself. "I'm sorry. Really. I didn't mean that the way it sounded. I know you knew my father, but . . ."

"But not well enough," he said, finishing her thought. "I understand." He held the door for her and stepped back to let her through. "It was nice seeing you again, Miss Matthews."

She started through, then stopped. Like her father, she wasn't one to let impulse overtake reason—at least not very often—but this was about to be one of those rare occasions. "Detective Matthews . . ."

"Abe," he corrected her. "Remember?"

This time she let the smile sneak out. "Abe," she repeated. "Then, please, call me Toni."

He returned her smile, and she couldn't help but notice that it was dazzling. She took a deep breath and plunged in. "I . . . well, maybe you could help me. I really didn't have anyone specific in mind to talk to, and since we've already met . . ."

The smile moved from his lips to his eyes, warming her even more than the morning sun, as they both stepped inside the building. "Let's go into my office. Down the hall, third door on the right. Let me get you some coffee."

~~~

Hi, Dad. It's such a beautiful day today that I thought I'd come and spend it with you. I even brought my lunch—and my journal, of course. Just like when you and I used to take the day off and go fishing, remember? You got the fishing gear together, I packed the lunch, and then we'd jump in the truck and head for the lake. And you'd tease me about bringing my journal along, asking me whether I planned to catch the fish or write letters to them. You always could make me laugh. . . .

Melissa set the pen down and leaned her head back against the huge pine tree that stood guard over her parents' gravesites, breathing deeply of the tree's pungent scent and listening to the trilling *caw-caw* of the bandit blue jay that rested in its boughs. In spite of her pain, it was peaceful sitting here. For some reason, she didn't feel quite as alone as she did at home, especially when Toni was gone and her father's absence seemed to echo from room to room.

This was the first time she'd seen her father's headstone in place, which somehow made her loss all the more final. "Paul Matthews," it read. "Beloved husband and father, July 25, 1946–May 21, 1999." Brief and simple, the way her father would have liked it.

She glanced over at her mother's grave, obviously not freshly dug like her father's, and wondered, *Is this what you've been waiting for, Mom? Are you and Dad finally together again after all these years? Are you happy? Are you in heaven, worshiping God, the way Pastor Michael says you are? Is there really a God? Can he hear me? Can you hear me?* She stifled a sob. *Mom . . . Dad . . . does God care that I'm talking to him, that my heart is breaking? Does he care at all?*

A lone tear escaped, and she wiped it from her cheek as she began to write. *I wish I'd known you, Mom, at least long enough so I could remember you. I see you in pictures with Dad and Toni, and some pictures where you're holding me. Everybody says I look like you, and I guess I do. But I don't remember you. I don't know what you smelled like, or how you felt. . . . Did you sing to me when you held me? Did you pray for me, Mom? I hope so. . . .*

I know you did, Dad. You told me so. But I never heard you. Carrie's parents both pray for her—out loud. I wonder why. Can't God hear us if we don't talk out loud? I sure wish I knew. . . .

She put her pen down again and took a sip of water from the bottle she'd brought along. The sun was almost directly overhead now, and even in the shade, the temperature was rising. If she and her dad had been out fishing, they would have come in with their catch of fish by now and be cooking them over an open fire. The thought sent a shudder through Melissa, and she gasped at the depth of pain it produced. Would it ever get any better, she wondered? Would she ever stop hurting and wishing things had been different, wishing that her dad hadn't gone to the lake, or that she had been out of school and had gone with him, or that someone—anyone—would have been with him that day out in the boat, or . . . ?

She shook her head, trying to clear her mind of the painful thoughts. As hard as she tried, they persisted. It was then that she noticed the flowers she had placed in the sunken vase between her parents' headstones were beginning to wilt. She reopened her bottle of water and slowly emptied the contents into the vase, pouring until the vase overflowed—even as she gave in to the pain and her eyes overflowed, watering the flowers with tears. What would she do? Would she live with Toni and Brad after they got married? Would she stay in River View forever? Or was there something else for her, something or someplace, maybe even someone who would someday ease her pain and help her find happiness again? Did she dare hope for that, or had her last chance for happiness died at the lake with her beloved father and dearest friend?

~~~

The coffee was hot, black, and strong. Not being much of a coffee drinker, Toni nursed the cup of liquid caffeine until it was tepid as she pored over the Julie Greene file with the attractive, attentive police detective. For the most part, she managed to keep her mind focused on the file rather than on Abe's nearness. But every now and then she would look up and catch those dark, penetrating eyes gazing at her. The concentration and concern for what she had to say was obvious, but was there more? Or was she reading something into his attentiveness that wasn't there? If so, why was she doing it? Certainly she wasn't interested in pursuing a relationship with him, nor did she wish to encourage any interest he might have in her, beyond their discussion about her father. Each time she found herself thinking along these lines, she immediately turned back to the discussion at hand, determined to block everything but professional thoughts about the charming, charismatic law enforcement officer sitting beside her.

"It all comes back to this," she said, pointing once again to the notation in the file that read *Eagle Lake, 6 A.M., Wednesday.* "I could ignore the rest of it, except for this. It just seems to be too much of a coincidence that Dad was—that he died—at Eagle Lake on a Wednesday morning. Then, when you start adding up all the other notations in the file—a missing teenage girl, a strange man named Carlo, Dad's suspicions about an illegal baby-selling ring and Carlo's involvement in it—not to mention the urgency in Julie Greene's grandmother's voice when she called and her belief that Dad had just been on the verge of finding out what happened to Julie. . . . When you tie all that in with the fact that Julie left her parents a note when she ran away, saying she was heading west to start a new life with Carlo, whoever he is . . ." She took a deep breath and looked up at the detective, who this time was gazing intently at the notations in the file.

"Detective—Abe—do you think my dad was on to something, that he was somehow getting too close to discovering something illegal, and—" She stopped herself, still unable to voice her suspicions.

Without looking at her, Abe rose from his chair and began to pace slowly across the small, windowless room that served as his office. A half-dozen strides took him to the other side, where he stopped for a moment, his broad shoulders straining against his white dress shirt. He turned back toward Toni. His face seemed chiseled in stone until she saw his jaw muscles twitch. For the first time since she'd met him, his eyes seemed expressionless. "I really can't say." His voice was slow and deliberate as he answered her unasked question. "But there's always an outside possibility, even though there really isn't anything concrete to suggest it." He walked back to his chair and sat down beside her. His face softened, and Toni's heart skipped a beat. "He had a heart attack. There's nothing suspicious about that, especially with what you've told me about his medical history. Without something more than your hunch, there's no sense calling in the county sheriff at this point, even though Eagle Lake is his territory. Still, if it will make you feel better, I'll be glad to help you any way I can—although strictly on a personal basis at this point. Nothing official."

Toni felt relief wash over her. So she wasn't just some emotional female overreacting to her father's death and letting her grief override her reason. As slim as the possibility was, there really might be something to her suspicions. And now there was an experienced, knowledgeable person willing to help her get to the truth. On the other hand, she realized how much easier it would be if Abe—or anyone, for that matter—could convince her that there was nothing to this Julie Greene connection, and she could just let the whole thing go. Deep inside, however, she sensed that she couldn't let it go, not until she knew for sure. And for now, at least, she had an ally.

"Thank you," she said, her voice barely above a whisper as she fought tears. "Thank you so much. I . . . I just didn't know where to start, what to do, or who to talk to."

She felt his hand cover hers. "You did the right thing," he said. "I'll get started on it right away, and I'll keep you informed of anything I might find out." He smiled. "Sound OK to you?"

"It sounds great," she answered, returning his smile. "Thanks, partner."

He laughed. "Partner. I like that. In fact, I like it a lot. Especially since you are, without a doubt, the best-looking partner I've ever had."

Surprised by the flush she felt creeping up her neck, Toni jumped to her feet, angry at herself for the thoughtless use of a term that somehow implied they were a team. "Well," she said quickly, glancing at her watch, "I'd better get going. I need to get some things done at my dad's office, and it's almost ten o'clock." She stuck out her hand. "Thank you for your time, Detec—Abe."

His smile disappeared, and his eyebrows went up again as he rose from his chair. "What happened? Is it something I said? You're the one who mentioned partners, so it can't be that. Is it the good-looking part you didn't like?"

Her flush deepened, and all she could think of was escaping from that tiny, stuffy office and getting outside into the fresh air. "I . . . I've got to go," she said. "Really. I—"

"I'll walk you out," he said, interrupting her as he opened the door to the hallway. She stepped out and hurried toward the exit, but Abe Matthews was right there beside her, holding that door as well. They stepped outside into the sunlight together.

"You're right," he said. "This is much better. It was getting pretty warm in there. I really do need a window in that office." He smiled, his demeanor much more professional than it had been a few moments earlier. "So, where's your car?"

Toni hesitated a moment, then remembered. "It's at home. It was such a beautiful morning that I decided to walk. And, as you know, it's not far from here to Dad's office. So, if you'll excuse me, I—"

"Now there's a great idea," he said, interrupting her again. "In fact, I had just been heading out the door for a quick walk myself when I ran into you earlier. Why don't I just walk with you? Would that be all right . . . partner?"

She opened her mouth to protest but couldn't think of a logical reason to say no. And so they fell into step together, down the stairs and out onto the sidewalk. The temperature was in the high seventies now, with a light breeze blowing in from the west. River View was slightly less than a couple of hours' drive from the coast—too far to smell the salt in the air, but close enough to reap the benefits of a cooling ocean breeze on a warm day.

The beauty of the rare, sunny weather, coupled with the therapy of their moderately brisk walk, soon eased the tension between them. They kept the conversation light, touching on everything from the flowers and birds they saw along the way, to the basketball finals, to the baby-sitting job that Melissa wanted to take for the summer. Suddenly, Abe stopped. Toni looked up at him, puzzled.

"Have you had anything to eat today?" he asked.

It was her turn to raise her eyebrows. "No. Why?"

His smile was back. "Because I'm starved. How about some lunch? Or is it too early for that? Breakfast, maybe? Brunch?" He paused, his dark eyes twinkling. "Some decent coffee?"

Toni laughed. "That was pretty terrible stuff you gave me back there. The truth is, I seldom drink coffee. I know that's practically heresy in this part of the country, but I just don't care much for it."

Abe shrugged. "OK. But you like food, don't you?"

She hesitated, but before she could answer, her stomach growled loudly. They both broke out laughing, and Abe took her by the arm. "That's it," he said. "I'll take that as a yes. Let's run across the street to the deli and see what we can find—besides coffee, of course."

The deli crew was between customers—cleaning up after the breakfast crowd and getting ready for the lunch rush. The place was practically empty. They slid into a booth and grabbed a couple of menus. Before they could browse the selections, a dark-haired waitress of about eighteen or nineteen, wearing a nametag that identified her as Melanie, appeared at their table. "We just quit serving breakfast," she informed them, her voice a bored monotone as she snapped her gum. "And lunch isn't ready yet. All's we got left is a few cinnamon rolls and some coffee."

Abe and Toni looked at each other and grinned. "We'll take the cinnamon rolls," Abe said. "No coffee."

"How many cinnamon rolls?"

"All of them," Abe answered as Toni suppressed a laugh.

Melanie sighed, scribbled something on her order pad, and turned to leave.

"And two big glasses of ice water," Abe called after her. "If you're not out, that is."

Toni's laugh escaped, but Melanie didn't even turn around.

By the time they'd finished their cinnamon rolls and ice water and Toni had wrapped up the three remaining rolls to take home to Melissa, it was almost eleven-thirty. Amazed at how comfortable she now felt in this man's company, she marveled at how freely she had shared with him about her life, including her mother's death, her insecurity at finding herself a surrogate mother to Melissa when she wasn't much more than a child herself, and her lifelong dream of writing novels. Just as the thought occurred to her that she hadn't even mentioned Brad or their impending wedding, she noticed the clock on the wall and reached for her purse. "I'd better get to the office before the day's over," she said. "And I need to let you get back to the station. As your new unofficial partner, I have a vested interest in making sure you stay caught up on your work so you'll be able to devote your off-duty hours to my dad's case."

Abe smiled as he rose from the booth and reached into his pocket to fish out some change for Melanie. Toni grabbed for the bill. "I'll get it," she offered, opening her purse.

"Not this time," said Abe, retrieving the bill from her hand. "This was my idea, so I'll pay. Next time you can get it. Fair enough?"

She hesitated, then shrugged. "OK. Fair enough. As long as next time doesn't include steak and lobster."

He feigned disappointment. "How did you know?"

She smiled and went to the door to wait for him while he paid the bill. As they stepped back out into the sunshine, Abe insisted on walking her the final block toward her father's office. Before they had taken a dozen steps, Toni was shocked to see Brad walking straight toward them, carrying a small picnic basket. He wasn't smiling.

Her eyes opened wide, and she stopped in her tracks. Eleven o'clock. She'd had a lunch date with Brad at eleven, and she'd completely forgotten about it. "I'm so sorry," she said as Brad drew to a stop in front of her. "I forgot all about—"

"So I see," Brad answered, the pain in his hazel eyes obvious. He glanced toward Abe, then handed the picnic basket to Toni. "I've got to get back to work," he said. "I'll talk to you later." Then he turned and walked away.

CHAPTER 3

The slight headache she'd had all afternoon seemed to be getting worse. She walked through the front door into her living room, relieved to be home at last. It had been a long day. In addition to the annoyance she felt toward herself for having forgotten her date with Brad, not to mention the resulting scene in which she and Abe had come face-to-face with him on the sidewalk, she had spent the vast majority of the afternoon stuck on the phone. On the positive side, however, besides having referred the last of her dad's former clients to other agencies, she had also managed to check out some of the details of Melissa's possible baby-sitting job, and she was anxious to discuss the findings with her younger sister. Assuming Melissa was in her room, Toni decided to go to the kitchen first to find a couple of aspirin and to decide what to fix for dinner. As she stepped into the kitchen, she stopped, surprised to see her younger sister standing silently in front of the open refrigerator.

"Melissa? Honey, are you OK?"

The slender, barefooted girl in the faded, cutoff jeans and oversized T-shirt, with auburn hair cascading down her back, didn't move. Toni came up behind her and laid her hand on her shoulder. Melissa jumped as if she'd been shot, turning toward her older sister with a look of wide-eyed fear that broke Toni's heart. How well she remembered that look. She had seen it in the mirror several times after her mother died, usually when she found herself sitting quietly in front of her dresser, remembering the touch of her mother's hands as she brushed Toni's hair or tucked her in at night. Then, a noise or a voice would suddenly snatch her back from her memory into the present, immersing her in an inexplicable, pin-pricking sensation of fear that shot through her body like a fiery bolt of lightning, and she would gaze in wonder at the terror-stricken girl in the mirror, trying to figure out who she was.

Now, as Toni stared into Melissa's fear-filled eyes, she was amazed to realize how much the young teen had grown recently. When had it happened? When had her baby sister gotten so tall that their eyes met on an equal level? Gently, she reached out and pulled the trembling girl to her. "I'm sorry. I didn't mean to frighten you. Are you all right?" Toni felt a shudder run through the fragile body as Melissa nodded, struggling to explain.

"I was just looking for . . . I wanted to surprise you and make dinner, but I . . . I couldn't figure out what to fix, and . . ."

Toni took Melissa's shoulders and gently held her out at arm's length. "It's OK. Really. We'll do something simple."

Melissa nodded again, tears pooling in her green eyes and hanging on her long lashes. "Will I ever stop missing him?" she whispered, her chin quivering. "Will it ever stop hurting so much?"

With all her heart, Toni longed to reassure her little sister, to promise her the pain would go away, but she couldn't lie to her. "No," she answered. "You'll never stop missing him, and I won't either. And it will never stop hurting, not completely anyway. But it will get better, that much I can promise you. It won't always hurt this bad."

Relief and doubt mingled on the young girl's face as she forced a smile. "Thanks. I guess you should know if anyone would."

"Yes. I should know." She took a deep breath and looked at the open refrigerator. "Tell you what. How about bacon and eggs? Nice and easy; what do you say?"

"Can we wait a few minutes? Maybe sit down and talk first?"

Toni closed the refrigerator door, then grabbed a tissue from the box on the counter and handed it to Melissa. "Sure. In fact, I've been wanting to talk to you anyway. How about in the living room?"

They walked to the couch as Melissa dabbed at her eyes and blew her nose. Toni hadn't realized how exhausted she was until she sank down into the comfortable cushions. Melissa plunked down beside her, next to the end table.

"What did you want to talk to me about?" asked Melissa, absently twirling a long strand of hair around one finger. "Is everything OK down at Dad's office?"

"Things are fine at the office. In fact, I got the last of Dad's cases referred to other agencies this afternoon, so things are coming together."

"Does that mean you've decided for sure to sell the agency?"

Toni shook her head. "No. I'm pretty sure I will, but . . . I just don't know yet. That's not what I wanted to talk about though."

Melissa raised her eyebrows. "Is it Brad? Is everything OK between you two?"

Toni winced at the mention of Brad. She had not talked with him since their awkward three-way meeting earlier that day. She needed to call him but hadn't yet gotten around to it. She made a mental note to do so before the evening was over.

"No," she sighed. "It's not Brad."

"Then, what is it?"

"You go first," said Toni. "What's on your mind?"

Melissa paused. "Well . . . I was just wondering . . . have you thought anymore about that baby-sitting job I told you about? I'd really like to do it. Please, Toni. I need something to do, something to . . . get me away from here. And I need to let Mrs. Johnson know—soon—before she gets someone else." The pleading look in her eyes faded to relief when she saw Toni smile.

"Sure," Toni answered. "I've thought about it. In fact, that's exactly what I wanted to talk to you about. I called Mrs. Johnson this afternoon and discussed it with her. We thought it might be good if we all got together sometime tomorrow morning over at her house, just to get to know each other a little better before making a final decision. What do you think?"

Melissa's eyes sparkled as she loosed the strand of hair and leaned forward expectantly. "I think that would be great! What time? Did she say? Is her little boy going to be there? His name is Tyler. I've seen him before, and he's really cute. Does this mean I can do it? I can start baby-sitting for her on Monday?"

Toni laughed. "No, she didn't specify a time, but I imagine around ten or so. I told her I'd call her in the morning and we'd figure out the details then. I don't know if her son will be there, but I imagine he will be. And we'll work out the rest at our meeting tomorrow. Fair enough?"

The phone rang before Melissa could respond. Beaming, the excited teenager reached over to the end table and grabbed the receiver. "Hello?"

Toni wondered briefly if it might be Brad, but then she heard Melissa say, "Yes, she is. May I say who's calling?" Toni watched her sister's face change from mild surprise to a puzzled frown as she handed her the receiver. "It's Abe Matthews, the detective from the police department. He says he wants to talk to you."

Taking the receiver from Melissa, Toni's thoughts raced in several directions at once. Had Abe already learned something about her father's death? If so, did she really want to hear what he had to say? And if it turned out that there was more to Paul Matthews's death than just a simple heart attack, what would she tell Melissa? Would this fragile teenager be able to handle such devastating news on top of the loss she had already sustained? Then again, how could Abe have found out something so quickly? But why else would he be calling? And regardless of his reason for calling, how was she to explain this call to Melissa? Brushing the questions aside, she took a deep breath, reminding herself not to call him by his first name.

"Detective Matthews," she said, trying to sound as impersonal as possible. "Hello. What can I do for you?"

A pause on the other end of the line confirmed that her impersonal touch had been convincing. "'Detective Matthews'?" he repeated. "What happened to 'Abe' and 'Toni'? Did I miss something, or aren't you the same lady I went on a cinnamon-roll-eating binge with today?"

Toni's smile sneaked out before she could catch it, and she glanced at Melissa from the corner of her eye. The look on her face was not an approving one.

"Yes, I . . . of course," she stuttered. "I just—"

"Ah, caught you at a bad time. Sorry."

"No, no, it's not a bad time. Not at all. Really. Melissa and I were just . . . talking."

"Well, I won't keep you, 'Miss Matthews.'" Toni couldn't tell if the slight hint of sarcasm in his voice was real or just a tease. She concentrated on looking disinterested as he went on. "It's just that I have to catch up on some paperwork tomorrow morning, but after that I thought I'd take a run up to Eagle Lake and do a little preliminary sleuthing. Any chance you might want to come along? If this were an official investigation, I couldn't invite you, being a family member and all. But since it's unofficial, I thought, why not? It's supposed to be another beautiful day, and it's such a great ride to the lake. What do you say? Can you come?" When she hesitated, he added, "Hey, partner, it may be unofficial, but it's still strictly business, I promise. I can go on up by myself if you think it would be too painful for you to see where—"

"No," she interrupted. "No, that would be fine. I'd be glad to. What time?"

She could hear the smile in his voice. "Pick you up about one-thirty?"

"Sure. See you then." She handed the receiver back to Melissa, whose eyes mirrored her confusion and disapproval.

"What was that all about?" she asked, replacing the receiver on the hook. Before Toni could think of a plausible answer, the phone rang again. This time she reached across Melissa to answer it.

"Hello?" Her voice was guarded, wondering if Abe had already changed his mind about taking her with him. As uncomfortable as the situation with the handsome police detective might be, and as unsure as she was about what to say to Melissa about Abe's phone call, she knew she wanted to be there when he did his so-called "preliminary sleuthing" at Eagle Lake. She had no idea what he might find, if anything, but whatever it was, she wanted to be in on it.

"Toni?" Brad's voice was a mixture of confusion and hurt. "Are you all right? You sound . . . different."

Toni felt a rush of relief sweep through her at the sound of the familiar voice she loved so dearly. "Brad," she said, his name a joyous exclamation that brought a smile to her lips. "It's so good to hear your voice. I've been meaning to call you."

"I wish you had," he answered, the hurt still evident in his words. "It's not like you to forget our plans. I'd really been looking forward to that picnic. I was worried when I got to your dad's office and found it locked. Then, when I looked up the street and saw you walking with that detective, talking and laughing . . ."

"I'm so sorry," she said, wishing she could say more, that she could explain why she had been with Abe, what they were talking about, and why she might very well be seeing quite a bit more of him in the near future. But this was not the time. Explanations would just have to wait. "Please forgive me," she added. "I guess I lost track of the time."

Toni knew Brad well enough to realize that the pause that followed meant he was restraining himself from saying something he might regret, and she loved him for it. Her headache was getting worse, and she was too emotionally drained to deal with an angry or jealous fiancé on top of everything else. Brad was just going to have to be patient and understanding with her throughout this time, whatever it might bring. She touched the solitaire diamond on her ring finger. "I love you," she said.

"I love you too," he answered, his voice cracking with emotion. "Truce?"

"Truce," she agreed, a surge of gratitude forcing a lump into her throat. Once again, from the corner of her eye, she glanced at Melissa. This time she was smiling.

"So," said Brad, "how do we go about celebrating this truce? Can we do something special? Tomorrow, maybe? You name it. Time, place—I'll be there. I'm at your disposal for the entire day. Can't beat an offer like that, can you?"

Toni's mouth went dry, and the lump in her throat seemed to grow. Now what? How was she going to explain to Brad, of all people, why she couldn't spend the day with him—especially with Melissa sitting right next to her?

"I . . . I can't," she said, struggling to get the words past her throat. "I've already . . . made plans. Melissa and I . . ."

The hurt was back in his voice, although it was obvious he was trying to hide it. "You and Melissa have plans? Is it . . . I suppose it's a 'girl thing,' right? Hey, no problem. How about Sunday? We can all go to church together—you and me, and Melissa too—and then out for a nice brunch afterward. How does that sound?"

At the moment it sounded absolutely wonderful—if only she could get past the guilt she felt over her deceptive answer. True, she and Melissa had plans for the next day, but only for the morning. How could she tell Brad—especially now, with Melissa right there and without first having a chance to explain to him about their awkward sidewalk meeting that morning—that she would be spending the following afternoon at Eagle Lake with Abe Matthews? She resolved to tell Brad as much as she could, as soon as possible. For now she would just have to let him think that her plans with Melissa included the entire day.

"Brunch on Sunday sounds perfect," she said, looking directly at Melissa. "The three of us." Melissa nodded happily. "You've got a date, counselor. Melissa and I will be looking forward to it."

"So will I." His voice softened considerably. "I miss you."

"I miss you too," said Toni, meaning every word. "See you then."

She reached over and hung up the phone, then leaned back against the couch and closed her eyes.

"He's pretty awesome, isn't he?"

Toni nodded. "Yes, he is. I can't imagine what I'd do without him."

"I hope you never have to find out."

Toni opened her eyes and looked at her sister. "What does that mean?"

Melissa shrugged and looked down. "Nothing. Just . . . I hope you two never break up or anything—that you get married like you've planned for so long."

"Why wouldn't we?"

She shrugged again. "I don't know." Then, looking up, the fourteen-year-old was suddenly very serious. "You're not dating that Abe Matthews guy, are you? I know he's a hunk and everything, but . . . but you've got Brad, and he loves you, and—"

Toni reached over and put her hand on Melissa's arm. "And I love him. Brad and I will get married, just like we've planned. You have nothing to worry about. I'm not dating Abe Matthews, no matter how much of a hunk he is, and I'm not going to do anything to jeopardize my relationship with Brad." She smiled, wondering if she should explain further, but decided against it, at least for the time being. "I promise. OK?"

Melissa smiled and nodded. "OK," she said. "Thanks, Sis."

~~~

The haunting images of the frightened teenager with the flowing blonde curls drifted through her mind as she tossed and turned, never quite certain if the images were vague, unconnected thoughts or snatches of a dream. In that surreal world between conscious thought and sound sleep, Toni agonized over the young, insecure girl, one moment cheering her on as the teenager seemed to rise to her full stature and stand steady on her feet, the next urging her to run before some illusive danger overtook and devoured her. Finally, just after midnight, Toni sat up in bed, her heart pounding in her ears, her nightgown drenched in sweat and clinging to her.

What was it about Julie Greene that she couldn't let go, even in her sleep? Was she truly obsessed with the girl as Brad had suggested? Or was it just that there was some macabre, intangible tie between Julie and Toni's father? Whatever it was, Toni shivered at the ominous undercurrent that seemed to permeate the entire matter. Then she wondered, Was the girl in the dream really Julie Greene, or could it have been Toni herself?

Either way, why did she feel such fear, as if she were stepping off the edge of everything familiar and dear into some nameless black hole from which there was no escape?

~~~

Saturday had dawned bright and sunny, just as predicted. The meeting at Mrs. Johnson's had gone well, and Melissa and Tyler had gotten along famously. Everyone agreed they were a perfect match, and the decision was made for Melissa to show up for work at the

Johnsons' home at 7:30 on Monday morning. To celebrate, the sisters had gone out for cheeseburgers and fries on the way back to their house.

They hadn't been home more than thirty minutes when Abe Matthews pulled up in his black '96 Honda Accord. As Toni grabbed her purse and headed for the door, Melissa had glared at her as if to say, "But you promised!"

"This is not a date," was all Toni had said as she hurried out the door and down the steps before Abe could get up the walkway. This was something she wanted to explain to Melissa on her own terms, when she felt the time was right—and with Abe there, the time was definitely not right.

As a result, the ride to the lake had started out in a somewhat stilted manner. But before long, Toni had found herself relaxing as she shared with Abe about Melissa's new job, her concerns for her younger sister since their father's death, and various other topics. She had scarcely noticed the scenery or how far they had come until Abe pulled the car to a stop in front of the small general store that marked the southwest entrance to Eagle Lake. The tiny dirt parking lot was full, which was not unusual for a sunny Saturday afternoon.

"Can I get you something?" Abe offered, shutting off the ignition and turning in his seat until he was facing Toni. It was the first time they had looked directly at each other since he had arrived to pick her up. The annoying flush was once again making its way up her neck and cheeks, and she scolded herself for acting like a foolish teenager. True, the man's dark, expressive eyes, his finely chiseled features, and his broad shoulders were hard to ignore—he was, after all, a "hunk," as Melissa had pointed out. But she was here with Abe Matthews on business—unofficial but very serious business—and not pleasure. Besides, she had a fiancé she loved very much and had every intention of marrying, just as soon as this situation with Julie Greene and her father was cleared up and she and Brad could get around to setting a date and making the necessary arrangements. So why was her heart racing as she looked at this handsome detective sitting so near her on the front seat of his car?

Abe raised an eyebrow. "A soda? Some juice?" He grinned. "I won't even ask about coffee."

Toni realized then that she had not responded to his offer to get her something from the store. How could she talk to him so comfortably and unreservedly over cinnamon rolls or while riding in the car, but the minute there was nothing to distract them and his eyes locked into hers, she suddenly turned into an insecure schoolgirl who could scarcely remember her own name?

She cleared her throat. "Juice would be fine."

He seemed to be waiting for something more. "Any particular kind? Or would you like to come in and pick it out yourself?"

"I . . . I'll come in," she said, grabbing her sunglasses from her purse and reaching for the door as she suddenly recognized her need for fresh air. Putting on the glasses, she breathed deeply as they weaved their way through a half-dozen parked vehicles and a small group of raucous teenagers standing in a circle just outside the store. As Abe held the squeaky screen door open and Toni stepped inside, the smell of popcorn assailed her nostrils. It was cool and slightly dark in the rundown wooden building, but the aisles were freshly swept and the shelves neat and in order. Toni had been here often, particularly when she was young. Everything about it—especially the popcorn smell— reminded her of her father. For as long as she could remember, her dad had never been able to hold out against her pleading for a bag of popcorn every time they walked through the door of this little store, even though he made quite a pretense of trying to do so. Now she was reminded, as she had been so many times since her mother's death twelve years earlier, how something as simple as the smell of popcorn could precipitate an entire new level of pain. Fighting tears, she was glad for the sunglasses that perched on her nose.

Anxious to put some distance between herself and Abe, she turned away from him and walked hurriedly toward the back of the store, where she knew she would find the refrigerated section that contained the cold drinks. As she pulled open the door and reached in to grab a plastic bottle of apple juice, she heard her name.

"Toni? Toni Matthews? Is that you, child?"

She knew the voice even before she turned around. "Maude," she said, transferring the juice to her left hand and reaching out with her right to greet the tall, stocky woman with the short, unkempt gray hair and the wrinkled white apron wrapped around her ample middle. "Maude Olson. I can't believe it. Don't tell me you and Simon are still running this place!"

Maude ignored Toni's outstretched hand and wrapped her in a bear hug, thumping her on the back as she talked. "Course we're still runnin' this place. What'd you think, we retired or somethin'? 'Sides, who else'd be fool enough to do it?" She let Toni go and stepped back to look at her. "My, my, you're just as purty as your mama, even though you don't look a lick like her. Who'd ever a-thought such a homely, skinny kid would turn out so purty!" She laughed. "I used to worry 'bout you when your mama and daddy first brought you up here. I told your mama, I said, 'You gotta start feedin' this child more. She's just too skinny.' Why, it's been years since I seen you up in these parts. Guess you was just too busy to come see us in the middle of all that fancy schoolin'. And you're still a might on the thin side. But I gotta admit, you look real good."

"She sure does," Abe agreed, coming up to the two women, "although you may be right about the skinny part." He flashed a smile at Toni.

"And just who might this be?" asked Maude, eyeing Abe suspiciously. She turned back to Toni. "Is this that lawyer fella I heard you was marryin', the one your little sister, Melissa, told me 'bout?" Before Toni or Abe could answer, she went on. "Now *there's* a girl that knows fishin'. Course, she's kinda skinny too, but a real sweetheart, that one. And, boy, does she favor her mama—in looks, that is. But it's her daddy she favors when it comes to just about everything else. Why, she's just like his little shadow."

Her voice trailed off and her smile faded, as the memory of Paul Matthews's death, right there at Eagle Lake, registered on her face. "Oh, honey, I'm so sorry," she said, enveloping Toni in another hug. "Here I am just runnin' on, and you grievin' like you are. I'm so, so sorry. When am I gonna learn to keep my big mouth shut?"

Toni swallowed the lump in her throat. "It's OK, Maude," she assured the woman, pulling away from her embrace and thinking again how grateful she was that she was wearing sunglasses. Ignoring the ringing that had started in her ears, she nodded her head for emphasis. "I'm OK. Really."

Maude pursed her lips and fixed her eyes on Toni. "First you lose your mama, then your daddy. How can you be OK?" She shook her head. "Nope. I don't believe it. Takes time to grieve, honey, and you ain't had 'nough time. 'Sides, even if you think you're OK, how 'bout your little sister? Why, that girl was always taggin' along after her daddy, followin' him ever'where. You tryin' to tell me she's OK? I 'magine she's hurtin' somethin' awful."

The ringing was growing louder, and Toni could feel herself slipping over the edge. She should never have come here, should never have exposed herself to questions she just wasn't ready to answer and to memories too painful to confront. If only she'd stayed in the car, but she hadn't, and now she was closer to the edge than she had allowed herself to get since her father's death. She was slipping, and there was nothing she could do to stop the fall.

Abe's strong arm around her waist pulled her back. She leaned against him gratefully, hiding behind her sunglasses as she heard Abe thank Maude for her concern and explain that they had to be on their way. Handing her a five-dollar bill to cover their drinks and telling her to keep the change, with his arm still around Toni's waist, he steered her toward the front door, past two older men examining fishing lures and a mother and child arguing over which cookies to buy. The ringing in her ears was fading, and she heard Maude call goodbye as they stepped outside into the bright sunshine.

"Thank you," she said as they made their way to the car. "I know Maude meant well, but . . ."

"But her timing wasn't the best." Abe unlocked her door and held it for her while she climbed in, then went around to the driver's side and got in beside her. "Maybe mine wasn't either," he added, looking into her eyes. Toni had slid her sunglasses off when she got into the car. Realizing that had been a mistake, she looked down at the juice bottle in her hand.

"I shouldn't have asked you to come with me," she heard him say. "I didn't realize this place was so full of memories for you. I'm sorry."

She shook her head and forced herself to look back up at him. "No. It's not your fault. I should have realized . . . I should have known . . . but . . . I'm all right now."

"Are you sure?"

"I'm sure." She held her gaze steady as long as she could. Then, opening her bottle, she took a sip. The cold apple taste was refreshing, and the drink was a good diversion. "Thank you for the juice."

He didn't answer. When she dared to look back at him, she was sure she saw a hint of tears in his eyes. "I really am sorry. I've been so caught up with the detective end of all this stuff—wanting to help you find out what happened to your dad, if there was any connection to this Julie Greene case—that I forgot how fresh all this is for you, and how painful. Forgive me."

The sincerity in his eyes was almost more than she could resist. With everything in her, she wanted to crumple into his arms and let him hold her while she cried, but her mind recoiled at the idea, not just because she knew she had no business in the arms of this man she hardly knew, particularly when she was already engaged to someone else, but also because she was afraid that, if she ever allowed herself to cry—really cry, not just shed a couple of tears—she might never be able to stop. Over and above all that, she had no intention of giving this man any more opportunities to see how emotionally vulnerable she was. Toni had always prided herself on being strong and able to stand up under pressure; she was appalled at how little of that strength she had exhibited lately. Taking a deep breath, she forced a smile. "Thank you for your concern. I really am OK now. Shall we . . . walk around the lake a little? Look around? Do some 'preliminary sleuthing,' whatever that entails?"

He returned her smile, but it wasn't very convincing. "Sure, partner. If you're up to it. Let's go walk around and see what we can find."

~~~

Toni couldn't decide if she was more disappointed in herself or in the fact that they hadn't found out anything new about her father's death. Although the remainder of the afternoon had been a pleasant one as they hiked the beaches and campgrounds surrounding Eagle Lake, and talked to the many fishermen and campers they came across, only one old man remembered having been there the day Paul Matthews died, and he couldn't recall having seen or talked with him. "Of course, my eyes ain't what they used to be," he had told them. "I may have seen a boat or two out on the lake that day, but I couldn't tell you who was in 'em. I fish mostly from the bank myself. Don't care much for boats." They had even gone by the cabin where Paul Matthews had stayed during his time at the lake, but they couldn't look inside because someone had rented it for the weekend. "Besides," Toni had explained to Abe, "Brad came up here after Dad's . . . death . . . and packed up his stuff and brought it home. There wouldn't be any sense in looking inside now."

Before leaving the lake, Toni had wrestled with the idea of going back to the store and asking Maude if either she or Simon had seen or talked to her dad the day of his heart attack, but by the time she worked up the courage to do so, the elderly proprietors had closed up shop and gone home for the day. "They tend to keep their own schedule," she explained to Abe. "They're always here early in the morning during fishing season, but they go home when they feel like it. If you need a quart of milk after that, you just have to drive down the road a few miles." Abe had smiled, saying it sounded like a nice, simple way of life.

Then they had gotten back into the car and headed for home. Toni was emotionally drained and spent most of the return trip staring out the window at the breathtaking grandeur that so many Washingtonians take for granted. The majestic firs towered above them on either side of the road, topped by a sky so blue it seemed unreal, a canvas painted by a master artist. *And so it is,* she reminded herself. *A world created by the Master himself, with so much beauty, and yet . . .*

"Hungry?" Abe asked, interrupting her reverie.

She turned toward him as he glanced over at her and smiled. She shook her head. "Not really. Just tired."

"Disappointed?" He was looking straight ahead now, but his jaw twitched as he awaited her answer.

"Yes. At least I think so."

Abe nodded. "I understand. If you want me to leave this thing alone, I will, since we really don't have any evidence of a crime, but if you want me to continue, just say so."

She paused, weighing her answer carefully. "I think I'd like you to continue, even though I'm not sure I want to know what you might find out. Does that make sense?"

"Sure it does. I'd feel the same way in your shoes."

Toni turned back toward the window, surprised to find they were only a couple of miles from the River View turnoff. She found herself looking forward to getting home, even though she knew it meant that she would have to give Melissa some sort of explanation for her trip with Abe. How complete that explanation would be she had not yet decided.

As they pulled up in front of the house, Toni was shocked to see the silver Lexus parked in the driveway. What was Brad doing there? Had he forgotten that she and Melissa had plans for the day? Suddenly, explaining the afternoon's outing to Melissa didn't seem nearly as difficult as explaining it to Brad.

Abe had no sooner parked his car on the street in front of the house than the front door opened and out stepped Brad and Melissa. Melissa still wore the hurt, accusatory look that Toni had last seen on her face as she had assured her younger sister that she was not leaving to go on a date with Abe. But as well as Toni knew Brad, she couldn't be sure about his expression. He was wearing what she called his "courtroom face," which could include angry, upset, confused, scared—but most of all, determined. She took a deep breath and stepped out of the car. Abe had already gotten out and come around to join her. Together they walked toward their welcoming committee.

Before Toni could open her mouth, Abe jumped in. "Brad," he said, extending his right hand. "It seems we keep running into each other. How are you?"

Stiffly, Brad shook Abe's hand. "Fine. And you?"

Abe smiled. "I'm doing fine, thanks." He turned to Melissa. "And how are you, Melissa? I haven't seen you in a while. How's your friend—Carrie, is it? You two must be glad to be out of school for the summer."

Toni could tell Melissa was trying hard to be polite without showing any disloyalty to Brad. "We're . . . fine."

As Toni wondered what to say or do next, Abe turned to her and said, "Well, I'd better get going. Thanks for coming along with me. I'll be talking to you."

She nodded. "Yes. Thank you."

No one spoke as Abe walked to his car, climbed in, and drove away. As the black Honda disappeared down the street, Brad gently took Toni's arm and turned her toward him. Even his courtroom face could no longer hide the hurt she saw in his hazel eyes. "We have to talk," he said. "Now."

CHAPTER 4

They had no sooner walked in the front door than Melissa picked up her diary from the coffee table, and without so much as a word or a backward glance, disappeared into her room. Toni could only imagine what must be going through her impressionable young mind, not to mention her very tender and vulnerable heart, but she would simply have to wait and deal with Melissa after she had explained things to Brad.

Toni looked up at Brad. He stared back at her, silent and unmoving, a myriad of unspoken questions and accusations reflected in his eyes. Toni could not remember a time, in all the years they had known each other, when she had sensed such awkwardness and tension between them. "Let's sit down," she said, determined not to have such an emotionally volatile conversation while standing in the middle of the living room. Not waiting for him to respond, she walked to the

couch and sat down at one end. Brad followed, lowering himself carefully onto the opposite end.

Even in his casual slacks and open-collared, short-sleeved summer
shirt, Brad looked neat—calm and unruffled, as if he had everything
under control. Toni knew better. They had known each other for so
long and shared so much that she could read him like a book. She
chided herself for the half-truth she had told him the day before and
for not having made more of an effort to confide in him sooner about
the reason for her involvement with Abe Matthews. But what was
done was done; it could not be changed now. She took a deep breath,
resolved to tell him everything and to see that nothing like this ever
came between them again.

"I'm so sorry. I really wanted to explain to you about what was
going on with Abe—"

There was a hardness in his voice she had never heard before as he
interrupted her. "Just what is going on, Toni? How serious is your
relationship with this . . . detective?"

She was fighting tears now, angry—not so much with Brad for asking such questions as with herself for putting him in the position
where he felt the need to do so. "It's not serious at all," she answered,
her throat constricting around every word. "At least not the way you
mean. What's going on has nothing to do with Abe and me, person-
ally. It's about Dad—about how he died, and whether or not there's
some connection between his death and the Julie Greene case."

Brad seemed incredulous. "The Julie Greene case? Are you still
harping on that? Toni, just because you have a P. I. license doesn't
make you one. You went to college to become a teacher, not an investigator. Besides, in case you've forgotten, your father had a heart
attack. That's how he died. Period. I know it's tragic, and I know it has
hurt you deeply, but there is nothing suspicious or sinister about it.
People die of heart attacks all the time, especially people with heart
conditions. You're really going off the deep end on this one if you
think you can somehow hang on to your dad by trying to turn his

death into some sort of mystery that needs to be solved. And now you're trying to tell me that the police department has sent this . . . detective . . . to investigate your father's death, based on nothing more than your suspicions about his involvement with some missing girl? Come on, Toni. You don't really expect me to buy that, do you?"

Toni felt a flash of anger at his insinuation that there was anything more to her relationship with Abe than a mutual interest to discover any previously undisclosed truth about how and why her father had died. But the anger subsided as she reminded herself that if she had been totally honest with Brad from the beginning, they would not be having this conversation.

"No. I am not trying to tell you that the police department has assigned Abe to investigate my father's death. He's offered to do it on his own time. Then, if we—if he—comes up with something concrete, he'll contact the county sheriff's office, since Eagle Lake is in their jurisdiction, to see about opening an official investigation. That's what we were talking about when you ran into us in town yesterday, and that's why we were up at the lake this afternoon, looking for evidence, but—"

"But what? You didn't find any, did you?"

"Not yet. But Abe said—"

"I don't really care what Abe said. You didn't find any evidence to confirm your suspicions today, and you're not going to find any in the future. This guy is just leading you on."

"That's not fair. He's only trying to help."

"Oh, that's right. I forgot. He's doing all this on his own, isn't he? Not in an official capacity, just as a 'friend.'" Brad spoke slowly and deliberately, but the sarcasm was obvious. "Out of nothing more than the goodness of his heart, Abe Matthews is sacrificing his free time to help you track down some unknown evidence on a case that isn't a case and isn't even in his jurisdiction. Am I just supposed to accept that and be relieved that you're doing nothing more than playing detective together?"

Toni was losing her battle for control. Even as she continued to remind herself that Brad was only reacting to a situation she herself had caused, her resentment at his tone and implications was growing. When she finally answered, her words were almost as slow and deliberate as Brad's had been. "We are not 'playing detective.' We are simply trying to find out if there is any connection between Dad's death and the notation in Julie Greene's file. And even though there's no real evidence to open an official investigation, at least I have an experienced detective who is willing to help me check this thing out. Brad, can't you see? Besides the fact that Julie's grandmother seemed so certain that Dad was right on the verge of getting a break in the case just before he died, doesn't it seem like more than a coincidence that he would leave a note about Eagle Lake and the exact date of his death in that file?"

"You don't know that it was the same Wednesday."

"That's true," she conceded. "But if it was—"

"If it was what?" Brad interrupted, his voice rising in volume and intensity. "Toni, your father had a heart attack. He wasn't shot or bludgeoned or stabbed. He had a heart attack. That's it. Nothing more. So what difference does it make if it was the same Wednesday or not? Why can't you just accept the fact that your father is gone and let this thing go?"

The silence hung between them as Toni absorbed the impact of Brad's words. She knew he wasn't trying to hurt her—even though he had—and that he was trying to help her face the truth and go on with her life—*their* life. But what if he was wrong? What if there *was* something to the notation in that file? Didn't she owe it to her dad to find out?

Before she could answer, Brad had reached across the divide on the couch and gathered her into his arms. After only a brief hesitation, she moved toward him and let him hold her.

"I'm sorry," he whispered. "I shouldn't have talked to you that way. It was totally insensitive and uncalled for. Forgive me?"

She nodded, her head resting against his chest.

"I should have known there was nothing between you and this Matthews guy," Brad went on. "Even if I don't know him, I know you. That should be enough. It's just that . . ."

She nodded again, blinking back tears. "It's OK. Really. And it's my fault for not telling you about this sooner. I meant to, but . . . it just always seemed that the timing was wrong." She looked up at him. "Forgive me too?"

His half-smile warmed her heart. "Of course, I forgive you. How could I ever stay mad at you?" He kissed her forehead, then pulled back and looked into her eyes. "But I'm still worried. I know this guy is a detective, and he may be a really nice guy, but . . . he's not blind. You're an attractive woman, and I can't help but think that his willingness to help you with this situation has at least something to do with his wanting to be around you. I'm sorry, but that's the way I see it."

She opened her mouth to protest, to tell him that there was absolutely nothing about Abe's behavior to indicate an interest in her as a woman—but she couldn't. Deep down, she, too, had suspected as much. But that didn't change the fact that she needed Abe right now. Besides, suspecting he was interested in her didn't make it so. His intentions could be completely aboveboard. She only hoped the same was true about her own. The realization shocked her, and she resolved to put such thoughts out of her mind.

"Whether Abe has any personal interest in me, I can't say for certain—although I doubt seriously that he does," she added quickly, hoping she sounded as convincing as she was determined to be. "Either way, this is strictly a professional relationship—and a temporary one, at that. As soon as we've settled this question about Dad's death and any possible involvement with the Julie Greene case, Detective Abe Matthews is out of my life."

Brad's smile widened slightly. "Sounds like a promise."

"It is."

"Then make me another one."

She raised her eyebrows questioningly.

"From now on, I want to be told about any and all aspects of this so-called investigation *before* they happen. No more of this 'after the fact' stuff, please. And if Abe decides to go snooping around on some investigative hunch and invites you to come along, will you at least think twice before saying yes? I'd rather not have you spending any more time alone with this guy than absolutely necessary. Fair enough?"

"More than fair." She reached up and put her arm around his neck, pulling him down to her for a kiss. He quickly obliged, sealing the promise. They didn't even notice that Melissa had come out of her room and was standing, motionless, in the shadow of the hallway.

≈≈≈

The weather had cooled off a bit, but the sun still peeked through the clouds as Abe pulled up in front of the general store at Eagle Lake. It was just before nine o'clock on Sunday morning, and only one lone vehicle—a rusty '78 Ford pickup with an empty gun rack in the back window—occupied the parking lot in front of the old building. Abe hoped he would find Maude Olson inside, feeling as talkative as she had been the day before when he and Toni were there.

Forcing his thoughts, once again, away from Toni Matthews and on to the task at hand, he stepped inside the dimly lit store and paused, taking a moment to let his eyes adjust. As they did, he looked around, but Maude was nowhere in sight. A slightly built older man, with a thin wisp of gray hair combed from one side of his head to the other in a vain attempt to disguise his baldness, stood behind the counter. He was handing some change to the only other person in the store, a middle-aged, heavyset man in a plaid shirt, overalls, and boots. As the customer pocketed his change, picked up his package, and walked past Abe to the door, the fish smell that wafted after him confirmed Abe's hunch that the man had probably already been out on the lake that morning. Abe stepped up to the counter.

"Hello," he said, as the older man eyed him curiously. "Are you, by any chance, Simon Olson, Maude Olson's husband?"

"Not by chance, by design," he answered, flashing a crooked smile. "And who might you be, and how do you know my wife?"

Reluctant to give the false impression that he was there in any sort of official capacity, Abe refrained from showing his police identification. "I'm Abe Matthews," he said. "I'm a friend of Toni Matthews. In fact, I was up here with her yesterday, and we talked with your wife."

Simon's blue-gray eyes lit up in recognition. "Aha. The wife told me you two was up here. First time that older Matthews girl's been up here in quite a while. Too bad 'bout her dad. That Paul Matthews was a real nice man. A regular 'round here, him and his whole family been comin' up here for years." He stopped suddenly and frowned. "What'd you say your name was?"

"Matthews. Abe Matthews. No relation to Toni."

Simon still looked puzzled. "I thought you was Toni Matthews's fiancé. Seems kinda strange, you two havin' the same name and all. Course, I 'magine it'll be right handy for her. Won't have to change her name when you get married."

Abe smiled. "I'm afraid I'm not her fiancé. Just a friend."

"You say that like you wished it was different."

Abe raised his eyebrows. "Oh, well, no. I just meant . . ." He cleared his throat. "Like I said, we're friends."

"From what the wife told me 'bout your visit yesterday, you must be real good friends. Sounded like you two was stuck together like glue. Can't say as I'd want my fiancée runnin' 'round with some other man she was all that close with. What's the future husband think of this so-called friendship?" He pursed his lips for emphasis as he waited for Abe to answer.

The memory of Brad and Melissa standing on the porch and staring at them as he and Toni walked toward the house from his car the previous day flashed through his mind. Although he didn't know it for a fact, he was pretty sure the "future husband" didn't like the relationship between Toni and Abe one bit. But he wasn't about to tell Simon Olson that.

Shrugging his shoulders as if it were no big deal, Abe said, "Actually, I'm a friend of the family—well, of Paul Matthews, that is. I brought Toni up here yesterday because she wanted to find out if anyone might have anything to tell her about her father's death—anything that she might not already know, that is."

The old man frowned again. "And just what's that s'posed to mean?"

Abe was getting frustrated. In spite of the cooler weather, he was starting to sweat. Things were not going at all as he had planned.

"Look, Mr. Olson, all I'm trying to do is find out for Miss Matthews—"

"'Miss Matthews'? I thought you just called her Toni. 'Sides, if somebody was hangin' on to me as close as my wife says 'Miss Matthews' was hangin' on to you, I'd sure be callin' her somethin' 'sides 'Miss.'"

Abe's jaws clenched as he found himself wondering why he had bothered to come back up here. He could have been sleeping in or going out somewhere for a nice breakfast. But no, here he was, off on some wild goose chase, following up on a flimsy clue in a missing girl's folder, all on the hunch of a young woman—a very attractive young woman, he reminded himself—who had a way of making him think that maybe, just maybe, there really could be such a thing as love at first sight. But if there was, why couldn't he have met her before she was engaged to someone else? He took a deep breath and tried again.

"Mr. Olson, all I want to know is, did you or your wife see Paul Matthews while he was up here on his fishing trip last month? In particular, did you see him the morning of his death?"

"Can't say I did," Simon answered. "But then, can't say I didn't, neither. What I mean is, I saw him while he was here, 'cause he always stopped by to say hello and shoot the breeze. But the day he died? Nope. Can't say I saw him that day. He died in the mornin', you know."

Abe forced a smile. "Yes, I know. OK, so you didn't see him the day he died. Did you see anything else that day, anything . . . strange or unusual?"

"Saw lots that day. Always do. But not much different from most any other day. Why?"

Abe shrugged again. "Oh, just curious." This conversation was going nowhere fast. He wished Maude were here. He had a feeling he could get a lot more information from her. Trying to appear disinterested, he asked, "So, where's your wife? Did she take the day off?"

"It's the Sabbath," Simon answered. "The wife takes that real serious. She's gone to church, and then she'll be goin' straight home. She don't do no work on the Sabbath. Don't believe in it."

Abe tried to ignore Simon's reference to the Sabbath. Although he had never practiced the Jewish religion of his ancestors, he knew enough to know that the Sabbath was on Saturday, not Sunday. But since he didn't observe it on any day, he decided against making an issue of it.

"Apparently it doesn't bother you like it does your wife—working on the Sabbath, I mean."

"I ain't never been much for goin' to church," Simon answered, folding his arms across his chest. "But I try to be a God-fearin' man. Don't smoke nor drink—never have. Don't cuss, neither. I figure that oughta count for somethin' with the Almighty. That, and havin' a religious wife like Maude. I s'pose if that's not enough to get me into heaven, then a whole lotta people ain't gonna be there."

Abe had never considered himself an authority on getting into heaven, but he was pretty sure that Simon was right about one thing: If there truly was such a place as heaven, there were a whole lot of people who weren't going to be there, himself included. It was a thought he did not allow himself to dwell on.

"Well, Mr. Olson," he said, pulling his keys out of his pants pocket and turning to go. "It's been nice talking with you."

"Leavin' already? What's your hurry?" The old man chuckled. "Got a hot date?"

Abe thought about his empty apartment. Then he thought about Toni and how she had undoubtedly made up with Brad by now and the two of them were probably out somewhere enjoying themselves as they made plans for their future life together.

"No. No date," he said, walking toward the exit. He was just about to open the door and step outside when Simon called out to him.

"By the way," he said. "Don't know if you're interested, but I did see somethin' sorta unusual the mornin' Paul Matthews died."

Abe froze in mid-stride. Turning back toward Simon, he fixed his gaze on the store's proprietor. "Yes?"

"Aha. 'Pears you're interested. Well then, just before the wife and I left home to open up the store that mornin'—'bout 4:30 or so—I went out back to have a little chew." When Abe raised his eyebrows, Simon went on. "Didn't say nothin' 'bout not chewin'—just said I don't smoke, drink, nor cuss. A man's gotta have some pleasure in life, don't he? And the wife won't let me chew in the house or the store. Says it's dirty. Anyhow, I noticed a car drivin' up toward Mr. Matthews's cabin—we can see it from our place, you know. It stopped a ways 'fore it got there and turned off its lights. Didn't see nobody get out. Course, I couldn't see who it was that far away. So I just went back inside. That was the last I saw of 'em, and I never thought no more 'bout it 'til now."

"Could you tell what kind of car it was?"

"Nope."

"Could you at least tell if it was a car or a truck? A van, maybe? Or an SUV?"

Simon shook his head. "Nope."

Abe sighed. It was obvious he had gotten all he was going to get from the old man. But at least it was something—not enough that he felt compelled to contact the sheriff about the possibility of opening an official investigation, and not even enough to pass on to Toni at this point—but enough to give him an excuse to pursue this case, as well as "Miss Matthews," a little further.

~~~

Melissa had awakened nearly an hour before her alarm went off. For the first time since her father died, she found herself looking forward to something.

Toni's eyes had opened wide when she walked into the kitchen and found Melissa sitting at the table, already dressed and eating a bowl of cereal. "Wow, you're up early," she had exclaimed, going to the refrigerator for some juice. Melissa had assured her that she'd had a good night's sleep but now was anxious to get started in her new job. Toni had teased her, asking if she would be as anxious to get up so early to go to work, day in and day out, five days a week, as the summer wore on. Melissa had laughed and declared that she would.

Now Melissa stood outside the front door, the early morning sun just beginning to warm her back, as she waited for Mrs. Johnson to answer the doorbell. Melissa tried to ignore the butterflies in her stomach.

The door opened wide and a smiling Beth Johnson stepped back to let her in. "Good morning, Melissa. How are you?"

"Fine," she answered, feeling a bit awkward as she suddenly wondered if she had been out of line to bring her backpack along, loaded with reading material and her journal. She didn't want Mrs. Johnson to think she was going to ignore Tyler.

"You can set your things in there on the table," Beth said, motioning toward the kitchen. "Tyler's still asleep, although I imagine he will be up any time now. You'll know he's awake when the cat comes out to greet you or you hear the sound of cartoons coming from the family room. Meanwhile, make yourself at home. Have you had breakfast?"

"Yes . . . thanks."

"Well, feel free to help yourself if there's anything else you'd like. The same goes for lunch. Fix whatever you want. Tyler will live on peanut butter and jelly sandwiches if you let him. You might try suggesting something else once in awhile, but don't force it. As long as he has some fruit or something with it, that's fine. Anyway, my work number's by the phone. I've got to run. See you about five-fifteen or so. Bye!" Then she was out the door.

Melissa put her backpack down on the table and stood looking around the unfamiliar kitchen. The ticking clock seemed unusually loud. She sat down, glad she had brought her journal. Getting it out of her backpack, she began to look over some of her more recent entries. She hadn't yet gotten around to writing anything new for the day when she heard a muffled sound, coming, she thought, from the area of Tyler's room. Walking quietly from the kitchen to the hallway, she made her way to Tyler's bedroom door, which was closed. The sound was louder now, although still somewhat muffled. She knocked softly.

"Tyler?" The noise stopped, but there was no answer. "Tyler? It's me, Melissa. Can I come in?"

After a slight pause, she heard a little voice say, "OK." She had no sooner cracked the door than Tyler's calico cat, Bozo, escaped through the opening and streaked down the hallway. Peeking inside, she saw that Tyler was still in bed, lying under a mass of tangled covers on the bottom bunk. Pictures of racecars and basketball players competed with Winnie the Pooh and Mickey Mouse posters for wall space. He was definitely an "almost seven-year-old" boy—as he was so quick to tell anyone who would listen—torn between wanting to grow up and become a "big boy" and clinging to the comfort of his little-boy world. Melissa smiled. Hidden at home, in the back of her top dresser drawer, was her very own Pooh blanket, which she had no intention of giving up any time soon.

"Hi, Tyler," she said, stepping into his room. "How are you this morning?"

Tyler sniffled. "OK." His voice sounded as tiny as he looked, buried under all those covers. Melissa walked closer to the bed. The big brown eyes that stared back at her from the pillowcase covered with rockets and spaceships were wet, and his face was red and puffy. She knew now that what she had heard was an almost seven-year-old boy crying. She sat down next to him on the bed.

"What's the matter?"

His chin quivered. "I miss my daddy."

Her heart skipped a beat. Fighting tears, she answered him. "I'm sure you do. I'm . . . sorry he's not here."

"He went away. Mommy says he still loves me, but he lives far away now, and he can't come and see me anymore." He stared at her, as if he expected her to say something that would make him feel better. Melissa didn't trust herself to speak.

"Lissa, do you think my daddy still loves me?"

Melissa thought of her own father, of all the wonderful memories they shared, and she couldn't imagine any father not loving his own child. "Yes," she managed to say. "I think he loves you. I'm sure he does."

Tyler smiled shyly. "Me too." Suddenly his eyes brightened. "I know his address. It's in the book by the phone in the kitchen. Will you help me write him a letter? I'm going to ask him to come home."

Melissa's eyes opened wide. "Oh, I don't know. . . . Do you think that's a good idea? I mean, would it be all right with your mom? I'm not so sure."

Tyler bounced up off the pillow and untangled himself from his blankets. "It's a great idea," he exclaimed. "Come on, let's go. I know where there's some paper."

Melissa watched him run out of the room with his straight brown hair sticking up in the air and his baseball pajamas rumpled and twisted around his sturdy little body. She sighed, then got up and followed him. It was obvious they weren't going to get anything else done until they had written a letter to Tyler's absentee father.

Beth Johnson had explained to Melissa and Toni on Saturday that her husband, Scott, had left about ten months earlier. He was now living with his new girlfriend in Austin, Texas, and although he had called Tyler fairly regularly in the beginning, his phone calls had tapered off to a trickle in the last few weeks. Tyler would not even consider the possibility that his father might not return. He talked about it daily and prayed every night for God to bring his daddy back. Melissa had felt bad for Tyler when his mother had told them about the situation, but nothing had prepared her for the look in his eyes when he asked her if she thought his daddy still loved him. Her heart ached as she followed her little charge into the kitchen. How was it possible that his father could have left him?

Tyler was already sitting at the kitchen table, a piece of paper in front of him and a pencil in his hand. Bozo, curled up on the small oval throw rug in front of the stove, eyed him intently. "I know how to write 'Dad,'" Tyler announced. "Watch." He held his tongue between his teeth in concentration as he carefully drew the letters. "There," he announced. "I wrote 'Dad.' How do I write 'I miss you'?"

As they worked through the letter, Melissa spelling the words and Tyler laboring over each one, she marveled at the little boy's naivete and faith that his father would respond to his plea and return. She wanted to believe he was right, but she doubted it. At the same time, she couldn't help comparing Tyler's plight to her own situation. Although she knew her father could never come home again, she also knew he had not left her by choice. That knowledge didn't make his leaving any less painful, but it kept her memories of him safe. Her dad had always been her hero, and he always would be. She knew Toni felt the same, to some extent. But Toni had Brad, so Melissa didn't see how her sister could miss their father quite as much as she did.

Melissa smiled as she remembered the scene in the living room on Saturday. She had felt a bit guilty for eavesdropping on Toni and Brad, but her relief at hearing them make up had far surpassed her feelings of guilt. When she had heard Brad apologize to Toni for the way he had spoken to her and Toni's response to Brad's apology, Melissa had known everything was going to be OK again.

When Brad had called earlier that afternoon, expecting to get the answering machine and planning to leave a message for Toni to call him when she got home, he had sounded surprised when Melissa answered. She had tried to cover for Toni, without actually lying, but Brad realized something was wrong and had come right over. Finally, through her tears, Melissa told Brad about Abe's phone call the previous evening and about Toni's going off with him in his car earlier that afternoon. After that, they had just sat together and waited.

Things worked out just as Melissa had hoped. After Toni and Brad had made up, Brad stayed for dinner. Then he came back and picked them up for church and brunch the next morning. Overall, it had been a very good weekend.

"There," Tyler exclaimed. "I'm done. Let's get an envelope."

Melissa smiled. "I'm afraid I don't know where they are."

"I do!" Getting up from the table, Tyler, barefoot, padded out of the kitchen, down the hallway, and into his mother's bedroom. Soon he was back with a box of envelopes.

"Here," he said, climbing back up on his chair. "Now you can help me write my dad's address. It's in this book." He handed Melissa his mother's address book. A sheet of stamps was stuck in the front.

They got the envelope stamped and addressed. Then Melissa promised him they would walk to the mailbox to mail it after he had his breakfast and got dressed, which started an immediate scramble for a cereal bowl and spoon. Before Tyler sat down to eat, he looked at the letter and frowned, then turned to Melissa, who was still seated at the table.

"Lissa, could we pray for it?"

Melissa was puzzled. "Pray for what?"

"The letter. Let's pray and ask God to get it there safe and to help my dad come home, OK?"

Melissa felt the familiar lump forming in her throat. She nodded. "Sure. You start."

Tyler closed his eyes. "Dear God, please take this letter to my dad. And please tell him to come home right away 'cause I really miss him. Amen."

Melissa tried to say "amen," but all she could do was grab a napkin from the center of the table and wipe her eyes.

CHAPTER 5

The dream was more realistic this time, the terror more pronounced. No more flitting images between waking and sleeping—only heart-pounding, sweat-inducing horror, as she ran, half-blinded with fear, from the nameless predator who stalked her. Her long blonde curls flew wild behind her, threatening to catch on the tree branches, as she crashed through the undergrowth near the water's edge. *Mom? Dad? Can you hear me? Where's Julie? I can't find her. Help me, Dad! I need you! Somebody, please help me! Brad, is that you? Brad? Abe. Oh, thank God, it's you. I knew you'd come. I knew you'd help me . . . but why? Why is it you? Why is it always you? Who are you, Abe? Who are you? What are you doing here? How did you get here? Can I trust you? Abe? Abe, don't go . . . Abe. Wait! Listen to me. . . . Don't go . . .*

Toni awoke shaking, crying, reaching for . . . something, but she was surrounded only by darkness and the overwhelming realization that her father was dead—and now, the absolute certainty that his death had not been from a heart attack. She shivered and drew the covers close around her neck as the haunting images of her terror-filled dream lunged at her from the night shadows. The pounding of her heart still echoed in her ears, and she recoiled in horror at the truth that imploded on her consciousness. She had no proof whatsoever, and yet she knew. She knew, beyond reasoning or understanding, that something evil had invaded her life, something much worse than she had ever imagined. And the knowing—yet not knowing—was the worst part of all. But one thing was certain. No longer could she dismiss her suspicions that something sinister and mysterious surrounded her father's death. Whatever it might be, there was a definite connection between Paul Matthews and the fifteen-year-old runaway from Colorado, a connection Toni sensed to be fraught with danger. And now—promises to Brad notwithstanding, and with or without Abe's help—she knew she would not rest until she had discovered that connection. She was, after all, a detective's daughter, and her father had taught her not to run in the face of danger. She owed it to him to solve the mystery surrounding his death, whatever the cost.

It had been a long week. The days had run together into one extended kaleidoscope of unanswered questions and unrelenting pain as Toni tried to outrun the terror that stalked her, particularly since her dream several nights earlier. Now it was Friday, and Toni hoped her meeting with Abe might answer some of her questions, although she doubted it would do anything about easing the pain.

She pulled up in front of the police station and parked her red '95 Ford Taurus in the only empty spot left on that side of the block. The mid-afternoon sun was beginning to break through the clouds that had hung over the area throughout the day. Toni, dressed in off-white

cotton slacks and a sleeveless print top, and remembering how warm
it had been the last time she was in Abe's office, decided against the
lightweight sweater she had brought along. She grabbed her purse
and climbed out of the car, surprised at the surge of emotion she felt
as she mounted the steps and opened the front door. Since waking
from her nightmare with the horrifying certainty that her father had
not died of a heart attack and that her life had been invaded by some
inexplicable evil, Toni had been unable to shake the sense of
encroaching dread that threatened to envelop her. She had done her
best to stay busy at the office, completing the referrals of her father's
clients, sorting through stacks of paperwork, deciding which to save
and which to shred, as well as spending time with Melissa and Brad.
On several occasions she had even tried to force herself to consider
her next career move but had been unable to concentrate long enough
to come to any sort of decision.

Abe had called a couple of times during the week, reassuring her
that he was continuing to look into the circumstances of her father's
death but had not yet come up with anything concrete. Apart from his
phone updates, however, Toni had not seen nor talked with Abe since
Saturday, when he brought her home from the lake. Now, as inappro-
priate as it was, she almost welcomed the excitement that pulsed
through her as she made her way down the hallway toward Abe's
office. It was the first real sign of life she had experienced in days.

His door was open. Abe sat at his desk, his head down as he studied the Julie Greene file, open on the desk in front of him. Toni's heart
leapt with encouragement as she realized that Abe truly did share her
concern about her father's death.

She raised her hand to knock, hesitating only momentarily as she
took in the outline of Abe's bent head, his hunched shoulders, his fingers tented together in front of his face. She wondered what went
through his mind as he gazed at the picture of this lovely, vibrant,
young girl, whose unknown fate was causing immeasurable pain to
her family. Had he been in law enforcement long enough and seen

enough of the seamier side of life that he had gotten used to such things? Was it possible that anyone ever came to that point? If so, what sort of person would he or she then be?

Abe raised his head slowly as she rapped on the door. It took a split second for his dark eyes to register recognition, but as soon as they did, a warm smile spread across his face and he rose to his feet. "Toni," he said, walking around to the front of his desk to escort her inside. "Come in. How are you? I'm so glad you called."

He closed the door behind her, and with his hand at the small of her back, gently steered her toward the only extra chair in the room, taking a moment first to reach out with his spare hand and pull the chair closer to his own before releasing her so they could both sit down. Toni did her best to suppress the shiver that ran down her spine as his hand rested against her back, but she was almost certain that her best had not been good enough. Did Abe sense the effect he had on her? Did he realize that she was attracted to him beyond anything that reason or propriety would dictate? She hoped not, and she resolved once again to diffuse any thoughts he might have along those lines.

"I'm fine," she said, striving to keep her tone of voice businesslike. "And I so appreciate your taking the time to see me. I hesitated to call because I didn't want to impose. . . ."

Abe's smile and dancing eyes implied that he was teasing, but his words were serious. "Impose on me anytime you want. Please. I'm never too busy for a visit from you. After all, we are still partners, aren't we?"

Toni concentrated on her breathing, even as she ignored his last remark. "Thank you. It's just that . . . I know you told me you're still checking into any possible connection between Julie Greene and my dad's death—which is obvious from her file sitting on your desk— and I know you said there wasn't anything tangible yet, but . . ." She paused, suddenly unsure of her purpose in coming to Abe's office. What exactly had she expected from this meeting? Did she think he was holding out on her, that he might tell her something in person that he hadn't told her over the phone? Or did she simply want to be near him? If it was her desire to be in his presence that had drawn her, was it merely because he represented a link to her father? Or was she losing her battle to resist seeing Abe as anything more than a detective who had agreed to help research her father's death? Taking a deep breath, she plunged ahead. "I . . . guess I just needed to see you, to ask if there's anything I should be doing besides just waiting around for you to discover something."

He was watching her as she spoke, and she resisted the urge to glance down and make sure her clothes were on right. Toni wished he would stop looking at her, that he would just answer her questions and stop staring in such a penetrating manner. At the same time, she felt caught up in his gaze, as if she couldn't move even if she wanted to. It suddenly occurred to her that he could be quite intimidating when questioning suspects. Finally he spoke, but even then his eyes never left her face.

"I'm afraid I don't have anything to add at this point, nothing major anyway. . . . Well, there is one slight thing, although nothing significant enough to warrant my contacting the sheriff. . . ."

Toni leaned forward in her seat. "You found something? What? What is it?"

Abe reached out and laid his hand on her arm. "Toni, listen to me. I didn't mention it because I didn't want you to read something into it that isn't there. But since you're here, I may as well tell you. Just remember what I said. It probably means absolutely nothing, OK?"

Toni nodded, relishing the touch of his hand on her arm, even as her heart raced in anticipation of what he was about to tell her. She was sure Abe was downplaying his discovery so she wouldn't overreact, but she was also sure that what he was about to tell her was more significant than he was letting on.

"I went back up to Eagle Lake on Sunday morning," Abe said. "I thought I might catch Mrs. Olson at the store, but she wasn't there. I did talk to Mr. Olson, though, and he told me he saw a vehicle drive up to your dad's cabin very early Wednesday morning, the day he had his heart attack. He couldn't see who was driving it, or even what kind of vehicle it was. He only told me as sort of an afterthought, as if it were no big deal. It probably isn't, which is why I wasn't going to mention it to you yet. But since you're here, well . . . that's it. That's all I've found out so far."

"That's all?" Toni was stunned. "What do you mean, that's all? Abe, doesn't that prove my dad didn't die of a heart attack? If someone else was there, doesn't that prove—"

"That doesn't prove anything," Abe interrupted. "Remember, according to the coroner your father died of natural causes. His own doctor was there with the coroner and said it was a heart attack. If there had been signs of foul play, that would be an entirely different thing and then Mr. Olson's observation would definitely be considered evidence. But under the circumstances, it's just an interesting point to note for future reference."

Toni was struggling to absorb what Abe was telling her. "Do you mean . . . even now, with what Simon Olson told you, we still don't have enough evidence to present to the sheriff?"

"I'm afraid so. We need something more, something that would cast doubt on the coroner's ruling of natural death, for Mr. Olson's information to mean anything. What we have right now is that a man with a known heart condition who died while out in his boat fishing—alone, mind you—may have had a visitor earlier that day. That in itself simply isn't suspicious, particularly at a lake during fishing season when many people drive up from town to fish very early in the morning. It's just not enough to justify an investigation. I'm sorry, Toni, but that's the way it is."

"But . . ." Toni was incredulous. For a split second she had been so sure that this piece of news was just what they needed to contact the sheriff's office and get an official investigation launched. Apparently that was not the case.

"I see," she said, a stab of fear piercing her heart as she realized that not even Abe was going to be able to help her discover the truth about her father's death. His hands were tied because of his official position, bound by lines he could not cross. As frightening as it was, she realized that this was something she was going to have to do on her own. Taking a deep breath, she rose from her chair, trembling slightly at the implications of the formidable task ahead of her. "Thank you for your help," she managed to say. "I appreciate all you've done, but I—"

"Hold on a minute," Abe interrupted, jumping up and taking her arm. Turning her toward him, he lifted her chin with his finger. "Where do you think you're going? You're talking like we're not partners anymore. Did I miss something here? I thought we were in this together."

The room suddenly felt warm and very still. Her heart was racing, and she couldn't decide if it was because of the way he was looking at her or because he had just offered her the tidbit of hope that she so desperately needed. "I . . . I thought you said . . ."

"What I said was that we don't have enough evidence to contact the sheriff's office and ask him to launch an official investigation into your father's death, but I didn't say anything about not continuing our own unofficial investigation, did I?"

Caught up once again in his gaze, it took her a moment to answer. "No," she said finally, her voice cracking as she fought the hot tears that stung her eyes. "I guess you didn't."

They stood that way for a few seconds longer, until Abe slowly released her arm and pulled away. Toni breathed a sigh of relief as she suddenly realized that, had he tried to kiss her, she would not have resisted. In fact, if he had not let go of her when he did, she might have initiated a kiss herself. Horrified, she sat back down, clasping her hands in her lap. She must not let him know what she was thinking or feeling. He must know only that she was grateful for his willingness to continue helping her discover the truth about her father's death.

Abe, still standing, laid a hand on her shoulder. "Are you OK?"

She nodded, then took a deep breath, wishing there were a window in the tiny office. "Yes. I'm fine. Really."

"How about a glass of water?"

"Please."

He was gone less than a minute, but she used the time to collect her thoughts and stabilize her breathing. She felt much more composed when he reentered the room carrying a paper cup full of cold water. Ignoring his touch as he handed her the cup, she resisted the urge to gulp its contents.

"So," she said once he sat down, "where do we go from here?"

Abe smiled. "I'm glad you've got that 'we' part figured out again. I've always found that one-sided partnerships don't work out too well."

Toni hesitated, not sure how to respond. Fortunately she didn't have to.

"OK," Abe said, reverting back to Toni's last question. "Where do we go from here? I can think of two things, at least as far as you're concerned. Didn't you tell me that Julie Greene's grandmother called you a week or so ago?" Toni nodded, taking a sip of water, and Abe went on. "Now, if you're not comfortable doing this, just say so, and I'll do it. But I think it would be best if you would, simply because of my official position here. I think you should call Julie's grandmother and see if you can get any more information at all out of her. Can you handle that?"

"Sure. I can do that."

"Good. I think she's our best shot at getting anything new to go on, even though I imagine your dad talked to her extensively and noted anything she might have told him in the file. But you never know. Sometimes you can talk to people several times and think you've heard all they have to say, and then suddenly they remember some nugget of information that makes all the difference. Since you have your P.I. license, you can quite honestly explain that you're trying to tie up any loose ends before turning Julie's account over to another agency. Then, too, you might want to call the girl's parents." He paused and glanced down at Julie's file. "Let's see . . . what were their names? Michael and Sarah Greene. Says here he's a minister." He looked back up at Toni. "Have you had any contact with them?"

"No. None at all. But I'll be glad to call them if you think I should."

"Try the grandmother first. She's the one who hired your father, and you've already had one conversation with her. It would make the initial contact easier. From the notes in Julie's file, your father seemed to feel the grandmother was the most helpful. The parents seemed to have a real hard time even discussing their daughter's disappearance. Of course, that's not difficult to understand. I can't imagine how hard this is for them."

Toni pressed her lips together and nodded as she held the water cup between her hands. Abe's reminder that Julie's father was a minister had suddenly opened an entirely different dimension of the situation that she had not considered before. "Her father's a minister," she mused aloud. "I'd forgotten about that."

"Is that important?"

"No, not really, but . . . I guess I hadn't thought until now how Julie's disappearance would impact the family spiritually. With her father being a minister, I can only assume she was raised in a Christian home, with countless opportunities to receive the Lord. . . ."

"I'm afraid you're one up on me there. I'm not very familiar with the details of the Christian faith—or any faith, for that matter. We went to temple occasionally when I was young, but not often enough that I ever understood much of it. I didn't even study for or have a *bar mitzvah*, although my Aunt Sophie tried to convince my parents that I should. I guess she was the only faithful Jew in the family."

Toni raised her eyebrows in surprise. "Abe . . . Abraham. Of course. I hadn't realized you were Jewish."

"By heritage, not by practice. I remember when I was about ten and my Uncle David, Sophie's husband, died. Aunt Sophie sat *shivah*; I didn't even know what that meant."

"What exactly does it mean?"

"I'm still not completely sure, but it has to do with a seven-day mourning period right after someone dies. Aunt Sophie was scandalized that she was the only one in the family who observed it, although I don't know why she was surprised, since she's also the only one who observes the Sabbath—*Shabbat,* as she calls it."

Toni smiled. "Your aunt sounds like an interesting lady."

"She is. You'd like her. I'll have to take you to meet her sometime."

"Oh, well . . . Does she live around here?"

"Just up the freeway in Centralia. Not far at all. It would be a nice drive, don't you think?"

Was that a generic question, or was he proposing that the two of them make a day of it and drive up there together? She decided to ignore the question and change the subject. "Do you have other relatives around here?"

"Only Sol, my uncle. Solomon Jacob Levitz, Sophie's—and my mother's—younger brother. Sol used to work right here at the station. He ended up taking an early retirement due to an injury he received in the line of duty. I'll have to introduce you to him, although I'll warn you ahead of time, he's nothing like Aunt Sophie. She's the religious one in the family; Sol's the heathen." He grinned. "I think you'll like him anyway. He's a bit overemotional and reactionary, but he's been like a father to me since my own parents died."

"Your parents? Oh, Abe, how awful. I'm so sorry. What happened?"

"Car accident. It was just after I went away to college. They were both killed instantly. It was terrible. Aunt Sophie sat *shivah,* of course, and I know she spent many hours praying for me—as she still does. But Uncle Sol, he stepped right in and helped me financially so I could finish my education. Eventually, once I had my foot in the door here, he put in a good word for me and helped me get into the detectives' division. I owe him a lot."

"I had no idea," she said, her heart constricting with compassion as she realized that this tough, handsome police detective understood better what she was going through than she would ever have imagined. "You must miss them terribly."

Abe, who to this point had shown little emotion as he related the story of his parents' death, suddenly had tears in his eyes. "Yes. I seldom talk about it. But with you . . . Well, I guess I knew you'd understand better than most."

"Don't you have any brothers or sisters?"

"Nope. It's just me."

Resisting the impulse to reach over and touch his hand, she said only, "Thanks for confiding in me. I've certainly learned a lot about you today."

Abe's jaws clenched, and it was obvious he was composing himself. "True. You now know my parents are dead, I'm an only child, and I'm Jewish—well, sort of."

Toni smiled. "How can you be 'sort of' Jewish? You're either Jewish, or you're not."

"In that case, I guess I am. And I guess it's safe to assume that you're not."

"Well, I don't sit *shivah* and I don't observe *Shabbat*." She took another sip of water and tried her best to sound casual. "But I do worship the God of Israel."

Abe raised his eyebrows. "Meaning?"

"I'm a Christian."

"Well, I figured that—especially after attending your father's funeral. It was pretty heavy on the religious stuff. But I can't say that I've ever known a Christian who talked about worshiping the God of Israel, even though I assume you mean that your religion is pretty much rooted in mine—or should I say, in Aunt Sophie's."

Toni smiled. "The God of your Aunt Sophie's faith is also the God of my faith. They're one and the same."

Abe looked uncomfortable. "I really don't know enough about any of it to discuss it intelligently. How about if we move on to the second thing you can do regarding this investigation."

The sudden shift of topic threw Toni for a moment. "The second thing?"

"The first being to contact Julie Greene's grandmother."

"Oh. Yes, now I remember."

"The other thing I would suggest—and this is not easy for me to say, but you're the only one who can really pursue this angle right now—is to consider having an autopsy done on your dad."

Toni was shocked. "An autopsy? My dad's been buried for almost a month."

"I know. And like I said, this isn't easy—and it may not even work. It's a long shot, but you could talk to the physician who was on the scene when the coroner certified your dad's cause of death and see if you can get him to support you in an attempt to have your father's body exhumed." He paused. "I'm sorry. I know this is hard, but it's the only way to find out if there was something other than a heart attack involved in your dad's death. If there was, then Mr. Olson's information might mean something. Would you . . . like to think about it for a while before making a decision?"

Toni nodded, unable to talk. Strangely, the only thing she could think of at the moment was how something like this would affect Melissa. As fragile as the girl's emotions were already, Toni wondered if she had the right to even consider exhuming their father's body for the purpose of an autopsy. But, as Abe had pointed out, what other option did she have at this point? She finished her water, then crushed the paper cup in her hand and dropped it into the trashcan.

~~~

Abe walked in to Matthews and Matthews Detective Agency less than five minutes after Toni and April Lippincott had arrived. He still had a hard time believing how quickly and easily this meeting had come together—how it had, in fact, fallen straight into their laps. After suggesting to Toni the previous Friday that she contact Julie

Greene's grandmother, he had not expected anything to come of it this soon, and certainly not anything as enlightening as a face-to-face meeting with the woman. Toni had called him first thing Monday morning, however, informing him that before she had even had a chance to telephone Mrs. Lippincott, the woman had instead called her, hesitantly expressing her concern that Paul Matthews's death might have something to do with his investigation into Julie's disappearance. After a lengthy conversation, April Lippincott had asked if she might fly out and meet with Toni. Toni, of course, had readily agreed. And now, here they were, late Wednesday afternoon, the three of them, meeting in Toni's father's office to discuss how to proceed from here.

Abe, his off-white shirt open at the collar and the sleeves rolled up above his wrists, walked straight toward the attractive white-haired lady sitting in the chair next to Toni's desk. He was carrying Julie Greene's file in his left hand. "Mrs. Lippincott," he said, extending his free hand. "Please, don't get up. I'm Abe Matthews. How are you?"

"I'm fine, Mr. Matthews," she answered, smiling as she took his hand, "and I'm glad to meet you. I've heard so much about you from Toni. Thank you. I won't get up. It's been a very long day, and I'm rather tired."

"I can imagine. It's certainly good to have you here."

Mrs. Lippincott's smile faded. "Thank you, Detective."

"Please, call me Abe. This is strictly an unofficial visit." He released her hand and turned to Toni, who was sitting at her desk, watching their exchange. What had she told April Lippincott about him? Had she mentioned anything personal, or had it all been strictly business? Why did Toni always have to look so beautiful? And those blue eyes . . . he pulled himself back. "Toni, thanks for including me."

"Glad to," she answered, offering him a half-smile. "Although I must admit, it was Mrs. Lippincott who first suggested it. When I realized she shared my suspicions about a possible link between Dad's death and Julie's disappearance, I mentioned that you were helping me try to get to the bottom of all this, and the next thing I knew, she had proposed a three-way meeting. Then, a couple of hours ago, I picked her up at the airport, and, well . . . here we are."

Yes, here we are, he thought, irritated with himself for the yearning he felt as he watched her every movement and hung on her every word. Why couldn't he have fallen for someone who didn't already belong to somebody else? He cleared his throat and sat down in the extra chair across from Toni, obviously placed there in anticipation of his arrival. Tearing his eyes away from her, he looked at April.

"Well, Mrs. Lippincott, how was your flight?"

Her pale blue eyes mirrored her fatigue. "All right, I suppose," she answered, smiling wearily. "But if I'm to call you two Abe and Toni, then you must call me April. I feel old enough as it is without you attractive young people making me feel any older."

Abe returned her smile. "April it is." He looked at Toni and raised an eyebrow. He was deferring to her, and she appeared to read his signal perfectly.

"So," she said, "where do we start? I've filled Mrs. Lipp—April—in on what Simon Olson told you about having seen that vehicle drive up to Dad's the morning he died. Beyond that and what little is in Julie's file, I explained that I have nothing more than a hunch, a gut feeling, I guess, that there's a connection between them. I see you've brought Julie's file."

"Yes, I did." Abe held out the file to April. "I realize you probably already know most everything that's in here, but I thought you might want to see it anyway."

April hesitated, then took the file and laid it open on her lap. She caught her breath as the picture of the smiling young girl greeted her. When she spoke, her voice was barely above a whisper. "She's so beautiful, my Julie. So beautiful . . . and so sweet. . . ."

Her voice trailed off, and Abe and Toni remained silent as April perused the notations in the file. After a few minutes, she looked up, her eyes moist as they settled on Toni. "You have a sister her age, don't you?"

"Yes. One year younger than Julie. Her name is Melissa."

April nodded, then turned to Abe. "What do we do, Detective? Excuse me . . . Abe. There has to be more to all of this than just coincidence. This mysterious Carlo person, notes in the file regarding a possible baby-selling ring, a vehicle seen near Paul Matthews's cabin the morning of his death, the notation about Eagle Lake, at the very place and on the day Toni's father died . . . and his death coming just days after I last spoke with him and he told me he thought he would have some answers for me very soon." She shook her head. "I just can't believe there isn't something going on somewhere, something more than a man searching for a missing girl and then dying of a heart attack. That's too easy, too simple—and too unbelievable. It doesn't make sense. There's got to be more to it. Don't you agree?"

Abe considered his words carefully before answering. He had learned over the years that what seemed to be a casual comment made in private could end up being a quote passed to the wrong person, causing problems down the road. As important as it was to him to continue working with Toni to try and resolve her questions about her father's death, he wasn't yet ready or willing to paint himself into a corner. Besides, there were too many aspects of this situation that could spell trouble for him if he didn't handle them correctly.

"I think it's possible. Unfortunately, at this point, it's not provable, and I have nothing concrete to approach anyone with as far as launching an official investigation. Now, if you have something more you can tell us . . ."

Mrs. Lippincott shook her head. "I'm afraid not, except for this: I'm not willing to let this matter go until we've exhausted every possible resource. Right now, Detective, I'm thinking you're our best resource." She glanced at Toni before continuing. "As I told Paul Matthews and as I told Toni, money is no object. I want to find my Julie, and if there's a connection here, then I think it will lead us to her." Her chin quivered and she blinked back tears. "Julie is my only grandchild—the light of my life. I cannot begin to tell you what her disappearance has done to me—and to my daughter and son-in-law. They are devastated. We've got to know the truth—where she is, how she is—even if she's . . . We *need* to know. That's why I'm here, and that's why I'm going to stay . . . until we know something. Can you understand that?"

Before Abe could answer, Toni spoke up. "I understand. I understand perfectly. I feel exactly the same way about my dad's death. I have to know the truth—all of it. I *have* to."

Abe looked from Toni to April Lippincott, then back again. His heart went out to both of them. He knew what it was like to lose a loved one—in his case, two at one time. At least, with his parents, there were no unknown factors to deal with. He sighed. Even if he had not wanted to pursue the case simply to stay close to Toni for as long as possible, he knew at that moment that he would have agreed to help these two women anyway. How could he turn them down? Besides, better that he be the one involved than some other detective who might go snooping around and dig up more dirt than necessary. There were some things that were better left buried, he reminded himself. Now, not only was his heart telling him to commit to this investigation, albeit unofficial, but wisdom and prudence dictated it as well.

"Like I told Toni the other day," he said, "you can count me in. I'll do what I can."

Mrs. Lippincott relaxed visibly at Abe's words. He only wished he could do the same.

～～～

It was the following Monday before Toni could get an appointment to see Dr. Jensen. Toni's father and Bruce Jensen had been friends for years, golfing and fishing together every chance they got.

He had also been Paul Matthews's personal physician. As a result, he was immediately notified when Paul was found dead, lying in the bottom of his fishing boat not far from shore at Eagle Lake. When the coroner arrived and certified Paul's death as being due to natural causes, Bruce Jensen was already there, confirming his patient's existing heart condition. So, it was Bruce that Toni had finally decided to call to discuss the possibility of having an autopsy performed on her father. The fact that April Lippincott had insisted on coming along, anxious to explain to the doctor why she agreed that there was a need for an autopsy, was comforting to Toni. April, although refusing Toni's offer to stay with her and Melissa, had spent quite a bit of time at their house since her arrival in River View, and both of the Matthews girls were growing quite fond of her.

Toni and April had barely settled into their seats in the waiting room when they were called in to Dr. Jensen's office. The fiftyish man with thick, silver-gray hair and steel blue eyes came around from behind his desk to greet them.

"Toni," he said, clasping her outstretched hand and laying his other hand on her shoulder. "I haven't seen you since the funeral. How are you doing? And how is Melissa?"

Toni smiled. Although Bruce Jensen had not been her personal physician since she graduated from high school, he had been the family physician for as long as Toni could remember. Melissa was crazy about him and jokingly referred to him as "Marcus Welby" after watching the medical series reruns on television.

"I'm fine, thank you." She turned to April. "Dr. Jensen, this is April Lippincott."

Bruce's smile was charming. "Mrs. Lippincott. What a pleasure. Please, sit down, both of you."

Toni and April lowered themselves into the two comfortable armchairs in front of the desk while Bruce settled into his own chair, facing them. "This is quite a treat," he said, still smiling. "To what do I owe this unexpected visit?"

"Well, as I told you on the phone, it's . . . personal," Toni explained. "It has to do with Dad's death. That's why April—Mrs. Lippincott—came along. Her fifteen-year-old granddaughter, Julie Greene, is missing. She ran away from home. Dad was investigating her disappearance when he died."

The doctor's smile faded. "Oh, I'm so sorry. I can't imagine how difficult it must be not knowing the whereabouts of a loved one, particularly one so young."

"Thank you," said Mrs. Lippincott.

Bruce looked back at Toni. "I'm . . . afraid I still don't understand what this is about. I guess I'm just not making the connection. You say you're here to talk about your dad's death, and Mrs. Lippincott is here because . . . ?"

Toni sensed April stiffen beside her. She took a deep breath. "Dr. Jensen, Mrs. Lippincott and I are here because . . . we think there may be some connection between my father's death and the fact that he was looking for Julie." She waited, but the doctor did not respond. "We . . . think my father may have been getting too close to finding Julie, and someone did not want that happening, so the person . . . what I'm trying to say is . . . I think maybe my dad's death was due to something other than a heart attack. I know that sounds farfetched, but . . ."

Bruce leaned forward. "Yes, it does. In fact, it sounds more than farfetched. It sounds impossible. Toni, you seem to be forgetting that your father was more than my patient; he was my friend. I was treating him for a heart condition. He was on medication for it, and he seemed to be doing well, but there are never any guarantees. I saw your father almost immediately after he died. It was obvious he'd had a heart attack. In fact, I was with the coroner when he certified his death as being by natural causes, and that was not easy for me, I might add. I cared deeply for your father. We'd known each other for years. Don't you think that if I had seen anything at all to make me think his death wasn't exactly what the coroner said it was, I would have brought up the need for an autopsy? But there was nothing, nothing at all."

"I know that, but—"

April interrupted. "Dr. Jensen, Paul Matthews was investigating my granddaughter's disappearance when he died. Days before his death, he told me that he thought he was about to find her. After his death Toni discovered a notation in Julie's file that said 'Eagle Lake, Wednesday, 6 A.M.' Mr. Matthews died at Eagle Lake on Wednesday morning. Doesn't that all seem a bit too coincidental to you?"

"Not at all," Bruce answered, his voice soft and reassuring. "Particularly since Paul was alone when he died, and there was absolutely nothing to indicate any sort of struggle or foul play. From what you say, the note didn't seem to indicate which Wednesday, did it? I think you and Toni are letting your grief and worry run away with you—and I don't blame you a bit. This is a terribly difficult time for both of you. But . . . we have to keep this in perspective. A vague note in a file hardly amounts to evidence of some sinister connection between two otherwise unrelated but tragic situations."

"Apparently that's the way the police feel too," said Toni.

The doctor raised his eyebrows. "You mean you've talked to them?"

Toni hesitated. She didn't want to cause problems for Abe. "Indirectly," she answered, "but there doesn't seem to be enough solid evidence to warrant an investigation."

Bruce smiled. "Well, then, you see? There really is nothing to this other than a coincidence or two and a couple of overactive imaginations—absolutely understandable under the circumstances, of course."

"Toni wants an autopsy done on her father." April Lippincott's abrupt statement startled Toni almost as much as it obviously did Bruce Jensen. The doctor's eyes opened wide and his face reddened slightly as the words hung in the air awaiting a response.

"An autopsy?" Although his voice was low, the words seemed to explode from the otherwise calm physician. He fixed his eyes on Toni as he spoke. "Do you realize what you're saying? You want to have your father's body exhumed? Toni, if nothing else, stop and think what this would do to Melissa. And for what? There is absolutely nothing to warrant such a drastic move."

"I think there is," said Toni. "And I was hoping you'd help me get the necessary court order."

Bruce's blue eyes turned to ice as he glared at her. "After all the years I have served as your family physician, not to mention your father's friend, and this is the thanks I get?"

Toni was puzzled. "What do you mean?"

"I mean," said Dr. Jensen slowly, "that you quite obviously do not trust my medical expertise. You don't trust my opinion—or the coroner's, for that matter—about your father's death being due to natural causes, more specifically, a heart attack. I find that quite offensive, not to mention hurtful." He stood. "If you'll excuse me, I have patients waiting." Without another word, Bruce escorted them from his office, then stormed away and left them standing in the hallway.

"My," said April, "that didn't go well at all, did it?"

"I'm afraid not." Toni shook her head. "I've never seen Dr. Jensen like that—never, in all the years we've known him."

"Well, my dear, I imagine it's safe to assume that we're not going to get any help from him."

Toni smiled halfheartedly. "It certainly looks that way, doesn't it?"

They walked down the hall and back into the waiting room, then out the front door toward Toni's red Taurus. April stopped just short of the car and turned, looking back toward the office.

"Is something wrong?" Toni asked.

"I believe there is," April answered, her back to Toni. "I think something is very wrong, and I think your Dr. Jensen just may have something to do with it."

CHAPTER 6

The late June weather was unseasonably cool with dark clouds threatening to bring even more rain to the already saturated city. From the sound of his uncle's voice when he had called, Abe thought Sol's mood probably matched the weather. He frowned as he rang the doorbell, wondering again what Sol was so upset about. It had been several weeks since Abe had been to visit his uncle, and he supposed it could be something as simple as feeling slighted by his only nephew's inattention, but he didn't really think so. For Sol to phone Abe at the station and demand that he come over "ASAP," it had to be something more serious than that.

Rosalie answered the door. Abe did his best to hide his dislike for his uncle's current live-in girlfriend, but he was sure she knew how he felt.

"Hello, Rosalie. How are you?"

The petite woman with the dyed red hair, the too-tight pants, and the stiletto heels smiled—a smile, Abe told himself, that was as phony as the rest of her. "I'm fine, Abe, thank you. Sol's in his office. Go on in. He's expecting you."

I bet he is, Abe thought grimly, *and I bet you know he's gunning for me, even if you don't know why. There's nothing you'd like better than for us to have a fight to help you separate him from the only real family he has left. Then you'd have him all to yourself. Well, it's not going to happen.* Aloud he simply said, "Thanks," and headed for his uncle's office, which was just off the living room.

Even though Rosalie had said that Sol was expecting him, Abe knocked anyway. He had always shown respect to his uncle, and he wasn't about to stop now.

"Come in." The command was gruff and clipped. Abe had guessed right. This was definitely something more important than his having neglected to visit. He opened the door and stepped inside.

Although Sol had always referred to this room as his office, it was really more of a den, a typical male lair filled with plaques and awards honoring Sol's law enforcement service, pictures commemorating his early days on the force, a big-screen TV that took up a large portion of one entire wall, a leather couch that still smelled new, and cigar smoke that always smelled stale. The only thing that validated the room's title of "office" was the mahogany desk in the corner, behind which sat a slightly overweight but still handsome fifty-three-year-old man, a few silver streaks in his dark, wavy hair and a half-chewed cigar clamped between his teeth. Sol Levitz was not smiling.

"Uncle Sol," Abe said, trying to sound as positive as he could. "It's good to see you. How are you?"

His uncle did not get up. "What do you mean, it's good to see me," Sol growled, the cigar scarcely moving as he talked. "It's been so long since you've been here, I'm surprised you recognize me. Sit down." He motioned toward the chair that had been placed in front of his desk.

Not a good sign, Abe thought. He sat down, but before he could say anything, Sol went on.

"So, you want to know how I am? Well, I'm glad you asked because that's just why I called you here—to tell you how I am." His dark, heavy eyebrows came together in a scowl, and he leaned forward. The heavy smell of his uncle's cigar assailed Abe's nostrils. There were times that smell brought pleasant memories to Abe's mind, but this was not one of those times.

"I'm worried, boy, that's how I am. Worried. And you're the one I'm worried about." Sol fixed his almost-black eyes on his nephew. Abe felt as if they were boring straight through to his brain, reading his thoughts. He wondered if his uncle could see that he didn't have a clue as to what it was that had Sol so worried. He wondered just how serious the offense might be that had caused the worry, and he wondered how this man, whom he loved almost as much as he had loved his own father, could be so unlike his two older sisters, Sophie, his aunt, and Rachel, Abe's late mother. The sisters, of course, had also been somewhat different from each other. Sophie was more outspoken than Rachel, who was two years younger, but both were kind and tenderhearted, generous to a fault. Sophie had remained faithful to her Jewish beliefs, while Rachel had given up practicing her religion after marrying her Gentile husband, Don, who claimed to be an agnostic. Sol, on the other hand, had not only stopped practicing his religion years earlier, he also claimed to have ceased to believe in God. Abe wasn't sure about that part. Was it really possible for anyone, regardless of how many heartaches and disappointments life dealt, to simply decide to stop believing in God? He doubted it. His mother used to say, "We may not go to temple, or sit *shivah,* or observe *Shabbat* like your grandparents and Aunt Sophie, but that doesn't mean there is no God. I believe he's probably out there—somewhere—but, like your father says, no one can know for sure, so we might as well just live our lives the best we can and see what happens."

That had frightened Abe, even as a young boy. It made him feel that life was nothing more than a continual shooting in the dark, having no idea what the target was or whether or not you were even getting close. Secretly, he had always hoped Aunt Sophie was right, that there was a God and that the Jewish people were his chosen ones. At the same time, he knew that probably meant that only the faithful Jews were chosen, which certainly left him out. Maybe Sol had opted for the easiest way after all.

Besides he reminded himself, *Uncle Sol has always been very good to me. Without his help, I never would have made it through college when Mom and Dad died, and I might not have become a detective. I've got to remember that this gruff exterior of his is just his way of hiding his pain over losing Patty and the baby, not to mention the injury and being forced to retire. . . . Life hasn't exactly been kind to him. It's up to me to get this situation—whatever it is—cleared up so we don't have anything between us.*

"I'm sorry," Abe said, his voice reflecting his respect and affection for the man sitting across the desk from him. "You're going to have to help me out here. I'm afraid I don't know what I've done to cause you so much concern."

Continuing to eye him, Sol removed the cigar from his mouth and placed it in an ashtray, then slowly sat back in his chair. "Does the name Toni Matthews mean anything to you?"

Abe flinched. How did Uncle Sol know about Toni? And just how much did he know?

Sol raised his eyebrows. "Ah, I see the name rings a bell somewhere in that hard head of yours. Would you like to tell me about her?"

"I . . ." Abe's mind was running in several directions at once. If Uncle Sol knew he was involved with Toni, then he knew everything. He had been one of the best police detectives River View had ever seen, and once he sniffed something out, he didn't stop until he had learned all there was to know. There was no sense trying to buffalo him.

"I met her a few weeks ago, not long after her father's funeral, when I stopped by his agency to return a book. I ran into her again the next day at the station, and we got to talking and . . ." He took a deep breath. "Toni thinks there might be something more to her father's death than a heart attack, and I'm trying to help her find out if that's the case. There's no real evidence but—"

"Of course there's no evidence," Sol interrupted, "real or otherwise. I didn't call you over here today to hear what this Toni Matthews woman thinks. I want to know what *you're* thinking, boy! Or maybe you aren't thinking at all, is that it? You see a pretty face and your brain flies right out the window. What's wrong with you, are you *meshugga?* Don't you know how much trouble you can get into, running around the countryside, looking for clues with the daughter of the man whose death you are supposedly investigating—especially when there's no official investigation? Not to mention the fact that it isn't even in your jurisdiction. You think I don't know what's going on in this town? I talk to people, you know. I get phone calls, especially from the station. I even checked the public record. Toni Matthews's father died of natural causes. It was certified by the coroner, and his own physician believes it was a heart attack. Nothing suspicious about that, nothing warranting any sort of investigation. If there were, don't you think the sheriff's office would be on it? But they're not, are they? What does that tell you?"

Sol relaxed in his chair, and his voice softened to that of the caring uncle Abe had known all his life. "What are you trying to do, boy, get yourself suspended? Ruin your career just when it's getting off the ground? After the good word I put in for you to help you get into the detectives division, now you're trying to sabotage your job? And for what? A woman—a woman who just happens to be engaged to someone else. What's the matter with you? There are a million women out there, good-looking ones too. So why this one? Why Toni Matthews?"

Abe's head was pounding almost as hard as his heart. He loved his uncle. He didn't like seeing him this upset; he knew it wasn't good for him. He also knew that the man took his duties as surrogate father very seriously. Even though Sol seemed to be overreacting, Abe had to admit that what his uncle said had a lot of truth to it. If he weren't careful, he could be putting his job in jeopardy by continuing this investigation, even though it was informal and on his own time. Still, he couldn't stop seeing Toni, not as long as there was any chance at all. . . .

"Uncle Sol, I'm sorry—"

"I don't want 'sorry,'" Sol interrupted, the concern evident in his eyes. "I want to know why you'd do something so unprofessional as to spend your time running all over creation with this woman, tracking down clues that don't exist. This isn't like you, boy. I always thought you had a good head on your shoulders. So why the sudden turn-around? What's so special about Toni Matthews?"

Abe hesitated, but he knew his uncle well enough to know that the best way to talk to him was just to spit it out. "Everything," he said, searching his heart for the answer and holding his gaze steady as he spoke to the man who had been his mentor and closest friend for slightly over ten years now. "Everything about her is special. I don't know how else to explain it. I know it doesn't make sense, and I know I'm walking a fine line here, trying to help answer her questions about her dad's death. But . . . I can't back off now. I have to see this thing through. I'm sure we'll get it cleared up soon and find out her dad's death was nothing more than a heart attack, just like you said. When I can convince Toni of that, that will be the end of it. It'll be over, I promise."

Sol squinted as if he didn't believe him. "No more Toni Matthews after that? Is that what you're telling me?"

"No. That's not what I'm saying. I can promise you no more unofficial investigation once I convince Toni that her father's death was a heart attack and nothing more, but I have no intention of not seeing her after that. In fact, I'm . . . hoping to make her a permanent part of my life some day."

The two men eyed each other for several seconds before Sol shook his head. "I had a feeling you were going to say that. It's written all over your face. All you have to do is hear her name and you go soft. You're a fool, boy, do you know that? A fool. Completely *meshugga*."

Abe wished he could deny it, that he could at least convince himself, if not his uncle, that he wasn't a fool. He wished he could assure the both of them that he knew without a doubt that Toni would someday give in to the feelings he was sure she had for him and break her engagement to Brad, but he didn't know that. He could only hope and continue to try to be involved in her life as much as possible. For now, it was all he had.

"You may be right," he said, "but it's what I have to do. I'll promise you something else too. I'll be careful, and I won't take this investigation any further than I absolutely have to."

Sol sighed, then nodded his head as if resigning himself to Abe's foolishness. When he said nothing further, Abe realized he had been dismissed. Slowly, he rose from his chair and walked out of the office and past Rosalie, who was sitting quietly on the sofa in the living room, undoubtedly having heard every loud word that made its way through the closed door. As he left his uncle's house and stepped out onto the porch, the first raindrops began to fall, splashing on his face as he made his way toward the car.

Brad's heart soared as he aimed the silver Lexus westward toward the rugged Washington coast. It had been a long time since he and Toni had been able to spend a full day together, and he didn't want to waste a minute of it. The faint smell of her perfume as she sat in the seat next to his teased his senses with every passing mile. He smiled as he remembered how radiant she had looked when he had met her at April Lippincott's hotel. Toni had gone to town early to have breakfast with April and had asked Brad to pick her up there so he could meet the elderly lady from Colorado. Toni had been singing April's praises since she arrived in town the previous week, but this was the first opportunity Brad had found to break away and meet her, if only for a few minutes. He had to admit, Mrs. Lippincott had seemed quite charming and genuine. He only hoped she would go back to Colorado soon. Her presence seemed to fuel Toni's obsession with the Julie Greene case and her father's death.

Before driving to the hotel, Brad had first popped into his office for a few minutes to clear up a few details and then had headed out the door before ten, his appointments having been canceled or rescheduled the previous day, as soon as he was sure Toni would be free to accompany him.

"On a Wednesday?" she had asked when he had proposed the beach getaway. "Why not wait until Saturday when you're off?"

"For one thing, it wouldn't be as much fun as playing hooky from the office for a full day. For another, this weekend is the Fourth of July, remember? If we go now, in the middle of the week, we'll beat the crowds. Besides, they're predicting one day of sunshine tomorrow but more clouds and rain by Thursday or Friday. Let's go while the weather's good and we can walk on the beach, find some secluded place, just the two of us. . . ."

To his delight she had agreed, and now they were on their way. It was a pleasant ninety-minute drive, and Brad relished the joy of being so close to this woman he had loved since he wasn't much more than a boy. Maybe today he would be able to broach the subject of setting a wedding date. He knew what she had said about not being ready to make any plans until this situation involving her father's death was settled, but Brad could not believe that resolving that issue could take much longer. As far as he was concerned, it was already settled, and Toni was a sensible young woman. Surely she would come to that same conclusion soon.

As the surrounding countryside changed from mountains, rivers, and tall evergreens to flatlands and marshes interspersed with farmhouses and barns in various stages of disrepair, Brad looked forward with longing to being able to hold Toni in his arms, privately and uninterrupted, while they planned their future life together. It was something they had done quite often in the past, before Toni's father died. Nothing had been quite the same since then. Brad knew that was to be expected, but he had somehow thought Toni's loss would draw them closer together. Instead, it seemed to have driven a wedge between them, particularly since Abe had come into the picture.

Abe Matthews. How Brad had come to resent the very sound of that name, and how ironic that Toni and Abe should have the same last name, even down to its spelling. Another reason to get going on their wedding plans, Brad reminded himself. The sooner he could get Toni's name changed from Matthews to Anderson, the better.

He pulled to a stop as they came to the coast road that ran north and south. "Tourist trap to the right or seclusion to the left?" he asked, glancing at her anxiously.

She smiled. "Left. Unless, of course, you'd like some company other than me."

Brad's heart jumped, and he leaned over to kiss her. "Not a chance," he whispered. As they headed south, the sun was now almost directly overhead, and he was thankful the weatherman had been right in his prediction for the day. Other than a slightly cool breeze off the ocean, the weather was a perfect seventy-five degrees, with only a few scattered clouds on the western horizon. The picnic lunch he had brought would not go to waste the way the last one had when he had run into Toni and Abe walking along the sidewalk toward her father's office. The pain of that memory, not to mention the vision of the two of them pulling up in front of Toni's house in Abe's car after having spent the entire afternoon together at the lake, squeezed his heart. It was the first time since he had known Toni that he had felt their relationship threatened by someone else. Until then, the only other man who had ever held a major place in Toni's life, besides himself, had been her father. When he died, Brad assumed that he would take an even more prominent place in Toni's heart than before. He had always been so sure that she belonged to him, that their future was secure, that God himself had ordained it so. Seeing her with Abe had stolen his sense of security, making him more determined than ever to move ahead with their wedding plans as quickly as possible.

Turning down a narrow road that led to a seldom-used campground and picnic area, Brad determined to put thoughts of Abe Matthews out of his mind. This was his day with Toni, and he was determined to make the most of it. They parked in a shaded area of the empty, unpaved parking lot and climbed out of the car. The cool, salty sea breeze washed over them as Brad removed the picnic basket, along with a blanket and a couple of towels, from the car's trunk. Toni, her short blonde curls gleaming in the sunlight, stood gazing out at the ocean. Her jeans were rolled up to mid-calf, and she wore a short-sleeved yellow blouse tucked in at the waist. It was all he could do not to pull her into his arms and kiss her, right there, and then insist that they set a wedding date before they did anything else. But he was determined to do everything right, to make this a perfect day, one that, if all went well, would not end until that wedding date had indeed been set.

He walked up behind her. "Do you want to eat lunch here on one of the picnic tables? Or shall we walk down to the beach and see if we can find a better spot?"

It took a moment before she turned, almost as if she hadn't heard him at first. When she did look at him, she seemed a million miles away. "I'm sorry. What did you say?"

"Lunch," he said. "I wondered if you wanted to eat it here or—"

Her eyes lit up, and her smile was warm as she interrupted him. "Oh, not here. Besides, I'm not hungry yet, are you? Why don't we take a walk first? I'll carry the blanket and towels, you carry the picnic basket. Should we take our windbreakers?"

Brad handed her the towels. "I'll carry the rest. And yes, I think we should take windbreakers. You know how the weather can change around here, and the wind is a bit cool."

They started down the path that led to the water, removing their shoes and walking barefoot as soon as they hit the dry sand. It was warm between their toes, slowing their pace. With all they were carrying, they couldn't hold hands, but Brad felt as if they were joined together nonetheless.

Less than a mile from where they had parked the car, they came to a small, secluded cove. The soft roar of the waves echoed off the sand dunes that dotted the driftwood-strewn beach. A rundown shack, which had undoubtedly once served as some sort of cabin, stood off to one side.

Toni stopped and looked around. "How about this? There's no one here but you and me and a few dozen seagulls."

"It's perfect," Brad agreed. "How about over here, against this dune?" When Toni nodded, he spread the blanket, hurrying to place their shoes on each corner to hold it in place against the breeze.

Toni sat down and opened the basket, then spread out the food in front of her—cheese, French bread, peaches, pickles, oatmeal cookies, and a thermos of iced tea. "You thought of everything," she said, smiling at Brad as he took a seat beside her. "Even my favorite fruit."

Brad leaned over and kissed her. "I know. I want it to be a perfect day for you. You've been through so much lately."

Toni dropped her eyes for a moment, then looked back up at him and smiled. "You always know just what to say and do, don't you?" Then, glancing toward the food, she said, "Shall we eat? I didn't think I was hungry when we got here, but that walk worked up an appetite. Will you pray?"

Brad took her hands in his. His heart was so full and there was so much he wanted to say, but he limited his words to asking a blessing on the food, reminding himself that they had all day. He didn't want to overwhelm her.

They had scarcely begun to eat when the mild breeze of a few moments earlier turned into a gusting wind, threatening to blow sand onto their lunch. Looking out to sea, they saw that the few clouds they had noticed on the horizon when they first arrived were multiplying and beginning to make their way inland. They snatched up the food and stuffed it back into the basket, grabbed their shoes, windbreakers, towels, and blanket, and headed for the shack. "Looks like we'll be eating inside, after all," Brad said as they stepped inside the doorless hut. "Is this OK? Or would you rather go back to the car and eat there?"

It was obvious from the trash strewn about the two rooms that they weren't the building's first visitors. Toni hesitated, then set her belongings down on top of a broken, dusty table. "This is fine. We can spread the blanket on the floor and finish our picnic in here. It isn't much, but it blocks the wind."

They sat in the middle of the larger of the two rooms, eating their lunch as the wind howled outside. Even inside the temperature was dropping, and soon they were wearing their windbreakers and huddling close together on the blanket. Brad decided that he couldn't have set a better scene if he had tried.

"I like this," he said. "How about you?"

"Umm. It's perfect. I'm glad we came."

"Me too. And we don't have to hurry home. No appointments, no worries, nothing. Just you and me."

"And Melissa," Toni added. "Don't forget, she'll be home from baby-sitting by five-thirty. I didn't leave her anything for dinner, so I'd really like to get home at least by the time she does so I can fix her something. Besides, I don't like having her spend her evenings alone. It gives her too much time to think."

Brad didn't answer. He loved Melissa and didn't want her feeling neglected, but he really had counted on spending the entire day with Toni—alone. He supposed he would have to settle for most of the day and then make the evening a threesome.

"No problem. We'll pick up something on the way home, and then we can all have dinner together. How's her baby-sitting job coming along?"

"She loves it. Thinks Tyler's the cutest kid around. But she gets pretty emotional over the way he talks about his dad leaving and how much he misses him." Toni began rewrapping the food and putting it back into the basket. "You didn't want any more, did you?"

"Are you kidding? I'm stuffed."

"Me too." Toni paused and looked at Brad, frowning slightly. "I'm concerned about Melissa—about the way she's questioning her faith since Dad died. She really hasn't said too much about it, but when she was telling me how Tyler keeps praying for God to bring his dad back and how she worries about what will happen when his prayers don't get answered, I hear a hint of cynicism in her voice—about God, I mean. I never heard that from her before. I'm not sure if she's actually questioning God's very existence or just whether or not he cares enough to become involved in our lives. Either way, I don't like it."

"I think it's healthy."

Toni raised her eyebrows. "You do? Why?"

Brad took her hand. "Sweetheart, she's at the age when she has to make her family's faith her own. It's an individual commitment we each have to make, you know that. She's been raised in church, yes, and she knows all the Bible stories. She knows the difference between right and wrong, good and evil, but Toni—she hasn't ever really accepted Jesus as her Savior, has she?"

Toni shook her head. "No. You're right, she hasn't. I think she believes—mentally—but she's never made a real heart commitment."

"Exactly. So we have to pray for her that God will use this tragedy of losing your dad to bring her to that place. She needs that close, personal relationship with her heavenly Father now more than ever."

Brad sensed Toni stiffen ever so slightly, and it puzzled him. Had he said something to offend or hurt her? He was sure she agreed with him, so what could be wrong? Maybe his talk of the heavenly Father had reminded her of her own loss. "Are you OK? Did I say something to hurt you?"

Toni drew her hand away and resumed putting the food into the basket. Her voice was quiet and subdued, but without a hint of tears. "I'm fine. Really. And you're absolutely right about Melissa. We will definitely have to pray, just as you said. We've got to help her get through all of this."

Brad laid his hands on her shoulders and gently turned her toward him. "And what about you? Will you let me help you get through it?"

The tears came then, but Toni blinked them back. "I want to. Really, Brad, I do. But . . ."

"But what?"

"Until Abe and I can find out the truth about what happened to my dad and Julie, I don't see how you and I can make any plans. . . ."

"You and Abe? You and I can't make any plans because of what you and Abe have to do first? Toni, please, listen to me. You don't need Abe. *We* don't need Abe. We were doing just fine before he came along. I don't understand why he has to be a part of all this. We already know what happened to your dad. If there's more to it, then let the authorities take care of it—officially. Otherwise, let it go. And let Abe go. Please, Toni. I don't trust him. Please."

"You don't trust him? What do you mean by that?"

Brad had not meant to say nearly as much as he had, particularly about Abe, but the words were out and there was no taking them back now. "Sweetheart, I love you. You know that. The last thing in the world I want is to see you hurt. This Matthews guy, I . . . I think he has more in mind than just helping you find out about your dad's death. You're an attractive woman. He's an attractive, single man. I know I haven't been in practice very long, but I have been around long enough to know that it is not standard procedure for a police detective to spend his off hours helping someone track down information about the death of a loved one. The whole thing is wrong, Toni. It's wrong, and you're going to get hurt. I'm concerned about you for the same reason you're concerned about Melissa—because I love you. Please, try to understand."

She didn't answer, but he knew her well enough to read the war of emotions just under the surface. He pulled her into his arms, and she didn't resist. "Please," he whispered. "At least promise me that you'll think about what I said. Please?"

"I promise," she answered, her voice hoarse with emotion.

As he buried his face in her hair, he realized the day had not accomplished anything near what he had hoped. Still, it was a start. For that, and for the feel of her in his arms, he was grateful.

Toni looked over her shoulder and then pulled her Taurus away from the curb. "I'm so glad you agreed to come for dinner tonight, April. Melissa and I really enjoy having you over. Her friend Carrie will be there too. Brad is also coming, so you'll get to know him a little better. That brief meeting you had with him when he picked me up at your hotel the other morning really didn't count."

"That's true, my dear. We scarcely had a chance to say hello before he whisked you away. It's obvious your young man is quite smitten with you. How was your trip to the beach? Did the rain hold off long enough for you to get back home?"

"Not quite. It was beautiful when we got there, so we walked down the beach and found a great place for a picnic. But the wind came up and we had to duck into an old abandoned shack to finish our lunch. The rain didn't actually start until just after we got into the car to leave. Overall, it was a nice day."

"Nice? That's all?"

Toni glanced sideways at April, who was looking at her questioningly. "I would have thought a romantic day at the beach with your fiancé would rate more than a simple 'nice.'"

April's gaze, as well as her words, made Toni uncomfortable, and she turned her eyes back to the road in front of her. "Well, of course, it was . . . wonderful. I always enjoy my time with Brad. He's so good to me."

"I would imagine." When April said no more, Toni stopped at a red light and decided to change the subject. Before she could think of anything appropriate, April said, "You're not in love with him, are you?"

Toni jerked her head to the right. April Lippincott's pale blue eyes were soft with concern as she awaited Toni's answer. "What do you mean? Of course I'm in love with him. I'm engaged to him."

"Have you set a date yet?"

"Well . . . no. But I told you the reason for that. I can't start making wedding plans so soon after my father's death, especially now when I'm still trying to find out if there was something more than a heart attack involved. I certainly can't think about getting married until we get to the bottom of all that."

"'We,' as in you and me? Or 'we,' as in you and your handsome detective friend, Abe Matthews?"

Before she could answer, the driver in the car behind her honked his horn. The light had turned green. "He's not my friend," she said, driving through the intersection. "He's just . . . a detective who happened to know my father and is willing to help me investigate his death—in an unofficial way, of course."

"Of course." April paused. "Although it does seem a lot of trouble for him to go to for someone who's not a friend." When Toni didn't respond, April went on. "I think that maybe your Detective Matthews would like to be even more than a friend to you. Don't you agree?"

Toni was beginning to feel frustrated. "He's not 'my Detective Matthews,' and I really don't care what he wants or expects from me. This is strictly a professional, platonic relationship—and a temporary one at that. Once we've resolved this issue about Dad—and Julie, of course—any relationship I might have with Abe is over."

"I see."

Once again, Toni glanced at April. She appeared to be absorbed in gazing out the window. Toni decided to drop the conversation. It seemed she was only getting in deeper the more she tried to explain and defend her relationships with Brad and Abe. What was it about this woman from Colorado? Was she somehow able to see beyond Toni's words into her very heart? Could she sense that Toni had begun to question those relationships herself?

Toni thought back to her trip to the beach with Brad a couple of days earlier. She had been so sure that a day alone, just the two of them, was all she needed to regroup, to get her thoughts and feelings about Brad back in order, back to where they had been before . . . before Abe Matthews had come into her life, but it simply had not worked. As wonderful as Brad had been that day, and as much as she had enjoyed their trip to the beach, she had known from the moment they arrived and she had stood gazing out at the ocean that it was Abe who absorbed her thoughts and tugged at her heart. It was Abe she had wished she were spending the day with, and she had hated herself for it.

After all, not only was she engaged to Brad, who loved her more and treated her better than any woman could hope for, but she scarcely knew Abe, and what she did know about him did not recommend him as her lifetime mate. Abe was Jewish, and not a practicing Jew at that. Knowing that the Bible taught that believers and unbelievers should not be "unequally yoked" together in a marriage relationship, Toni clearly recognized that there was no point in pursuing a relationship with Abe, even if she were free to do so—which she wasn't. So, she had turned her attention and energy to Brad, hoping to make their day together so special that she would forget all about her "handsome detective friend, Abe Matthews," but it had not turned out that way. Although she had continued to insist to Brad—as she did with April—that Abe meant nothing to her beyond his professional help in finding out the truth about her dad's death, she wondered if they believed her any more than she believed herself.

As they pulled into her driveway, April looked over at Toni. "I've been thinking," she said. "I've been here more than a week now, and we really haven't been able to come up with any new ideas or clues about your dad's death or Julie's whereabouts. I know I said I was going to stay until we did, but . . . maybe it's time for me to go home. Maybe I need to find another private detective to search for Julie and let you get on with your life."

"Oh, April, no." Toni shut off the engine and reached over to lay her hand on April's arm. "We can't give up, not yet. There's got to be something we can do, some way to find—"

"Maybe," April interrupted, "but I'm not so sure anymore. If something doesn't turn up in the next day or so, I believe I'll go on home."

Just then Melissa and Carrie came running out of the house. Toni opened the door of the car and stepped outside to greet them. "Hello, you two. What's up? Where are you headed in such a hurry?"

"Over to Carrie's," Melissa explained. "She forgot her overnight bag. We'll only be a few minutes." She turned to April, who had just opened her car door, and helped her out. "Hello, Mrs. Lippincott. How are you?"

"I'm fine, Melissa. How are you?"

"Great. I'm really glad you could come. I wanted you to meet my best friend, Carrie. She's spending the night tonight."

Carrie, her short black hair and brown eyes a contrast to Melissa's fair coloring, smiled shyly. "Hello, Mrs. Lippincott. It's nice to meet you."

"The pleasure is mine, my dear. I'm looking forward to getting to know you this evening at dinner."

"Speaking of which," Toni interjected, "did Brad happen to call and say when he'd be over?"

"He sure did," Melissa answered. "In fact, he should be here any minute now. He said he'd stop on the way and pick up some charcoal to barbecue the steaks."

"Oh good, he remembered. OK, girls. Don't be late getting back. We'll start the coals as soon as Brad gets here—assuming some last minute clouds don't sneak in and dump some more rain on us."

The girls laughed and started down the driveway while April and Toni headed for the front door.

"Oh, by the way," Melissa called out.

Toni turned.

"Dr. Welby called."

"Melissa's name for Dr. Jensen," Toni reminded April, then looked back toward Melissa and Carrie. "Did he leave a message?"

"Only that you should call him at home."

"Thanks. I will." Toni held the front door for April. "Please make yourself comfortable. I'd better make that call right away. I really can't imagine what he wants to talk to me about, especially after the way he practically threw us out of his office the other day."

Mrs. Lippincott sat down at the far end of the couch, while Toni settled down next to the end table with the phone. Taking a quick peek in the address book for the doctor's home phone number, she picked up the receiver and dialed. Bruce Jensen answered on the third ring.

"Dr. Jensen, this is Toni Matthews. Melissa said you called."

"Yes, I did. Thank you for calling back so quickly. I wanted to apologize for my behavior toward you and Mrs. Lippincott on Monday. I was so shocked by your request that I'm afraid I overreacted. Please forgive me."

Toni hesitated, surprised by the unexpected apology. "Why . . . of course. I . . . I appreciate your call. Thank you."

"No need to thank me, Toni. I should have been more concerned about your feelings in the matter and less concerned with my own. I was very close to your father, as you know, and although my loss doesn't begin to compare to yours, I did take his death very hard. As a result, I'm afraid I wasn't very considerate. I've been rethinking our conversation and your request for my help in getting a court order to have your father's body exhumed for an autopsy. If that's something you still want to pursue, then I'll see what I can do."

Toni was stunned. She had just about given up on being able to have an autopsy done on her dad, and now the one man who could help her get it done was offering his help—the same man who had summarily tossed her and April out of his office earlier in the week. "I . . . yes. Yes, I am still interested in pursuing the autopsy." Toni looked at April, whose face registered the same puzzled shock that Toni felt.

"Fine. I'll make some phone calls Monday morning and see what I can do. I'll get back to you as soon as I know anything."

"Thank you. I . . . I don't know what else to say."

"You don't need to say anything. It's what I should have done when you expressed your concern. I must say, I still don't share that concern, but I'll do whatever I can to put your mind at ease. It's the least I can do for the daughter of a man who was one of my best friends for so many years."

When Toni hung up the phone, she sat motionless until April spoke. "Was that . . . what I think it was? Did Dr. Jensen just offer to help you get that autopsy on your father?"

Toni nodded. "Yes. Can you believe it?"

"Well, I must admit, his call couldn't have been more timely. I certainly can't leave town now, can I?" She sighed and shook her head slowly. "I never would have imagined. . . . Who would have thought, after the way he reacted to our visit on Monday, that he would do such an about-face? It seems I may have misjudged the man after all."

"Maybe we both did," Toni agreed. "I only wish I knew what to expect now. Do you suppose I should call Abe and tell him?"

"That would probably be a wise idea, since he's the one who suggested this move. Before you do that, however, have you thought about what you're going to tell Melissa? She and her friend will be back soon."

Toni's eyes opened wide. "I'd forgotten about that. Oh, April, I'm not looking forward to it. Please pray that she'll understand, that she won't—"

She was interrupted by the doorbell. "Brad," she said. "He's here with the charcoal. I suppose I'd better tell him before I tell Abe or Melissa." Toni looked at April. "Something tells me this dinner isn't going to turn out quite the way we'd expected."

CHAPTER 7

As soon as Toni opened the front door, Brad stepped inside and planted a kiss on her forehead. "Hi, beautiful. Sorry it took me so long, but I ran into my parents at the store when I stopped to pick up the charcoal. When I told them I was on my way here for a barbecue, they wanted to know when I was going to bring you over again. They reminded me they haven't seen you since the funeral, so I told them we'd try to come by after church on Sunday. Is that OK?"

"Oh. Well, sure, I . . ."

"Good. Let me take this charcoal out to the grill, and then I'll give you a real kiss." He stepped past Toni into the living room, then stopped. "Mrs. Lippincott. I didn't realize you were here. I mean, I knew you were coming. I just forgot. . . ."

April Lippincott smiled. "That's quite all right. You don't need to apologize or explain yourself. I can certainly understand why you'd forget about me, with your mind on kissing your fiancée. We all have our priorities, don't we?"

Brad grinned. "You're absolutely right, but I'm very glad to see you again. Excuse me while I go and put this charcoal down. I'll be right back."

As he walked into the kitchen and out the back door onto the covered porch, April and Toni exchanged looks. "Go ahead," April said. "I'll wait here and give you two a chance to talk."

"Thank you. I suppose that's best." Toni followed Brad outside, praying silently as she went that God would give her the right words and that Brad would understand. "Hi," she said, coming up behind him.

Brad turned. He had laid the bag of charcoal next to the barbecue, and his hands were free. Taking her in his arms, he said, "Hi, yourself. Did you come out here to collect your kiss?"

Before she could answer, his lips were on hers, but he stopped as soon as she stiffened. Pulling away, he looked down at her, his eyebrows drawn together in a puzzled frown. "What's the matter? Is something wrong?"

"No . . . well, yes. Not really, but . . ." She took a deep breath. "Oh, Brad, I'm so sorry. I know I should have said something to you about this before, but . . . I wasn't sure I wanted to do it at first. Then, when I decided to go ahead with it and went to see Dr. Jensen, he almost threw us out of his office, and—"

"What are you talking about?" Brad interrupted. "Go ahead with what? And what do you mean, Dr. Jensen almost threw you out of his office? You said 'us'? Who was with you? I don't have a clue what you're talking about."

Toni sighed and shook her head. "I know . . . Brad, please, let's sit down so I can try to explain this." They moved to the porch swing and sat down side by side. "I guess the best way is to begin at the beginning, which was a couple of weeks ago, when I met with Abe at his office to see if he had come up with anything new about Dad. That was the day he told me about Simon Olson seeing that vehicle pull up and park near Dad's cabin. You do remember I told you about that?"

Brad nodded.

"Well, what I didn't tell you—because I just wasn't sure whether or not to pursue it—was that Abe also suggested that I . . . consider trying to have Dad's body exhumed for an autopsy." Toni held her breath, watching Brad's face as her words sunk in. His intense concern quickly changed to a look of incredulity—not encouraging to Toni, but admittedly the reaction she had expected.

"An autopsy? Toni, have you lost your mind? What are you thinking? No, wait. It's not you, is it? It's that Abe Matthews again. He's the one who's putting these crazy ideas into your head, like keeping the agency open, now an autopsy. I told you he was dangerous. I warned you. . . ."

"Brad." She laid a hand on his arm. "Please, listen to me. Abe has nothing to do with my indecision about selling the agency. And as far as the autopsy, yes, he suggested it, but simply because it's the only possible way to prove what really happened to Dad. That doesn't make him dangerous, and it doesn't make the idea crazy either. There really is no other way, can't you see that?"

"What I see," Brad answered, his hazel eyes growing hard, "is that this phony detective is using your father's death to try to get to you. He's twisting your thinking and playing on your emotions, and I don't like it one bit. You've always been so sensible, Toni. What kind of hold does this guy have on you that he can turn you around so completely? Are you blind? Can't you see he's just leading you on, dragging this thing out any way he can to buy himself more time to win you over? And from the looks of things, he's doing a pretty good job." He shook his head. "I can't believe you're falling for it. I just can't believe it."

"Brad, that's not it. Really. It's not like that at all. Abe suggested the autopsy because there was no other way to prove how my father died. The only reason I didn't tell you about this sooner is because I wanted to think about it for a while before deciding what to do. Then

April came to town and we got to talking and decided to go see Dr. Jensen together, to try to persuade him to help us, but he refused and—"

Brad interrupted her again. "Do you blame him? What did you expect? It's the most ridiculous idea I've ever heard. I'm glad somebody had the good sense to talk you out of this."

"Actually, I . . . I'm planning to go ahead with it, that is, if Dr. Jensen can help me get the court order. He called earlier and said he'd thought it over and would see what he could do to help."

Brad stared at her without speaking, his courtroom face now firmly in place. Toni wondered what was going on behind his emotionless mask. When he finally spoke, she knew he had made up his mind, and there was no use trying to change it.

"I'm going to say this just once. I believe I've been very patient with your obsession over your father's death and some imagined connection with Julie Greene. I've been more than patient about putting off setting a wedding date. I've even been patient about this Matthews guy who has repeatedly stuck his nose into our business and disrupted our lives. But I'm through waiting patiently. Do you understand? I'm not insisting that you set a wedding date if you're not ready, but I am insisting that you drop your involvement with this detective. I want him out of your life—out of *our* lives—once and for all. Is that clear?"

"But, Brad, he's only trying to help. . . ."

"The only thing Abe Matthews is trying to help is himself—to my fiancée. Well, it's not going to happen, do you hear me? You're going to have to make a choice, Toni. Him or me. It's as simple as that." He stood up and looked down at her. "Call me when you've made up your mind." The back door slammed behind him as he went back into the house. In less than a minute, she heard him start his Lexus and pull away.

Her head was spinning as she slowly rose from the swing and opened the door. She had forgotten April Lippincott was there until she walked into the living room and saw her sitting on the couch where she had left her only minutes earlier.

April looked at Toni questioningly. "I assume he didn't take it very well."

Toni shook her head. "Not at all." Plunking down on the couch next to April, she sighed. "How did things get turned upside down like this? A couple of months ago, I thought I knew exactly where my life was headed. With all those years of college finally behind me, I was going to try to get a teaching job and start planning my wedding. But now . . . I just don't know what to think."

The front door opened then, and Melissa and Carrie walked in. They were uncharacteristically quiet.

"What happened?" Melissa asked. "Did Brad forget the charcoal? We saw him driving away just now."

Toni looked from the girls to April, then back again.

"Excuse me," April said, lifting herself off the couch. "Carrie, would you come out back with me for a few minutes? It's such a nice evening, and I thought maybe you and I could spend a little time getting better acquainted."

Carrie hesitated, looking confused. "Yeah, sure. I guess so," she said, following April into the kitchen. When they were gone, Melissa fixed her eyes on her older sister.

"What is it? What happened? Is it you and Brad? Did you break up?"

Toni patted the couch beside her. "Sit down."

Melissa joined her. As Toni took a moment to steady herself and plan her words, Melissa grabbed her arm. "It's that Abe Matthews, isn't it? He's causing problems between you and Brad. I knew that was going to happen."

"No. Not really. He's involved, but—"

"I knew it. I knew it! I wish you'd never met him. I wish he'd never come to Dad's office and messed up our lives. Wasn't it bad enough that Dad died? Now we're going to lose Brad too."

"Melissa, honey, please. Calm down. It's not at all what you think."

"Then what is it?" Melissa was crying now, and Toni felt as if she might join her any minute. She decided she had better say what needed to be said and get this thing settled before it got any worse.

"It's about Dad. I've . . . decided to try to have his body exhumed for an autopsy."

Melissa recoiled, drawing her hand away from Toni's arm as her green eyes opened wide. "An autopsy? You mean . . . cut Dad open?"

"Sweetheart, if there were any other way . . ."

"Any other way for what? Why do you want to do this? Why?"

"Because I . . . I think maybe Dad didn't die quite like the coroner and Dr. Jensen thought he did."

Melissa looked thoroughly confused. "You don't think he had a heart attack? I don't understand."

"You know that Dad was trying to help Mrs. Lippincott find her granddaughter, Julie, when he died, don't you?"

Melissa nodded slowly. "Yes, but—"

"Abe and I—and Mrs. Lippincott—think maybe Dad was getting too close to finding Julie, and that somebody . . ." Her voice trailed off as she searched desperately for a gentle way to voice her suspicions. There seemed to be none, so she plunged ahead.

"We think that—"

Before she could finish, Melissa jumped up from the couch. "You think Dad was . . . killed? Murdered?"

"I think it's possible. Yes."

Once again, Melissa began to shake her head. "No. No, it's not possible. Dad was not murdered. He had a heart attack. Dr. Jensen said so, and he knows more than you or that stupid Abe Matthews. It's his fault, isn't it? They're going to cut my father open because of him. I hate him. I hate him!" She spun on her heel and ran out of the room.

When Toni heard the bedroom door slam shut, she leaned her head back on the couch, letting the tears spill over onto her cheeks.

Oh, God, she prayed silently. *Where are you in all of this? What is going to become of us? What do I do now?*

∾∾∾

"Abe! Abe Matthews, is that you?"

Abe turned at the sound of the familiar female voice. The attractive redhead was standing halfway up the flight of stairs behind him, carrying a sack of groceries. How long had it been? One year? Two?

"Karen. What are you doing here?"

"I live here. Just moved in last week. Don't tell me you live here too."

"For about six months now. What about you? When did you get back into town?"

"A couple of weeks ago. I decided big-city life just wasn't for me. So I got my job back at the restaurant, and here I am." She shifted her groceries. "Listen, why don't you come on up? Have you had dinner? I could fix a salad, maybe an omelet . . ."

"Oh . . . thanks, but I need to, uh . . . take a shower and unwind. It's been a long day and I'm really tired."

Karen flashed a smile. "No problem. Listen, you go on home, and I'll get some things together and be over in a flash. That way you won't even have to leave the house. I'll bring dinner to you. You shower, I'll cook, and we can spend the evening together—just like old times. Which apartment is yours?"

"Nineteen. But—"

"See you in a few," she called, turning to run up the stairs to her apartment.

Abe sighed. Karen never was much of a listener, not exactly a deep thinker either. But then, he reminded himself, he hadn't dated her for her mind. He shook his head as he made his way to number nineteen. *How do I get myself into these things? It's not like I was looking for it.*

There was a time I would have welcomed the company—and anything that went with it. But now . . .

He unlocked the door and let himself inside. The spacious one-bedroom, ground-level apartment was sparsely decorated, not because he couldn't afford more, but because he just wasn't much for "knickknacks," as he referred to anything from wall hangings to porcelain statues. Flipping on the living room light, he went into the kitchen for a cold soda, then checked his answering machine by the phone next to his recliner for messages. There were none, a fact that brought mixed emotions. He was glad he didn't have to return any unwanted calls but disappointed that Toni hadn't phoned—not that he had really expected her to. She had never called him at home in spite of the fact that he had given her his number and encouraged her to do so any time. Still, there was always the chance. . . .

He hadn't seen Toni all week, although he had called and talked with her on the phone a couple of times. He considered calling her again, even though he had nothing new to report, but before he could pick up the receiver, his doorbell rang.

He did a double take when he opened the door and saw Karen standing there, dressed in very short, very tight cutoff jeans and a revealing halter top. And just as she had been when he had seen her standing on the stairwell near her apartment a few minutes earlier, she was carrying a sack of groceries.

Abe forced a smile. Even though they had dated a few times a year or so before—"old times," as she called it—he had never been more than mildly interested. Karen, however, had always made it abundantly clear that she was quite interested—and quite available. And, although he wasn't very proud of it, he had taken advantage of her availability. Now, as he stood there, wishing he could think of some gracious way to get rid of her, he realized that a lot of guys would have envied him such a problem.

"Hungry?" she asked, stepping inside before he could invite her. "I am. I had the day off today, so I'm really looking forward to fixing us a nice meal. Why don't you go ahead and jump in the shower, and I'll get started? It'll be fun catching up on the last year, won't it?"

Abe doubted that but decided he might as well let her go ahead and cook dinner, especially since she had already invited herself in and was walking toward the kitchen with her groceries. Once dinner was over and they had "caught up," he was definitely going to have to set her straight on some things.

The warm water eased his tired muscles as he stood with his head directly under the nozzle and let the soothing streams wash down his face and body. It had been a long day—a long week, in fact. However, as busy as he had been, he had never stopped thinking of Toni, wondering what she was doing and whether or not she was thinking of him, hoping she wasn't getting any closer to making those final wedding plans with Brad. He looked for reasons to call her but restrained himself from doing so as often as he would have liked. With nothing new to report on her father, he was hard pressed to find a believable excuse for phoning her more than every two or three days. Even then, it was difficult to maintain a businesslike attitude. Occasionally he got away with slipping in a teasing remark about their "partnership," but the minute he stepped over the line, even slightly, she pulled back. How he longed to tell her what was really in his heart, but he knew if he pushed too hard, too fast, he could lose her completely.

Stepping out of the shower, he toweled dry and slipped into a pullover sports shirt and jeans. If it hadn't been for Karen, he probably would have spent the evening sitting around in his robe and watching TV, but he wasn't about to wear anything that might encourage her in any way. This was one relationship he intended to end before it got started.

He looked in the mirror. *You're slipping, old man. There was a time you would have relished a situation like this. It's pretty obvious why she's here. If only it were Toni instead of Karen . . .*

As he opened the bathroom door, he heard Karen's voice. "I'm sorry, he's in the shower right now. Can I take a message?"

He frowned. What was she doing answering his phone? He should have made it clear to her that any calls that came in should go on the answering machine.

"Toni Matthews? Sure, I'll let him know you called just as soon as—"

He grabbed the phone out of her hand before she could finish her sentence. "Toni? What's up? Are you OK?"

"Abe? Your . . . friend . . . said you were in the shower."

"I was, but . . ." Silently, Abe cursed his timing. How would he explain this? Not that he owed her an explanation. She, after all, was engaged to someone else. Still, the last thing in the world he wanted was to alienate her or give her any reason to resist her feelings for him and draw closer to Brad.

"I just wanted to let you know that Dr. Jensen called earlier this evening," she said, her voice slightly more detached than usual. "He apologized for the way he acted when April and I went to his office this past Monday, and then he offered to speak to the coroner about having Dad's body exhumed for the autopsy. I understand that avoids the necessity of getting a court order."

Abe was surprised. From what Toni had told him about her visit to Dr. Jensen's office, it had seemed highly unlikely that he would change his mind. She was right too; the doctor's intervention would circumvent the need for a court order. So why wasn't he feeling more hopeful? Hadn't he been the one to suggest this move in the first place? Of course, Toni had no idea how he had wrestled with the idea of even mentioning an autopsy. Even though he had been reasonably sure she wouldn't be able to get the court order on her own, there was always the possibility that Dr. Jensen would be willing to intervene. If she chose not to or was unable to enlist the doctor's assistance, they would run into a dead end in the pursuit of information on her father's death, which ultimately meant an end to his excuse for prolonging their relationship. If, on the other hand, an autopsy was done, the results would also affect their relationship. A confirmation of a heart attack would bring their informal investigation to a screeching halt; evidence of foul play would necessitate turning the case over to the county sheriff, which technically left Abe out of the picture. Whatever the results of Toni's quest for an autopsy, he knew his days in "partnership" with Toni were numbered. Still, he had promised to help her, and suggesting an autopsy had seemed to be his only option at the time. All he could do now was to try to make the best of whatever time he had left with Toni—and Karen's answering his phone certainly hadn't helped his chances any.

"That's good news," he said, wishing he could say so much more. *Karen's nothing to me, just someone I used to date. I'm not interested in her at all. I just happened to run into her and she invited herself over and . . . I wish it were you. I wish you were here with me. Not just for tonight, but always. . . .* "I appreciate your letting me know."

"Sure. Well, I'd better go. Have a nice . . . evening." The phone clicked in his ear, and she was gone. When Karen came up behind him and laid her hand on his shoulder, it was all he could do not to throw her out of his apartment. But dinner or no dinner, she was leaving. Immediately.

~~~

Apart from her parents' deaths, this had been one of the most painful and trying days of Toni's life. What she had planned as a pleasant evening had deteriorated into a quick succession of arguments, disappointments, and confusion. After Brad's ultimatum and subsequent departure, Melissa, too, had decided to leave, opting to go home with Carrie to spend the night at her place. On top of that, Toni had then called Abe to let him know of Dr. Jensen's change of heart, only to find herself shocked—and more than slightly jealous— over the female voice on the other end of the line. Although she had tried to convince herself that the woman was probably nothing more than a casual friend, she had a problem believing that someone who was nothing more than a friend would be at Abe's apartment answering his phone while he took a shower. Still, she had reminded herself, what right did she have to expect that Abe would not be involved with someone? What she had perceived as his interest in her might have been nothing more than her overactive imagination. Worse yet, it might have been indicative of the way he treated all women. Where did she get off thinking she was special to him? Maybe she was letting this "partner" thing take on more meaning than Abe had ever intended. Maybe her phone call at that particular time was more than simple coincidence. Perhaps it was God's way of reminding her that she had absolutely no business becoming emotionally involved with someone who did not share her faith. Brad had given her an ultimatum, and it was obvious that she needed to put Abe Matthews out of her life before she ended up losing the man who truly loved her.

By the time all this had transpired, neither Toni nor April had felt much like barbecuing, so they fixed a salad and nibbled at it, while they discussed their uncertain futures in light of the evening's events, beginning with Dr. Jensen's offer to help secure an autopsy. Finally, when the rehashing of these subjects began to wear on them, Toni had taken April back to her hotel and had come home, fully resolved to call Brad and tell him she had made her choice. With Dr. Jensen's help, she would move ahead with the autopsy. Regardless of the outcome, Abe Matthews was out of her life. It was the right thing to do, and it would seal her decision to voice it to Brad.

But Brad didn't answer his phone. Even his answering machine was unavailable, undoubtedly turned off, she decided, because he did not want to hear from her yet. She supposed he wanted to give her more time to think things through and to come to the right decision, but she didn't need more time. The decision was made, and there was no turning back.

Wearily, she climbed into bed, determined to shut out the distressing events of the day and escape into a restful sleep. More than an hour later, she knew that had been nothing more than wishful thinking. She turned on the light and reached into the drawer of her nightstand. Pulling out the well-worn Bible, she fluffed her pillows and leaned back.

Oh, Lord, she prayed silently, *I've been neglecting this time with you lately. I'm so sorry. I'm paying the price, aren't I? I'm hurt and confused. I don't know what I want or where I'm going. I don't even seem to know who I want! Brad loves me, but . . . what about Abe? Oh, God, I know he's wrong for me, and he probably doesn't really care about me at all. But . . . how do I stop thinking of him? How do I stop myself from feeling what I feel for him? I just don't know what to do. The only thing I know for sure is that I have to continue pursuing the truth regarding Dad's death. Maybe then I'll be able to find some peace and get on with my life. Maybe . . . but . . . what if I still don't know what I want, even then? Help me, Lord. Lead me. . . .*

She opened her Bible to the fifty-fourth chapter of Isaiah, and her eyes fell on verse 6:

"For the Lord has called you

Like a woman forsaken and grieved in spirit, . . ."

She caught her breath. *Oh, Lord, I know those words were written to Israel, but they describe exactly how I feel! Even though I know Brad loves me and wants to marry me, I have felt absolutely forsaken and grieved in spirit, ever since Dad . . .* The rising pain in her chest threatened to overwhelm her. It was a pain she had been fighting for weeks, a pain she had been terrified would envelop her entire life if ever she gave way to it. Yet here it was, calling to her, as if God himself were bidding her to come, to yield herself . . .

When she finally stopped resisting, the tears came in torrents, washing over her in great engulfing waves as she dropped the Bible onto her lap and buried her face in her hands. Yet, in the midst of the crushing agony, a peace came, a silent promise that the resurrection that followed death would also defeat the pain and loss that had seemingly invaded every area of her life.

"Oh, Lord," she cried aloud, "I miss him! I miss him so much. I miss my father...."

I am your Father.

The words had been nothing more than a whisper in her heart, but they reverberated through her very being with a truth that released a sense of inexplicable joy within her. Even as she wiped the tears from her face, she began to laugh—softly, gently, but with conviction.

"Yes," she said. "Yes, You are my Father. My Father..."

She looked again at the open Bible on her lap, reading another portion of the same chapter:

"For a mere moment I have forsaken you,

But with great mercies I will gather you."

She closed her eyes. *Oh, Father. Gather me. I feel so scattered....* As she sensed a warm blanket of love wrap around her, she realized that she had never before experienced the absolute truth that her heavenly Father loved her ... completely, unconditionally, unendingly, undeservedly. She knew, from that moment, that whatever happened, she was going to be all right.

Suddenly she remembered what Brad had said to her at the beach about Melissa's needing her heavenly Father more now than ever before. *No wonder his comment made me so uncomfortable. How could I help lead my little sister to her heavenly Father when I was so out of touch with him myself?* She grabbed a tissue from the nightstand, blew her nose, and leaned back against the pillows. "I've believed in you for as long as I can remember," she whispered, "and I've known you as Savior for years. But ... I never knew you in this way, did I? As my Father. I've missed so much because of it.

"Help me, Lord. Help me to draw closer to you as Father, to better understand what that means. I feel like a child just beginning to learn the truth about something I thought I already knew. Teach me, Lord. Teach me. Help me to sort through the confusion of my life, to rest in your peace...."

Secure in her Father's arms, she soon drifted off to sleep. For this night, at least, there were no dreams of a teenage girl with long blonde curls running for her life.

CHAPTER 8

Toni could not remember a time when she had come from church with such mixed emotions. Spiritually, she felt stronger than she ever had before. Throughout the service, the words of the songs and sermon seemed to come alive and take on entirely new meaning as she focused on the new aspect of her relationship with God, that of Father and daughter. However, the problems in her other relationships seemed more painful and pronounced than ever as she sat next to Melissa, who had scarcely spoken to her since learning of Toni's intentions to seek an autopsy on their father. In addition, Toni could see Brad, two rows ahead and across the aisle from her, sitting next to his parents. It was the first time since their late teens, except during their college years when they were gone from River View, that they had not sat together during a Sunday worship service. Toni's heart ached at the realization, particularly because she knew she had no one to blame but herself.

She and Melissa had run into Brad while they were walking to the church from the parking lot. Toni had been hopeful that this would be her chance to tell him of her decision to cut off all ties with Abe. It was, after all, Independence Day, and the Anderson and Matthews families always went to the Fourth of July church picnic together. This would be the perfect opportunity to talk things through and get their relationship back on its old familiar footing. Brad, though polite, had been cool and aloof, speaking to her briefly and giving Melissa a quick hug, then veering off to join his parents.

Oh, Father, Toni had cried silently, as she watched him walk away. *I really need you right now. Help me. Show me what to do.*

In answer to her cry, she felt wrapped, once again, in the cloak of her heavenly Father's love. Slipping into the pew, she had determined not to let anything—or anyone—rob her of her newfound peace with God. Melissa, however, had not made it easy, sitting several inches away from Toni, as if she were too angry even to touch her.

Help Melissa too, Toni had prayed. *Help her to turn to you, Lord. She needs you so desperately.*

Later, stepping out of the church into the warm, late-morning sunshine, Toni had asked Melissa what they should fix to bring to the picnic that afternoon. Melissa had informed her coolly that Carrie's family had invited her to go with them and that she would prefer to do so if Toni had no objections. Toni did—mainly that she felt rebuffed and rejected—but decided not to voice them.

So she headed for home, alone. Strangely, however, she didn't feel alone—at least, not entirely. Even amidst the confusion and uncertainty of her botched relationships, she still sensed the peace and joy that had filled her since she first recognized God's presence in her life as Father. Surprising herself, she smiled as she drove, humming one of the choruses they had sung at church.

As she pulled into the driveway, she wondered if April Lippincott was home from her church service yet. Toni and Melissa had taken April to their church the first Sunday she had been in town, but it had been a bit too contemporary for the elderly woman who was more comfortable in a traditional worship setting. And so, although they shared the same faith and worshiped the same God, Toni had recommended another church to April. Unlocking the front door and walking into the empty house, Toni decided to give April a call to see if they could get together sometime later in the day.

She walked toward the phone on the end table in the living room and saw the light blinking on the answering machine. She pushed the button, hoping maybe Brad had arrived home ahead of her and had called to say he'd had a change of heart and would like to get together with her for the picnic. The male voice on the machine was not Brad's, however.

"Hi, Toni. It's me, Abe. Did you get my message from yesterday? I . . . was hoping to get a chance to talk with you about . . . well, just about things in general, I suppose, but especially about Friday night when you called. It's just that . . . I know I don't owe you an explanation, but I really would like to explain anyway. I guess you're at church right now, but if you get a chance, would you call me when you get home? Please."

The aching in her heart to return his call, to hear his explanation for why that woman had been in his apartment answering his phone while he took a shower, and to find out what else he wanted to say to her was almost more than she could resist. But she had ignored his phone message on the previous day, and she would ignore this one as well. The very fact that his words were so personal—as was her reaction to them—was confirmation enough that she needed to cut off all contact with him if she ever hoped to patch up her relationship with Brad. *Help me, Father. Change my heart. I have no right to feel the way I do about Abe, but my attraction to him seems to grow stronger every day.*

Forgetting her intention to call April, she forced herself away from the phone and walked to the kitchen to see about making herself something to eat. She had just about decided on a tuna sandwich when the phone rang again. Picking up the receiver from the wall phone beside the kitchen table, her heart jumped when she heard Abe's voice respond to her "hello."

"Toni? Hi. It's me again. I know I should have waited till you called back, but . . . I was afraid you wouldn't, and I . . . really need to talk to you." He paused. "Toni? Are you there?"

"Yes," she said, her voice shaking almost as much as her legs. She pulled out a chair and sat down, knowing she would need all the strength she could muster to keep her focus where it needed to be. *Help me, God.* "Yes, I'm here."

"I would really rather have this conversation face to face, but right now I have some things to say that can't wait, so I'm just going to spit it out. I know I'm out of line on this. I know you're engaged, but please hear me out, will you? I can't keep these things to myself any longer. I think you already know what I'm going to say, but . . . I have to say it anyway. I'm in love with you. I've tried to talk myself out of it so many times, but it just doesn't work. I can't think about anything or anyone but you. That woman who was here when you called, it wasn't what you thought. She's just an old friend I ran into and—"

"You don't have to explain," Toni interrupted, trying desperately to divert the conversation, even as her heart cried out to hear more. "Really. It's none of my business, and it doesn't matter because—"

This time it was Abe's turn to interrupt. "It does matter. It matters a lot. I don't want you to think that I would say I'm in love with you while I'm spending time with someone else. Toni, from the moment I met you, there hasn't been anyone else. I've tried to fight it, but I—"

"Stop, Abe. Please." Her voice was still shaking, but she was determined. If she didn't end this conversation right now, she knew she would say things she would regret. She could not let him know how she felt. This relationship was wrong, and it was up to her to put an end to it, once and for all. "I don't want to hear any more. We can't talk like this. In fact, we can't . . . talk at all. Abe, our relationship is over. It should never have started. It was wrong from the beginning, I know that now. Please forgive me if I encouraged you in any way. I appreciate all you've done to try to help me, but you know I'm engaged to Brad. You and I can never—"

"I know you're engaged to Brad, but . . . are you in love with him?"

Toni's heart skipped a beat. "What do you mean? I just told you, we're engaged."

"That's not what I asked you. I asked if you're in love with him. Maybe I'm just believing what I want to believe, but I think . . ." He paused, and she heard him take a breath. "I think you're in love with me, not Brad."

Oh, Lord, what do I do now? She felt as if her heart would explode as the heat rushed up her neck to her cheeks. How she longed to tell him the truth—that he might very well be right, that it was just too soon to be sure, that she wanted desperately to spend time with him, to pursue their relationship, to find out—but she couldn't. No good could come of it, and she was not going to allow this to go any further.

"You're wrong," she said, her voice steadier than she had imagined it could be. "I'm not in love with you, Abe. I'm . . . in love with Brad, and I intend to marry him. Please, don't call me anymore."

She hung up the phone, buried her face in her hands, and cried. "Oh, Father," she sobbed, "forgive me for lying. Forgive me. But what else could I do?"

~~~

The phone was ringing as Toni unlocked the door. It was early Tuesday afternoon, and Melissa was still at her baby-sitting job. Fumbling with her keys and purse, Toni pushed the door open and hurried to the phone. She still had not been able to talk with Brad, even though she had left several messages on his machine at home and had called his office first thing that morning. The receptionist had said he was "unavailable" and that she would let him know that Toni had called and would like him to call back. As she grabbed the receiver, she hoped this would finally be her opportunity to begin to set things right between them.

"Toni? Dr. Jensen here. How are you?"

Her disappointment over not hearing Brad's voice was quickly replaced by anxiety over what Bruce Jensen might have to say. "I'm . . . fine, thank you. And you?"

"I'm doing well. And how's Melissa? Is she beginning to cope with her loss?"

"I . . . believe so." She wanted to scream, "Forget the formalities and just get on with it." But she restrained herself. "Have you got some news for me?"

"As a matter of fact, I do. As I'm sure you know, with yesterday being a legal holiday, I wasn't able to do anything about the autopsy. I put in a call first thing this morning—and, I might add, pulled a few strings with the coroner—and we got a green light. I won't bother you with all the details, but the legalities will be taken care of quickly, and the autopsy will be done as soon as possible. If all goes well, we should have the results sometime early next week."

Toni felt as if her stomach were in knots. This was what she had wanted, the only possible way to prove that her father's death had been more than a simple heart attack. But now, with the procedure set in motion, the possible repercussions were overwhelming. Still, there was no other choice.

"Thank you," she managed to say. "I really appreciate it."

"No problem. As I told you before, I should have been more con-siderate of your feelings and desires in this situation when you first mentioned it to me, but you really caught me off guard when you and Mrs. Lippincott came to my office. I hope you understand."

"Of course. I know it's not a common request, but I felt—"

"No need to explain yourself. If this will put your mind at ease and help you get on with your life, then I'm glad I could be of help. I'll be in touch. Goodbye."

Toni hung up the phone and sank down onto the couch. *What now? When the results come back on the autopsy, showing there was some sort of foul play involved in my father's death—and I know there was—then what? There will undoubtedly be an investigation, but what happens then? How will this affect Melissa? How will it affect me ... and Brad? Oh, Father, help us. Carry us through this difficult time.*

≈≈≈

The sunshine was beginning to peek through the clouds as Toni mounted the steps to the neat but modest building that housed the legal offices where Brad, as a junior partner, occupied a small space, in comparison to the spots held by the two senior partners. One of those two senior partners was Brad's father, George Anderson, a well-known and highly respected attorney in River View. The other senior partner, Carolyn Summers, was among the minority of female attorneys in the Southwest Washington region. She was also George Anderson's sister and Brad's aunt. True to his dependable nature, Brad had carried on the family tradition just as his parents had always expected he would.

It was Friday afternoon, and Toni had finally gotten up the courage to call Brad's office on Thursday and make an appointment with him. It seemed to be the only way to force a discussion—and, presumably, a reconciliation. She had hoped to get in to see him earlier, but the receptionist had told her that this was his first available time. Chagrined, she had taken it, amazed that their relationship could have deteriorated so drastically that she had to make an appointment to see her own fiancé.

Now she was here. Although Toni had known Catherine, the receptionist, for years, Toni felt awkward when she walked in. It was apparent that Catherine knew there was trouble between Toni and Brad, so Toni limited her greeting to a brief nod, then took a seat in the waiting room.

She had chosen her clothes carefully, her sleeveless silk blouse a pale pink, Brad's favorite color. Her gray summer slacks and pink sandals coordinated perfectly. Even her hair had cooperated, the short but often unruly locks falling right into place. She knew she was doing the right thing. Now if she could only put Abe out of her mind. . . .

The receptionist's intercom buzzed. "Yes? Certainly. I'll send her right in." Catherine looked up at Toni. "You can go on in now."

He's not even going to come out to meet me . . . not going to make it easy on me one bit. Well, I suppose I deserve it. "Thank you," she said, then rose and walked past the receptionist's desk and down the hall to a room that had always seemed so welcoming and familiar. Now, even before she knocked, it felt foreign and somewhat intimidating. She was grateful that Brad did not make her wait long. "Come in," he called as soon as she had rapped on the door.

Taking a deep breath, she opened the door and walked in. Brad, still sitting behind his desk, looked up, his smile strained, his courtroom face showing signs of stress. It was the shock of sandy blond hair falling across his forehead that tugged at her heart though. Dear, faithful, patient Brad. He had always been there for her—and for Melissa too. She had always known he would be, and had taken him for granted. Was that not to be the case any longer?

He rose slowly and walked around to the front of his desk to greet her. *Surely he's not going to shake my hand,* she thought. He didn't, but his welcoming embrace was stiff, as was Toni's response.

"How are you?" he asked, his voice controlled but just husky enough to betray his emotions.

"Fine," she said as they released each other. "And you?"

Brad nodded. "OK. Busy."

"Yes. So I heard . . . from Catherine. I've been trying to reach you all week."

"I'm sorry. It's just . . ." He stopped, indicating the chair in front of his desk. "Please, sit down." As she did, he went back to his own chair behind the desk.

Where do I start, Father? Show me what to say. "I've missed you." That, at least, was not a lie. Brad had been so much a part of her life for so many years that she truly had missed him, even though it didn't begin to compare with the longing she felt for Abe.

The courtroom face was crumbling. "I've missed you too."

His voice was softer now, and Toni was sure she saw a hint of tears in his eyes. She was going to have to do something to break the ice. "This is really awkward, isn't it?"

He nodded. "I hate it. We've always been so close."

"Yes. Always. It's my fault. Can you . . . forgive me?"

The courtroom face was dissolved completely now. "I already have. I'm not angry anymore. It's just . . ." He closed his eyes briefly, as if gathering his strength, then took a deep breath. "I need to know what you've decided about Abe . . . and me. Who is it going to be, Toni? You can't have it both ways."

"I know that." She spoke softly, willing herself not to cry, determined that he not realize the depth of her feelings for Abe or how very painful it was for her to deny them. "I had no intentions of my relationship with Abe coming between us. I just wanted his help with . . . well, there's no sense rehashing all that. You already know. The point is, I have told Abe that I do not need his help anymore and that he is not to call me or—"

"You told him that?"

Toni nodded. "Yes."

Brad jumped up from his chair and hurried to Toni's side. Kneeling beside her, his eyes wet with tears, he took her face in his hands. "Oh, Toni, I love you so much. I've been so miserable without you."

The joy on his face broke her heart almost as much as the pain she had seen there earlier. True, she had missed Brad, but the only reason she had been miserable was that she had been trying so desperately to convince herself that Abe was no longer a part of her life, that he never could be, that she must go on without him and work things out with Brad. Had it not been for the strength she drew from her deepened relationship with her heavenly Father, she knew she would not be sitting here having this conversation with Brad. She would, instead, be exactly where her heart longed to be—in the arms of Abe Matthews, telling him of her true feelings for him, begging him to forgive her for lying—and praying that God, in turn, would forgive her for her disobedience.

Rising to his feet, Brad lifted her from her chair and took her in his arms. Holding her close, he nuzzled her hair and whispered her name, as he had done so many times before. But instead of responding, she simply stood there, feeling safe and protected in his arms and grateful that he was happy, but unsure what to do next. With her left thumb, she fingered the diamond on her ring finger. *Should I bring up the wedding? Maybe even get out the calendar and set a date? Nothing would make him happier. . . no, not yet. I need to give my heart more time.*

Releasing her, Brad held her at arm's length and gazed lovingly into her eyes. His joy was almost contagious—almost. Still, she truly was happy for him. She smiled up at him as he leaned down to kiss her. This time she forced herself to respond, reminding herself that this was right—it was what God had purposed for them.

Pulling back to look at her once again, his hazel eyes lit up with obvious excitement. "It's Friday night. Let's go out and celebrate. Somewhere romantic and . . ." He stopped. "Or would you rather do something quiet at your house, something that would include Melissa? We never did have our barbecue last week, did we?"

Toni was grateful for his thoughtfulness about Melissa. She was also grateful that his suggestion would buy her some time. It would be a lot easier to avoid discussing wedding plans if dinner was a threesome around the barbecue rather than a candlelit dinner for two.

"That's a wonderful idea. Melissa would love it. She's really missed you. Nothing would make her happier than to see the two of us back together again."

"I'm with her," Brad agreed, pulling her close to his chest. "Nothing could make me happier either. This is where we belong, sweetheart. Together, always."

Toni blinked back the tears that threatened to spill over, glad he couldn't see her face. "Yes. This is where we belong."

Toni was in shock. How could she have been so wrong? It had been so obvious; she had been so sure. And now . . .

Pulling into the hotel parking lot, she berated herself for not first going to Brad with the news, but she couldn't . . . not yet. As kind as she knew he would be about it, she just wasn't ready for any I-told-you-so's. She would have to face them sooner or later, particularly from Melissa, but not until she had talked to someone else who would be as shocked as she was.

She wondered if Abe knew. She had been tempted to call him, but she knew she would only be using the news as an excuse to hear his voice again. Then where would they be? Back to dancing around their emotions, pretending that they didn't exist? Back to Abe's declarations of love for her, with Toni forced into lying about her own feelings for him? Then, of course, there was the possibility that Abe had rethought his feelings, particularly after her rejection, and would not even want to talk with her. No, it was best to leave that relationship where it was and let it die a natural death, painful as it might be. Besides, if Abe had not heard the news by now, he certainly would before long.

When Toni had called, just fifteen minutes earlier, April told Toni to come straight up to her room. Toni had jumped into her car and driven right to the hotel. Now, she stepped into the elevator and punched the button for the third floor, anxious to get April's reaction, hoping she would have some sort of logical explanation. How could she? How could anyone? It made no sense, and yet, facts were facts. Toni supposed she and April would simply have to accept them and move on.

"Hello, my dear," April said, greeting her at the door. "Come in. You look almost as frazzled as you sounded on the phone. Can I offer you a cold soda, some juice? I have a small refrigerator here."

"No ... thank you." Toni sank into one of the two chairs in the corner of the room next to a small table. April came over and joined her. Sitting in the chair next to hers, April reached over and laid her hand on Toni's arm. "What is it, my dear? What's wrong? Are you all right? Is something wrong with Melissa?"

Toni shook her head. "No. No, Melissa and I are fine. It's ... the autopsy report. It came back this morning. I found out just before I called you." She looked into the elderly woman's eyes. "April, we were wrong. I still can't believe it, but ... we were wrong."

April frowned. "What do you mean? I don't understand. Surely you aren't saying ..."

"I'm afraid so. The autopsy report proves that Dad died just as Dr. Jensen said he did—from a heart attack. It was verified by the medical examiner. No signs of foul play. Nothing. Just a heart attack. Exactly what Brad has been telling me all along."

"That's impossible. How can that be? How can your father's death and the notations in Julie's file be nothing more than a coincidence? It's simply not possible."

"According to the medical report, it is."

April shook her head. "I was so sure."

"So was I. But we were wrong. Brad, the doctor, the coroner, Melissa—they were all right. I guess we should have listened to them." She sighed. "So, now what? Where do we go from here?"

April was silent for a moment, staring at her hands folded in her lap. When she spoke, she did not look up. "I'll go home, I suppose. There's no reason for me to stay here any longer. Today's Tuesday. I can catch a flight out tomorrow. The sooner the better, I suppose. I need to hire another agency to look for my granddaughter. Surely there's someone who can find her." She looked up, tears shining in her pale blue eyes. "Surely there is, don't you think?"

Toni's heart went out to her. Although the news was confusing to Toni, she had forgotten that it was another dead end in the ongoing search for April Lippincott's only grandchild. Still, they needed to look at the positive side.

"Maybe," Toni ventured, "this is good news. After all, if there was no foul play involved in Dad's death—and I truly am glad of that—it's likely there's none involved in Julie's disappearance either. We were basing all this on the supposition that Dad was killed because he was searching for Julie. Now we know that's not the case. If we look at this in the right way, it's really a positive thing for both of us."

April's smile was tentative. "I suppose, and we do need to look at the positive, don't we? After all, we've both been praying, along with others, and God does care more about both of our situations even than we do."

Toni thought of the words she had heard in her heart slightly over a week ago. *I am your Father.* "That's so true. In fact, in the midst of all this, I feel as if I've drawn closer to God than ever before. I only hope the same will be true for Melissa. She seems so far from God, so cynical, even, about his existence. I've been praying that God would reveal himself to her and use her pain to bring her to a place of putting her faith and trust completely in him."

"As have I," said April. "Ever since I met Melissa, I have prayed that way, exactly as I've prayed for Julie for years. My granddaughter was raised in a Christian home. Her parents are devout believers. My son-in-law, as you know, is a pastor. He and my daughter . . ." Her voice cracked, but she went on. "They've been praying, as has their entire church. Surely God . . ."

Toni took April's hand. "God knows where Julie is, and he's keeping her safe in his hands. I'm sure of it."

April nodded. "If I didn't believe that, I don't think I could go on."

Toni waited a moment, then said, "I'll miss you when you're gone. Even though you'll be working with a new agency to find Julie, will you stay in touch with me? With us? Melissa will miss you too."

"Of course, my dear, and I will keep you updated on any developments in our search for Julie." Her smile was sad. "Perhaps we'll see each other again sometime."

"You're absolutely right. When Julie is home safe and sound, Melissa and I will want to meet her. And you . . . well, you have to come back for my wedding, you know."

"Yours and Brad's?"

Toni was puzzled. "Of course, mine and Brad's. Who else . . .?"

April shrugged her shoulders. "Just wondering . . ."

"I told you, there was never anything between Abe and me beyond his helping me find out about my father's death. And now we know about that, don't we? So there's absolutely no reason for me to see Abe Matthews again. I'm marrying Brad . . . and I'm very happy about it."

"Of course you are, my dear," April agreed. Toni only wished she sounded more convinced. It was, after all, a *fete accompli*. There was no turning back now. As soon as she could bring herself to discuss details with Brad, they would set a date, and very soon she would be Mrs. Brad Anderson. Melissa would be thrilled.

CHAPTER 9

Abe had always enjoyed the scenic drive up Interstate 5 from River View to Centralia—until today. As he steered the Honda toward his Aunt Sophie's hillside home on this sunny Sunday morning, all he could think of was how he had wanted to bring Toni along to meet her. Now, of course, that would never happen, which was why he was making the trip in the first place.

It had been a long, soul-searching week. From the time he had poured out his feelings to Toni the previous Sunday until today, he had replayed her words of rejection over and over in his head, asking himself countless questions. Had she really meant what she said? If so, how could he have been so dense as to completely misread her feelings for him? If she had not meant what she said, what was her purpose in lying to him? Would she really go through with marrying a man she didn't love simply because she didn't want to hurt him? Was it possible that she was unsure of which of them she loved? Or, was it him? Was there something about Abe Matthews that prevented Toni from pursuing a relationship with him?

Regardless of how many times he asked himself these questions, he always came back to the same conclusion. Whether Toni was truly in love with Brad or not, she had said she was going to marry him, and that was the end of the discussion and the end of Abe and Toni's relationship. The problem was, it did not end what he felt for her. For the first time in his thirty-one years of life, Abe was in love. He had found someone he cared about more than himself, but he had found her too late.

And so, unsure of what to do next, he had decided to visit Aunt Sophie. It had been several months since he'd been up to see her, so she was thrilled when he called to ask if he could visit. "By all means," she had exclaimed. "Come ahead. Will you come in time for *Shabbat?*" He had told her he would not but would arrive midmorning on Sunday.

He wondered at his sudden desire to talk with his aunt. Although he loved her and had many fond memories of her, he tended to avoid spending any time with her that might lead to a discussion of her faith—which almost any conversation with Sophie did, sooner or later. Since meeting Toni, however, faith seemed to be the exact topic he needed to understand. Here she was, a Christian Gentile, talking about worshiping the "God of Israel." What had she meant? Maybe if he understood that, he might better understand this woman who had captured his heart, even though understanding her wouldn't make any difference at this point. Still . . .

Thinking of Toni—which he did most of his waking moments— reminded him of the autopsy results he had learned about on Friday. He wasn't sure yet just what he thought or how he felt about those results, but he hadn't really been surprised by them. Even with the notation about Eagle Lake in Julie Greene's file, Abe had considered it a long shot that there would be any connection between her disappearance and Paul Matthews's death. Yet, Toni had been so sure that there was more to her father's death than a simple heart attack, and her confidence had begun to rub off on him. Now the whole thing was behind them, including his excuse to stay in touch with her.

Another wave of pain washed over him. He had tortured himself with the reliving of their last phone conversation until he actually came to the point of crying out to God to help him. That cry of desperation had shocked him. He had spent most of his life trying not to think about God, but it seemed that wherever he turned these last few weeks, he was reminded that the concept of God could not easily be dismissed.

As he exited the freeway and turned right at the narrow road that led up the hill overlooking the city, he wondered about the real reason for his visit. Was he here to see if he could gain insight into Toni's faith in God and how that affected the way she thought and lived, hoping against hope that such an understanding would somehow give him another chance to win her away from Brad? Or was it possible he was here to gain insight into the need for God in his own life? The very thought jolted him. That he was even asking himself such a question was a monumental step for a man who had been taught that if God existed at all, he certainly was not involved with or relevant to his life.

He parked the car in the street and walked up the sloped walkway to Sophie's house. As he rang the doorbell, he noticed the *mezuzah* on the doorpost. He vaguely remembered seeing it before, but he had never paid much attention to it. Waiting for his aunt to come to the door, he studied it more closely. Mounted on a royal blue background, three Hebrew letters, outlined in gold, stood above a golden scroll, which he assumed depicted the *Torah,* or Jewish Law. The concept of the scroll representing Jewish Law was something he was familiar with; the Hebrew letters he could not identify. He wondered at their significance.

The door had no sooner opened than he heard the familiar greeting. "*Avraham!* You have come. *Baruch ha Shem!* Praise be to *Adonai!* Come in, come in."

His heart caught at the familiar smile, the dark brown eyes, the gray hair gathered into a bun at the nape of her neck. How she reminded him of an older, more matronly version of his mother. Taking him by the hands, she pulled him inside and wrapped him in a hug. He could almost feel some of the tensions of the last weeks melting away.

"You have stayed away too long," said Sophie, releasing him so she could step back and examine him. "I have missed you. You look a little thin. Have you been eating enough? What is it, they work you so hard at the station you don't have time to eat?"

Abe laughed. "If I walked in here weighing three hundred pounds, you'd say I was too thin. I've been eating just fine, thank you. In fact, I can guarantee you, I have not missed any meals since I last saw you."

Sophie shook her head. "I don't know. . . . It seems to me you need a good wife. That's what's wrong with you, you know. Thirty-one years old and not married. Shameful." She tsk-tsked her disapproval. "What's the matter, they don't have any nice Jewish girls in River View?"

"Aunt Sophie, please."

She threw her hands in the air. "I know, I know. It's none of my business. So I'll drop it . . . for now. Let's go into the living room and sit down. Are you hungry? Have you had breakfast? I could make some *latkes.*"

"Maybe later, thanks."

As they sat down across from each other in the living room, Abe suddenly felt uncomfortable. How in the world was he going to explain why he had come if he wasn't sure himself? Before he could decide how best to approach the subject, Sophie gave him her "poor neglected me" look, guaranteed to put a guilt trip on him, even when he wasn't at fault.

"So, how is *Shlomo,* my only brother, Solomon, who lives less than an hour away but never calls or visits?"

"Uncle Sol is fine. Just . . . busy. I'm sure he doesn't mean to ignore you, Aunt Sophie."

She raised her eyebrows. "No? Well, he may not mean to ignore me, but he certainly does. And what's he so busy doing? He's not working anymore. Does he still have that . . . friend living with him? I suppose she's the one taking up all his time these days."

Abe decided it was time to change the subject. "I'm not sure what he's been doing, but I'm sure you'll hear from him soon. So . . . how have you been? You're looking beautiful, as always."

Sophie laughed, a clear, tinkling laugh that sounded so much like his mother that he shivered. "I'm fine, thank you for asking. And you, I see, are still the great diplomat and flatterer. All right, no more talk about *Shlomo.* You always were quite a charmer, which makes it that much harder for me to understand why you haven't found a wife. You have a good job, you're handsome . . . what's wrong with the women in your town? Are they blind?"

Abe's heart constricted. His aunt was smiling—he knew she meant well—but it was as if she had plunged a dagger into his chest. Should he take a chance, just jump in and tell her about Toni, about her rejection of his love and his confusion over her comment about the God of Israel? Or should he prolong the small talk, try to ease into the conversation . . .?

"What is it, *Avraham?* You look . . . wounded. Did I say something? Is there something going on I don't know about?" She frowned. "Wait a minute. You came here for a reason, didn't you? It wasn't just that you missed your poor old aunt. There is a purpose for your being here, is there not?"

Things hadn't changed much. Since he was a child, it never took Aunt Sophie long to nail him to the wall when he had something on his mind. He couldn't fool her then, and it was obvious he couldn't fool her now. He might as well tell her everything.

"Actually, there is someone. Her name is . . . Toni. I met her several weeks ago when I went by to drop something off at her dad's office. He was a private investigator."

"Was? He's not anymore?"

"He . . . died, had a heart attack just a few weeks before Toni and I met."

"The poor girl. She must still be in mourning. Did she . . . sit *shivah?*"

"If you mean, is she Jewish, no, she's not. That's what I want to talk to you about."

Sophie raised her eyebrows. It was obvious, even before she knew the details, that she disapproved of his being involved with a Gentile, even though his father had been a Gentile and Abe himself had never been a practicing Jew. Still, as Sophie had said many times through the years—although never around Abe's father while he was still alive— "It's important not to pollute the family bloodline anymore than it already is. It is forbidden for Jews to intermarry with the *goyim,* and there is good reason for that." He had never before cared enough to ask what that reason might be. Today he cared enough.

"Why is it so important that Jews and Gentiles don't marry? Mom married my dad, and he was a Gentile."

"Exactly. And I liked your father, you know that. He was a kind and gentle man, a good husband and father. But he was not Jewish. He was not even a God-fearer. He led your mother away from the Holy One—blessed be he—and from her faith."

"But what if . . . what if the Gentile is not Jewish, yet worships the God of Israel?"

This time Sophie's frown went deep, and Abe could sense the explosion that was coming. "Impossible! A *goy* who worships the Holy One of Israel—blessed be he. It cannot be! Who is this Toni, this woman who has beguiled you to think that she, a *goy,* worships *Adonai?* Has she converted? Is she a proselyte then?"

"No, Aunt Sophie. She's . . . a Christian."

She said nothing. Her face became devoid of expression—except for her eyes. He could see the tears forming, but he knew they were not tears of compassion or joy or even of understanding; they were tears of anger—and betrayal. He braced himself for the onslaught.

"You would do this to your *mishpacha?* You would bring, not only another *goy,* but a . . . *Christian*"—she spat out the word as if it were a curse—"into our family? What is wrong with you, *Avraham?* Is it the influence of your father, the *goy* who didn't know what he believed and didn't think it was important? Wasn't it bad enough that you chose to follow in your mother's footsteps and abandon the faith of *Avraham avinu,* after whom you have been named? Now you must further pollute our bloodline by bringing a persecutor of our people into our very midst? Do you have any idea what this would do to your grandparents if they were still alive?"

"Aunt Sophie, I am not bringing Toni into our family. She . . . rejected me for someone else—another Christian Gentile."

Sophie clasped her hands in front of her and looked up into the heavens. "Oh, praise be to *Adonai!* He has delivered us from such a curse."

Abe sighed. How was he ever going to steer this conversation back to what he had originally intended? It was obvious Sophie did not believe Toni could possibly worship the same God as the Jews worshiped, so that tack would never work. He supposed he had better approach it from a personal angle.

"My relationship with Toni is over. Actually, it ended before it ever got off the ground. But . . . something she said got me to thinking about . . . my faith. Lately I have come to realize I don't know much about it, that I don't understand—"

Sophie bounded out of her chair, rushed over to Abe, and grabbed his face in her hands. "How I have prayed for this day! At last you are returning to the faith of our fathers. You have made me so happy." She planted a kiss on his forehead, then laughed aloud. "What a glorious day!"

Abe was glad he had made Sophie so happy, but he still didn't have any of the answers he was looking for. "Aunt Sophie, I need to know more about—"

"Of course you do," she agreed, hurrying to the bookshelf against the far wall. "And so you shall." She pulled a somewhat tattered volume from the shelf and brought it to him. "This copy of the *Tanakh* belonged to your Uncle David. He had more than one copy, of course, but this one is in English, so you can read it."

Abe remembered having his own copy of the Scriptures—the *Tanakh,* as Aunt Sophie called it—when he was a boy, but he had no idea what had happened to it over the years. His grandparents had presented it to him and encouraged him to read it, and he had tried, but he couldn't understand it, so he had relegated it to a lower shelf in his room. That was the last time he recalled seeing it. Since his parents had not taken or sent him to the synagogue nor allowed him to attend regularly with his grandparents, he had thought no more about it—until now. Was it possible that the answers he was looking for might be found in this ancient book? If they were, since he was so unclear on his questions, would he recognize the answers even if he found them?

Suddenly he remembered the *mezuzah* on Aunt Sophie's front door and wondered about its connection with the book he held in his hands. "Aunt Sophie, your *mezuzah* . . . The scroll represents the *Torah,* right?"

Sophie, back in her chair once again, nodded, her dark eyes shining. "Yes. The sacred teachings of *Adonai.*"

"The Hebrew letters above the scroll. What do they mean?"

"They represent *Adonai's* name, to remind us that it is he who gave us *Torah.*"

"I see." He looked back at the book, wondering how it was possible that he could say the words "I see" when he felt like a blind man. Would he ever truly be able to see? Was it even possible that he might someday understand? If he did, would it bring him any closer to the woman who held his heart in her hands, the woman who claimed to worship the God of Israel, despite Aunt Sophie's comments to the contrary? Was there yet any hope for him, or was this simply an exercise in futility?

~~~

Toni awoke in a sweat, her heart pounding furiously. The nightmares had returned. Since learning of the autopsy results the previous week, she had found herself terror-stricken, once again running through her dreams, chased by an invisible stalker, and awakening to a sense of imminent danger. What she had thought would finally bring her peace and restore some sense of direction to her life— obtaining concrete evidence of how her father had died—had done just the opposite. She felt more confused and lost now than she had when she first learned of her father's death. Tonight's episode was the third nightmare in a week, and each time, whether searching for Julie, her father or mother, or even for Brad, it was Abe—always Abe—who seemed to appear just before she crossed back into reality.

Why, Lord? Why Abe? Why is it always Abe? And why are the dreams back? I thought, once I began to feel secure in our Father-daughter relationship, that the dreams had disappeared. But now . . .

Oh, Father, are you trying to tell me something? Or is it just my overactive imagination, combined with my grief over losing Dad . . . and Abe? If only I had never answered that call from April Lippincott, never looked into Julie's file. . . . How different things would be right now. Dad would still be gone, but Abe would never have been a factor. And my relationships with Brad and Melissa would be solid, the way they once were. But I did answer that phone call, didn't I? And I did look into the file. Now, even after the autopsy, I can't seem to let go. It's as if . . . as if someone is calling me, compelling me to continue. Continue what? What is there to continue? If Abe couldn't come up with anything else, and if the autopsy proves Dad had a heart attack, what else can I do? Where would I go from here?

Groaning, she rolled over onto her side and pulled the covers up around her neck. Why was it, whenever she awoke from one of these dreams, that she felt as if something evil were lurking right there in her room? The feeling reminded her of the times in her childhood when she'd had a nightmare and woke up crying. Her mother would always come and hold her, rock her, pray for her, and sometimes even sing to her until she fell asleep again. When Toni's mother died, Toni was fourteen—certainly old enough to deal with nightmares alone but not old enough to ward off the pain and fear that came from her dreams when she saw herself safe in her mother's arms, then felt her slipping away. Screaming, she would try to hold on, but she was never strong enough. Then she would wake up sobbing as the crushing grief threatened to suffocate the life right out of her. Those nightmares of losing her mother had long since faded, but now these . . .

Where was she to go from here? Was there any hope that she would someday escape this endless maze of unresolved pain, this over-whelming loss that made no sense? Would her relationships ever return to normal—whatever "normal" might be? Although she and Brad seemed to be making progress—Brad, at least, seemed happy enough—her longing to be with Abe had not diminished. And her relationship with Melissa, although having improved somewhat since she and Brad had reunited, was still strained. In addition, she could not seem to move forward with her plans, either for the wedding or her career. She had convinced herself that she needed to put what was left of the agency up for sale but had not yet taken any action to set that in motion. As for securing a teaching position, it was far too late in the year to hope to obtain anything for the fall term. She might, at best, be able to get on somewhere locally as a substitute, which at this point, she thought might be the wisest solution. Yet how could she teach anyone anything when she couldn't even concentrate on the simplest matters? Her days—and now, many of her nights—were consumed with perplexing and frightening thoughts of her father, Julie, Brad, Abe, and Melissa. There had to be an answer, some sort of resolution to this painful limbo in which she found herself. Whatever that answer was, she had yet to figure it out.

"Oh, Father," she sighed, "show me what to do. Give me some direction, some guidance. Open a door, or . . . close one. Please, show me something."

Tyler was thrilled. Not only had Melissa agreed to make peanut butter and jelly sandwiches for lunch, she had suggested they have a picnic in the backyard. Their sandwiches and apples quickly consumed, Melissa now sat on the top step of the back porch. She wrote in her journal as Tyler played on his swing set, alternately soaring back and forth through the air on a swing, then sliding gleefully down the slide. Periodically he would call out, "Lissa, look what I can do!" Then he would perform some slight variation to his last trick, going backward or headfirst down the slide, or twisting the chains of the swing and then letting go and spinning in circles. Each time Melissa would applaud his efforts, then return to her journal.

It's really a beautiful day today, Dad. I wonder if you can see that from heaven—or wherever you are. I know if there's such a place as heaven, you're there. But . . . what if there isn't? What if Pastor Michael and Toni and Brad and . . . even you . . . are wrong? What if you just die and . . . that's it? Nothing else. Just darkness. No hearing or seeing or . . .

Melissa shivered in spite of the warm sunshine almost directly overhead. Ever since finding out about her father's autopsy, she hadn't been able to get warm. She thought that maybe she felt cold inside, the way she imagined her father might feel. Then she wondered if he felt anything at all. She certainly hoped he hadn't felt anything during the autopsy. She began to write again.

I'm so mad at Toni for doing that. Wasn't it bad enough that you died? Did she have to make them cut you open? And for what? Just to

prove to her what everybody else already knew, everybody but that Abe
Matthews. I wish she'd never met him. I'm glad she's finally back with
Brad, but . . . it's not like it used to be with them. I can tell. I think Brad
can too. I wish they'd hurry up and get married.

"Lissa, are you going to come to my party?"

Melissa looked up. Tyler, his cheeks red and his dark hair damp
with sweat, stood directly in front of her.

"What party?"

Tyler rolled his eyes. "My birthday, remember? I'm finally going to
be seven."

Melissa smiled. "Sorry, I forgot. It's in September, isn't it?"

"Yep." Tyler nodded excitedly, his eyes dancing. "Two more
months, right after school starts. We're going to invite some of my
friends from school and all my cousins. We're going to have hot dogs
and chocolate ice cream and cake and . . . what else? Oh yeah, punch.
And we're going to play games and have prizes . . . right here in the
backyard, unless it's raining. It's going to be so much fun. You're coming, aren't you? Please?"

"I wouldn't miss it. I'm sure it's going to be a really special day."

Tyler's smile lit up his entire face, then slowly faded away. "I just
wish my dad was coming. Mom says Texas is too far away. Have you
ever been to Texas?"

Melissa shook her head. "No, I haven't."

"Me neither. I think I'd hate it there. Do you think my dad likes
it?"

"It's hard to say, especially since I don't know your dad, remember?"

"Oh, yeah. But . . ." His chin came up and he looked quite serious.
"I've been praying, Lissa, every day and every night, and I think God's
gonna bring my daddy home for my birthday."

Melissa swallowed, determined not to let him see her tears. She
nodded in silent agreement as he turned to walk back to his swing set.
Oh, God, if you're up there . . . if you're listening and if you care at all,
please don't let that little boy be hurt again. He's already been through

so much, losing his father the way he did. And now, with his birthday coming . . .

The realization hit her like a sledgehammer. How could she have forgotten? Had she purposely blocked it out? Toni hadn't mentioned it either, but maybe that was to protect her. In spite of Toni's bizarre behavior lately, she had always been very protective of her little sister, and Melissa appreciated it—most of the time. Sooner or later, Melissa would have thought of it though. It was, after all, only two days away. Sunday, July 25, would have been Paul Matthews's fifty-third birthday. There was a time that fifty-three had seemed almost ancient to Melissa. Now it seemed young, far too young for her handsome, fun-loving father to die—far too soon for him to leave her behind.

Melissa began to write again, struggling to see through the tears that blurred her vision. *How different today would have been if you were still alive, Dad. Toni and I would be planning something special— a party, or maybe a cookout. Brad would be there, for sure. Things would be so good, so happy and fun, like they used to be. Oh, Dad, I miss you so much. How am I ever going to stop hurting like this?*

~~~

Once again Melissa had opted to go home after church with Carrie and her family. Once again Toni had acquiesced, although she was more than slightly surprised that Melissa had not mentioned their father's birthday or said anything about going to the gravesite. She had, however, promised to be home in time to go to Brad's parents' house for dinner. The Andersons had extended the invitation right after church that morning, and the sisters had readily agreed. It would be the first time they had been over there since before their father's death. Brad had been ecstatic, inviting them to spend the entire afternoon with him before going to his parents' home. Surprisingly, not only Toni but Melissa had declined, Toni mumbling a vague excuse about having something else she needed to do, Melissa wanting to spend time with Carrie.

Toni, however, knew before she drove out of the church parking lot exactly what it was that she was going to do before going to the Andersons' home for dinner. It was her father's birthday, and she had always spent that day with him. Today would be no exception. Stopping off at home just long enough to change into some cool cotton slacks and a sleeveless blouse, Toni headed straight to the cemetery. Parking her Taurus in the shade, she carried her Bible, a sports bottle full of cold water, and an old blanket to her parents' gravesites. Spreading the blanket in the shade of the huge pine tree, she sat down near the twin headstones, laying her Bible and the water bottle on the blanket beside her. She fought tears as the fresh earth on her father's grave reminded her that, at her insistence, he had only recently been exhumed for an autopsy.

"Hi, Dad," she said softly. "I . . . I know you're not really here, but . . . I just wanted to say happy birthday. I don't imagine you have to worry about birthdays anymore, since you'll never grow old." Her voice cracked. "But I can't help remembering. . . . Birthdays were always such a special time at our house, thanks to you, and Mom, of course. Now I wonder if . . . they will ever seem special again, if anything will ever seem special. . . .

"Oh, Dad, I've made such a mess of things. I truly have. I never should have talked Dr. Jensen into helping me get that autopsy. What did it prove? Only that you had a heart attack, just as Dr. Jensen suspected. And now Melissa . . . she's so hurt and confused. This autopsy thing sure didn't help, and she's so angry at Abe and at what she sees as his part in influencing me to pursue the autopsy, not to mention what my involvement with him almost did to my relationship with Brad. Fortunately, that relationship has been patched up—at least, I guess it has. Brad seems happy anyway. Now if I could just get past my feelings for Abe, then maybe—"

I am your Father.

The abrupt shift in focus from her earthly to her heavenly Father jolted her as the memory of those words echoed in her heart almost as clearly as the first time she had sensed them. But she was puzzled. What did God mean? What was he trying to say to her with that reminder?

Trust me.

She gasped. It was obvious now that God was doing more than simply reminding her of what he had previously said. He was trying to help her understand something, but . . . what? What was it she didn't seem to understand? God had said he was her Father, that she was to trust him. . . . As the realization began to wash over her, she sensed a melting of something deep within, a fear that she had not been able to name—until now. It was the fear that, since her mother's death and then her father's, she must carry the weight of responsibility for herself and for Melissa on her own shoulders, a responsibility she felt totally inadequate to handle. As she meditated on her Father's words, she realized that concept was exactly what he wanted her to grasp. Of course, she was inadequate. She was never meant to carry such responsibility. God wanted only that she recognize him as her Father in every sense of the word: faithful, dependable, omnipotent, loving—more even than her earthly father had ever been. In addition, he would never leave her nor forsake her, a promise Paul Matthews had never made to her because it would have been impossible for him to keep.

It's you I should be talking to, isn't it? You I should be calling Father and pouring my heart out to. As wonderful and loving as my dad was, only you can answer my deepest longings and lead me where I need to go. I'm sorry, Father. I'm so sorry. . . .

As she sat there crying softly, she felt a hand on her shoulder, and she knew who it was without turning to look. Toni prayed that the sight of the fresh earth on her father's grave wouldn't make their already strained relationship worse.

Melissa sat down on the blanket beside her, graciously saying nothing about the visible reminder of the autopsy. Silently, together they honored their father's birthday. Toni thanked her heavenly Father for restoring their relationship, and asked him to bring Melissa to the same realization that he had given to her. It was a full fifteen minutes before either of them spoke.

"I'm not cold anymore," Melissa said.

Toni wasn't sure what her younger sister meant, but she sensed it was a good sign. She nodded and smiled.

"I wasn't going to come," Melissa explained, staring at her father's headstone. "That's why I went to Carrie's after church, so I wouldn't have to think about . . . Dad's birthday. It didn't work though, so here I am."

Toni reached over and squeezed her hand. "I'm glad."

"Me too. I've missed you. It's been . . . lonely."

"I know, and I'm so sorry about—"

Melissa interrupted her. "It's OK. I wish you hadn't done it, but . . . it's OK."

They sat in silence for a few more minutes. Then Melissa asked, "How soon do we need to go home and get ready to go to the Andersons'?"

"Not for a while yet. We've got plenty of time."

"Good. I'd like to just stay here—together—if we could."

"I think that's a good idea," Toni agreed.

With their backs against the rough trunk of the faithful sentry that overshadowed their parents' graves, they rested, each lost in her own thoughts but no longer grieving alone.

CHAPTER 10

"Toni, Melissa. It's so good to see you again." Barbara Anderson, color-coordinated in her pink seersucker dress and white summer beads, welcomed the Matthews sisters in her usual warm manner. With a brief hug and a peck on the cheek for each of them, the tall, slender, neatly-coifed blonde ushered them into the spacious house and then out onto the patio, where Brad and his father, George, a slightly older and balding version of his son, were sharing barbecue-detail. Both wore short-sleeved shirts and cotton slacks, and each had donned an apron for the occasion. Brad's was bright red, with no design or lettering, while George's blue apron boldly announced, "You may kiss the cook." Toni immediately went to him and planted a kiss on his cheek, laughing as she explained that she was taking his apron at face value.

"I knew there was a reason you wanted that apron instead of this one," Brad complained to his father. "Could I borrow it for a minute?"

George laughed. "Since when do you need a special apron to get a kiss from your fiancée?"

Toni smiled as Brad took her into his arms and kissed her, and everyone applauded. "You're right," said Brad. "Forget the apron." He kissed her again, then turned to Melissa. "And what about you? Do I get a kiss, or do I need the right apron?"

"No problem, Bro." Melissa and Brad hugged, then exchanged pecks on the cheek before Melissa went to George for a greeting as well. The official welcomes completed, Barbara took cold drink orders from everyone and headed back into the house. Toni was right behind her.

"Let me help you with those," she offered. "You can't possibly carry that many lemonades and iced teas by yourself."

"Don't be silly, dear. I'll just put them on a tray. You go on out and enjoy your visit." Barbara, who was standing in front of the open refrigerator, turned to look at Toni. Her blue eyes were serious. "You and Brad haven't been spending as much time together as you used to. I was hoping this evening might help remedy that. Please, go on. He came over right after church, and he's been pacing ever since, waiting for you to get here. He's missed you, you know."

Toni nodded. "I know. I've missed him too."

"Good. I'm glad to hear it. You two were meant for each other. George and I, we love you as if you were our own daughter. Melissa too. We're already family as far as we're concerned—especially now that your father is gone. We'll just be glad when our family ties are official, and you and Brad are finally married."

"Thank you. I appreciate that." Toni gave her future mother-in-law another quick hug, then hurried back outside, reminding herself as she went how very blessed she was to be loved by such a kind and considerate man as Brad, as well as his wonderful parents. Seeing Melissa joking and laughing with Brad and his father, she realized how much her little sister needed the Andersons right now. She smiled, grateful that she and Melissa had mended some of their differences.

"So, what's on the grill tonight?" she asked, walking up to the happy threesome. "Perfect weather for a cookout, isn't it?"

"Couldn't be better," George agreed. "It took awhile, but I think summer has finally arrived in the Northwest. We've got some tri-tips going here, marinated in my own special recipe, the one Melissa always raves about."

"Are you ever going to tell us how you make that?" Melissa pleaded. "Toni and I have tried to figure it out, but ours is never quite the same."

George smiled. "Well, I don't know. I don't share my secret recipe with just anyone, you know."

"I'm not just anyone. I'm the *only* sister of your *only* future daughter-in-law."

Brad reached over and tousled her hair. "With credentials like that, you've got my vote."

"Thanks a lot, Bro," Melissa pouted, patting her hair back into place with exaggerated movements. "But just because we're almost family doesn't mean you can mess up my hair."

"You tell him, Missy," George laughed. "Don't let him get away with that."

"Are you kidding?" Brad asked. "These two never let me get away with anything. In fact, they gang up on me all the time and pick on me constantly."

Just then Barbara joined them with a tray of cold drinks. "Why do I find that more than slightly difficult to believe? These two sweet, innocent young ladies picking on you? Not likely, I'm afraid."

"You see?" said Brad, looking to George for support. "We're out-numbered. We don't have a chance."

"What's this 'we' stuff? Where did you get the idea that I'm siding with you here? I'm not as stupid as I look, you know. I may be barbe-cuing the meat, but I know who does the rest of the cooking at this address—and I like to eat too much to alienate her."

As the good-natured bantering continued throughout the evening, Toni tried with all her heart to enter in. She thought she had been doing a pretty good job until she caught Brad giving her a sideways glance during dinner, studying her as if trying to figure out what she was really thinking. *He knows,* she thought. *He knows. What am I going to do?*

She leaned over on the picnic bench where they were sitting side by side and kissed his cheek. "I love you."

Brad smiled. "I love you too." His smile was strained though, and Toni found herself wondering what it would be like to live their entire lives this way.

∾∾∾

The life is in the blood. . . .
It is the blood that makes atonement.

It was Tuesday evening, and in the two days since Abe had received his Uncle David's *Tanakh* from Aunt Sophie, he had spent his after-work hours reading the first five books, referred to in the contents as the *Torah* section. Before going on to the next section, the *Nevi'im,* which consisted of the writings of the prophets, he couldn't help but think about what he had read so far and how blood seemed to be such a central part of the Jewish faith. From the first book of *B'resheet,* where God had come down to the garden to provide coverings from the skins of slain animals for Adam and Eve, the common thread of blood atonement seemed to run through the pages. Abe felt that he was beginning to get a glimmer of understanding, but there was not yet enough to tie it all together. He wondered if he would be able to do so by the time he had read his uncle's *Tanakh* in its entirety. Of course, his detective mind wasn't about to overlook anything. Taking notes, he searched for clues as he read. Already in his investigation he had discovered one thing for certain: There was no possible way to reconcile the writings in this book with what his parents had taught him. Whether or not there truly was a God he could not yet say for sure; but if there was, then what people believed about him and how they responded to those beliefs did matter. From his readings so far, it was obvious that the God of his ancestors was not an impersonal deity who left those whom he had created to their own devices. The God of Israel, whom Toni claimed to worship, had given promises to his people, but those promises had conditions. He had given *Torah*—teachings, or laws—to the Israelites. Obedience to *Torah* brought blessings; disobedience brought curses. How could it not be important for people to know about these things before making any sort of rational decision about the role of God in their lives?

Abe sighed as he flipped through the remaining pages. So much to read. So much to learn. So much to understand. Would the rest of the puzzle pieces fall into place as he worked his way through to the end? Would there be a clear explanation for why God emphasized blood so much in the first five books of the *Tanakh,* and why—at least to Abe's limited knowledge—blood was no longer an issue in the modern practice of the Jewish religion? After all, faithful Jews, such as Aunt Sophie, still observed *Shabbat* and the festivals as prescribed in *Torah.* Why not the sacrifices? He vaguely remembered his grandfather telling him something years earlier about the animal sacrifices coming to an end when the Temple was destroyed, but he didn't remember his grandfather saying anything about what replaced those sacrifices. Were there inconsistencies in this book that was supposedly given by God himself? If so, Abe would find them—and he would reject the Jewish faith in its entirety. If not . . .

He closed his eyes as a shudder ran through his body. If there were no inconsistencies to be found, what sort of radical changes would be required of him as he adopted this ancient faith of his fathers?

∾∾∾

The sun was just beginning to peek over the horizon as Brad brought his cup of coffee to the terrace and settled into a lounge chair. He was not, by nature, a morning person, but he had trained himself to wake early, convinced that there was merit to the "early to bed and early to rise" theory. This morning, however, his earlier than usual rising had nothing to do with this theory or a busy agenda. Since the barbecue at his parents' home three days earlier, he had not been able to shake the feeling that although he and Toni had reconciled and she had assured him that Abe Matthews was out of her life once and for all, they were growing farther apart by the day. The thought terrified him. How could he fight what he could not see or hear, what he could not even identify? He knew the problem still revolved around the loss of Toni's father, but it was more than that. It was, whether Toni would admit it or not, a lingering attraction, even an attachment, to Abe that kept her at a distance from Brad. Even when he kissed her, it was obvious that her mind—and quite possibly her heart—was somewhere else.

He closed his eyes and tilted his head to the sky, hugging his coffee cup with his hands as the first rays of sunlight touched his face. *What am I going to do, God? How do I get through to her? How can we recapture what we had before . . . before her dad's death, before Abe? There must be a way. There has to be. . . .*

His heart constricted with the pain of missing her. It was worse than when he had given her the ultimatum and then forced himself to stay away from her so she would see the need to put Abe out of her life and return to him and to the way things used to be. At least then he had been sure she would see things clearly, that she would make the right choice. It seemed that she had, but now . . .

He sipped his coffee, his eyes still closed. *I'll call her as soon as I know she's up. I'll convince her to go with me Friday night—just the two of us this time—somewhere really special. Quiet and secluded, and very romantic.*

Oh, Toni, don't you understand? We were meant to be together. We've always known it. We've talked about it and praised God for it. For years we've planned our future together. Please, please don't throw it all away now. Not now . . .

~~~

After Melissa had left for work on Friday, Toni spent the morning doing some laundry and cleaning before going to the office. Even though she had finished referring her father's clients to other agencies, there were still stacks of paperwork and years of files to sort through and either pack into storage or run through the shredder. Once all that was done, she could then take the next step, which was putting the agency—or what was left of it in the way of furniture and equipment—up for sale. It was a decision she had already made and was going to have to act on sooner or later, but even after the results of the autopsy, which should have settled the issue of her father's death once and for all, she was still reluctant to make the move. She wondered if it might be because she saw the next logical step after putting the agency up for sale as setting a wedding date with Brad.

Oh, Lord, what's wrong with me? Brad is such a fine man. I know he'll be the perfect husband, but . . .

Sighing, she unlocked the front door of the office. It was just after noon on Friday, and she and Brad had a date for dinner later that night. She knew the conversation would eventually get around to discussing wedding plans, and she wondered how long she would be able to use her dad's death as an excuse for prolonging the inevitable.

Oh, Father, forgive me—and help me! What a terrible way to think of my future marriage to Brad.

Walking straight through to the inner office and flipping on the light, she surveyed the mound of files and paperwork piled on her desk. Determined to make at least a sizable dent in the pile before the day was over, she resolved to put thoughts of Brad and their wedding out of her mind. *One thing at a time,* she reminded herself, putting her purse in the bottom drawer and plunking down in the chair. The mound in front of her seemed to grow the longer she looked at it. She reached out and picked up a file, but before she could get it open, the phone rang.

"Matthews and Matthews. May I help you?"

"Toni Matthews?"

Toni frowned. She didn't recognize the somewhat muffled male voice, but there was something vaguely, even eerily familiar about it. "Yes, this is Toni Matthews. How may I help you?"

"Don't worry about helping me. You'd better think about helping yourself."

"Excuse me?"

"Just mind your own business and everything will be OK."

Toni was getting angry now. "Is this some kind of joke? Who is this?"

"This is definitely not a joke, and it doesn't matter who I am. What matters is that you remember what I said. Mind your own business. Don't start poking your nose in where it doesn't belong. Understand?"

"Look, I don't know who you are, but—"

The caller hung up before she could finish her sentence. Fighting the creeping sense of fear that had become the recurrent aftereffect of her recent nightmares, she jumped up from her desk and walked to the water cooler in the front office. Her hands shaking slightly, she filled a paper cup to the brim and drank it, then tossed the crumpled cup in the trash.

Just some crank call, she told herself. *Probably some kid who's getting bored with summer vacation and has nothing better to do.* Yet, whoever it was knew her by name—and he had certainly not sounded like a young kid, or even a teenager. If only her dad had not been so old fashioned, so prone to hang on to anything that still worked, rather than trade it in on a newer model. A caller I.D. would have been a big help right now, although she imagined the caller, whoever he was, hadn't been stupid enough to call from home.

She returned to the inner office, stopping in front of her desk with her back to the door. *Oh, Lord,* she prayed, closing her eyes, *is this something I should be concerned about, or am I making a big deal out of nothing? Could this possibly have anything to do with the evil I've sensed lately?*

She felt a hand on her shoulder as a low voice spoke her name. With a frightened yelp, she turned to find herself staring up into Abe Matthews's stunned face. His dark eyes were wide with concern as he took her by the arms.

"Are you all right? I'm sorry I scared you. What's wrong? You look so . . . frightened. Has something happened?"

Her heart was pounding so hard that she thought it would burst as she fought the impulse to fall into his arms, to beg him to hold her and to forgive her for lying to him, to confess what she truly felt. How she longed for the strength and safety she knew she would feel in his embrace, the release she knew would come if she could just tell him the truth. But, of course, she couldn't.

"I'm fine," she said, cringing as she lied to him once again. "You just . . . startled me, that's all. Really."

"I'm sorry. I know I'm the last person you expected to show up in your office—or anywhere in your life. I called you at home, and when you weren't there, I decided to take a chance and come by here."

For a brief moment, Toni considered closing her eyes, relaxing, and allowing him to pull her close—which she was sure he would do with just the slightest encouragement. The moment passed, however, and she knew she had better change the subject quickly, before it was too late.

"I . . . assume you're here for a specific purpose?"

The look of concern faded a bit from Abe's face, and she could tell he was making a concerted effort to be businesslike. "Actually, yes, I am. Can we sit down?"

Tearing her eyes away from his, she turned and walked toward the chair behind her desk. Abe pulled an extra chair over near hers, then waited until she sat down. Her legs were still shaking as she lowered herself into her seat. What was this about? She had clearly told him that she intended to marry Brad and that they should not see each

other anymore. Yet, he had come. Did he intend to try again, to tell
her of his love for her, to beg her to reconsider? If so, would she be
strong enough to reject him twice? She doubted it, and found herself
hoping—as futile as it would be—that he would do just that.
However, he didn't. As he sat mere inches away from her, his eyes
locked into hers, she had to summon all her strength to focus on his
words.

"Toni, something has happened. I heard about it this morning. A
fisherman found a body . . . late yesterday evening, tangled in some
reeds on the north side of Eagle Lake. Apparently it had been in the
water a while, several weeks anyway. They haven't been able to identify her yet, but—"

Toni interrupted him. "'Her'?" Fear gripped her heart as she felt
herself slipping to the edge once again. Instinctively she grabbed Abe's
hand and clung to it with every ounce of strength she had. "What do
you mean, 'her'? It's a woman's body?"

Abe nodded. "A young woman—a girl, really, at least as far as they
can tell at this point. There'll be an autopsy, of course, and . . . if no
one steps forward to identify her right away, they'll have to try to
identify her through dental records or DNA or . . . Toni, it's going to
be on the local news, so I wanted to tell you about it before you heard
about it somewhere else."

Toni's head was spinning. "Do you think . . . ? Could it possibly
be . . . ?"

"Julie?" Abe's jaw twitched. "I hope not, but . . . we have to consider
the possibility."

"Oh, Abe." Hot tears sprang to her eyes as she thought of April
Lippincott. "What are we going to tell April?"

"That's why I'm here. Even though we don't know it's Julie, I really
should have called the sheriff's office as soon as I heard about it and
told them what we know about her, including the information about
your dad's investigation—not that they can't identify her without
our help. If it's Julie, she's already listed as missing in the nationwide

computer system, and they'll have her dental records on file. I still need to notify the county right away, but I thought it might be easier for April if you called before the authorities contact her or Julie's parents, or I can call her if you'd rather. I don't mind doing that if you don't feel up to it."

Toni was suddenly aware that she was clinging to Abe's hand. Embarrassed, she released him and reached for the phone. "No, that's all right. Really. I'll do it. I just . . ."

As visions of the attractive blonde-haired girl flashed through her mind—first the picture of the smiling teenager in Julie's file, then the image of the terrified girl in Toni's dreams, running for her life—Toni's resolve crumpled, and she buried her face in her hands and began to weep. She was vaguely aware that Abe was kneeling beside her, his arms enfolding her, as he rocked her gently and stroked her hair, assuring her that everything was going to be all right. How she longed to believe him. But even now, in the arms of this man she was so fiercely drawn to that she could scarcely breathe, this strong yet gentle one to whom she could never speak of love, she doubted that anything would ever be right again.

CHAPTER 11

The view was breathtaking. Toni only wished she could enjoy it. Brad had phoned ahead and reserved the best table at their favorite restaurant, about thirty minutes northeast of River View. Sitting beside him and gazing out the window at the setting sun, Toni realized that prior to the events of the last few months, nothing would have made her happier than being right where she was, right at this moment. Tonight, however, her heart was heavy, her smile strained, as Brad, sitting very close to her on the booth's cushioned seat, held her hand, occasionally whispering endearments or kissing her cheek. She was relieved when the waiter brought their salads.

After Brad had given thanks for the food, she began to toy with the greens on her plate. She'd had no appetite since Abe had told her of the discovery of the body at Eagle Lake. Even though he had assured her that the body had not yet been identified, she somehow knew that it was Julie. She had sensed that Abe knew it as well, and she had been grateful for his arms around her as she cried, even though she knew she'd had no right to welcome—nor encourage—his embrace.

Toni's call to April, once she had composed herself enough to make it, had been difficult at best, even with Abe at her side, ready to step in and help if she broke down. She had made it, though, and April had taken the news somewhat stoically, undoubtedly praying that the autopsy would prove that the body was not Julie's. After the call, Toni sat silently, trying to imagine what April and Julie's parents would go through while awaiting the report. Abe had sat next to her, allowing her as much time as she needed to compose herself. When he had finally spoken, there was no mention of his own feelings, only concern for hers and for April and her family. His unselfish support had endeared him to her all the more. When he had gone, leaving her with a gentle kiss on the forehead, she had wavered between admiration for his compassion and disappointment at his restraint.

"Earth to Toni. Come in, please."

Brad's voice shook her from her reverie, and she turned to find him smiling at her hesitantly. "Are you OK in there? Are you even in there?"

Another forced smile. "I'm fine. Really. I was just thinking about . . ." She sighed. "Have you listened to the local news today? Did you hear about the body they found at Eagle Lake?"

Brad's smile faded. "Actually, I did have the news on earlier while I was getting ready to pick you up, but I only heard fragments. Have they identified the body?"

"Not that I know of. At least, they hadn't when I heard about it earlier today. I called April Lippincott and told her, just in case."

Brad frowned. "Just in case what? Why would you call Mrs. Lippincott?"

"In case the body is . . . Julie's."

"Julie Greene's? You mean, they think . . .?"

"I only know they think the body is that of a young woman—possibly a teenage girl—and that she had been in the water for quite a while. We couldn't help but think that it might be Julie because—"

"Wait a minute," Brad interrupted. "Who's 'we'? You mean you and April?"

Toni felt her cheeks flush. She had not intended to mention Abe's involvement, but it was too late now. "No. Abe and I. He . . . came by the office this afternoon to let me know about the body. He didn't want me to hear about it on the news, and he thought I might want to be the one to call April, which I did."

Brad dropped his head and sat silently for a moment. When he looked at her, there were tears in his eyes. "So he's back. Somehow, I knew that."

"He's not . . . back. Not the way you mean. There's nothing, Brad. Nothing between Abe and me. There never was, and there never will be. He just came to let me know. That's all."

"I want to believe that. I really do, but . . ."

"Believe it. I'm going to marry you, Brad. Abe has no part in my life."

His eyes searched hers, as if trying to see below the surface. Why couldn't he just accept her words at face value? Why did he have to look at her that way? Her heart ached as she wondered just how much he could really see. Were her feelings for Abe so evident? Did the longing she felt for him inside show on her face? She prayed not. She did not want to hurt Brad, and she knew there was absolutely no future for her with Abe. The matter was settled. What could she do to convince Brad of that fact?

"I've been thinking," she began, praying silently for the strength to get through what she was about to say. "Maybe you're right. Maybe we do need to at least pick some sort of target date for our wedding and get started on the plans. . . ."

As the realization of what she was saying began to dawn on Brad, a smile spread slowly across his face, and the tears that had threatened earlier now shone in his eyes. "Toni, do you mean it? Can we finally set a date?"

She nodded. "Yes. It's time. I know that."

"When? Where? How? You name it. Whenever and whatever you want is fine with me. Just, please, don't let it be too long."

Her mind was racing. She had come this far; now she had to deliver. When? What would be a realistic date? She thought of spring but sensed that was too far away. Not only would Brad be disappointed at having to wait almost another year, but it would give her too much time to think, to change her mind . . . too much time to run into Abe, to risk her resistance breaking down. No, it must be sooner.

"How about this fall? November or December? Sometime before Christmas. We could have a small ceremony, either at the church or maybe your parents' home, or . . . whatever you think is best. But small. I definitely want it to be small . . . and simple. No big social affair. It's just too soon after . . . Dad's death."

Brad slipped his arm around her, pulled her close, and kissed her. Toni returned his kiss, glad they were seated next to each other in a high-backed booth, affording them an element of privacy. She knew their decision would become common knowledge soon enough, but she just wasn't ready to advertise it unnecessarily.

When he released her, his hazel eyes were dancing. "I've got my day-timer in the car. After dinner, let's pick an exact date so we can make the announcement official."

Toni hesitated. "Do you mind terribly if we put that off, just until after . . . after the autopsy results? I'd like to have that settled first, to know whether or not the body is Julie's. I know that might sound strange, but it's important to me. Please?"

Brad's look was tender. "Of course." He smiled. "You've made me the happiest man in the world. Do you know that?"

"I'm glad," she said and meant it, even as she wondered if she would ever be able to share in that happiness.

~~~

It was Wednesday morning, and Toni was just about to run into town to pick up some groceries when the phone rang. Her heart soared the minute she heard Abe's voice on the other end of the line. She immediately scolded herself for her feelings and tried to focus on his words rather than on the way she had felt when he held her as she cried, or the lingering sweetness of his kiss on her forehead. . . .

"I'm sorry to bother you at home, but would it be all right if I came over for a few minutes? I won't be there long, I promise, but I really need to talk with you about the autopsy results."

"The results are in? Is it Julie?"

"I'd really rather tell you in person. If this isn't a good time, or if you'd rather I not come over there . . ."

"No, this is fine. Really. I'll be here."

She hung up the phone, her heart racing even as she scolded herself for her overreaction. Why should it matter if Abe stopped by for a few minutes? This was business, after all. Strictly business. Even as she tried to convince herself, she hurried to the bathroom mirror to check her makeup and hair. *Why? Why can't I just let this thing go? What kind of hold has this man got on me? Even before I met Abe, I never felt this way about Brad. Oh, if only I could!*

Going to the kitchen, she checked the refrigerator for cold drinks. Almost a full pitcher of iced tea. Good. And plenty of ice cubes in the freezer. Cold drinks could be a handy distraction. That would help. At least it would give her something to do, something to look at besides his eyes.

She got the glasses out of the cupboard and set them on the table, then began to pace back and forth across the kitchen floor. Why had he insisted on telling her the results in person? Why couldn't he have told her over the phone? There were only two possible reasons as far as she could see. First, the body had been identified as Julie Greene, and Abe knew she would take the news hard. He was right, of course. Second, he wanted an excuse to be near her. Both sounded likely.

Oh, Father, help me! I don't want to have these feelings for him, but I do.

The doorbell rang and she jumped. Nervously running her fingers through her hair, she patted it into place, then walked, as calmly as she could, to the front door. When she opened it and looked up at him, his broad shoulders straining against his short-sleeved, pale blue cotton shirt, she was sure he was even more handsome than the last time she had seen him. Ignoring the echo of her heart pounding in her ears, she pushed open the screen door.

"Come in, please. How are you?"

He stepped inside, near enough that the faint smell of his aftershave made her heady. He was staring at her, the concern obvious on his face. "I'm fine. The important thing is, how are you?"

"I'm . . . OK. Thanks. Shall we sit down?" Without waiting for an answer, she led the way to the couch in the living room, being careful to leave a sizable space between them. "I have some iced tea. Would you like some?"

"No . . . yes. I mean, sure, that would be fine. Can I help you?"

She was already up and moving into the kitchen. "I can get it. I'll only be a minute." She took deep breaths as she poured the tea, hoping that would help calm her nerves and that he wouldn't notice how badly her hands were shaking. Also, she thought it was amazing that he couldn't hear her heart beating, as loud as it sounded to her. *Help me, Father,* she prayed, then picked up the glasses and walked back into the living room.

Abe was no longer seated on the couch. He was standing with his back to her, looking at the picture on the mantle. It was a family picture, taken less than a year before Toni's mother died. Abe turned as she entered the room and placed the glasses on coasters on the coffee table in front of the couch.

"Nice picture," he said, walking back to join her. "Your mother was very beautiful."

Toni nodded, carefully taking a seat at the far end of the couch near the end table. "Yes, she was. Melissa looks a lot like her."

"I can tell." He sat down in the middle of the couch next to her and picked up a glass of iced tea. Looking across the room at the picture, he said, "Obviously beauty runs in your family."

Without commenting, she reached for the other glass, but he stopped her with his free hand. She looked up into his eyes.

"I love you, Toni."

She felt the tears come then, tiny pinpricks at the back of her eyes, but she fought them. "Don't," she whispered. "Please."

He withdrew his hand. "I'm sorry."

For a moment neither spoke. Instead, they kept their eyes averted and searched for a way to break the silence. Finally, Abe said, "I suppose I'd better tell you why I came. The autopsy, I mean." Once again, their eyes met.

"It was Julie, wasn't it?"

Abe nodded.

"Does April know?"

"Yes. She helped them with the identification. Of course, Julie's dental records were already on file, which would have been enough, but April told them about a ring she had given Julie, an heirloom that she always wore. It was still on her finger when they found her."

"Oh, Abe. Poor April."

"Are you OK?"

"Yes . . . I think. I don't know. I expected this, I suppose, but . . ."

He nodded. "Me too. Still, I kept hoping . . ."

She took a deep breath. "What happens now? Where do they go from here?"

"There'll be an investigation, of course, especially since she was a runaway and your dad had those notes in her file regarding his suspicions about a baby-selling ring—which, by the way, reminds me of something else I read in the report."

She raised her eyebrows. "Something else? What do you mean?"

"According to the medical examiner, Julie died from drowning, but . . . she also had just had a miscarriage. It seems she'd been experiencing some major bleeding, and it doesn't appear that she was being treated medically. There may be some sort of connection there; I'm just not sure what it is yet. The county will be following up on that."

"A miscarriage. A fifteen-year-old pregnant girl having a miscarriage, and now she's dead. It just doesn't seem possible. Does . . . April know about all this yet, including the miscarriage?"

"I'm not sure, but I would imagine she does. Someone from the sheriff's office has probably filled her in by now. This must really be rough on her and the rest of Julie's family."

Toni swallowed. "To wait all those weeks and months. To hope and pray, and then . . ." The tears came again, and this time she couldn't stop them. "I feel so sorry for them."

Before she knew it, she was in his arms, crying softly against his chest. She wasn't sure which of them had first reached out for the other, but it really didn't matter anymore. Her heart ached for April and her family, and yet she felt as if she could stay right where she was forever. If only it were possible . . .

He lifted her head with his finger, gazing down at her with such longing that everything else faded from her mind. When his lips met hers, there was no fight left in her. She knew she was where she wanted to be, not just for this moment, but always. Lost in a depth of passion she had not known before, she was shocked, even angered, when the phone rang, invading her territory and interrupting her world just when it seemed that world was finally beginning to make sense.

She pulled away, suddenly embarrassed and ashamed at the realization that she had crossed the line she had said she would never cross. If Abe had questioned her feelings for him before today, those questions had been answered emphatically. Denying them at this point would be futile.

She reached for the phone beside her. "Hello?" Her voice was shaking so badly that she could scarcely speak as she berated herself for having allowed this situation to occur. Surely she had seen it coming. Surely she could have done something to stop it, but now it was too late. Now Abe knew, and her options were narrowing.

"Toni? Sweetheart, is something wrong?"

"I . . ." Brad. Why Brad? Why now? Was this God's way of stopping her before she compounded her mistake? If so, why couldn't Brad have called just a few moments sooner? "I'm . . . fine. Really. I was just . . . talking with a . . . friend." *Oh, God, forgive me.*

"If you're busy, I can call back later."

"No. No, I'm not busy. This is fine."

"Well, if you're sure. Actually, I just called to see if I could pick you up for lunch later. Do you have plans?"

She looked at Abe. He knew she was talking with Brad, yet he kept his eyes locked on her, drawing her, calling her to himself. There was no more denying that he had captured her heart, but would that be enough? Could she choose to walk away from Brad, from the life they had planned together, from the promises she had made? She was sure these same questions were running through Abe's mind.

"Lunch would be fine. What time?"

"About twelve-thirty or one, OK?"

"Sure. See you then."

She hung up the phone, then sat staring at the receiver, her back to Abe, until he took her by the arms and turned her toward himself. He waited until she looked up at him.

"I was right, wasn't I? It's me you love, not Brad."

She wanted to answer, but she didn't trust herself to speak. She wanted to explain to him about the Bible's prohibition against a believer marrying an unbeliever. She wanted to tell him that, her relationship with Brad aside, she was still confused, and it was too soon to speak of love and of commitments. She also longed to tell him that she had never before experienced such depth of feeling for anyone. She wanted to tell him all these things, but she could not. She could only look into his eyes, praying for God to intervene.

"Tell him," Abe said, his voice soft but firm. "Even if you can't tell me, tell Brad how you feel. Please."

"I . . ." Her heart was breaking, but she knew what she had to do. "I can't. I can't, Abe. Don't you see? I promised him. Just the other night, in fact. An autumn wedding. It's . . . the right thing to do. It's what I *have* to do. Please, try to understand. I'm going to marry Brad."

The hope and joy faded from his eyes as he slowly released her, then rose from the couch and walked away. He didn't stop until he had crossed the room. When he looked back, his voice cracked as he spoke. "Goodbye, Toni. I wish you all the best—both of you."

~~~

It had been two days since Toni had made it clear to Abe that in spite of her feelings for him she was going to go through with her wedding to Brad. For two painful days, with little or no sleep, Abe tried desperately to transfer that information from his brain to his heart. He didn't feel as if he had made much progress, and the effort was beginning to take its toll on his physical and mental alertness. Sitting at his desk that Friday morning, nursing his third cup of coffee, he tried once again to focus on the tasks before him. When he heard someone open his door without knocking first, he looked up, startled to see his uncle standing in the doorway, frowning down at him.

"You look terrible," Sol announced as he studied Abe's drawn face. "Your eyes look like roadmaps. What's wrong with you, boy? How come you're not getting any sleep?" Without waiting for an answer, he pulled up a chair and sat down.

"Uncle Sol. It's good to see you."

"Wish I could say the same about you. What's going on? You been pulling extra duty or something?"

"Not really. I—"

"Is it that Matthews woman again? You haven't been out with her, have you? I heard you talked to her before going to the sheriff with what you knew about the Julie Greene case. That wasn't very smart."

Abe studied his uncle. He could tell he was concerned but not nearly as upset as he had been the time he called Abe to his house.

"No, I wasn't out with Toni. As for going to her first when I heard the body had been found at the lake, it was the right thing to do, at least for her sake. Besides, all that's been taken care of. The sheriff's office has the girl's file, and everything's under control."

"I know the county has the file. And if you mean 'everything's under control' because they're investigating her death, that's right. I'm not so sure you're under control though, and I don't like it."

"Uncle Sol, you don't have to worry—"

"Since when, I don't have to worry? Am I your uncle, or what? If I don't worry about you, who's going to do it? Listen, that's why I'm here. I've been talking to some of the key people on this case, and they're considering bringing you in as part of a countywide task force since you're already familiar with the situation. Even though there's no obvious connection between the girl's drowning and the heart attack that killed your girlfriend's father—"

"She's not my girlfriend."

"Yeah, yeah, OK. Anyway, since you got the file from Toni Matthews and it was her father who was investigating the girl's disappearance, it seemed logical to get you involved in the investigation." He looked at Abe questioningly. "Can I safely assume you aren't already 'unofficially' involved?"

"I'm not involved in the Greene case, and I'm not involved with Toni Matthews. Is that what you wanted me to say?"

Sol shrugged. "Just want to know what we're dealing with here. Look, it's nothing personal against this Matthews woman, it's just that I don't want to see you do anything stupid—not that it would be the first time."

Abe's jaws twitched. He had a feeling his uncle was referring to more than his recent involvement in trying to track down information on Toni's father's death. He decided to let it pass. It was a topic they had not discussed in many years, and he wasn't about to reopen it now.

"So, they want me as part of a task force on the Julie Greene investigation. You didn't have anything to do with that, did you?"

Sol raised his dark eyebrows in surprise, the picture of innocence. "What do you mean? I'm just a retired cop. What have I got to do with anything that goes on around here?"

Abe smiled in spite of himself. "Probably a lot more than you let on, and don't give me that innocent look. I know you, remember? I know how you can drop hints, make suggestions, even call in favors."

"So sue me. Look, I'd rather have you involved in this thing officially than risk seeing you poke your nose in where it doesn't belong and get it chopped off. Do you get my drift?"

"OK. No problem. I'll keep my nose where it belongs."

"That would be a relief." He got up from his chair and turned to leave, then stopped. "I understand this girl had a miscarriage before she died. What do you make of that?"

"I don't know. Why?"

Sol shrugged. "No reason. Just . . . wondering. Thought maybe it might tie in somewhere with that suspected baby ring that Matthews guy mentioned in the file."

"I don't see how. Why? You don't think . . . ?"

"Not anymore than I have to, boy. At least, not about things that are none of my business. Might be a good idea if you learned to do the same."

He paused, staring down at Abe as if waiting for his nephew to absorb the full impact of his comment. Then he walked out, pulling the door shut behind him.

～～～

It was not quite noon on Saturday, and the sun had already burned off the morning clouds, promising a perfect day for a picnic. Toni, seated at the kitchen table, wished she could absorb some of Melissa's excitement. She watched her little sister, dressed in typical teenage attire of baggy shorts and T-shirt—which did not completely hide the burgeoning woman underneath—scurrying around, filling the picnic basket with more food than the three of them would ever eat in one afternoon. She had to admit, though, that Melissa's nonstop chatter since early that morning was beginning to get on her nerves.

"I'm so glad we're doing the food this time," said Melissa, folding some napkins and tucking them into the basket. "It seems like Brad's always doing everything. He takes us out to eat or brings something over here or has us over to his parents' house. He deserves to be waited on for a change. And he loves your fried chicken. I just hope he likes my potato salad."

"I'm sure he will. Besides, when have you ever known Brad to turn down food of any kind?"

Melissa laughed. "That's true. Do you think we have enough fruit and cookies?"

"I think we have more than enough of everything."

The phone rang and Melissa raced to answer it. "Mrs. Lippincott. How are you? I'm . . . really sorry about Julie. Just a minute. I'll put Toni on."

Toni, still seated, took the phone. "April, how are you?"

"As well as can be expected, thank you. And you?"

"Oh, we're . . . fine. We're just waiting for Brad to pick us up and take us on a picnic."

"How nice. Do say hello for me." She paused. "I thought you would want to know that we will be having the memorial service for Julie on Wednesday afternoon. The associate pastor will be speaking rather than my son-in-law. He decided he just wasn't able to handle it."

"I . . . can imagine." Toni reached for something else to say but came up empty.

"Toni . . ." April sounded hesitant. "I was thinking that after the service next week I might come back to River View. I know there's nothing I can do there, and I certainly don't want to be in the way, but I just want so desperately to be near where the investigation is taking place. Oh, I hope this doesn't sound macabre, but . . . I want—I *need*—to see where they found my Julie." Her voice broke. "I hope you can understand."

Toni's heart went out to the woman. She wished she could reach through the phone and hold her close. "Of course I understand, and you won't be in the way at all. In fact, Melissa and I have missed you since you left. We would love it if you'd come back for a while. But there's only one thing."

"What's that, my dear?"

"No hotel this time. You're staying with us."

"Oh, no. I don't want to impose. . . ."

"No imposition—and no arguments. You just let us know when you're coming, and we'll have the spare room ready for you."

"Well, if you're sure . . ."

Toni looked at Melissa. She was smiling and nodding her head. "Positive," Toni said. "We're already looking forward to it."

She had no sooner hung up the phone than Brad arrived. Melissa let him in, and after giving him a quick hug, went to her room, ostensibly to retrieve her journal, but, Toni thought, more than likely to give her and Brad a few moments alone. Brad took immediate advantage of the opportunity, gathering Toni into his arms and kissing her tenderly before gazing down into her eyes.

"I was hoping we'd have a minute or two to ourselves," he said, smiling excitedly. "The autopsy report is in, Julie's case is officially under investigation, and now we can set a wedding date. Why not pick one right now? Today. Then we can make it official by telling Melissa before we tell anyone else. What do you say? When can I finally start calling you Mrs. Anderson?"

Toni swallowed. She *had* promised to settle on a date as soon as the autopsy report was done, and now she couldn't think of a single reason to postpone it any longer. "Let's go into the kitchen and look at the calendar."

Brad's eyes opened wide. "Seriously? Right now?"

"Right now."

Toni took the calendar off the wall by the refrigerator and laid it on the kitchen table. Then they sat down and flipped the calendar open to the month of November.

"I assume you'd prefer a Saturday?" Brad asked.

"Is that OK with you?"

Brad leaned over and kissed her again. "Sweetheart, any day—or night—is OK with me. Just pick a date so I can start the countdown."

She smiled, then looked back at the calendar. "Thanksgiving is on the twenty-fifth. How about Saturday, the twenty-seventh?"

"A Thanksgiving wedding. What a great idea. That's perfect."

"What's perfect?" Melissa asked, walking up behind them.

Brad turned to look at her, his eyes shining. "Toni and I have set a wedding date. Saturday, November twenty-seventh, two days after Thanksgiving. What do you think?"

Melissa squealed with delight, dropped her journal on the floor, and threw her arms around both of them. "That's incredible! Oh, I am *sooo* happy! Where's it going to be? What time? Do I get to be a bridesmaid?"

Toni and Brad laughed. "Take it easy," Toni cautioned. "Let me get used to all this one step at a time."

Melissa was soon chattering nonstop again, but this time about the wedding. As she and Brad carried everything out to the car, Toni started out the door behind them, only to be stopped by the phone. She had no sooner picked up the receiver than she wished she hadn't. The familiar muffled voice greeted her on the other end.

"You're doing real good there, Toni, minding your own business. Keep up the good work and no one will get hurt."

"Who is this?" Toni demanded, resolving to get a caller I.D. installed on their phone first thing Monday morning.

"I told you before, it doesn't matter. The only thing that matters is that you pay attention to what I told you. Understand?"

The phone clicked, and Toni stood staring at the receiver. How long was this going to go on? She had tried repeatedly to convince herself that it was some cruel joke, that it was best to ignore the calls until whoever it was got tired of making them. Now she was beginning to wonder if she should report the calls to the police.

Her heart jumped. If only things were different with Abe. If only she could talk to him, tell him about the calls, he would know what to do. Should she . . .?

Brad honked the horn just as Melissa yelled through the screen door, "Are we going on a picnic or not? Come on, let's celebrate!"

Celebrate? How do I do that? With one last glance at the phone, she turned toward the front door. "Coming," she called. The mysterious phone calls would just have to wait.

CHAPTER 12

Abe's muscles ached, and his stomach felt empty. Glancing at his watch, he was amazed to see how late it was. He hadn't realized how long he had been sitting in his recliner and reading. It was almost eight o'clock Sunday evening, and he had spent the majority of the weekend in that very spot, studying his uncle's *Tanakh*—and trying not to think of Toni. Having finished *Mal'akhi*, the last of the prophets, he closed the book, stood up, and stretched. Before getting into the last of the three sections, the *K'tuvim*, or writings, he had some thinking to do. He decided he could best do that on a full stomach.

When he opened the refrigerator, he realized his options were severely limited. He could have a bowl of cereal with very little milk or leftover spaghetti. In spite of the fact that the spaghetti was several days old, it was an easy choice. Popping the bowl of pasta into the microwave, he opened a can of soda and sat down on a stool at the counter to await the bell that would announce his feast.

What is it, he wondered, that tied the messages of all these prophets together? What did they have in common? It seemed that most of them spent the majority of their time calling Israel to repentance and warning them of the consequences if they did not respond—which, time and again, they didn't. It also seemed that these prophets believed in the future appearance of a literal, physical Messiah who would redeem and restore their nation. That had really grabbed Abe's attention because it seemed that so few Jewish people still hoped or believed in a coming Messiah, at least not a literal one. There were, of course, exceptions, Aunt Sophie being one of them. But Uncle Sol and so many others—even some of the religious Jews—had relegated the idea of a Messiah to a type of government or social order, manmade and militarily protected. What little thought Abe himself had ever given to a Messiah had been pretty much restricted to that same viewpoint. Now he was suddenly faced with the realization that if the words of the *Tanakh* were true, if they were to be taken literally and not figuratively, then God really had promised to send a Messiah, and as far as he could see, that Messiah had to be an actual person. If that were the case, what was taking so long? Where had this Messiah been through all the long, dark years of Israel's history? Hadn't his people suffered enough for their so-called sins? Now that the nation had been reestablished and the Jews were going home again, which was so clearly prophesied throughout the *Tanakh,* particularly in *Yechezk'el* 37, why didn't this Messiah appear to establish his kingdom and assure the peace and safety of the promised land? Wouldn't this be the obvious time for him to arrive on the scene?

The bell dinged and he retrieved his dinner from the microwave, then returned to his perch at the counter. Steam rose from the bowl as he stirred the stale contents. He really needed to get to the grocery store soon. He had planned to do so this weekend, but he had gotten so engrossed in reading that he hadn't bothered. Now that the cupboards were bare, he had no choice, short of another home-delivered pizza. And, as much as he enjoyed pizza, even that was beginning to get tiresome.

He sighed, thinking how nice it would be if he could call Toni and invite her out for dinner somewhere. How many times he had dreamed of being able to do just that. At least before, he could hope. Now even his hopes were gone. It wasn't much consolation knowing that she had feelings for him but was unwilling to break her commitment to Brad. He supposed he admired her for that, but such an admirable trait only made it harder to let her go.

Still, let her go he must. He had to move on with his life. Although he certainly wasn't yet at a place where he could consider dating other women, he could at least find something else to fill the huge empty space in his heart. For now, he supposed, that would have to be his job, and of course, his studies in the *Tanakh*.

He took a bite of spaghetti and shook his head. It amazed him that he was spending so much time reading anything, let alone the sacred Scriptures. Beyond a mild curiosity as a child, he had never had any interest in the book. Now, here he was, researching it in detail as if it were the most important case he had ever investigated.

Grabbing a piece of scratch paper from beside the phone, he began to make some notes. *Blood sacrifice,* he wrote, *key issue in the Torah section. A call to repentance and the promise of a coming messiah, key issues of the prophets.* Studying what he had written, he wondered how it all tied together. Blood sacrifice, call to repentance, coming messiah. Would the final section, the writings, give him the answer? He hoped so. He sensed that he would be terribly disappointed to have spent all this time studying the ancient book only to find that it did not contain whatever it was he was searching for.

That's the problem, he mused. *Maybe it would be easier to figure out the answer if I just knew what it was I was looking for. I wish I could talk to Toni about it, ask her what she meant when she said she worships the God of Israel, ask her opinion on the* Tanakh, *or the Old Testament, as she probably calls it. I wonder if she even has an opinion on it. Do Christians read it much? Or do they stick to their so-called New Testament? Aunt Sophie once told me the New Testament is full of a lot of lies about the prophet Jesus and his followers, and a lot of anti-Semitism. If that's so, how can someone who believes in it say she worships the God of Israel?*

Laying his fork in his bowl, he buried his face in his hands. "I don't understand, God. There is so much I don't understand. If you're real, if you're there, if you're listening, please . . . show me. I really want to know the truth."

～～～

The Portland airport was as much a mess as ever. Toni wondered if they would ever finish the remodeling that had been going on for years. April's flight from Colorado Springs had been delayed, and Toni had spent the better part of two hours waiting at the terminal. She checked her watch again. Almost three o'clock. The plane should be arriving at the gate any minute. If all went well, they could still make it home by five o'clock, in plenty of time to relax a bit before Brad showed up with their dinner. In response to Melissa's pleas, he had agreed to bring Chinese food, which was fine with Toni. It meant she wouldn't have to go home and cook, and she was sure April would be too tired from her trip to want to go out anywhere.

It was almost 3:15 before the announcement of April's flight came over the loudspeaker, and closer to 3:30 before Toni was able to welcome her with a warm embrace. "April, it's so good to see you again. I just wish—"

"I know, my dear," April interrupted, her voice laced with a sad resignation. "I wish the circumstances were different too. But we can't change the facts, can we?" She stepped back and looked at Toni. "You look wonderful, as always. I'm sorry you had to wait so long. Some sort of delay on the runway as we were leaving."

"No problem. I'm just glad you could come. Melissa and I are both looking forward to having you stay with us."

"That's so kind of you. I must admit, I believe I'll enjoy the company. I really wasn't looking forward to that empty hotel room again. It's . . . hard to be alone right now. I'm sure you understand."

Toni nodded. She understood all too well. "Of course I do. Let's go pick up your luggage and head for home, shall we? Brad's coming over later with Chinese food—Melissa's special request."

As they began to walk toward the baggage claim, April linked her arm in Toni's. "So Brad is still in the picture, is he?"

Toni looked at her, surprised. "Still in the picture? April, we're getting married in November—November twenty-seventh, two days after Thanksgiving."

"Ah, so you've set a date. I suppose that means you've worked through your feelings about your detective friend."

"My . . . detective friend?" Toni forced herself to keep walking, resisting the impulse to stop in her tracks and insist that April leave Abe out of the conversation. There was no sense confirming what the woman already suspected. For the first time since inviting her, Toni wondered if having April stay at the house had been such a good idea. She seemed to have a very annoying ability to look past Toni's words and right into her heart, and she certainly had no trouble speaking her mind. This could prove to be an interesting visit, Toni decided. "Why would I have to . . . work through my feelings about Abe before setting a wedding date? What does Abe have to do with my marrying Brad?"

It was April who stopped walking. Turning to Toni, she raised her eyebrows questioningly. "Maybe nothing. Maybe everything. I should think you could answer that question better than I, my dear. You're the one caught in the middle, after all."

"What makes you think I'm caught in the middle? I've never even been out on a date with Abe. Brad and I have known each other for years, practically all our lives. It's as if we've always known we would end up together, and we're a perfect match. Everyone says so. He comes from such a wonderful family, and he's so good to me—and to Melissa. Why would I even consider anything else?"

April shrugged, then turned and began to walk toward the baggage claim area once again. "I can't imagine. Just thought I'd ask."

The subject did not come up again until they were almost home. By then Toni's nerves were frayed from the afternoon rush-hour traffic. It had taken a lot longer than expected to retrieve April's luggage, get it loaded into the car, and snake their way through the airport exit and onto the busy freeway. Throughout that time they had discussed all sorts of topics, including how the rest of Julie's family was doing, what the memorial service had been like, what, if anything, new had come up with the investigation, how Melissa was doing with her baby-sitting job, and even the weather in Colorado versus the weather in Washington. Toni had begun to believe that they had left the subject of Abe Matthews behind them, but it was not to be.

"What did you say Brad was bringing over for dinner, my dear?" April asked. "Chinese food, was it? I haven't had that in years. My late husband, Lawrence, used to take me out to eat Chinese food all the time. We had one particular restaurant that was our favorite. They served the best egg rolls! I haven't really felt much like going back there since he died. Funny. He's been gone almost fifteen years now. You'd think I'd have stopped missing him by this time, but I suppose it just doesn't work that way, does it? Not when you truly love someone. The pain eases over time, but you never really stop missing them."

Toni's heart constricted as she thought of her parents. Her father's death was so fresh, her mother's a more distant memory. April was right though. She still missed both of them. "I don't think you've ever mentioned your husband before," Toni observed, glancing at April. "Lawrence must have been very special."

April smiled. "A wonderful man. Very special indeed. We had almost forty years together, and I wouldn't have traded a day of it. Oh, our marriage wasn't perfect, of course. We had our differences, but our love for each other just seemed to grow stronger over the years. I can still look at his picture, even today, and my heart races like a schoolgirl's. Can you imagine?"

Toni's eyes were back on the road as she determined not to let April see the tears she was fighting. Before she met Abe she might not have been able to relate to what April was saying. She loved Brad, but she knew it was nothing like what April had described as her feelings for Lawrence. Now, the very mention of Abe's name, or even of something that reminded her of him, made her feel exactly like the schoolgirl April had mentioned.

"Are you all right, my dear? You seem a bit shaken."

What was it with this woman? Were there no secrets safe from her? "I'm fine," Toni replied, forcing a smile as she again glanced at April. "Really. Just a bit tired from all this stop-and-go driving."

"I see."

Toni turned her eyes back to the road, wondering just how much April did see. Was there any point in continuing this charade, or should she just come out and tell her what she was really feeling? Maybe the benefit of an older woman's wisdom would be useful to her right now. She certainly wasn't doing very well on her own.

"Actually . . ." Her voice trailed off, and she tried again. "You're right. About Abe, I mean . . . and about Brad. I truly do love Brad. He's a fine man, and I know he'll be a wonderful husband. But . . ."

"You're not in love with him."

Toni pressed her lips together and shook her head. "No, I'm not." She felt a burden lift from her shoulders as she spoke the words. Still, it pained her to make such a confession, as if she were betraying this kind, gentle man with whom she had promised to spend the rest of her life. "But . . . April, I'm already engaged to him. I can't just go back on my word. It would break his heart, not to mention Melissa's. Everyone, including Brad's family, expects us to go through with this. They're all so excited."

"A noble reason to get married, I suppose—pleasing others. But is it the right reason?"

Toni opened her mouth, then closed it again. She realized she didn't have an answer to April's question, and it frightened her. She had been so sure that marrying Brad was the right thing to do, regardless of how she felt about him . . . or about Abe. Did she dare bring up her feelings for Abe? She had told April she did not want to discuss him, and yet, deep inside, she so longed to pour out her heart, to tell someone how she really felt. . . .

They had finally reached the River View exit. Toni eased off the freeway, glad to escape the Friday afternoon traffic, which, although no longer bumper-to-bumper, had continued to be heavy all the way from Portland. As she drove toward home, the familiar streets and landmarks failed to comfort her as they usually did. She felt lost, disconnected somehow, as if she had left something very important behind but had no idea how to retrieve it.

She pulled up to a red light and stopped, then turned to April. "I don't know what to do about Abe. I . . . think I'm in love with him. I can hardly stand to be away from him, but . . . it's an impossible situation. I'm engaged to Brad, and Abe's not even a Christian. I can't possibly pursue that relationship. What should I do? I'm so confused."

April's pale blue eyes were soft as she reached over and patted Toni's hand. "I can't tell you what to do, my dear. It's not my place, although you're absolutely right about not pursuing a relationship with an unbeliever. But . . . must it be an either-or situation? Since you can't follow your heart concerning Abe, does that mean you must go through with your marriage to Brad?" She paused, eyeing Toni questioningly. "Maybe you need to deal with one relationship at a time. Clear up one before trying to figure out what to do about the other."

Toni's heart caught in her throat. What was April implying? "Do you mean I should break my engagement with Brad because I'm not in love with him? Is that what you're saying?"

"The only thing I'm saying, my dear, is that you need to pray about this and then listen for God's answer. Only he knows what the future holds and what his purposes are. There truly is no peace or joy apart from his plan for your life, you know."

I am your Father. The memory of those words echoed in Toni's heart as she turned onto her street and pulled up to the house. There, parked in front, was Brad's silver Lexus. He was early—and they were late. There would be no time to relax before dinner, no time to collect her thoughts or pray before facing him, and she needed to do both before she even considered discussing this subject with him. As she parked the car in the driveway, once again April reached over and patted her hand, and Toni realized how very glad she was to have this wise woman in her life right now.

～～～

Toni, seated at the kitchen table, was still shaking when April walked into the room. It was midmorning on Monday. Melissa had gone to babysit Tyler, and April had been out for a walk. Toni had opted to stay home, hoping to have some quiet time to spend reading the Bible and praying. She had not been able to think of anything all weekend except April's advice regarding her relationship with Brad. Yet, she had still not been able to bring herself to broach the subject with Brad or even to seriously consider breaking off the engagement. She had been sitting at the table, reading from the Psalms, when the call came. The familiar voice had reminded her of his warning to mind her own business. He had also told her that if she did not heed his warning, or if she told the police about his calls, someone she cared about was going to get hurt. It was the first time he had threatened someone other than herself, and Toni was devastated by the implications.

"It's getting warm out there," April announced, taking a glass from the cupboard and heading for the refrigerator. After pouring some lemonade, she came and sat down opposite Toni at the table. "But warm or not, it's certainly beautiful. I don't know when I've seen such a glorious profusion of roses and gladiolus. They're everywhere! The Northwest may be gray in the winter, but it certainly makes up for it in the spring and summer, doesn't it? I can't help but wonder if . . . my Julie . . . experienced any of the beauty of this part of the country before she . . ." Her voice trailed off, and with downcast eyes, she took a sip of lemonade, then looked at the Bible lying open in front of Toni. "I see you're reading from the Psalms. It's my favorite book in the entire Bible." When Toni didn't respond, she frowned. "Are you all right, my dear? Is something wrong?"

Slowly Toni brought her thoughts into focus. She had been watching April and had heard her speaking but had not been concentrating on her words. "I . . . I'm sorry. What did you say?"

"I asked if you're all right. Obviously you're not. What is it? What happened?"

"I . . . had another phone call."

April raised her eyebrows. "A phone call? From whom?"

Toni shook her head. "I don't know. He's called several times over the last couple of weeks. He doesn't identify himself, but . . . his voice is vaguely familiar. I just wish I could place it, but I can't. He keeps warning me to mind my own business. I kept hoping it was just some sort of prank caller, but today he said that if I don't listen to him and do what he says, someone . . . close to me . . . could get hurt."

"Oh, my dear. What do the police think about it?"

"I . . . haven't told them. I'm afraid if I do, he might—"

April looked shocked. "Toni, you must tell them. You can't handle this alone, and you can't assume this caller isn't serious. Why, if it were just some sort of prank, I wouldn't think it would amount to more than a call or two, but repeated calls over a couple of weeks? You simply can't ignore this. Let the police check it out. If there's nothing to it, then you needn't worry, but you can't just keep it to yourself. That's exactly what he's counting on."

"April, what if . . . what if I call the police and he finds out? He might follow through on his threat and hurt someone . . . maybe even Melissa. I just can't take that chance."

April pursed her lips and squinted her eyes, as if she were thinking. Finally she said, "Then you must tell Abe. If you won't tell anyone else, tell him. You can trust him, can't you?"

Toni caught her breath. "Abe? Oh, April, I don't know. . . ."

"You have to tell someone, my dear."

Closing her eyes, Toni weighed her options. Up until now she had kept the phone calls to herself, choosing to ignore them and hoping they would stop. They hadn't though, and now he was threatening people she cared about. April was right; she could no longer handle this alone, but she was too frightened to risk bringing the police into it. That left only one option that she could think of, one that filled her with very mixed emotions.

"I'll call him," she said softly. "It will be easier to tell him on the phone than . . . in person."

"Good. I'll go sit outside on the porch swing and give you some privacy."

She got through to him right away. Even the sound of his voice brought tears to her eyes, but she determined to focus on nothing but the purpose of her call. "Abe, it's . . . me, Toni. I'm sorry to bother you, but . . ." She took a deep breath. "Something has happened."

The surprise and concern in his voice were evident. Yet Toni couldn't help but notice that she didn't hear the familiar tone of hopefulness that had always before marked his conversation when she surprised him with a phone call. "Toni, are you all right? What do you mean, something has happened? Do you want me to come over?"

"No. No, really. It's not necessary. It's just . . . Abe, I've been getting some phone calls. Anonymous calls. Threats, really. I . . . don't know who it is, although the voice is somewhat familiar. He warned me not to tell the police, but I—"

He interrupted her before she could finish. "I'm on my way. I'll be there in ten minutes."

"But—"

The phone clicked in her ear, and he was gone.

~~~

Abe rubbed his eyes. It was getting late and he was tired. Sitting in his car in the dark, hidden in the shadows but just close enough to see her house, he was in an uncomfortable position in more ways than one. He shifted in the seat and checked his watch. Ten-thirty. He wondered how late he should stay. It was Friday night and Toni's car wasn't parked in its usual place in the driveway. Because he hadn't seen anyone in or around the house since he had parked there an hour earlier, he assumed that Toni, April, and Melissa had all gone out somewhere together.

The previous nights, ever since Toni had told him on Monday of the threatening phone calls she had been receiving, he had driven by her house several times after dark and then had gone on home once he was satisfied that everything seemed to be OK. Tonight was different though. It was Friday, and as no one was home, he decided to stick around a while and keep an eye on things. He wondered if the three of them had gone out alone or if Brad was with them. Because Brad's Lexus wasn't parked in the driveway or in front of the house, he doubted it, but it was possible that they had picked him up at his place. The thought pained him, but he was determined to push past it. After all, Toni had made it perfectly clear that regardless of her feelings for him, she intended to go through with her marriage to Brad. Even on Monday, when he had gone to her home to discuss the phone calls, she had given him no indication that her intentions had changed. And he had certainly not broached the subject, particularly with April Lippincott there. Even had Toni been alone, he had already decided, before he ever set foot in her house that day, that he would never again speak to her of his feelings—unless, of course, she brought up the subject first. He had served the ball into her court, and she had been adamant about not playing the game. So it was settled. Now all he could do was hover in the shadows, ready to protect her if she needed him.

A car approached from the left, and Abe watched it closely. It appeared to be a late-model Taurus, so maybe they were coming home. That would be a relief, although he would probably still stay awhile, just to be sure everything was all right. He felt his shoulders relax as the car turned into Toni's driveway and stopped. Disappointment swept over him when he realized that April was driving, with Melissa in the passenger seat. Toni was not with them. April and Melissa got out of the car, talking and laughing, and went inside the house. Abe had not been able to make out what they were saying, even with his window down, but now he had to reconcile himself to the fact that Toni was undoubtedly off somewhere with Brad.

Meshugga. Is that what Uncle Sol calls me? Crazy. He's probably right. I must be, to sit here like this, waiting for her to come home while she's out with her fiancé. She's got him to protect her. She doesn't need me. And April and Melissa are here now, so when she comes home, it won't be to an empty house. Why don't I just leave?

Abe didn't leave though. Instead, he poured another cup of coffee from his thermos and sipped it, waiting and watching . . . and wondering. Where were they? What were they doing? What were they talking about? When she was with Brad, did her mind ever wander? Did she ever think of him the way he thought of her, day and night, until the pain forced him to pull his thoughts away and center them on something else, at least for a little while? How he had wanted to ask her those very questions on Monday as he sat in her house and listened to her explain about the phone calls. April had sat at Toni's side, watching him with a sadness that Abe assumed was due primarily to Julie's death but might also have had at least something to do with what she sensed was going on—or not going on—between him and Toni.

Instead of asking Toni anything personal, he had asked only those questions that were pertinent to the phone calls she had been receiving. It struck him that the calls had begun right about the time Julie's body was discovered at the lake and that this last call—the one threatening those close to Toni—had come just after April had come to stay at Toni's home. It had been difficult, but Abe had finally made Toni understand that they could not keep this between themselves. It had to be reported, especially in light of Julie Greene's death and Toni's father's connection with her before his own death. Although the autopsy results on Paul Matthews tended to minimize the connection between the two, Abe felt the calls were suspicious enough to warrant a police report, a trace on Toni's phone, and a little extra surveillance on his part.

So, here he sat, waiting for the woman he loved to come home from what was more than likely a date with the other man who loved her—and with whom she planned to spend the remainder of her life. Uncle Sol was right. He was *meshugga,* no doubt about it.

Abe took another sip of coffee and thought again about their conversation on Monday. Toni had been so frightened at the idea of filing a police report and of putting a trace on the phone, concerned that the caller would find out, explaining that he had warned her not to go to the police. Abe had assured her that she was much safer with the police knowing exactly what was going on than trying to handle something like this on her own. Once he had explained to her that it simply wasn't an option for him not to report it, particularly now that he was part of the taskforce investigating Julie's death, she had finally agreed. Now if she would just get another phone call from this creep so they could try to get a lead on who he was. . . .

He sat up straight. Another car was headed his way. He watched it closely until he could make it out. A silver Lexus pulled up and stopped in front of Toni's house. Abe groaned. He had known that

Toni was probably with Brad, but this was one time he would have liked to have been wrong.

Once again he glanced at his watch. Just after eleven. He supposed he should find some consolation in the fact that at least they weren't out late.

Brad got out of the car and hurried around to the passenger side to open the door. Toni climbed out, and as they walked toward the house together, Abe heard the clear sound of her laughter. At the front door, Brad pulled her close and kissed her, and then she went inside.

As Brad turned to walk back to his car, Abe slammed his fist on the steering wheel. "*Meshugga*," he said. When Brad had driven away, Abe started his car and drove down the street in the opposite direction.

CHAPTER 13

"What a lovely idea," April exclaimed as they sat around the picnic table in the Andersons' backyard. "Sunday brunch outside, and how nice of all of you to include me."

"It's our pleasure," Brad answered, smiling across at her.

"Absolutely," Melissa chimed in. "Besides, you're practically family now."

April turned to Melissa, who was seated to her right, and gave her a quick hug. "Thank you, my dear. That is quite a compliment."

Toni sat at the end of the bench, next to Brad and across from Melissa, the late morning sun almost directly overhead. A light breeze kept the temperature comfortable as the six of them talked and laughed and munched on fresh fruit, pastries, muffins, and sliced ham. A large iced pitcher of orange juice and a carafe of coffee, which Barbara Anderson refilled each time they approached the half-empty mark, sat on either end of the table. George and Barbara sat across from each other, on the opposite end from Melissa and Toni, ready to spring into action if anyone looked as if they needed anything, but with the bounty of food in front of them, Toni couldn't imagine what that could be.

She and Melissa had picked up April after church and brought her along with them, arriving just after eleven. Brad was already there, helping his parents with last-minute preparations. He had greeted them at the door, giving April a warm handshake, Melissa a kiss on the forehead, and Toni a brief hug and a tentative kiss, promising to do better when they were alone. Toni had responded to his kiss as best she could, hoping the opportunity to be alone with him would not materialize so that he could not follow through on his promise.

The topic of the day, from the moment they had arrived, had been the upcoming wedding. Even as Toni continued to remind them of her wish for a small, simple ceremony, the plans seemed to expand. It had already been decided that Melissa would be the maid of honor, and she was determined to wear a pale blue dress with matching heels and to carry a bouquet with tiny white roses and blue ribbons. So it was decided. The wedding colors would be blue and white. Now the big question was, where would Brad and Toni be registered? Although Toni insisted that registering wasn't necessary for such a small affair, Barbara would have none of it.

"Don't be silly," she said, smiling as if she thought Toni were teasing. "Of course you must register somewhere. How will people know what you need if you aren't registered?"

"We don't need anything," Toni protested. "Really. Melissa and I have a house full of things, and Brad has his own place too. We haven't decided where we'll live yet, but between us we have more than enough of everything."

Barbara laughed. "Oh, Toni, surely you don't mean to start your married life with used towels and cracked plates. This is a momentous occasion, a once in a lifetime affair. You want to start fresh, with everything new and chosen especially for the two of you." She looked at her husband for support. "Isn't that right, George?"

George, who was about to pop a piece of pastry into his mouth, stopped and looked around. "If you say so," he answered. "I'm afraid I'm not the one to ask about that. As far as I'm concerned, a package of paper plates and a couple of pillows, and you're ready to set up housekeeping."

Everyone laughed as Barbara shook her head. "You're impossible." She turned to April. "What do you think, Mrs. Lippincott?"

"Call me April, please, and with all due respect, I'm not sure it matters what I think." Smiling, she looked from Barbara to Brad and Toni. "It seems to me that Toni and Brad should do whatever they feel is best. It's their wedding, their future home. There are so many decisions to make, even for a small wedding, aren't there? I imagine the two of them should be the ones to make those decisions." She raised her eyebrows at Toni. "Isn't that right, my dear?"

There she goes again, thought Toni, *reading my thoughts. Oh, April, pray for me to do the right thing. Pray for me to know what that is and to have the strength to do it.* Out loud she said, "I guess you're right. I hadn't realized how much was involved."

"Well, let us help by taking some of the pressure off you," said Barbara. "I know we can have the reception in the fellowship hall at church. I'll be glad to make those arrangements . . . if you don't mind, of course. I wouldn't want to interfere."

Toni knew when she had lost the battle. She only hoped she hadn't lost the war. "You're not interfering at all. The fellowship hall will be fine. Thank you."

Melissa, her smile lighting up her entire face, poured herself another glass of orange juice. "This is so great. I can't believe this wedding is finally going to happen. I've been waiting for it for so long."

"You think it's been a long wait for *you*," said Brad. "You should be in *my* shoes. We're talking *years* of waiting, but I can finally count the days, and there are exactly ninety-seven of them if anyone cares to know."

"Ninety-seven!" Barbara looked shocked. "I knew it was close, but I guess I didn't realize just how close. I can see we're going to have to get moving on this thing right away. Toni, have you looked at wedding dresses yet? We really should pick that out first thing, in case there are alterations to be made. Pastor Michael will perform the ceremony, of course. Now that we know your colors, we'll have to get started planning flowers and decorations, not to mention lining up the rest of the wedding party. We can't have poor Melissa standing up there on the platform by herself. We'll need a flower girl, a ring bearer, a best man—"

"Slow down, Mom," Brad interrupted with a smile. "Can we finish eating first?" He turned his head to look at Toni. "We don't want to overwhelm the bride all at once."

Toni smiled her appreciation. "Thank you. And you're right. It is a bit overwhelming."

The conversation turned then to more mundane topics, such as the weather, clients at the Anderson and Summers law offices, George's and Brad's predictions for the upcoming football season, and what to do with all the leftover food. Before long, however, George mentioned that he thought they had forgotten to discuss the most important aspect of the wedding—the honeymoon.

"I know we agreed not to wear out this wedding subject, but I just have one thing to say," he explained. "Barbara and I have hoped and prayed for this day almost as long as Brad. You know, Toni, that we've considered you part of the family for a long time. We're glad it's finally going to be official. As a welcoming gift, Barbara and I would like to offer you two a cruise—anywhere you'd like to go—for your honeymoon. Over the years, I've heard you both talk about how much you'd like to take a cruise someday, so why not for your honeymoon? Will you let us do that for you?"

Toni felt as if her head were spinning. A honeymoon cruise. She hadn't even gone that far in her thinking. She hadn't let her thoughts go beyond the wedding itself. But here it was. This was it. A lifetime commitment. Her chance to back out was running short. She heard Melissa comment on what an awesome idea the cruise was. Brad, too, had responded enthusiastically. Now, with all eyes turned on her, the only thing she could think of was the date she and Brad had been on this past Friday, just two nights earlier. Throughout the evening she had forced herself to smile and laugh, to talk as animatedly as she could about their plans, even to respond—albeit briefly—to his good-night kiss at her front door. The entire time, however, her mind had been on Abe. Where was he? What was he doing? Was he thinking of her? As Brad had kissed her goodnight on the front porch, she had sensed somehow that Abe was nearby, even though she knew that was impossible. Then she had spent half the night tossing and turning in her bed, berating herself for dwelling on a man she could never have.

Toni glanced at April, the only one at the table who knew what Toni was going through at the moment. The dear woman's pale blue eyes were full of compassion. *Not right now, April. Not here. Not yet.*

She looked at Brad. His face was apprehensive. She tried to smile reassuringly as she looked from Brad to George, and finally, to Barbara. "What a generous gift. Thank you both, so much. A cruise would be wonderful. We'll . . . have to think about . . . where we want to go."

Brad kissed her on the forehead. "Your choice," he said smiling. "It's all up to you now."

In spite of the warm sunshine, Toni felt a chill pass over her. If only Brad knew how she agonized over such a heavy responsibility.

Melissa was tired. She had stayed at Carrie's much later than she should have the night before, having gone over there right after the brunch at the Andersons'. As soon as she had arrived and told Carrie about the cruise Brad and Toni were going to take, the two girls had gotten so excited and caught up in discussing wedding plans and possible honeymoon destinations that they had not paid attention to the time. Now, as Melissa sat outside on the back step watching Tyler run through the sprinkler to keep cool, she thought she might join him if she just weren't so sleepy.

She yawned, then picked up her journal and began to write. *It's so romantic. I wish I knew where they were going to go for their cruise. I know where I'd go—the Bahamas. Or maybe the Virgin Islands. Or Jamaica. Maybe someday I'll—*

She jumped as the portable phone beside her rang loudly. Melissa always brought it outside with her just in case someone called, but almost no one ever did. She wondered now if it might be Tyler's mom calling to say she had to work late.

It wasn't. When an unfamiliar male voice asked for Janice, Melissa replied, "You must have the wrong number."

"Oh." The caller sounded dejected. "I'm . . . sorry to have bothered you."

"No problem," said Melissa, ready to punch the "off" button, but the caller stopped her.

"Um . . . Excuse me, but . . . can I talk to you for a minute? I'm a talent scout for a filmmaker down in Hollywood, and. . . . Well, the reason I was calling for someone named Janice was because she answered an ad I had placed in the paper. We're looking for extras for a movie that's going to be filmed near here. It doesn't pay much, but it's a great way to break into the industry, maybe get discovered some day, you know what I mean? You have a nice voice, and I wondered if you would be interested in getting into something like that."

Suddenly Melissa was wide awake. Someone was asking her if she wanted a part in a movie, something she had dreamed about for as long as she could remember. Surely he wasn't serious.

"This is a joke, right? You're playing a trick on me. Who are you, really?"

"Oh, no, ma'am, this is no joke. I'm quite serious, I assure you."

The man sounded serious; he sounded nice, too, and he had called her "ma'am." That was a first. Maybe it wasn't a joke after all.

"Well, I . . . I don't know. I'd . . . have to talk to my older sister about it."

"Tell you what. Take some time to think about it first, but keep it to yourself until you decide. I'll call you back next week sometime. Then, if you're interested, we can both talk to your sister. How does that sound?"

It sounded great, but Melissa didn't want to appear foolish, in case the caller really was playing a joke on her. "I . . . guess so," she answered, trying to keep her voice casual.

"Good. Like I said, I'll call back next week, maybe Tuesday or Wednesday. Will you be there?"

"Sure. I'm here every day, Monday through Friday, baby-sitting."

"Great. Remember, keep this to yourself until we talk next week. Deal?"

Melissa hesitated. She didn't even know this guy's name, and here she was making a deal with him. She had a feeling Toni would not approve. Still, what could it hurt? It wasn't like she was committing to an audition or anything. Besides, if the call turned out to be a prank and she didn't hear back from him, she wouldn't be embarrassed at having told someone about it.

"OK. I'll keep it to myself until you call back. But . . . what's your name? I don't even know who you are."

"Oh, sorry. Of course. My name is Carlo. And you are?"

"Melissa. Melissa Matthews."

"Pleased to make your acquaintance, Miss Matthews. I'll look forward to talking with you next week."

It wasn't until she had clicked off the phone that she realized he hadn't told her his last name. *Oh well,* she thought. *I'll find out next week, unless, of course, he doesn't call back. Either way, I guess it doesn't really matter right now.*

~⌢~

It had been two months since Abe had visited his Uncle Sol, although he had seen him a couple of times when he had stopped in at the station. He had been surprised when Rosalie called over the weekend and invited him to dinner on Wednesday, even though he was sure she had done so at Sol's request. Abe didn't particularly care for the redhead who currently shared his uncle's home, but then he doubted she cared much for him either. Still, if Uncle Sol got it into his mind that he wanted Abe there for dinner on a particular night, Rosalie probably didn't have much say in the matter. But, sitting now at Sol's table, Abe had to admit—although grudgingly—that Rosalie had done a good job on the roast, and she had even baked an apple pie for dessert.

When they couldn't eat another bite, the two men retired to Sol's office, leaving Rosalie to clean up. Abe was glad to escape her company. His uncle could be difficult and more than a little demanding, but Abe loved Sol and enjoyed being with him—most of the time— as long as it didn't include Rosalie.

They had no sooner settled onto the leather couch than Sol lit up a cigar. As he had so many times over the years, he offered one to Abe. As always, Abe declined.

Sol shook his head. "You don't know what you're missing, boy. There's nothing like a good cigar after a big meal. Settles your stomach."

Abe doubted that but decided not to comment on it. "So, how have you been feeling? Has your leg been bothering you much?"

"Nah. No more than usual, anyway. But when the weather turns cool in a month or so, then it'll start acting up. I can just about walk without a limp during the summer, but the dampness kills me." He puffed his cigar and frowned. "You know, before I took that bullet I used to love the rainy winters up here. Now they just remind me of the creep that left me hobbled and forced me into retirement. Maybe I should move to Tucson or Phoenix; what do you think?"

"I think you'd hate it. You never liked hot weather."

Sol chewed his cigar. "I suppose you're right. Guess I'll just stay here and be miserable."

Abe suppressed a smile. Maybe he didn't like Rosalie much, but he almost felt sorry for her during the long, gray winter season. He could only imagine what it would be like to live with Uncle Sol, especially when he was cooped up in the house for months with a bum leg. Maybe she earned her keep after all.

He thought of some of the other women who had occupied his uncle's home since the death of Sol's wife, Patty, and their only child, an infant son named Michael, both of whom were killed in an auto accident nineteen years earlier when they were hit by a drunk driver on their way to a restaurant to meet Sol for dinner. Sol had blamed himself for not driving the extra fifteen minutes from the station to pick them up rather than asking them to meet him. When the driver had gotten off with a two-year suspended sentence and several hours of community service, the grief-stricken man had been furious, going on a two-week drunken binge and threatening to kill the driver if he ever saw him face-to-face.

Fortunately that didn't happen, and Sol had settled down and returned to work after that one binge, giving up drinking all together. Shortly thereafter, a parade of attractive although somewhat cheap-looking women had begun to make their way through Sol's life, living in his home for weeks or months, until he tired of them and moved them out in favor of a new playmate. None of them had been any-thing like Patty, Abe thought—not as genuinely pretty, and certainly not as sweet or intelligent. "Bimbos" was how Sol referred to them, and Abe thought it an appropriate description. Rosalie fit the bill per-fectly, although, he had to admit, she seemed to have more staying power than any of her predecessors, having been with Sol slightly over a year now. Abe wished his uncle would stop wasting his time with these cardboard cutout imitations and meet a real woman, one he could love and who would love him in return. The one time Abe had suggested it, Sol had told him in no uncertain terms that he had experienced real love once and that it was irreplaceable, so he had no intention of looking for the impossible. Abe felt a stab of pain as he wondered if he had already found his one true love and then lost her before ever having the chance to experience the joy of having her in his life, even for a little while, as his uncle had with Patty.

Sol interrupted his thoughts. "So, what's new with the Greene investigation? Anything?" Sol frowned. "You don't think this miscarriage thing is anything we need to worry about, do you? On a personal level, I mean."

Abe was puzzled. A personal level . . .? How could Julie's miscarriage have anything to do with them on a personal level? Suddenly his heart skipped a beat as a long-buried memory flashed into his mind. Surely his uncle wasn't referring to that incident years earlier. . . . Did he really think there could be a connection? Abe felt a shudder ripple through his body. It had never occurred to him that he would have to worry about that awful experience raising its ugly head again at this point in his life. Was it possible that he was involved in an investigation that might uncover evidence that could lead to his own undoing?

"I . . . hadn't thought of that."

"I did. We've got a lot to lose, boy, if you get my drift—especially you. I managed to bail you out once, but I'm not so sure I could do it again now."

Abe nodded slowly, and his jaws twitched. His uncle was right. He was going to have to handle this investigation very carefully.

"Thanks for the warning. I'll keep my eyes open."

"Good. So, anything new on the case?"

Abe was amazed at how easily and quickly his uncle could change course. It took him a bit longer to catch up, but he determined to block out the painful memory of his youthful indiscretion—and the fear of its resurrection—and refocus on the matter at hand. "Not really," he said, his voice almost back to normal. "Although, just about the time the girl's body was found, Toni Matthews started getting some strange phone calls. You know, anonymous, vague threats, that sort of thing, telling her to mind her own business and no one would get hurt. She ignored them until a couple of weeks ago when the guy threatened to hurt someone close to her. That was right after Julie Greene's aunt, April Lippincott, came to stay with Toni and her sister. That's when she told me about the calls, and we put a trace on her phone. There haven't been any more calls since then, so we really don't have any leads on that."

Sol frowned and took his cigar out of his mouth. "You still think there's some sort of connection between Paul Matthews and the Greene kid? I thought the autopsy cleared all that up."

"More or less. Still, I thought it was worth following up, just in case."

His uncle grunted and stuck the cigar back between his teeth. "Just in case what? In case she needs someone to hold her hand while she waits for the phone to ring? Sounds a little too convenient, if you ask me. She gets all these phone calls until you put a trace on her line, and then they suddenly quit? And she just happens to report those calls directly to you instead of the department? Wise up, boy. She's making a play for you, can't you see? Are you blind, or just stupid?" He raised his dark eyebrows. "Or are you being stupid on purpose? Maybe you're more than just a little bit willing to accommodate the lady, maybe even donate your free time to serve as her personal bodyguard. Is that it?" Still chewing his cigar, he added, "You got it bad, don't you, boy?"

Abe thought of the nights he had recently spent driving by Toni's house and parking in the shadows to watch and make sure she was home, safe and sound. The familiar stab of pain came as he remembered the night he had seen Brad bring her home, then kiss her goodnight on the porch.

"Yeah, Uncle Sol. I got it bad, OK? But I've got to get over it. She's just not interested, and she's definitely not making a play for me. She made that perfectly clear. She's engaged to somebody else, and that's that. So, can we change the subject?"

Sol shifted his cigar from one side of his mouth to the other. "Whatever you say. So what's up with Sophie? You talk to her lately?"

There he went again, changing gears without missing a beat. Abe sighed with relief as he felt his shoulders relax a bit. Aunt Sophie was definitely a much safer topic than his past indiscretions or his feelings for Toni. "Actually, I went up to see her last month. She's fine, as always. You know Aunt Sophie. She never changes."

"Yeah, I know. Ever the religious fanatic."

Abe was surprised to find himself defending his aunt. "She means well, you know. She . . . gave me one of Uncle David's books, an English translation of the *Tanakh*."

Sol's eyebrows shot way up. "You're kidding. What did she do that for? She doesn't expect you to read all those fables and old wives' tales, does she?"

"To tell you the truth, that's exactly what I did. Just finished it, as a matter of fact."

"You read the whole thing? Cover to cover?"

Abe nodded. "I did, and I thought it was very interesting."

Sol, the cigar perfectly still between his clenched teeth, studied him for a moment. "And did you come to any life-changing revelations?"

"Not yet. I'm still thinking about it."

Sol shook his head. "You really are *meshugga*, aren't you? Absolutely *meshugga*."

Abe didn't argue with his uncle, nor did he tell him what he planned to do next. It was such a radical step he could hardly believe it himself.

~~~

Toni had managed to avoid Brad since the Sunday brunch at his parents' house. Now it was Friday night, and he had been insistent about coming over to take her for a ride—alone. "Just the two of us. Please. We need some time alone . . . to talk."

Toni knew he was right, but she had dreaded the evening ever since she had hesitantly agreed to it the previous day. Now it was here. Brad was waiting for her at the door, Carrie was spending the night with Melissa, and April was thrilled to supervise the pajama party. Toni had no excuses. Waving goodbye to April and the girls, she had headed out the door to join Brad, but not before noticing the wary glance she got from April.

This time I know what she's thinking. That's a switch. It's usually April who reads my mind. She's wondering if I'm going to tell him or if I'm going to keep my mouth shut and go through with this wedding just to keep from hurting him. Oh, April, I don't know! I just don't know. Pray for me. Please pray. . . .

"Where are we going?" she asked as soon as they got in the car. "You really weren't very specific on the phone."

Brad pulled away from the curb, keeping his eyes on the road as he answered. "That's up to you. I thought maybe we'd take a ride, and then, I don't know, go get something to eat . . . unless you're hungry now, that is. We can eat first if you'd like."

"No. I'm . . . really not hungry at all. A ride would be fine."

Her mind raced and her heart ached as they drove out of town and up into the surrounding hills. The daylight hours were getting shorter, but it was only a little after seven, and it wouldn't be dark for at least another hour. She studied his profile, a profile that had been dear and comforting to her for so many years, one that was almost as familiar to her as Melissa's or her dad's. She swallowed the lump that came automatically with the reminder of her father. How she missed him. If only he were here to talk to and advise her. . . .

I am your Father. Once again, the memory of her heavenly Father's words rose up within her, filling her with a sense of peace, as if he were assuring her that he was in control, that she could trust him to deal with this seemingly impossible situation. She relaxed in her seat.

Brad stopped the car on a rise overlooking River View. It had always been one of their favorite spots to park, to gaze at the peaceful scene below with the mighty Columbia River providing a clear-cut border between Oregon and Washington, and to observe the town where they had grown up and where they would someday live as man and wife and raise a family together. But now everything had changed. The river and the town were the same, Brad's love for her was as strong as ever, but Toni's father was dead, her mind was in turmoil, and her heart belonged to someone else. Her future life with Brad loomed, empty and meaningless, in front of her, even as he reached over and took her left hand in his.

"I thought we could sit here and watch the sun go down together," he said. "We haven't done that in a while."

Toni, staring out the window in front of her, forced a smile. "That would be nice."

They sat in silence for several minutes, Brad still holding her hand as Toni prayed for a miracle that would settle the question of their future together, once and for all. Suddenly Brad lifted her hand to his lips and kissed it. "Toni, look at me."

The tone of his voice was distant and unfamiliar, as if it belonged to someone she didn't know. She turned her head. The shock of sandy blond hair fell across his forehead, giving him a vulnerable look that tore at her heart. How could she hurt him? How could she ever disappoint him and break their engagement? After all, she had promised. . . .

"Sweetheart," he said, "I've been doing a lot of thinking . . . and praying . . . about us. About our marriage, our future, our relationship. I . . ." His voice caught, and Toni saw a hint of tears in his hazel eyes. "It's taken me a long time, but I've finally realized that I've been trying to impose my will on you, and . . . even on God. I've been praying that he would change your heart, cause you to love me as you once did . . . or, at least, as I thought you did. But . . ." He dropped his head for a moment. When he looked back up, the tears were clinging to his lashes. "I just haven't wanted to face the truth. I kept thinking that . . . if I just loved you enough, if I just prayed hard enough, and believed . . . then you would love me again, and things would be the way they used to be. We'd get married and everything would be wonderful, the way we'd always planned. But sitting here with you now, I realize that . . . things have changed. You've changed. Whether it has anything to do with Abe Matthews or not, I'm not sure, but . . ."

He paused as he choked on his words. Toni's heart raced and she wondered what he would say next. Never had she experienced such a roller coaster of emotions in such a short span of time. She found herself hoping that maybe, just maybe, Brad was going to do for her what she could not do for herself and spare her the agony of being the one to break their engagement. The next minute she felt devastated at the thought of truly letting go of Brad, of never having him in her life again. His presence had always been so steady, so safe and reassuring.

"I . . . can't marry you, Toni." The tears were spilling over onto his cheeks. "I want to, more than anything in this world. But . . . it's not right. I know that now. Your heart is somewhere else, and I . . . have to let you go. It's the hardest thing I've ever done, but . . . I can't let you go through with this. I know you don't want to hurt me, but . . . that's not a good enough reason for us to get married."

Still holding her left hand, he caressed the diamond on her ring finger. "Why don't you give this back to me? Let's make it a clean break. It'll be . . . easier that way."

Toni felt her own tears coming then, and she didn't even try to hold them back. As she removed the ring from her finger and placed it in Brad's hand, she knew she was letting go of a huge piece of her life, and the pain was immense. But when Brad kissed her gently, for the last time, she felt, once again, the comforting presence of her heavenly Father, and she knew, whatever the future might hold, that Brad had made the right decision. She would always love him for that.

CHAPTER 14

It had been a beautiful drive up to the lake, with just a slight hint of approaching autumn in the air. The early morning sun was beginning to burn through the clouds, promising to warm the temperature quickly as the day progressed. They pulled into the dirt parking lot in front of the store, and Toni started to open the door, then looked over at April, who was sitting very still and staring straight ahead.

"April? Are you OK?"

Slowly, she turned her head and looked at Toni. "I'm . . . all right. It's just . . ."

"I know. It affected me the same way when Abe first brought me up here after . . . my dad . . ."

April nodded. "Of course. If anyone would understand, you would. Thank you . . . for bringing me here. It's something I need to do."

"We really don't have to go into the store if you don't feel up to it. We can just go on over to the north shore."

"No, I'm fine. I would like to get something to drink to take with us since we're not sure how long we'll be there. But . . . I do have one request."

"Of course. What is it?"

"If we run into the owners or anyone else you know, would you mind not mentioning that I'm Julie's grandmother? I really don't feel up to talking to anyone about it, and I'm sure we wouldn't find out anything from anyone around here that the sheriff hasn't already discovered in his investigation, so there's really no point."

"I agree. We won't say a word. We'll just get a couple of cold drinks, do our best to avoid getting hung up in a lengthy conversation with Maude or Simon, and get right out again."

Once inside the store, the familiar smell of fresh popcorn tugged at Toni's heart. She could almost see her father standing at the counter, buying her a sack of it as she waited anxiously at his side, mouth watering. She didn't let herself dwell on the memory though. She and April went immediately to the back of the store, picked out their drinks, and headed for the front counter to pay for them. As the only other customer in the store pocketed his change and began to walk toward the door, Toni spotted both of the Olsons standing side by side behind the counter. Apparently she and April weren't going to be able to avoid at least a minimal conversation with them. It was Maude who caught sight of them first.

"Why, Toni Matthews, you're back. Look, Simon, it's Toni Matthews, come back to visit us." The stout woman stepped out from behind the counter and enveloped Toni in her familiar bear hug. "Oh, child, it's so good to see you again. How are you?" She released her and stepped back. "As purty as ever, I see. Look here, Simon, ain't she a purty little thing?"

The thin man with the ever-present wisp of gray hair combed over the top of his head squinted at her. "You're right, Maude. A mite skinny though. How ya doin'?"

"I'm fine, thank you, Simon. It's good to see you both again." She turned toward April. "This is my friend April. We're just out for a ride and thought we'd stop by for a minute and get something cold to drink. April," she said as she slipped an arm around her, "Maude and Simon Olson."

April smiled. "How do you do?"

Maude raised her eyebrows. "And howdy-do to you too. It's nice to meet you, I'm sure."

Simon nodded in greeting, studying Toni's companion with curiosity. "How come you didn't bring your other friend? Abe, was it? The one Maude first met when he come up here with you? We seen him a few times since then, working with some other fellas on that Julie Greene case. You know, that girl that drowned up here not long ago. I s'pose you heard 'bout that."

Toni glanced at April and saw that she was struggling to maintain her composure. "I . . . yes, I heard about it. As for Abe . . . Detective Matthews . . . I really wouldn't know. I would imagine he's working today." She opened her purse, hoping to get the transaction accomplished and get April out of the store and back to the car quickly, but Maude wasn't about to let them go that easily.

"You know, when I first seen you with that young man—and a mighty handsome young man he is, I might add—I thought sure he was the fella you was engaged to. Imagine my surprise to find out otherwise. Why, you coulda knocked me over with a feather, 'specially the way you two was hangin' on each other. When I told Simon 'bout how close you two seemed to be and then he found out he wasn't your fiancé after all, why, we was both shocked."

"I 'spect that Abe Matthews fella wished he was," Simon added. "Your fiancé, that is. Like I told him, it'd sure be easier on you. Wouldn't have to change your name when you got married." He chuckled at his own joke. "I'd say he's got some real strong feelin's on that subject. Weren't too hard to tell that. Had it wrote all over his face. Can't help but wonder how that fiancé of yours feels 'bout havin' somebody like him hangin' 'round all the time, carryin' a torch for you and all."

Toni was now as anxious to get out of the store for her own sake as for April's. Laying a five-dollar bill on the counter, she said, "Well, April and I really have to run. It's been nice talking with you."

In what seemed to Toni like slow motion, Simon rang up the sale on the old cash register, then pulled the change out of the drawer and handed it to her. "So, when are we gonna meet this here fella you're plannin' to marry?" he asked.

"That's right," Maude agreed. "When you gonna bring him on up? Why, we'd love to meet him, size him up a bit." She looked at Simon and winked. "Maybe even compare him to that detective fella, right, Simon?"

Simon laughed, and his eyes twinkled with mischief. "Aha. Now, that's a right good idea. You do that. Just bring 'em both up here together and let us look 'em over side by side."

Toni stuffed the change in her purse and grabbed April by the arm. "Good seeing you," she said, ignoring their last comments as she steered the older woman toward the door. "Goodbye."

They were out the door and headed across the parking lot before either one of the Olsons could do any more damage. Once inside the car, they both collapsed into their seats, quickly closing the doors behind them.

"That was terrible," Toni declared. "I am so sorry. This was definitely a bad idea. We should have brought an ice chest full of cold drinks from home and avoided this place entirely."

"It's all right, my dear. I'm fine now. I know they meant well, but . . . I do believe it was harder on you than it was on me."

Toni looked at her. "It was pretty bad," she admitted, "but you're right. They meant well."

April laid her hand on Toni's arm. "There's something you haven't told me, isn't there? You've been so withdrawn all weekend, ever since your date with Brad on Friday night. Did something happen?"

The tears sprang to Toni's eyes so quickly that she realized there was no use trying to hide anything from this perceptive woman. Besides, she had to tell someone sooner or later.

"It's over. The engagement, I mean."

April's eyes opened wide. "You did it? You broke it off?"

Toni shook her head. "No. Brad did."

"Oh, my dear . . ."

"It was hard, but . . . I'm grateful. It was the right thing to do. He had the courage to do it, even if I didn't."

"He's quite a man, isn't he?"

Toni closed her eyes and took a deep breath. "Yes, he is, and it hurts to lose him, even though I'm relieved that it's over. Does that make any sense?"

"Of course it does. Have you told Melissa?"

"No. I've been putting it off. I know it's going to break her heart. But . . . I suppose I should get it over with. The sooner the better."

"Yes. You don't want to risk having her hear it from someone else."

"You're right. I'll tell her tonight."

April squeezed Toni's hand. "I'll be praying."

They drove to the north side of the lake to the approximate area where Abe had told Toni that Julie's body had been found. They parked the car, and at April's suggestion, got out and walked to the shoreline.

"I need to sit here a while," April said, settling down on a rock near the water. "I need to think . . . and pray . . . and maybe say goodbye again."

Toni nodded. Walking away several yards, she, too, found a rock to sit on, nearer the trees where she could hear the breeze soughing in the branches. She looked at her watch. It was only 9:30. They had come early so April could spend as much time as she needed to sort through her feelings. As April Lippincott poured out her pain to God, Toni spoke to him of her feelings for Abe, begging God to change her heart, to help her to stop thinking of this man day and night, wondering where he was, what he was doing . . . and if he still thought of her. Her faithful heavenly Father had answered her prayers and resolved her relationship with Brad. Would he now intervene and somehow help her deal with her feelings for Abe?

≈≈≈

It wasn't often that Abe got a weekday off, but he had been putting in a lot of overtime lately, so this Monday morning, instead of being in his office, he was at the mall, pacing, and waiting for the stores to open. Actually, he was waiting to get into one particular store, and he was more than slightly nervous about setting foot in the place since he had never done so before. He had thought it over for days, however, and he knew it was the next logical step, not to mention his only viable option at this point. He just hoped he wouldn't see anyone he knew, either while he was waiting or once he was inside the store. How would he ever explain what he was doing?

Some of the stores began to unlock their doors, raising the iron gratings that protected the entrances. Abe checked his watch. The sign in the front window had said the store would open at ten o'clock. It was now two minutes after. What was the holdup?

Finally Abe spotted some movement inside. The lights had come on, and a middle-aged woman was unlocking the door. Resisting the urge to turn and run, Abe took a deep breath and walked inside, amazed that something as harmless as an excursion into an unknown store could make him more edgy than tracking a danger-ous criminal. The difference, of course, was that he was trained to track criminals. He was experienced at it. This was all new to him, and very uncomfortable.

"Good morning." The woman who had unlocked the door greeted him with a smile. "Is there anything I can help you with?"

"Oh, no thanks. I . . ." He glanced around the store. Soft music played in the background, but if it was meant to soothe him, it wasn't working. Where would he start? Was there some sort of arranged order here? An alphabetical or topical listing, or . . . He decided he had better swallow his pride and ask for help or he might be there all day. "As a matter of fact, there is. I . . . was wondering if . . . do you have . . .? Well, what I need is a . . . New Testament."

"Certainly. Is there a particular translation you'd like?"

Abe flushed. He hadn't realized there was more than one. Back to swallowing his pride again. "I really don't know," he admitted. "I've . . . never even seen one before, let alone read it. Do you have any suggestions?"

Her smile was warm as she turned toward a large shelf full of books behind the counter. "Let me show you a couple of our better ones, and you can choose."

With the clerk's guidance, Abe made his choice in record time and was out the door before any other customers arrived. Relieved, he clutched his purchase and hurried to his car. He wanted to get home and begin reading as soon as possible.

≈~≈

Melissa sat curled up on the couch in the family room while Tyler watched cartoons. She had taken him to the park after lunch where they had spent the better part of the afternoon. Now, it was just a matter of waiting another hour or so until Tyler's mom got home. With her journal on her lap, she fought the tears that had been threatening her all day.

I'm so mad, she wrote. *Why did Toni do this? She says it was Brad's idea but that they both agreed it was for the best. I don't believe her. I think it's that Abe Matthews again. She's been different ever since she met him. Why did he ever have to come into our lives? Brad and Toni were so happy before he showed up. I really hate him. I bet if he wasn't around, Toni and Brad would still be getting married. Why is my sister so stupid? I don't even want to go home tonight.*

When the phone rang, she tossed her journal on the floor and got up to go into the kitchen to answer it. Her heart jumped when she heard the familiar voice, and she wondered how she could have forgotten about his promise to call back this week.

"Melissa? This is Carlo. How are you?"

She hesitated briefly. "I'm . . . fine."

"Good. I've been thinking about you and wondered if you'd come to any decision about trying out for the part. I know this is only Tuesday, so if you need more time, it's no problem. Have you given any more thought to what we discussed?"

Melissa had thought about little else all week . . . until Toni had dropped the bombshell on her last night. Before that she had decided that if Carlo followed through on his promise and called her back, she would tell him she was definitely interested and see about setting up an appointment for him to meet with her and Toni. Now she wasn't so sure she wanted Toni involved. After all, if Toni could make life-changing decisions without consulting anyone else, why shouldn't she have the same right? It wasn't like she was running off to Hollywood or anything. It was just a bit part in a local movie. How could it hurt?

"Actually, yes. I've thought about it a lot. I think I'd like to give it a try . . . if you really think I could do it, that is."

"Of course you could. Why couldn't you? Like I told you, it's just for an extra, that's all. You probably won't even have any lines. You'll basically just be part of the background scenery. You should be able to handle that, shouldn't you?"

"I guess so, but I really should tell you, I'm . . . only fourteen."

"Hey, no problem. We need people of all ages for this film. I tell you what we'll do. Why don't we meet for a few minutes sometime soon, maybe even this evening if you have time. I'll give you a few more details, and then, if you're still interested, we'll talk about getting parental permission."

"I . . . don't have any parents."

"Oh, I'm sorry. That's right. You mentioned something about talking to your older sister, didn't you? Is she your guardian?"

"Yes."

"You . . . haven't already talked to her about this, have you?"

"No. You asked me not to until you called back."

"Good. Well then, what do you say? When can we get together? Did you tell me you're baby-sitting? If you get off soon, I can meet you somewhere before you go home. I'll even buy you a hamburger."

Melissa felt a slight stab of fear as she realized she was actually considering meeting with someone she knew nothing about, but it wasn't like she was going out on a date with him or anything. It was strictly a meeting to find out some details so she could decide if she wanted to try out for the part or not. How dangerous could that be? She decided she would meet with him but pass on the hamburger.

"Sure. I guess so. But . . . just for a few minutes. I won't have time to go eat anything."

"No problem. Where are you now? Is there somewhere nearby where we can talk? I have my car and can meet you wherever you like."

She thought for a moment. "There's a park just a couple of blocks from here, on Washington and Eighth. Do you know where it is?"

"Absolutely. What time?"

Melissa glanced at the kitchen clock. Mrs. Johnson was due home in about forty-five minutes, and she was never late. "How about in an hour?"

"Great. I'll be looking forward to it. I'll be driving a red BMW, and I'll park by the playground."

"I'll be there. Goodbye, Carlo."

She hung up the phone, her heart hammering in her chest. She had never done anything so daring before, and she knew Toni would be upset with her. But then, why should she care what Toni thought?

"Lissa?"

Melissa jumped. She hadn't heard Tyler come in. He was standing at her elbow, staring up at her, his brown eyes opened wide.

"Who's Carlo?"

She smiled reassuringly. "Nobody special. Just a friend. Listen, how would you like me to color with you until your mom gets home?"

Tyler's face lit up. "I'll be right back." He ran out of the kitchen and down the hall toward his room, undoubtedly, Melissa thought, to retrieve his colors and coloring book. Her stomach was feeling a bit queasy, and she hoped coloring with Tyler might help keep her mind off her upcoming meeting with Carlo. She couldn't help but wonder if this meeting could be the beginning of the greatest adventure of her life.

It had been a long day, and an emotional one at that. Toni had been amazed to realize just how many gifts and mementos Brad had given her over the years, and what a sentimental attachment they held for her. But she had determined, after telling Melissa the previous evening that the engagement was off, that she would gather together all the things that reminded her of Brad and store them away somewhere. It wasn't that she wanted to be rid of them—she might, in fact, bring them back out some day, when her heart was ready—but she did feel the need to get them out of sight so she could think more clearly about her future. There were a lot of decisions to be made, and although they didn't all center around Abe Matthews, it was his face that dominated her every thought, regardless of which aspect of her future she was considering.

Toni was glad she had gone ahead and secured a position as a substitute teacher for the fall. The extra money to supplement what her father had left them certainly couldn't hurt; and besides, she needed something constructive to do now that things were just about cleared up at the office. She also wanted some free time to sort through her feelings for Abe and to come to some concrete decisions regarding the agency, teaching, and possibly even writing her first book.

Carefully wrapping a ceramic vase that Brad had given her for her birthday two years earlier, she placed it in the box along with several other wrapped items and decided to call it a day. It was getting late and she needed to see about getting dinner started before Melissa got home, which should be any minute now. April was sitting outside on the back porch swing, reading, and Toni decided not to disturb her. Although April was always more than willing to help with anything and everything around the house, Toni thought that she probably needed some quiet time to herself. The previous day at the lake had been a draining one for both of them, although they agreed it had been cathartic as well. Still, it had not begun to prepare Toni for Melissa's extreme reaction to her announcement regarding her broken engagement with Brad.

Toni sighed, walked into the kitchen, and pulled some ground beef out of the refrigerator. A quick pot of spaghetti and a tossed green salad with garlic bread, one of Melissa's favorite meals, just might help reopen the communication lines between them. At least, she hoped so. Melissa had not spoken to her since she had run to her room in tears the previous night.

Dinner was almost ready to put on the table when April walked in from outside. "Oh, my dear, you should have asked me to help. I've just been sitting out there on the porch swing, reading and drowsing a bit. Actually, I must have been drowsing more than I realized, or I would have heard you in here. You really should have called me. Here, let me at least set the table."

"I didn't want to disturb you. I know what a comfortable spot that is out there. It's one of my favorite places."

"I can see why." April was already taking plates and glasses out of the cupboard and carrying them to the table. "Where's Melissa? Isn't she usually home by now?"

Toni checked her watch. "I was just thinking the same thing. She always lets me know if she's going to be late, but maybe she just forgot. I'll call over there and check."

Tyler's mother answered on the second ring.

"Beth? Oh, you're home. This is Toni. I thought maybe you had to work late and Melissa had stayed over a little longer."

"Hi, Toni. No, I got home at the usual time, and she left right away. That was almost an hour ago. You mean she's not home yet?"

Toni felt the first prick of fear as she remembered the caller's warning a couple of weeks earlier. There had been no further calls since Abe had placed a trace on her phone, and she had hoped that was the end of it. Now she wasn't so sure.

"No. She hasn't come home, and she hasn't called. That's not like her. She didn't say anything about going anywhere else, did she? Maybe over to Carrie's?"

"Not to me, but just a minute, let me ask Tyler. He's in his room. I'll be right back."

Toni tapped her fingers on the table as she waited anxiously for what seemed an interminable amount of time but was actually only a couple of minutes. When Beth came back on the line, she sounded a bit hesitant.

"Toni, I'm . . . not real sure about what Tyler said. You know how kids' imaginations can be sometimes. At the same time, I've never known him to lie. He said Melissa was talking to her friend on the phone and that they were going to meet at the park."

"You mean, Carrie?"

"No. Tyler said it was someone named . . . Carlo. Do you know anyone by that name?"

Toni gasped. Surely, it couldn't be . . . and yet Carlo was just too strange a name for a little boy to come up with on his own. As desperately as Toni wanted to believe that this was just some sort of freakish mistake on Tyler's part, she knew better. She had never been so terrified in all her life.

"I'll . . . I'll call you back. Thank you, Beth."

"But—"

Toni hung up the phone and looked at April. "Something's happened to Melissa. Something awful. I . . ."

She burst into tears, and April hurried to her side, lowering her into a chair. "Toni, what is it? What's happened to Melissa? Please tell me."

Struggling to control her breathing, Toni looked up at the concerned woman standing over her. "It's Carlo," she whispered. "I think Carlo has gotten to Melissa somehow. Oh, April, what are we going to do?"

April's face paled and she sat down next to Toni. "Oh, dear God, no. Not Melissa. What makes you think it's Carlo? Are you sure?"

"No, not completely, but . . . Tyler overheard her talking on the phone with someone named Carlo, making plans to meet him at the park—over an hour ago." She rose from her chair and started toward the front door. "Do you suppose there's any chance they'd still be there? We could drive over there . . ."

"Hold on, my dear. Before we go running out looking for her, we've got to call the police. Maybe you should call Abe directly, since he's already working on Julie's case."

Toni nodded, suddenly aware of how much she needed Abe to be there with them, to lend her his strength and to assure her that Melissa would be all right. "You're right. I need to call Abe." She went to the living room to get the address book. Sinking down onto the couch, she dialed his home number. *Please, Abe. Please be there!*

"Hello?"

"Abe, it's Toni. Please, I need your help. It's Melissa. I . . . think something terrible has happened to her."

CHAPTER 15

It was less than fifteen minutes before Abe arrived, but it seemed an eternity to Toni as she paced the living room, stopping every few moments to peek out the window. April sat on the couch, her face ashen, her hands clenched in her lap. When Toni heard Abe's car door slam, she had the screen door open before he had mounted the steps. The moment he saw her face, he stopped. "What is it? What happened to—"

"Do you remember Carlo, from Julie's file? I think he's got Melissa."

Abe's dark eyes opened wide. "Carlo. You mean . . .?" His jaws clenched. "Let's go inside. I want to know everything. Don't leave anything out. Do you have some paper I can write on? I want to get this down while it's fresh."

Toni went to the kitchen and retrieved a pen and some notepaper. Abe nodded in greeting to April, who was still seated on the couch. Toni sat down next to her while Abe sat across from them in an armchair, perched on the edge of the seat, pen and paper in hand. He grilled Toni on every detail, and she answered as best she could, with April filling in on occasion. When they had exhausted what little information the two women could give him, Abe reached over and laid the pen and paper on the coffee table, then looked at Toni. The compassion and concern on his face were the only rays of hope Toni could see in this terrible situation.

"I'm going to call the station," Abe announced, his voice soft but firm.

"But, what if—"

"I know what you're thinking, but there's always a much better chance of getting someone back safely when the police are involved."

"But you are the police. Can't you . . .?"

Abe shook his head. "No. Not only do I have a professional obligation to report this, but it's much too big a deal for me to handle on my own. Toni, I can't go into detail, but you know I've been working on Julie's case, and . . . Let me just say that this apparent 'Carlo connection' could turn into something a lot bigger than anything we might have imagined. That's all I can tell you right now. I'm sure Melissa is going to be fine, but if this guy Carlo—or anybody else—has her, we've got to play by the rules. In fact, if it starts looking more like a kidnapping than a runaway situation, we'll have to call in the state police, maybe even the FBI. There's too much at stake to take any chances."

His eyes held hers until she nodded in agreement. "I know you're right. I'm just so scared. Not knowing where she is, or what's happening to her . . ."

"I know, sweetheart. I'll do everything I can. I promise."

Even in the midst of her pain and fear, Toni caught the endearment. She doubted that Abe was even aware he had uttered it, but

April had noticed. Toni could tell by the way she straightened up and looked from one to the other, but she said nothing.

"I'm going to call the station now," Abe went on, "and then I want you to give me a list of all of Melissa's friends, anywhere she might have gone. We'll start calling around just to make sure she didn't stop somewhere on the way home."

"Abe, that's not like her. She wouldn't do that without letting me know."

"I'm sure that's true, but it's something we have to do."

As Abe made the call to the station, Toni jotted down names and numbers on the notepad Abe had been using. She understood his point that the calls to Melissa's friends had to be made, but she knew in her heart that it was a wasted effort. Whoever Carlo was, and whatever part he had played in Julie's death, he now had Melissa—somewhere. *Oh, Lord, you know where she is. Please, please keep her safe!*

Abe hung up the phone and turned to her. "They'll be here in a few minutes. They'll probably ask you some of the same questions I asked, but just cooperate with them. We need all the information we can get, and sometimes, by repeating it, you remember something you forgot the first time." He looked at the paper in her hand. "Got your list ready?"

"Yes, but . . ." Toni paused. There was something she had to do, something more important even than making the necessary phone calls to Melissa's friends. "Do you mind if I make one quick call first? I need to talk to someone at church, to request prayer . . ." Her voice cracked. "I need to know people are praying for Melissa."

Abe's jaw twitched and he nodded. "Sure. Go ahead."

Toni had no sooner hung up the phone after calling the church than it rang. She jumped, then looked at Abe questioningly.

"You can answer it," he said. "We've still got a trace on it."

"Do you think it might be . . .?"

"It could be anybody, but if it's about Melissa—Carlo or anyone else—talk slowly and carefully."

Her hand shaking, Toni picked up the receiver. Beth Johnson's concerned voice greeted her, asking if she'd heard anything from Melissa. When Toni said she hadn't, Beth said Tyler had found Melissa's journal on the floor in the family room and asked if she should bring it over or just wait and give it to Melissa the next day. Sensing that the journal could be important, Toni covered the mouthpiece of the receiver with her hand and explained to Abe what Beth had said.

Abe thought a moment. "You're going to have to tell her something, especially since she's expecting Melissa to show up tomorrow. Let her know you've called the police, but downplay it as much as you can for now, and tell her I'll send someone over to pick up the journal in a little while. Let her know that the officer who comes over will want to ask Tyler a few questions, just to see if he remembers anything other than the name he heard Melissa mention on the phone."

Toni relayed the message and once again hung up the phone.

"Tell me about Melissa's journal," Abe said. "Did she write in it a lot?"

"Every day, about everything."

"That's good. There may be something in it that will help us. Once I get someone to pick it up, I'll start reading through it right away. I know it's probably very personal, but right now we can't worry about something like that. We'll also get someone over to the park to see if we can find anyone who saw anything, although it may be too late to learn much there."

The doorbell rang then, and Abe offered to get it. "It's going to be OK. You and April just take a deep breath and relax. There will probably be two officers. I'll walk you through it, so don't be nervous. When we finish with them, I'll help you make those calls to Melissa's friends, and then I'll get that journal and start reading."

Toni nodded, grateful for his presence and his knowledgeable assistance. She couldn't imagine having to face this ordeal without him, and she couldn't imagine losing Melissa.

~~~

The thin, rough blanket that covered her did nothing to ease the cold she felt deep inside. In some ways, the blanket made things worse, scratching her bare legs. If only she had worn long pants today instead of shorts. If only she hadn't answered the phone at Tyler's, or gone to the park, or gotten into Carlo's car . . . but she did, and now here she was, the ropes around her ankles and wrists feeling tighter with each passing minute. How long had she been here, lying on her side on this lumpy, uncomfortable cot? The blindfold over her eyes prevented her from knowing whether it was daylight or dark. With her hands tied behind her, she couldn't turn onto her back, and her left arm was beginning to feel numb. Awkwardly, she struggled to roll onto her stomach, which helped only slightly.

She strained to hear a sound—any sound. Being alone in the darkness was the most terrifying thing she had ever experienced. Still, she reminded herself, it was better than what could have happened. She shivered as she thought of Carlo's hands on her when she had first gotten into his car. She was sure he was going to rape her, right there in front of the park, but he hadn't. Before she could scream or reach for the door handle and get out, almost before she had even realized she was in danger, he had grabbed her and held a knife to her throat, then forced her to climb into the back seat of the two-door car. After flipping the front door locks, he told her to lie down and keep quiet. The only sound she had made for the next few minutes was a soft, whimpering cry. Then the car had stopped. Melissa had tried to peer out of the window from her prone position, but before she could see enough to identify where they were, Carlo was blindfolding her. The next thing she knew, her hands and feet were tied together. In a matter of about fifteen minutes, she had gone from being an excited fourteen-year-old girl, hesitantly climbing into a shiny red sports car driven by a handsome Hollywood talent scout, to a terrified captive with no idea whether she would live or die, or what she might suffer in the process.

How could she have been so stupid? She had asked herself that question countless times both as she lay blindfolded in the backseat of the car during the remainder of the drive, which she estimated at anywhere from thirty minutes to an hour or more, and as she lay here on a cot that smelled as awful as it felt. Why hadn't she talked to Toni first, or at least insisted that Carlo come to the house, instead of going alone to meet him at an almost deserted park? What would happen to her now? Did anyone have any idea where she was? Were they looking for her? Would they find her in time?

Fighting tears, she rolled back onto her side just as she heard a door open and shut. Not having seen the place where she was being kept, she couldn't visualize where the door was in relation to her own position, but she was sure it must be in an adjacent room. She strained to hear every sound, identifying more than one set of footsteps and at least three voices. One of them was Carlo's. It was a voice she knew she would remember for the rest of her life—however long that might be.

"What took you so long?" she heard Carlo say. "I fell asleep waiting for you. Don't worry, everything's under control. She's right in there."

Melissa's skin crawled as she realized Carlo had been sleeping in the next room the entire time, as she lay, tied up and helpless, on this filthy cot. But maybe it was a good sign that he had left her alone. Maybe that meant he wasn't going to hurt her or . . .

She froze as she heard another door open, this time very close by. "So you really did it," said a loud male voice heavy with sarcasm. "Gee, I hope she didn't put up too much of a fight for you."

She heard Carlo laugh. "Hey, nothing to it. It was like reeling in a fish. She was even easier than the Greene kid. With her I had to promise love and romance in sunny California before she'd give me the time of day."

"Yeah, and look at all the trouble that one brought us. I suppose you're going to get this one pregnant too?"

Carlo laughed again, and the door closed. Melissa shuddered at the unknown man's question even as she concentrated on listening to what they were saying. Her heart leapt when she heard a woman's voice, even though it was too soft to make out the words. Surely a woman wouldn't allow any harm to come to her. This must all be about a ransom. But what did they expect to get? She and Toni weren't poor, thanks to their father's wise planning over the years, but they certainly weren't rich either. So why had she been singled out?

As she wriggled again in a vain effort to get comfortable, the blindfold slipped up slightly and she was able to see a faint slit of light. Anxiously, she rubbed her face against the bed, over and over, until the blindfold was high enough that she could see out from under one side. She glanced around the tiny room. It was dirty and totally devoid of furniture, except for the cot where she lay and an old wooden chair. A lone light bulb hung from the ceiling, dimly illuminating the room. It appeared that she was in a very old cabin somewhere—if only she knew where. The room didn't even have a window.

The door opened again, and Melissa caught her breath. Footsteps approached, but they were too light to belong to Carlo or the man with the loud voice. Peering out from under the blindfold, she saw the figure of a woman come into view.

"Hey, kid, you need to go to the bathroom or anything?"

Melissa was puzzled. The voice was familiar, but she couldn't place it. Tilting her head up, she caught sight of the woman's face, and found herself looking into the eyes of her dad's former secretary.

"Lorraine," she gasped, "what are you doing here?"

"Well, well, aren't you the clever one?" The woman grabbed her, digging her nails into her arm as she tugged the blindfold back into place and tightened the knots. "Don't think it's going to make any difference knowing who I am. You won't be telling anyone about it, I guarantee you. Now, do you need to go to the bathroom, or not?"

"Yes. But why—"

"Just shut up while I untie your feet. I'm going to walk you to the bathroom, but don't even think about trying anything. Look, it wasn't my idea to bring you here, OK? So just play it smart. There's no sense in your leaving this world any sooner than you have to. Do you understand?"

Melissa nodded. Her heart hammering, she allowed the woman she had called Lorraine to walk her to the bathroom, hoping she would at least leave the ropes off her ankles when she brought her back to bed, but she didn't. She gave her a few sips of water, then retied her and went to rejoin the men. Once again Melissa lay in the dark and listened to the voices in the next room.

"Now that you two are here, I'm going out for a walk," she heard Carlo say. "I'm sick of being cooped up in this place. I need some fresh air." Another door slammed, and Melissa heard Lorraine's voice, although she couldn't make out what she was saying.

"That guy's nothing but trouble," the man said. "I know you had a thing for him once—that's why we brought him in. You're finished with him though, aren't you? I used to think he might be useful to us somehow, with his good looks and smooth talk. But between his drinking and his bad temper, he's becoming more of a liability than an asset. He blew it with the Greene girl, you know that? Thought he was so smart, dumping her in the middle of the lake at night when she was too weak to make it back to the beach, and then sitting there in the boat and watching, just for kicks, while she went down for the last time. He's a sick man, really sick. If he was going to kill her, why didn't he just do it and get rid of her somewhere else? We just about had everything under control after the Matthews autopsy, and then the girl's body turns up on shore, and wham! A full-blown investigation."

Lorraine spoke again, but Melissa couldn't tell whether she was agreeing with the man or defending Carlo.

"Yeah, I know," the man with the loud voice continued. "Technically, she drowned. There's no actual proof of anything else, just like with the heart attack for Matthews, but there are too many loose ends now, too many unanswered questions, especially with Matthews's daughter and her lovesick sidekick—Abe, of all people—nosing around. Once that Greene girl was identified, I knew we were in trouble. All these years of playing it safe, and good old Carl had to mess us up. And now this. Where does he get off making these kinds of decisions without checking with us first? A stupid move like this could end up bringing the Feds in. That's all we need."

The man paused, and Lorraine said something as Melissa wondered who Carl was. Had he meant to say Carlo? If only she could hear what Lorraine was saying, maybe then she would understand what they were talking about.

The man went on. "I say we do it as soon as he gets back, while the others aren't around. Those three buffoons are likely to go soft on us, and we can't afford to make any more mistakes. There's just too much at risk. I've poured years of my life into this operation, and I'm not about to see it go down now. Our only hope is to get to Abe before the cops get to us. He's our ace in the hole. As soon as we take care of old Carl out there, I'll call Abe and tell him what we expect from him, unless he wants to go down with us. You can stay here with the kid while I'm gone."

The outside door opened then, and Melissa heard Carlo's voice. "Turning into a nice night out there, full moon and everything. Nothing like a walk in the moonlight to make a guy feel . . . romantic, if you know what I mean." He laughed. "Hey, listen, why don't you two go ahead and take off? I'll stay here and . . . take care of our little fish. She just might be getting lonely in there."

"You've been drinking," the other man said.

"Sure," Carlo answered. "Why not? Puts me in a more romantic mood."

"Come on, Lorraine," said the other man, his voice filled with disgust. "Let's take off."

No, don't go, Melissa cried silently. *Please, don't leave me here alone with Carlo. Please!*

The door to Melissa's room opened, and she heard Carlo's footsteps approaching the bed. The smell of alcohol assailed her nostrils, and she tried to move away as Carlo sat down beside her.

"What's the matter, little one? You don't like Carlo anymore?" He grabbed her arms and leaned toward her until she gagged from the smell of his breath. "I think you'll like me again before the night is over."

"Get away from me. Don't you touch me!"

"Oh, you're not going to fight me now, are you? I saw how you looked at me when you climbed into my car. I'm not such a bad looking guy now, am I? Why not just make it easy for both of us and—"

His voice stopped mid-sentence, and his grip on her arms loosened. Suddenly he was on top of her, heavy and unmoving. Terrified, Melissa began to scream.

"I'll get him off of her," she heard the man say. "You shut the kid up. She's making me nervous."

"You heard him," Lorraine said as Melissa felt Carlo's body being lifted off hers. "You'd better shut up if you know what's good for you."

"But . . . what happened?" Melissa's voice was shaking as she choked back the tears. "What happened to Carlo? What did that man do to him?"

"The same thing he'll do to you if you don't keep your mouth shut. Carl didn't play it smart, and he paid the price. Raymond did you a favor."

Melissa understood then that Carlo—or Carl—was dead, and from what she had heard earlier, it had something to do with the way he had handled Julie's death as well as the fact that he had brought her here without the others' knowledge or approval. What she didn't understand was why Lorraine was involved. The few times they had met she had not seemed the type, but Melissa was sure it wouldn't do any good to ask, so she took Lorraine's advice and kept her mouth shut.

"Come and help me get him out of here," the man named Raymond said.

Melissa listened as the two of them dragged Carlo's lifeless body out of the room and shut the door behind them. Then, what little control Melissa had left collapsed, and she sobbed hysterically, begging God to send someone to help her before she ended up being dragged out of the room like Carlo, or floating facedown in the lake like poor Julie.

~~~

Abe was finally home, but he knew he wouldn't get much sleep that night. For the first time in weeks, he lay back in his recliner, planning to read something other than the Holy Scriptures. With Melissa's journal resting on his lap, he thought over the events of the day. Prior to Toni's call, he had been focusing on the Julie Greene case. The more he dug into it, the more he began to wonder if he was following a trail that would ultimately lead him back to the past he thought he had covered up. Was it really possible, after all these years, that the nightmare he had experienced so long ago was still going on, in one form or another? He had been so sure it was all behind him, that the people involved had long since moved on to greener pastures. Uncle Sol had been so careful to attend to the details and to protect him. . . .

Abe shook his head. This was no time to be thinking of himself. An innocent fourteen-year-old girl was missing, very possibly in the hands of the same people who had been responsible for Julie Greene's body ending up in the lake. He closed his eyes, remembering the times he had seen Melissa. Although their coloring and personalities were different, there was still a strong resemblance between Melissa and Toni. The family picture on their mantle was fresh in his mind as he recalled Marilyn Matthews, their mother, the only member of the family he had never met. Such a beautiful woman, and she had died so young. Toni had already lost so much. He couldn't bear to think of her losing her little sister as well.

He opened his eyes and began to flip through Melissa's journal. Later he would start at the beginning and read straight through, but for now, he would start with the final entries, hoping Melissa had written something about her relationship with this Carlo person. There had to have been previous contact between them, or she would never have agreed to meet with him alone. Somehow the man had been able to establish enough trust to lure her to the meeting. How had he done it?

Although Abe had sent an officer to talk with people at the park, there was almost no one there, and the few who were had come long after Melissa's meeting with Carlo. And, as he had expected, he and Toni had come up empty on their phone calls to Melissa's friends. Although they still had no proof, it seemed the girl was in the company of a man who apparently had little or no regard for human life, and Abe could do nothing but pray for her safe return.

It hadn't surprised him when Toni wanted to call her church to request prayer for her sister. What surprised him was that he had also begun to pray for Melissa, silently, the moment Toni had called and asked him to come over. In fact, praying seemed to be becoming an automatic reaction for him lately, as if he were talking to someone he actually believed existed, someone who could hear him and who cared enough to answer his requests. There were still a lot of unanswered questions regarding his emerging faith, but he felt sure he had made a lot of progress since he first began his quest.

He came to Melissa's final entry and began to read. *I'm so mad. Why did Toni do this?* Abe frowned. What had Toni done to make Melissa mad? *She says it was Brad's idea but that they both agreed it was for the best. I don't believe her. I think it's that Abe Matthews again. She's been different ever since she met him. Why did he ever have to come into our lives?* Abe's emotions were on a roller coaster. He couldn't help but rejoice that Toni truly had been different since meeting him; it confirmed his belief that her feelings for him ran as deep as his did for her, but he hadn't realized that Melissa so deeply resented his intrusion into their lives. *Brad and Toni were so happy before he showed up. I really hate him.* Abe winced but read on. *I bet if he wasn't around, Toni and Brad would still be getting married.* Abe's eyes opened wide. What was this? Toni and Brad were no longer getting married? The engagement was off? When had this happened? What had caused it? He read the final sentences. *Why is my sister so stupid? I don't even want to go home tonight.*

Abe groaned. He was beginning to see why Melissa had been so vulnerable to this creep, why she would do something so totally out of character as to meet with him alone. The girl's final journal entry lent some support to the runaway theory, even though Abe had a hard time believing that Melissa had disappeared of her own volition.

He closed his eyes and sighed. If only he had never come into Toni's life, had never pursued her or told her of his love for her, quite possibly she and Brad would still be engaged and Melissa would be home where she belonged, but he had disregarded Toni's prior commitment to another man and had selfishly tried to win her away. Now the engagement was over, but he was no closer to achieving his objective of winning Toni for himself. If anything, he had pushed her further in the opposite direction. Once she read Melissa's journal, she would reject him completely; and if it turned out that there was some connection between his past and what had happened to Julie and Melissa, she would most certainly hate him as much as her younger sister already did.

The phone on the table next to his chair rang, and he looked at his watch. It was after midnight, too late for a social call. Maybe it was Toni saying she had heard from Melissa. He wouldn't even allow himself to think that it was bad news.

"Hello?"

"Abe, how are you? I didn't get you out of bed, did I?"

Abe frowned. The voice was vaguely familiar, but he couldn't place it. He glanced at his caller I.D. It read "Unavailable."

"No, I was up. Who is this?"

"Just an old friend, someone who wants to see you stay out of trouble. You've got a good career going in law enforcement, and I'd sure hate to see it ruined over things that happened a long time ago. You know, things when you were young and not quite so careful."

Abe was getting angry now, but he cautioned himself not to over-react. "I'm . . . not sure I know what you're talking about."

"I think you do, and I think you'd better start playing things our way if you want to stay out of trouble . . . and if you want that Matthews kid to make it home alive."

Abe's heart began to race. So there was a connection between the past and all that was going on now with this so-called Carlo person. . . . "Is this Carlo? Is that who you are? Because if I'm going to talk to you, I want to know your name and—"

"So you know Carlo, do you?" the man interrupted. "Well, isn't that interesting? It really is a small world, isn't it? Listen, Matthews, let's cut the small talk. You're in no position to ask questions or make demands. If you're smart and if you don't want the kid to end up like the one they found up at Eagle Lake, you'd better pay attention. I don't know what you have to do or how you're going to do it, but you'd better find a way to derail this investigation, do you hear? Keep the Feds out of it and stall it as long as you can. We need time to relocate, to move our main headquarters and get rid of evidence, if you know what I mean. We all have lives here in River View, and we have no intention of giving them up. With a little bit of time we can relocate the business without having to relocate ourselves. We've got a lot at stake in this, and it seems to me that you do too. Am I right, Abe?"

Abe felt sick. The guy was right, whoever he was. He had more at stake here than he had ever dreamed possible. But how could he purposely stall the investigation, put off tracking down Julie's killers and finding Melissa, knowing that her life hung in the balance? Yet, if he didn't cooperate, he could be signing her death warrant. He had no doubt that the people involved in this ugly business wouldn't blink an eye at destroying the life of one more young girl. He had no choice but to play along with them.

"I'll . . . do what I can, but it's not like I'm the only one working on this investigation, you know. Even without the Feds involved, I can't make all the calls on my own."

"I'm not worried about the others. I'm worried about you, Matthews. You're the key here. And I'm telling you, you'd better cooperate. I don't care how you do it, just do it. Understand?"

The man hung up and Abe replaced the receiver. Closing his eyes, he leaned back in his chair. "Oh, God," he whispered. "What am I going to do? Please show me. I don't care about myself, but . . . please, don't let Melissa get hurt. I've already lost Toni, but don't let her lose Melissa now. Please, God . . ."

CHAPTER 16

Toni was angry. She hadn't suspected Abe could be so insensitive. "How can you even ask me that? You know Melissa didn't run away. Besides, the officers already asked me that very question yesterday, and I told them then that it was impossible."

"I know, and I'm sure you're right, but just like we had to call her friends to make sure she wasn't with one of them, I have to ask you again if she might have run off because she was . . . upset. The final entry in her journal stated that she was mad at you and didn't want to come home. That, combined with what Tyler Johnson overheard her saying on the phone not long before she left to come home, might tend to reinforce the runaway idea rather than an abduction."

Toni flushed. She had not yet read Melissa's journal and hadn't realized how much of their personal lives might be revealed in its pages. Looking at Abe sitting across from her in the armchair facing the couch, she wondered what else he might have discovered as he read Melissa's writings. Still, she had to admit that he was right. As he had said the previous day, privacy was not the issue right now. Melissa's well-being was the only thing that mattered.

"I'm sorry. I didn't mean to overreact. It's just been so . . . hard."

Abe nodded. "I know, and I don't mean to make it harder on you. I'm just—"

"Doing your job. I understand." She paused, then asked, "Did you . . . learn anything else from reading Melissa's journal?"

"Not really, only that she had spoken to him on the phone once last week and he claimed to be a Hollywood talent scout. He offered her a chance for a bit part in a film and told her he'd call her back this week for her answer. She seemed pretty excited about it but mentioned that he didn't want her to tell anyone about his offer until he talked to her again." Abe shook his head. "Sounds like he set her up real good."

"You see? Even if she voluntarily went to meet him, it was because he misrepresented himself. A Hollywood talent scout—no wonder she fell for it. She's always . . ." Toni paused as her voice cracked. "She's always dreamed of being in the movies some day. And now . . . Abe, shouldn't we be getting a call from this Carlo guy? A ransom note, some sort of demand or threat like I was getting before?"

Abe studied her silently, his jaws clenched as if he were wrestling with something, trying to decide whether or not to tell her about it. Finally, he said, "You never know with these things, Toni. Each case is different." He paused, then asked, "So, where's April?"

Toni was surprised by the abrupt change of subject but realized that he was probably trying to help her get her mind on something else, even if only for a few moments. "She's taking a nap. Neither of us got much sleep last night."

"I can imagine."

"Abe, what if . . .?" Her voice trailed off and she felt the tears returning. It seemed that just when she thought there were no tears left to cry, a fresh supply emerged from some bottomless well. By the time they spilled over onto her cheeks, Abe was at her side, sitting on the couch and holding her hand in his.

"Don't say it. Don't even think it. You can't, Toni. You'll make yourself crazy. You've got to believe she's going to be all right." He paused, and she looked up at him. There was a hint of tears in his dark eyes, and his voice was filled with concern. "You've been . . . praying, haven't you?" he asked. "You and some people at your church?"

She nodded, surprised at his question.

"So have I."

This time she was shocked. She knew he cared, but she had no idea that he prayed. This was a whole new side to Abe Matthews that she had not seen before. What had brought about such a change?

"I know what you're thinking," he said. "It surprises me, too, and I don't know that my prayers count for much, but I figure they can't hurt."

She gave him a weak smile. She knew he wasn't a Christian, but she was touched—and more than a little impressed—that he would turn to prayer at a time like this. "Thank you," she said. "That . . . means a lot."

For a moment neither of them spoke. Then Abe cleared his throat and let go of her hand. "Well," he said, standing up, "I guess I'd better get going."

Toni started to stand but suddenly felt dizzy. Instinctively she reached for Abe to steady herself. Abe caught her by the arms and lowered her back to the couch. "Are you all right? Can I get you something?"

She shook her head. "I'm fine. Really. I just . . . haven't had enough sleep, I suppose."

"When was the last time you ate something?"

Remembering the uneaten spaghetti of the night before, she realized it had been more than twenty-four hours. "Yesterday, at lunch. I . . . really haven't thought about it since then, but I'm not hungry. I just need to lie down for a few minutes."

"Good. You do that, right here on the couch, but I'm going out to the kitchen and fix you something to eat."

"But I'm not—"

"I don't care whether you're hungry or not. I'm going to fix you something, and then I'm going to sit here while you eat it."

She gave him another weak smile as she stretched out on the couch. "All right. Please, don't go to a lot of trouble. Anything will do."

"That's good, because anything is what you'll get. Cooking is not my strong point."

As she lay there listening to him rummaging around in the refrigerator and cupboards, she wondered at the poor timing that seemed to characterize their relationship. She had thought, once she was free of her commitment to Brad, that she would be able to think about Abe more objectively. Now, if anything, she felt less objective than ever. Her heart yearned for this man yet condemned her selfishness for even thinking about him at a time when her sister's life could be in danger. Besides, there was still the major obstacle of Abe's not being a believer. Still, he had said he was praying . . .

He came in quietly, carrying a tray, which he set on the coffee table. "I thought you might have fallen asleep," he said as he sat down beside her.

"Then I'd miss your meal."

"You wouldn't be missing much, I guarantee you."

"I have to admit, I'm so tired you'd think I'd drift off, but . . . I can't keep from thinking about . . . everything."

"I know. Here, I made you some soup. I thought that might be a little easier on your stomach than leftover spaghetti. It's canned, of course. Like I said, cooking isn't my thing."

"Soup is fine. Really. It's . . . sweet of you to do this for me."

For the first time since she had known him, Abe appeared self-conscious. She thought he might even be blushing a bit. She looked away to give him a chance to regroup. Sitting up, she tasted the soup. "Chicken noodle. Not bad."

"Thanks. It's one of my few specialties."

She had taken only a couple of spoonfuls when the phone rang. Reaching over to grab the receiver, she prayed it was something good about Melissa.

"Toni? How are you? I just heard about Melissa. Is there any news?"

"Brad. I . . . No, nothing yet, I'm afraid."

She glanced at Abe. He had suddenly become engrossed in study- ing the carpet, undoubtedly even more self-conscious than he had been a few moments earlier.

"Is there anything I can do?" Brad asked. "We're all praying, of course, but . . ."

"Thank you. Prayer is the most important thing right now. We're . . . all doing a lot of that."

There was a pause. Finally Brad said, "Well, I'm sure you have a lot going on right now, so I'll . . . let you go. Please . . . call me if there's anything you need, or . . ."

"I will. Thank you, Brad . . . for everything."

She hung up the phone and looked again at Abe. He raised his head and fixed his eyes on hers. There was a sadness in his expression that only increased the longing in her heart. Should she tell him that she and Brad were no longer engaged? Would he misunderstand, take it as an encouragement to once again pursue their relationship? The last thing in the world she wanted to do was to give him false hope, and yet she didn't want him to hear about it from someone else.

"I . . . need to tell you something." She swallowed and took a deep breath. "Brad and I are no longer engaged."

She wasn't sure what she had expected, but she had definitely thought she would see some sort of visible reaction. Instead, Abe didn't move, and the sadness in his face remained.

"I know," he said finally. "I read it in Melissa's journal. She was . . . very upset about it—to the point of not wanting to come home."

Of course. She should have known that Melissa had written about it in her journal. "When I . . . told her about it Monday night she ran to her room in tears. We haven't . . ." Toni's voice cracked again, and the tears returned. "We haven't spoken since. Oh, Abe, it's my fault, you know. All of this is my fault."

As he gathered her into his arms, she leaned against his chest, grateful for his strength and longing for his love, but all she could do was cry as he reassured her time and again that it was not her fault, that it was his, and that he was so very, very sorry.

～～～

By the time Abe dragged himself into his apartment that evening, he was exhausted. In addition to the guilt he felt about not telling Toni—or anyone else—about the call he had received the previous night, he'd had little or no sleep since Melissa's disappearance, and it was starting to catch up with him. He knew he should get to bed as early as possible, but ever since he had left Toni's house a few hours earlier to go to the station, he'd had a nagging feeling that there was something he had to take care of before the day was over. He only wished he knew what it was.

He checked his answering machine, but there were no calls that needed to be dealt with before morning, so he grabbed a frozen dinner and put it in the microwave. Collapsing into his recliner with a stack of mail, he flipped through it, tossing most of it into a wastepaper can near his chair. The only two pieces worth keeping were bills, and they could wait.

Closing his eyes, he rehearsed the events of the day, particularly his time with Toni. How ironic that she was finally free from her engagement to Brad, but he wasn't free to pursue their relationship because he knew that as soon as his past came to light—which he was sure it would any day now—she would want nothing more to do with him. He had never imagined that he would have to pay so dearly for his youthful indiscretions more than ten years after having committed them.

When the microwave bell rang, he plopped down on a stool beside the kitchen counter to eat his dinner. The New Testament he had purchased on Monday morning, just two days earlier, sat on the counter beside him. Could this be what had been nagging at him, the thing he needed to do before he went to bed that night? He had spent the entire day on Monday studying it, taking notes and pondering what he had read, but it had almost seemed to introduce more questions than it answered. Still, as tired as he was, it was as if it were calling to him.

He picked it up and began to read where he had left off Tuesday morning before going to work. It was a book called Hebrews, and it caught his attention right away. Although he had recognized references to the *Tanakh* from the moment he began reading Matthew, the connection in Hebrews was astonishing. There were many references to the sacrificial laws and the need for blood sacrifices, the high priest, the tabernacle, the failure of the Jewish people to listen to and obey God's teachings and the warnings of his prophets. . . . Was this what he had been looking for? Was he finally going to get his questions answered? His dinner forgotten, Abe began to underline key verses and words, making notes on a piece of paper as he read. By the time he had finished reading Hebrews, he was astonished. He laid down his pencil and looked at the notes he had made. It was clear that he had been right about what he had surmised from reading the *Tanakh:* the shedding of blood was absolutely necessary for the forgiveness of sins. He had wondered what his people did to atone for their sins now that there was no more Temple in which to offer sacrifices. Here, in black and white, was his answer. According to the writer of Hebrews, the previous sacrifices of bulls and goats and other animals were only temporary coverings for the people's sins, offered in anticipation of the perfect sin offering yet to come. That perfect offering, if he was to believe what he had just read, was God's only Son, Jesus, or *Yeshua* in Hebrew.

He closed the book and stared at his notes. Did he believe what he had read, or didn't he? That's what it all boiled down to now. If he did believe it, then he could see only one course of action. Moving back to his recliner where it was more comfortable, he reopened the book and flipped back to the first four books, the Gospels. Determined to know the truth, he began to reread Matthew, studying carefully every word that this Jesus spoke. By the time he was finally halfway through the Gospel of John, he was reading with tears in his eyes.

God, is it true? Is this Jesus really your Son? He says right here that he is the only way to get to you, the Father. If that's so, it's because of his blood, isn't it? He didn't deserve to die because he never sinned, so his blood . . . The tears were streaming now, and he could no longer see the words to read them. He set the book in his lap and covered his face with his hands. *His blood was the acceptable sacrifice, wasn't it? The eternal, unblemished sacrifice that Hebrews talks about. That's why there's no more temple, no more sacrifice of bulls or goats. It's not necessary anymore because . . . Oh, God, is it possible? Did his blood pay for my sins too?* **For mine?** *Because if it did, then maybe you can forgive me for all the years . . . all the things I did . . . and didn't do . . . everything. I need your forgiveness, God. Please, because of what your Son did, forgive me . . . and please, please don't let Melissa and Toni be hurt because of what I did. Protect them, God, please . . .*

≈≈≈

Melissa had lost all track of time. Lorraine came in occasionally to take her to the bathroom or give her something to eat or drink, but she wouldn't answer any of her questions or converse with her in any way other than to warn her to shut up and not try anything funny, as if she could, Melissa thought. The only respite she had from the horribly uncomfortable position on the cot was when Lorraine took her to the bathroom. Even her meals were eaten sitting on the bed, blindfold intact. Her wrists and ankles were raw from the ropes that chafed her constantly, being untied only long enough for bathroom or meal breaks. Even then, Lorraine was right beside her every minute. At times, as Melissa lay in the ever-present darkness, she wondered if she might go crazy before they killed her. She had almost begun to believe it would be easier that way.

How she longed to be back in her own room, to see Toni again and to tell her she forgave her and loved her, even if she didn't marry Brad. Now she would probably never have the chance. Poor Toni. This must be awful for her. She assumed Toni had called the police and that they were looking for her—at least, she certainly hoped so—and she wondered if Abe was involved in the investigation. The man named Raymond had spoken as if he knew Abe, as if he had something on him and thought he could get him to help them somehow. Melissa didn't like Abe much, but she had never thought of him as the criminal type. Surely he couldn't be as dangerous as the people who held her captive.

She tried not to allow herself to think of what these same people had done to Julie, or what Lorraine and Raymond had done to Carlo, although she had wondered at how Carlo had died. It had been quick and instantaneous, as if he had been shot, and yet she had heard no sound. Could it be that they had used a silencer, the kind she had seen so often on TV and in movies? Whatever their method of assassination, it had become quite obvious to her that if she had any chance at all of getting out of her situation alive, it would have to be because someone else found her and rescued her. Did anyone even know where she was though?

You know, God. You're the only One who knows. Please, please help me. Send someone. Show somebody where I am, please!

A door opened and closed, and she heard men's voices in the adjacent room with Lorraine. Melissa froze. Had Raymond returned to kill her? Who was with him?

As before, she could not understand Lorraine's words when she spoke, but most of what the men said was clear to her. She recognized Raymond's voice, but who were the others? She strained to hear, and Raymond spoke first.

"Well, it looks as if everything's been going all right here while I was gone."

Lorraine said something, and then another male voice said, "And just what are we going to do with the girl? We can't let her go home even if Abe buys us the time we need. She's already recognized Lorraine, and if she figures out Bruce is involved—"

Before he could say another word, Raymond interrupted him. "Shut up, will you? She doesn't need to know about him if you don't go blabbing. Don't you think she can hear you in there? She's young and stupid, but she's not deaf."

Bruce? Who was Bruce? She tried to think who she might know by that name.

Lorraine was talking again, and then the man Raymond had reprimanded earlier jumped in. "Wait a minute. Why do we have to kill her? I tried to warn you about leaving that Greene girl with Carl, but you wouldn't listen, and look what happened. First he gets her pregnant—which would've been fine businesswise, if she hadn't lost the baby—but the next thing we know, Carl's involved again, and as usual, he messes up. Now we've got the law breathing down our necks, and it can only get worse since he went and grabbed the Matthews girl. I don't know how he thought that was going to help, but now we're stuck with her, and we've got to do something before they decide this thing really is a kidnapping and bring the Feds in. Then even Abe won't be able to help us. Look, you said the kid's attractive, right? And she's young. That means she's worth more to us alive than dead. If we play it right, we could sell her for what we usually get for a healthy baby. For pleasure, for breeding—either way, we come out ahead. I say, don't kill her. Set up a buy. Get her out of the country. What do you think, Frank? You're the legal expert."

"Sounds good to me. The longer we keep her here—dead or alive—the higher the risk the Feds'll come in. I say, get her out as soon as we can."

Melissa's heart pounded in her chest as she fought to control her breathing. What were they saying? What did they mean, "set up a buy"? For pleasure, breeding . . . surely they didn't mean to sell her to someone as a slave for sex or to have babies. She had heard of things like that, but certainly not in today's world.

"I agree," said another voice, one she hadn't heard before . . . at least, not here. The voice was familiar though. "I've done a lot of things I never thought I'd do since I got involved in this business, but I've known that kid since she was a baby. I can't be a part of killing her. Still, we can't let her go, even if Abe does manage to buy us the time we need. I say, sell her and get it over with. As long as Abe keeps believing her life and his career depend on his playing along with us, I think he'll do what he can to hold the Feds off till we're safe. After that, we can count on his silence because he'll be in as deep as we are, but we've got to move fast. Even Abe can't buy us that much time."

Bruce . . . Bruce Jensen? Dr. Welby? Melissa was horrified. *No, it can't be! He's my friend. He was Dad's friend. He wouldn't be involved in something like this. He couldn't . . .*

Raymond spoke up again. "OK, it's settled. What's this, Thursday morning? We should be able to work this out with the same contacts. Lorraine, you make the arrangements today. See if we can get her out of here by nightfall and out of the country before the weekend. We'll get busy shredding documents and erasing files and making arrangements with our contacts outside the Northwest to move the main operation to one of our other locations. We've got a lot to do if we're going to cover our trail and keep the business going somewhere else while we keep hauling in the profits. If we play this thing right and clean up our trail in time, we can all stay here in the community where we've been known and respected for years. Who's going to suspect any of us? We've got to get this thing done quick though. Agreed?"

There seemed to be a general consensus that the plan was a good one, and within minutes Melissa heard the door open and shut again.

Because she no longer heard Lorraine's voice, she could only assume that the woman had gone to arrange the transaction that would sell her, like a piece of chattel, to the highest bidder. The tears flowed then, soaking the blindfold over her eyes. She now knew that it was Thursday morning and that she had been here almost two full days. She couldn't even imagine where she might be in two more days, or what she might be forced into doing. She almost wished that Carlo were still around. Maybe he would have just killed her and gotten it over with.

∾∾∾

It had been another sleepless night for Toni, and she had stumbled around the house dazed for most of the morning. Finally, just before noon, she had allowed April to convince her to lie down and take a nap. Almost immediately she had drifted off into a fitful sleep, plagued with visions of a young girl running for her life. This time the girl wasn't a blonde composite of Toni and Julie Greene. This time the girl's hair was auburn, flying out straight behind her as she ran like the wind. Regardless of how fast she ran though, darkness seemed to be closing in on her. Toni tried to call to her in her dream, *Hurry! Run faster!* But her voice wouldn't work, and she was helpless to assist the terrified girl. She awoke in a sweat, her heart and head pounding simultaneously.

As she lay there, trying to steady her breathing, the phone rang. She glanced at the clock next to her bed. It was three o'clock. She was shocked that she had slept so long. She grabbed the receiver next to her bed, her heart skipping a beat when she heard Abe's voice.

"Toni, I want you to listen to me very carefully—and I want you to pray like you've never prayed before. Do you understand?"

Toni was puzzled. She detected a hint of excitement in his voice, but it was tainted with sadness or fear or . . . something. And he wanted her to pray. What was this sudden obsession with praying that seemed to have gripped him? "Yes, I guess so. But what—?"

"I think I'm on to something. It's so farfetched that I don't want to say anything to anyone else until I've checked it out, but I'd feel a lot better if I knew that someone was covering me . . . with prayer, I mean, and you're the only one I know to call for that."

This man who had so captured her heart was becoming more complex by the day. "Abe, what are you talking about? Yes, I'll pray for you, but what's going on? Have you found out something about Melissa? Is that it? If it is, you've got to tell me."

"I can't. At least not now, but I will just as soon as I've found out for sure myself."

She looked at the newly installed caller I.D. on her phone. It read "Unavailable." "Abe, where are you calling from?"

"I'm at home. I was in the office earlier but got to thinking about some things and decided to come home for a while and see if I could make some sense out of my hunch, and I think I just may have done it. As soon as I can make a couple of quick phone calls, I'm leaving, but I'll call you as soon as I know anything, I promise."

"This has something to do with Melissa, doesn't it? I want to come with you."

"No way. I need you to stay right where you are and pray. Let me handle the rest of it."

"But I—"

He hung up before she could say another word. For the first time in two days she felt hopeful. Her exhaustion was forgotten as a surge of adrenaline urged her out of bed. Impulsively she slid her shoes on and grabbed a purse, then hurried from her room, almost colliding with April as she dashed down the hall.

"My dear, what—?"

"I've got to go," she announced, heading for the front door. "I'll call you as soon as I can." Halfway out the door she stopped and turned back. "Pray, April. I don't even know what to ask you to pray for. Just pray."

Jumping into her car, she backed out of the driveway and steered toward Abe's apartment. She had never been there before, but she knew where it was and that it wouldn't take long to get there. Maybe she could catch him before he left. Surely if he saw how determined she was, he would take her with him.

She drove the short distance in record time, only to find herself perplexed by the seeming maze of separate buildings within the complex. Parking as close as she could to the building she assumed would house his apartment, she hurried to the front to look for number nineteen. It was two doors down. Rushing toward it, she pounded on the front door. She was shocked when it creaked open. She couldn't imagine anyone as careful and well-trained as Abe not closing and locking his door if he weren't there. Maybe he was still inside.

She pushed the door open and called out. "Abe? Abe, it's me, Toni. Are you in here?" There was no answer. She told herself she should leave, but curiosity tugged her inside. Stepping into his living room, she glanced around, calling his name a couple more times just in case. Still no response. She walked toward the hallway, thinking he might be in the bedroom. "Abe?" There were four doors off the hallway—a bathroom, two bedrooms, and a closet. She knocked on each door and checked them all. Finally she returned to the living room, telling herself she had no business snooping through his apartment and that she should have stayed home and prayed as he asked her to. Before heading back to the front door, she noticed a couple of books lying on a table next to the recliner. Picking them up to see what they were, she sat down in the recliner, stunned. The older, larger book appeared to be a copy of the Old Testament, although in a slightly different order than she was used to. The other one was a New Testament, filled with underlined verses and comments written in the margins. A small notebook, full of questions and observations, sat on the table next to them.

Could these be Abe's, she wondered. *Could these books and notes explain his sudden interest in praying?* Ignoring her guilt feelings over invading his privacy, she began to read through the notes. It appeared he had been on quite a spiritual journey, a search for answers that, if the notes told the true story, had ended in the greatest discovery anyone can ever make. On the final couple of pages she read a note that brought tears of joy to her eyes.

Wednesday morning, September 1. This is it! This is the truth I've been looking for. Jesus, the way, the truth, the life. The perfect sacrifice. Now I understand. Thank you, God!

"Oh yes, thank you, God," she said aloud. "Thank you for leading him to your Son."

As she wiped the tears from her eyes and prepared to go back home and pray as Abe had asked her to do, some additional notes caught her eye, notes written after the Wednesday morning entry she had just read.

Where is she, God? What's the connection here? What am I missing? Baby-selling ring. 1988-1999, at least. Must be bigger than I ever imagined. Who's the key guy? Sol took care of all the legal connections for me, so I don't even know who the lawyer was, but there had to be one, probably local. And a doctor, no doubt. Who else, God? Who?

The final entry, written just below the preceding note, consisted of just three words, written in capital letters and underlined several times: *SOL! EAGLE LAKE.*

What exactly the notation meant, Toni had no idea, but she was sure it had to do with the hunch he was following up on today. If Abe had gone to Eagle Lake to look for his uncle or for Melissa or for any other reason, then she would go too.

As she headed out the front door, being careful to close it behind her, she realized how quickly Abe must have run out of the house, probably just minutes before she had arrived. How would she ever find him? It was a big lake, full of forest service roads, side trails, campgrounds, and cabins. He could be anywhere.

Help me, Father, she prayed as she climbed into her car. *I have no idea where to go. But you know, Lord. You know where he is, and you know where Melissa is. Oh, Father, keep her safe, and please lead me to Abe. We've got to find her quickly, before it's too late. . . .*

Pulling out into the street, she headed for the northbound freeway, praying as she drove, sensing in her heart that God was directing her. It wasn't until she was approaching the entrance to Eagle Lake that she knew exactly where to find Abe.

CHAPTER 17

It had been almost two hours, a long wait in the cover of the surrounding trees, but Abe didn't dare allow his impatience to push him into doing something foolish. If his hunch was correct, and with a Ford Explorer and a Buick sedan parked in front of his uncle's old fishing cabin, this would not be a good time for him to march up to the front door and knock. He only prayed that the vehicles parked out front belonged to some of Sol's fishing buddies and that they were all there for a perfectly legitimate and innocent reason. As badly as he wanted to find and rescue Melissa, he didn't want it to be here.

He glanced at his watch. It was almost four, and his stomach was beginning to rumble. He wished he'd had lunch before he left, or at least thought to bring along something to eat and a thermos of coffee. He had left so quickly that, apart from his nine-millimeter and his cellular phone, he had come empty-handed. He was glad that, despite the cloudless sky, the temperature was fairly cool. Resigned to a long wait, he was about to settle down on the soft dirt around the towering pine that served as his cover when he thought he heard a sound in the trees behind him. Crouching down with his gun in his hand, he turned toward the sound, waited—and listened.

"Abe?"

The voice was nothing more than a whisper in the breeze. He wasn't even sure he had heard it.

"Abe, where are you?"

The voice was slightly louder this time and definitely more familiar. Keeping his own voice low, he answered. "Toni, is that you?"

"Yes. Where are you?"

"Stay still. Don't move. I'll come to you."

Walking carefully, noiselessly, in the direction of her voice, he found her less than fifty feet from where he had been standing. He could hardly believe his eyes.

"What in the world—"

"I told you. I wanted to come with you."

"And I told you to stay home and pray. How in the world did you find me?"

"My dad was a private detective, remember? He trained me well."

Abe stifled a smile. He admired her determination—or *chutzpah,* as Aunt Sophie would call it—but was less than thrilled to have her show up unannounced to complicate the situation. He shook his head. "You're really something, you know that? You just might make a detective yet."

She smiled. "I know. Can I stay?"

"Would you leave if I asked you to?"

"No."

He hesitated. "Come on. Let's get back over here where I can keep my eye on the cabin but where they can't see us. Just keep quiet and do what I tell you. Got it?"

"Yes, sir."

Abe studied her face. "Are you trying to be funny?"

"No, sir." This time he saw the corners of her mouth twitch. He shook his head again and took her by the hand. "Come on, Miss Private Eye. You can tell me your story while we wait."

Back in the shelter of the huge pine, Abe resumed his watch while Toni explained how she had ended up at his side. When she got to the part about letting herself into his apartment, he was shocked and more than a little disgusted with himself for being so careless as to have left his door unlocked. When she got to the part about finding his notebook next to his *Tanakh* and New Testament, she really had his attention.

"I know I shouldn't have read it," she said, "but I remembered what you said about privacy not being the issue right now, and that Melissa's safety was the most important thing. When I saw your note about your uncle and Eagle Lake, I decided you must have come up here to look for him, or Melissa . . . or something. Anyway, I jumped in my car and headed up here without a clue as to how I was going to find you—until I came to the entrance to the lake, that is. Then I remembered that day when you brought me up here and you told me how your uncle used to bring you here to his cabin to go fishing. You even showed me where it was, remember? I have to admit though, it took me a while to find it again. This place is really hidden."

So that was it, but how had she known to leave her car behind and walk in? Surely she hadn't seen his Honda—he had left it well-camouflaged. The idea that her Taurus might be parked in plain sight somewhere made him nervous. Before he could ask her about it, she answered.

"Don't worry. I knew I shouldn't come driving up to the cabin and announce my arrival. Private detective training 101. I parked it behind some trees in a nearby picnic area and walked the rest of the way. The hard part was figuring out where you were. I didn't know if you were inside or . . ." She paused, her blue eyes searching his. "Abe, what do you expect to find in there? What's going on in that cabin?"

"I wish I knew," he said, trying not to get swept away with his emotions. He had to keep focused on his reason for being here, and there was nothing that distracted him more easily than gazing into the depths of Toni's eyes. "Those two vehicles out front tell me there are several people in there—assuming they're not out on the lake fishing somewhere—but I have no idea who they are. It's probably nothing more than that, an innocent fishing trip, but . . ."

"But you think Melissa might be in there, don't you?"

He hesitated. "I think it's possible."

"Abe, we've got to get her out."

"First we have to make sure she's there. If she is, then I've got to call for backup."

"Just how do we find out?"

"We wait. Somebody has to go in or come out of there sooner or later."

Toni's eyes were still holding his, and he had to fight the impulse to take her in his arms. What was she thinking? What was she feeling? Even in the midst of her concern for her sister's welfare, was she wrestling with the same impulses? If she knew what he had come to suspect about his Uncle Sol—and why he suspected it—would she ever want to be in his arms again? As much as he wanted to believe that the faith they now shared, as well as the forgiveness each of them had received from God, would enable her to forgive him and to give their relationship a chance, he seriously doubted it. Maybe there were some things that were so bad only God could forgive them.

"I know there's more to all this than you're telling me," she said finally, "and I won't push you to tell me now. But when it's all over, I want to know . . . everything."

He swallowed, then nodded. "All right. I owe you that." He turned away, momentarily too ashamed to look at her. As he did, the cabin door opened and a woman stepped out. She looked familiar, but he couldn't place her. Then, as Toni peered around him, she gasped.

"Lorraine Murdock," she whispered. "My dad's secretary."

Of course. That's where he had seen her before. "Didn't you say she quit just before he died?" he asked, his voice barely audible as the woman climbed into the driver's seat of the Buick.

"Yes, and with very little explanation. Something about moving away unexpectedly with her boyfriend, Carl something-or-other. I can't remember his last name, only that he was quite attractive and . . . I don't know, smooth, I guess . . . in a slimy sort of way, if you know what I mean. I never could understand what she saw in him."

"Hmm. How well did you know her?"

"Not well at all. She only worked for Dad for a few months, after Claire took an early retirement to take care of her grandchildren full-time. Claire had been with Dad since soon after Mom died, but Lorraine . . . Come to think of it, it was Dr. Jensen who recommended her to my dad. He said she was fairly new in town, one of his patients, and that she'd mentioned she needed a job and had secretarial experience."

Abe raised his eyebrows. "Bruce Jensen recommended her to your father? That's interesting."

Toni looked puzzled. "Why? What does Bruce have to do with . . .?" Her eyes opened wide. "Oh, Abe, you don't think . . ."

Abe looked back toward the cabin as the Buick pulled away. He remembered thinking that at least one doctor had to be in on this baby-selling business and wondering who it might be. "I don't know exactly, but things sure are starting to fall into place here, especially when you consider the doctor's involvement in your dad's autopsy and his original reaction to your request for one."

Toni clutched his arm, and once again he was fighting his impulses. "Abe, surely someone like Dr. Jensen, someone who's known us most of our lives, wouldn't . . ."

"I pray not," Abe answered, steeling himself against his own mixed emotions as he kept his eyes trained on the cabin door. He had to stay clearheaded. Now that Lorraine had left, it was possible that someone else could surface at any moment, and he needed to be ready to make split-second decisions. "Just like I pray my uncle isn't part of this. But no matter who's involved, Toni, if Melissa's in there, we're going to get her out."

Her hand still on his arm, Toni was quiet for a moment, then said, "Abe, I read something else in your notebook. I . . . read what you wrote about Jesus, about his being the perfect sacrifice, the only way to God. . . ."

Abe's resolve melted, and he turned to her, his voice soft. "You know then. You know that I prayed and asked God to forgive me for my sins because of . . . what Jesus did, because of his blood sacrifice, because I came to believe that he is Israel's Messiah, and . . . the Messiah of the Gentiles."

She nodded, her eyes filling with tears. "Yes. I know." Gently, she reached up and laid her hand against his cheek. "And I'm so glad. I . . ."

He kissed her then, gently, tenderly, without thinking or reasoning, and she returned the kiss in such a way that all else faded from his mind. Could it be? Was there still a chance for them even after what he had done years earlier, and which, undoubtedly, was about to come to light? He longed to believe it, longed to—

He heard men's voices coming from the direction of the cabin, and he released her, turning toward the sound. There, walking down the steps toward the Explorer were three men. Abe's heart sank as he recognized each one. As he had suspected, Bruce Jensen was one of them, as was Frank Madson, a longtime River View attorney. The third man, his dark wavy hair streaked with gray, was Sol—Solomon Jacob Levitz, his very own uncle whom he had loved and admired since he was a little boy. *Oh, please, God,* he prayed silently. *Please let there be some other explanation for all this. Three old friends on a fishing trip, or . . .* But what was Lorraine Murdock doing there? Wasn't she supposed to have left town with her boyfriend, Carl? If these men were here on a fishing trip, why would she . . . ?

Wait a minute. Carl . . . Carlo. What had Toni said about Lorraine's boyfriend? He was attractive and smooth in a slimy sort of way.

Suddenly Abe had a hunch that Carl and Carlo were one and the same. The description would fit a guy like that perfectly, and Carlo would be just the kind of name that would entice a naïve young girl.

"She's in there," he said. "I know it now."

"How do you know? Who were those other two men with Dr. Jensen? Did you recognize them?"

The men climbed into the Explorer, with Frank Madson in the driver's seat, and drove away as Abe turned back toward Toni. How foolish he had been to think, even for a moment, that she would be able to forgive his part in all this. Even if Melissa was still alive, and even if he could get her out of there safely, it would never make up for what Toni and her sister had been through.

"I'm so sorry," he whispered. "I am so sorry, Toni."

"What do you mean?" Her eyes were searching his again. "Abe, I don't understand."

"I'll . . . explain it all to you . . . afterward. I promise. First, I've got to take advantage of the situation. I'm going to take a look in there while they're gone and see if I can see anything."

He turned to go, but she grabbed his arm. "Abe, tell me. Who were those other two men?"

Abe's jaw twitched. "One was Frank Madson, an attorney. The other was . . . my uncle."

Her eyes grew wide. "Abe, what do you think that means? Is Melissa . . . ?"

"I'm going to find out. You wait here . . . and don't move. Do you understand?"

She nodded. "Be careful. I'll be praying."

His jaw twitched again, and he was gone.

~~~

Melissa lay very still in the darkness, wondering how long it would be until Raymond came in to take her to the drop-off point she had heard them discussing before the others left. Apparently Lorraine had made the necessary arrangements earlier in the day and then returned to tell them about it. It seemed Melissa was to be flown out of the country on a private jet early the next morning. She never did hear them mention her final destination, only that it was somewhere in the Middle East and that she had "brought a good price." For a long time afterward, Melissa had listened to them discussing their own future plans, amazed at how they could so easily go on with their lives knowing that she was being sent away to live—and possibly die—in some foreign land where she knew no one and had no chance of ever escaping and returning home. She had heard Bruce Jensen ask Lorraine when she planned to return to Seattle, and Melissa had judged by the doctor's response to her answer that it must be right away. The others seemed to indicate that they planned to stay right where they were, confident that Abe had held off the law long enough for them to cover their tracks and return to their respectable lifestyles, and that he would continue to keep his mouth shut in order to protect himself.

What amazed Melissa most of all, though, was that such an operation could be going on right in the middle of River View, a relatively small, uneventful town where she had always felt safe, and where, she imagined, most of its residents felt the same way. Still, here were several apparently prominent and respected citizens of that very town involved in what she had deduced to be an extremely profitable baby-selling scheme, one that had been going on for several years and extended to countries all over the world. Somehow, because of her father's involvement with Julie Greene, who had voluntarily but ignorantly become a part of this enterprise, Melissa had landed right in the middle of the whole mess. Now she was going to pay a huge price, possibly even greater than Julie's.

In between crying and praying, Melissa thought a lot about Julie Greene. Julie hadn't been much older than she, and yet she had allowed Carlo to get her pregnant. Had she realized that her baby, once born, would be taken from her and sold to the highest bidder?

Or had she naively believed that Carlo would someday marry her and they would all be a happy little family? What must she have thought when she began to hemorrhage and realized she was going to lose the baby? Did she beg Carlo to get her some medical help? Had he refused? Or had he waited until she was too weak to resist and then pretended to be taking her for help, only to take her instead out to the middle of the lake, drop her over the side, and watch her drown? How terrified and betrayed Julie must have felt in the last few moments of her life. If April knew the details of her grand-daughter's death, it would be even harder on her than it already was. Melissa prayed she would never find out. What about Toni? What would happen to her once she was faced with the fact that her sister might never come home again? Poor Toni. First Mom, then Dad, and now . . .

Still bound by a blindfold and ropes, she rolled to her stomach, buried her face in the pillow, and sobbed. Where was God? Why didn't he help her? Why didn't he send someone to rescue her?

Abe had made his way around to the right side of the cabin. He remembered a big window on that side, one that would give him a full view of the main room and the small kitchen area. There was no window in the back room, and only a tiny one in the bathroom. This window offered him his best chance of finding out who, if anyone, was still in the cabin.

Standing beside the window, he leaned over just enough to get a look inside. It appeared that there was only one occupant, sitting in an old armchair with his back toward the window. Abe couldn't see the man's face, only his arms hanging down at the sides of the chair and his feet spread out in front of him, as if he were asleep. Abe certainly hoped he was because it meant he might be able to catch the guy by surprise. There was no way to ascertain if anyone else was inside, and he still wasn't absolutely positive that Melissa was there, but he felt he had no choice but to try to find out before any of the others returned. In the meantime, he wasn't going to take any chances. It was time to call for assistance, just in case.

Soundlessly making his way to the back of the cabin, he pulled his tiny cellular phone from his pocket and made the call, then crept back toward the front door, stopping along the way to peer in the window once more to be sure the man was still in his chair. As he silently stepped up to the front door, he hesitated, wondering if he should wait for the deputies, but he realized it would take too long. With the others gone and the cabin's only occupant—other than Melissa, if his guess was right—asleep, this was as good a time as any to attempt a rescue. Gun drawn, he breathed a silent prayer, grabbed the doorknob, and threw the door open. In a split second he had his gun pointed straight at the startled man in the chair. As Abe's brain registered recognition, the final puzzle piece fell into place.

"Raymond Johnson," he said. "Well, now I'm beginning to get the full picture. A doctor, a lawyer, an ex-cop, and the county medical examiner. You guys really had all your bases covered, didn't you?"

"Abe, listen—"

"Don't move, Ray, not until I tell you. First, drop your gun on the floor in front of you, then kick it, nice and easy, to the side. Good. Now I want you to move real slow, do you understand?"

The slightly overweight man with the full head of gray hair nodded. "Sure, I understand. No problem. Abe, think about what you're doing. You haul us in, your past is tomorrow's headlines."

"That's just something I'll have to live with, won't I? Now, I want you to get up very slowly and carefully and walk over to the door to the next room. Move it."

Raymond did as he was told.

"Now open it and step inside."

As the door opened and Raymond stepped into the other room, Abe caught sight of Melissa on the cot. His heart lurched at the pathetic, terrified girl, trussed and blindfolded and trembling with fear. "Untie her," he ordered. "Now! The blindfold too."

Raymond removed Melissa's ropes and blindfold, and she stared at Abe, blinking her eyes to adjust to the light, her expression a mixture of relief and apprehension.

"Abe?" Her voice sounded as tiny and helpless as she looked. "Is it really you? Did you come to . . . help me?" She was crying now as she rubbed her wrists and ankles.

"Of course I came to help you, sweetheart. You're going to be OK now. Do you understand? I'm going to get you out of here. I'm going to take you home."

"Are you sure?" Her crying had turned to whimpering. "You're not one of them, are you? You're not just here to take me to the plane so they'll keep quiet about your past?"

Abe winced. So she knew. If she had hated him before, what must she think of him now? He thought of the kiss he had shared with Toni just moments earlier and realized it would probably be their last. She would never forgive him for his part in this. It was just too much to ask.

"I'm not one of them, Melissa. I promise. You're going to have to trust me. I didn't bring my handcuffs, so I need you to help me use those ropes to tie up Raymond so we can get out of here."

Her eyes grew big, and she recoiled as she looked at her former captor. "I can't. I can't touch him. He's a . . . a murderer. He killed Carlo, right here in this room."

Raymond spoke up then. "I saved you from him, kid. He was going to rape you, you know that."

"You killed him because of what he did to Julie and because he took me without telling you. You weren't trying to help me. You and the others were going to sell me—I heard you planning it."

Dear God, thought Abe, *what has this poor girl been through?* "OK, Melissa. If you can't do it, that's all right. Listen to me very carefully, and don't move until I tell you. Toni is outside behind some trees, not

far from here. If you go to the front door and call her, she'll hear you
and come. Can you do that?"

Melissa had stopped whimpering, and her eyes had grown very
large. "Toni's outside? She's right outside the cabin, waiting for me?"

Abe nodded. "Yes. Now go on to the front door and call her."

As Melissa hobbled toward the door, she froze. The sounds of a
vehicle pulling up in front of the cabin sent a chill down Abe's spine.
He knew it was still too early for the sheriff to arrive. If the Ford
Explorer had returned, he and Melissa were in very serious trouble.

CHAPTER 18

With her heart in her throat, Toni had stayed hidden behind the tree, watching Abe's every movement. When he had finally burst into the cabin, she'd had to remind herself of her promise to stay put and pray. There was no longer any doubt in her mind that her little sister was being held captive inside. Her every impulse screamed to go in after Abe, to find Melissa and get her out quickly. She had restrained herself though—until the Explorer returned. She didn't have to be able to see what was going on inside the cabin to know that this was not a good development—for Melissa or for Abe.

She watched the three men get out and walk to the cabin. *Dear Lord, what now? I can't just stay here and hide. I have to do something.* Once they were inside, she took a deep breath, gathered her courage, and began to move as quickly and quietly as she could, from tree to tree toward the cabin. When the trees stopped just a few feet from the front door, she tried to ignore the pounding of her heart as she stealthily made her way across the final distance. As she approached, she could hear their voices.

"Give it up, Abe. Just drop the gun, and you and the girl will be OK. You know you can't take us all before one of us gets you."

"Listen to him, boy. Don't be *meshugga* . . . please."

Toni hadn't recognized the two voices, but she was sure the second must have been Abe's uncle. How awful this must be for Abe, finding out that his own flesh and blood was part of such a horrible crime as kidnapping and who knew what else. She didn't dare let them see her, but she knew she had to do something to distract them and at least give Abe a chance to make a move. Spotting a good-sized rock on the ground beside her, she picked it up and tossed it a few feet, plastering herself up against the outside cabin wall as the rock landed with a loud thud.

"Hey, what was that? Somebody else must be out there." The voice belonged to the man Toni assumed was Abe's Uncle Sol. In a matter of seconds, he cautiously poked his head out the door, but before he could step outside to take a closer look, Toni heard some scuffling noises coming from inside, followed by a scream. As Sol turned back, Toni followed him. She knew the scream had come from Melissa, and nothing was going to keep her out of the cabin now. As she stepped inside behind Sol, she saw her sister huddled on the floor with Abe crouching over her protectively, his gun aimed at the four men. In that split second, as she stepped into the cabin and sized up the scene in front of her, Abe turned his head toward her, and a man Toni didn't recognize, apparently the one who had remained in the cabin when the others left, snatched a gun from the floor. He fired a soundless shot at Abe at the same instant that Sol dove for the man, putting himself in the direct line of fire. As Sol fell to the floor, other gunshots followed, and Toni threw herself down and prayed that God would cover and protect them.

In a matter of seconds, Toni heard the sound of men moaning mixed with the sobs of her hysterical sister. Daring to raise her head, she saw that Abe still crouched next to Melissa, gun in hand, although he was holding his right shoulder and blood was seeping through his fingers. All the others, except Bruce Jensen, lay wounded on the floor. Bruce stood, ashen faced, in their midst.

Springing to her feet, Toni ran to Melissa. She glanced briefly at Abe, who nodded to her that he was all right, so she reached down and grabbed the sobbing teenager. When the girl finally realized who it was that was trying to lift her from the floor, she sat up and fell into her arms, weeping uncontrollably. Toni rocked her gently, stroking her hair. "It's OK. It's going to be OK, honey, I promise. I'm here now. Shhh. We're going to go home soon. It's OK."

Finally, looking over at Abe, she asked quietly, "Are you all right?"

"I'm fine, but . . . I need to call for an ambulance and . . . check on my uncle. Can you keep an eye on the doctor? He doesn't look like he's going anywhere—none of these guys do—but I don't want to take any chances."

Silently she nodded, taking his gun and repositioning herself so she could watch her father's longtime friend and their family physician, who stared at her blankly, even as she cradled Melissa in her lap. Abe used his cellular phone to call for an ambulance, then went to his uncle, who seemed unable to move. The other two men moaned as they lay on the floor but didn't appear to be as seriously injured as Sol.

"Uncle Sol, can you hear me?" Abe, still clutching his right shoulder, was gently resting his right hand against his uncle's face. Sol's eyes were closed.

"I . . . hear . . . you," Sol answered, his words coming in gasps.

"You've got to hang on. Please. Help will be here soon."

"I . . . couldn't . . . let them . . . kill you."

"I know. You saved my life." Abe was crying now. "Don't leave me, Uncle Sol. Come on, you can make it."

Sol didn't answer, and his breath was becoming more ragged. Abe looked up frantically. "Jensen," he shouted. "Get over here and help me. He's dying."

Bruce Jensen slowly turned toward Abe's voice, dazed but unresponsive.

"I said, get over here," Abe ordered. "We need your help. Can't you hear me?"

Sol's eyes fluttered open. "It's . . . too late . . . *meshugga*. Too late. You . . . take care . . . of yourself. I . . . can't . . . do it . . . anymore. . . ."

His voice trailed off, and his breathing stopped. Toni's heart convulsed as she felt herself torn between staying with Melissa and going to Abe. As a sheriff's car pulled up in front of the cabin, she watched Abe lean over his uncle and sob on his lifeless chest. Her own tears streamed down her face and dropped onto Melissa's hair as the terrified, exhausted young girl cried as if she would never stop.

"I still can't believe I'm home," said Melissa, smiling across the table at April and Toni as they ate their late Saturday morning breakfast. "Even after sleeping in my own bed for two nights, I still think I'm going to wake up in that awful cabin."

"Well, you're not," Toni assured her, reaching out to pat her hand. "You're home, safe and sound, where you belong."

"And thank God for it," added April. "He definitely protected you."

"That's for sure," Melissa agreed. "If Abe hadn't gotten there when he did . . ." She shuddered as the memories threatened to overtake her once again. "I don't even want to think about it."

"Then don't," said Toni as she refilled Melissa's juice glass. "Just concentrate on getting your strength back. Tuesday will be here before you know it, and then it's back to school for you."

Melissa nodded excitedly. "I'm looking forward to it, but I'm going to miss baby-sitting for Tyler. I feel so bad that I wasn't there for our last week together."

April set down her coffee cup. "I've been meaning to ask, what did Mrs. Johnson do about that?"

"I talked to Tyler yesterday evening," Melissa answered. "His grandma was going to start baby-sitting when school opens up next week anyway, so she just started a few days early."

"And how is Tyler?" asked Toni.

"He's fine. He was so excited when I called. He said he was praying for me, and he knew I'd come back home soon. He . . . also said he was still praying for his dad to come back in time for his birthday in two weeks. I really didn't know what to say to him about that. If his dad's not there, it could ruin his whole birthday."

"Well then, my dear," said April, "we shall just have to join him in praying for his father to come, won't we?"

Melissa hesitated. She didn't want to sound as if she didn't trust God, especially after what he had done for her, but this was different. "I guess so. But . . . what if he doesn't come?"

"It isn't our responsibility to get him there," April explained. "It's just our responsibility to pray." She smiled. "I think we can leave the rest to God. He's bigger than we are and much wiser. He'll know how to work things out so Tyler's faith isn't damaged, regardless of the circumstances."

Melissa dropped her eyes for a moment. Would it be disrespectful or inconsiderate to ask April how she could still pray even after what had happened to Julie? She looked back up. "I thought about that while I was . . . while I was gone. About how you prayed for Julie, I mean—to come home safe, just like you prayed for me. But . . . she didn't, and you still have faith in God. I'm not sure I understand."

April smiled. "It's taken me a lot of years to learn that my faith in God doesn't depend on what he does for me, but rather on who he is. I have come to understand that he is always faithful, he is always right, and he is always in control, no matter what happens. I have walked with him now for almost sixty years, my dear, and he has never once deserted me, even though I often wondered where he was and what he was doing. Give yourself a little time to walk with him as I have, and then you'll also begin to understand."

Melissa nodded, returning April's smile. She so appreciated her wisdom and advice. She would certainly miss her when she returned to Colorado. Before she could ask her when that might be, the doorbell rang.

"I'll get it," she announced, bounding out of her chair and heading for the front door. She pulled it open and grinned. "Abe. I thought it might be you. Toni said you called this morning and that you might come over."

Abe, his right arm in a sling, smiled as he walked in the door. "Oh, she did, did she? Well, I'm glad she warned you. I think I scared you the last time I showed up unannounced."

Melissa laughed. "Are you kidding? Only for a minute, when I wasn't too sure why you'd showed up, but once I realized that you came to get me out of there, I was never so glad to see anyone in my whole life."

Abe gave her shoulders a quick squeeze with his free arm and kissed the top of her head. "Believe me, I felt exactly the same way when I saw you."

"Come on," said Melissa, taking his left hand in hers and leading him into the kitchen. "You're just in time for breakfast."

"Breakfast? At eleven o'clock? I was hoping for something more along the lines of lunch."

"Lunch will just have to wait," said Toni, smiling up at him as he joined them. "We all slept in this morning. Have a seat. Would you like some coffee?"

Abe raised his eyebrows. "You made coffee? I thought you never touched the stuff."

"She doesn't," said April, "but I do, and I made it."

"Then I'll take some." Abe sat down next to Melissa while Toni filled a cup for him. "I never trust coffee made by someone who doesn't drink it."

"Toni used to make it for Dad," said Melissa. "I tasted it once. Trust me, it was terrible."

"Thanks a lot, little sister."

"No problem. By the way, Abe, how's your arm?"

"It's OK. Just babying it for a while, you understand." He cut his eyes toward Toni, then back to Melissa. "Thought I'd get all the mileage out of it that I could."

"Don't count on getting any sympathy from me," Toni said. "You look entirely too healthy to qualify for that sort of thing."

"Thanks. You look pretty great yourself."

Toni flushed, and Melissa grinned. Only a few days earlier she would have been furious over such an interchange between the two. Today she watched them and knew it was right. Even though Toni and Brad had always been able to joke around together, something had been missing. Whatever that something was, it was definitely there between Toni and Abe. She was glad for them.

It was apparent that Abe had noticed the pink tinge of Toni's cheeks, but he graciously declined comment and changed the subject. "Well, believe it or not, I already have some updates for anyone who's interested." Melissa could tell that included all of them, as they each sat up, alert and receptive, all eyes focused on Abe. "It looks as if it's going to be a long, drawn-out investigation, especially since we're discovering that this baby-selling ring extends far beyond the Northwest into several other countries, just like you said, Melissa. They may even have dabbled in the slave trade. The authorities have picked up Lorraine, and she and Bruce Jensen can't seem to talk fast enough. They're hoping for the possibility of a lighter sentence, I suppose. They spent all day yesterday filling in the blanks for us, giving us information that could have taken weeks, or even months, to track down. Even though the investigation will take quite a while, it would have been worse without their cooperation. I can't remember when we've been able to get so much information in such a short time—and with so little effort on our part."

Toni shook her head. "It's still so hard for me to believe that Lorraine was involved in something like this. Even though she only worked for Dad for a short time, I never would have thought she could do anything so awful."

Melissa felt her recently restored confidence beginning to dissolve as the memories came flooding back. "She was . . . right there, in the room, when Raymond killed Carlo. Or Carl . . . whatever his name was."

Abe squeezed her hand. "It's OK," he said softly. "It's over now."

She nodded, smiling up at him gratefully. "Thanks to you."

"Hey, I couldn't have done it without your sister's help, you know."

"That's right," Toni agreed. "And don't you forget it, Detective Matthews. Maybe the next time I offer my assistance you won't run off without me and force me to track you down like the good private detective's daughter that I am."

Abe looked across the table at Toni. "You really did show up at the right time . . . 'Detective Matthews.' That rock-throwing ploy of yours distracted them just enough for me to be able to get Melissa down on the floor and, to some degree, out of the line of fire."

"When you threw me on the floor, I screamed because I didn't know what was going on," said Melissa. "Everything was happening so fast. I didn't even see Toni come in."

"That's because I wasn't inside the cabin for more than a couple of seconds before I was on the floor too. I'm glad to know my timing was good because I sure wasn't much help other than that."

"Yes, you were," Melissa insisted. "After the shooting was finally over and you came and lifted me up off the floor, that's when I knew I was going to be OK."

Toni smiled at Melissa's reassurance but seemed to be studying Abe's face. "Are you all right?" she asked softly.

Abe's jaw twitched, and Melissa realized he was thinking of his uncle. This time it was her turn to comfort him. She reached over and took his hand. "You saved my life and . . . your uncle saved yours."

Abe nodded and smiled at her. "Yes, he did. It seems he was always running interference for me, especially since my parents died. This wasn't the first scrape he got me out of." He paused, then fixed his eyes on Toni's. "In fact, I'd like to talk to you about that, if I could. Would this evening be OK? We could grab a bite to eat somewhere and . . . talk. Maybe about six or so?"

Melissa watched their eye contact. It was obvious that the two of them knew more about this particular subject than either she or April.

Toni nodded. "Six would be fine."

"Well," said April, looking at Melissa, "it appears as if it's just the two of us for dinner tonight. Any ideas?"

Melissa grinned. "Pizza?"

"Why did I even ask? All right, pizza it is." She turned toward Abe. "By the way, what about your uncle's girlfriend . . . Rosalie, is it?"

Abe nodded. "Rosalie, yes. It seems she was oblivious to any of his illegal dealings, at least from what we've learned so far, but she sure is clamoring to know about his will. Didn't waste any time asking about that."

"I see," said April.

As they talked and visited, Abe continued to fill them in on some of the details that had emerged over the previous thirty-six hours. It seemed that Lorraine had been involved in the illegal organization in another town, and when Paul Matthews had mentioned to Bruce Jensen that he had been hired by a woman in Colorado to find her missing granddaughter, Bruce had helped Lorraine get the recently vacated secretarial job at Matthews and Matthews so she could monitor Paul's progress. When he got too close to the truth, Bruce knew his friend well enough to know that he would never back off. That's when it was decided that Paul Matthews must be eliminated. Just before Paul was to go on his annual fishing trip to Eagle Lake, Lorraine gave her notice, saying that she planned to marry her boyfriend, Carl, and move out of state. The truth was that she didn't want to be anywhere in the vicinity if anyone started asking questions about her former boss's untimely death.

"That must have been about the time I ran into Lorraine and her so-called fiancé," said Toni. "I had just gotten home from college and had told Dad I would fill in at the office for him until he found someone to replace Lorraine. I was on my way back to work after lunch one day, and I saw Lorraine climbing into the passenger seat of a car parked in front of the office. Apparently she had come to pick up her final paycheck."

"Don't tell me," Melissa interrupted. "It was a red BMW, right?"

Toni nodded. "Yes, it was, and I guess I don't have to tell you who was driving it. Lorraine introduced him—somewhat reluctantly, I might add—as her fiancé, Carl. He didn't have much to say, just enough that his voice sounded vaguely familiar when he started making his threatening phone calls. Then they took off as quickly as they could. Guess they didn't want me getting too close a look at him."

"I'm sure that's true," said Abe. "Then, just before your dad left for his vacation, Bruce Jensen called him and arranged to meet him at the lake to do some fishing. Would anyone like to guess what day and time they were going to meet?"

Toni's face grew pale, and her eyes opened wide. "Wednesday morning at six o'clock?"

"You got it."

"But . . . why would Dad write that down in Julie's file?"

"That's the beauty of it. The best we can tell, he must have had Julie's file open when Bruce called. He jotted down the time and day, then got busy doing something else and forgot where he'd left the information. He called Bruce back later that day to confirm everything and told him he had misplaced the note. So your one piece of evidence, the one and only thing that linked your dad's death to Julie's disappearance and started your obsession with this whole case, was nothing more than an accident." Abe raised his eyebrows and looked around the table, focusing primarily on Melissa. "Or, so it would seem."

Melissa was shocked. "You mean . . . Dad didn't put that note in there on purpose? It had nothing to do with Julie?"

"Nothing at all."

"Then . . ." The realization dawned on her slowly. "Then maybe . . ." She looked from Toni to Abe and finally to April. "Do you think God planned for Toni to find that note?"

April smiled. "I think it's possible. As I told you earlier, walk with him a while, and soon you'll understand a lot more about his ways. What you don't understand, you'll simply accept because you'll have learned that he is faithful."

Although there was still so much Melissa couldn't understand, she was beginning to see a pattern and a purpose in things that had once seemed so meaningless. Still, there was one thing that didn't make any sense at all. She looked at Abe. "If they were planning to . . . murder my dad . . . what did Dr. Jensen's fishing date with Dad have to do with all this? If Dad died of a heart attack . . ."

"He didn't," said Abe, pausing a moment as the others absorbed his words. "Toni was right from the beginning. If anyone other than Raymond Johnson had performed the autopsy, we would have known that long before this, but between him and Bruce Jensen, they were able to keep their little secret."

Toni's face was still pale. "But . . . if Dad didn't die of a heart attack, what happened to him? He was out in the boat fishing, alone, in the middle of the lake. How could anyone possibly have gotten to him and . . . killed him . . . in such a way as to make it look like a heart attack?"

"Dr. Jensen was his physician, right? He was well aware of your father's heart condition. He also knew your father well enough to be familiar with many of his habits, particularly when it came to fishing." He turned to Melissa. "I'll bet you know those habits, too, don't you?"

Melissa nodded, wide-eyed.

"What's the first thing your dad did when he got up in the morning and got ready to go out on the lake to go fishing?"

"He packed some food and fixed a thermos of coffee."

"Exactly, and Bruce knew that. When he got to your dad's cabin, he offered to make the coffee while your dad prepared the food. Being a doctor, he had access to medications, including digoxin, pills that dissolve easily in hot liquid like coffee and can be fatal to someone with a heart condition. Bruce knew he could put enough digoxin in your dad's thermos to kill him, and he also knew your dad wouldn't drink it until he was out on the lake fishing—alone."

This time it was April who spoke up first. "But . . . I thought you said Dr. Jensen was going to go fishing with him."

"That was the supposed plan. Just before the two men left the cabin to go to the lake, however, the doctor's beeper went off—compliments of Lorraine—and he used his cellular phone to make a call, only to learn of an 'emergency' that required his immediate presence at the hospital. Apologizing, he got into his car and drove away, promising to return for the fishing outing the next day. Needless to say, that never happened."

Toni shook her head. "This is all too incredible. Who would ever have thought . . .? Bruce Jensen, our own doctor, Dad's friend. How could he have done something like that?"

Abe sighed. "Survival, I suppose. I don't imagine he took any pleasure in doing it, but he had convinced himself it was necessary to protect the organization and to keep himself out of prison. Funny how he seemingly had no stomach for a gun battle at the cabin, but he had no compunction—or, at least, none he couldn't overcome— over murdering his own friend, so long as he wasn't there to see it."

"What do you mean," Toni asked, "about his having no compunction he couldn't overcome?"

"Do you remember the vehicle Simon said he saw driving up to your dad's cabin before daylight on the day he died, and how it stopped a short distance away?"

"Yes."

"That was Bruce. Apparently he was struggling with guilt at the idea of killing your father, so he stopped to gather his courage before going on up to the cabin and carrying out his plan."

"Bruce Jensen," Melissa mumbled. "Dr. Welby. He killed my dad." She looked at Abe. "It just doesn't make any sense. I heard him tell the others that he couldn't be a part of killing me, but he thought . . . selling me . . . was a good idea."

Abe squeezed her hand again. "The man has some strange principles, that's for sure." He turned and looked at April. "By the way, I did find out something about Julie that I think you might want to know."

April's eyes widened, as did Melissa's. She couldn't imagine that Abe was going to tell April the horrible details of Julie's death.

"The last couple of weeks before Julie died, she had started asking to be allowed to call home, to speak with you and her parents. Carlo refused, of course, but Julie continued to ask him. She also asked Lorraine to help her get him to change his mind. Of course, Lorraine didn't even bother to try, but she told us that Julie was becoming quite an annoyance at the end. She was . . . talking about Jesus, about going to church and getting right with God, and she spent every spare minute praying and repeating Bible verses she said she'd learned as a child."

April's eyes filled with tears, which quickly overflowed onto her cheeks. "She was praying and reciting Bible verses?"

Abe nodded, and Toni embraced April, as the two of them cried together. Melissa, watching them, thought how much easier it must be now for April to continue trusting the God who had been with her granddaughter, even at the last moment of her life. It was a lesson she vowed never to forget.

~~~

Abe had been tense all day. Even now, seated across from Toni in a booth at a small downtown café with his right arm still in the sling, his stomach felt as if it were in knots. Just how understanding and forgiving was this woman whom he loved so deeply? Before the evening was over, he would know.

They had both opted for a light dinner of soup, salad, and bread, each of them, Abe supposed, for similar reasons. Abe had encouraged Toni to order something more substantial, but she had laughed and reminded him that it was her turn to pay, that she had "owed him" ever since their cinnamon roll binge at the deli way back in June, and that she therefore preferred to keep the dinner tab as low as possible. Abe had laughed, too, even as his stomach churned in anticipation of what was to come. Although Toni couldn't possibly imagine the scope of what he was about to tell her, she had undoubtedly been preparing herself all day to hear it and was therefore as disinterested in eating as he was. So they each toyed with their food, talking about everything but what was really on their minds.

"How is your . . . aunt doing with the news of Sol's death?" Toni asked. "You said the funeral is Tuesday, right?"

Abe nodded. "She's pretty devastated, almost as devastated as she was about my news."

Toni frowned. "Your news?"

"I told her about . . . discovering Israel's Messiah. She was nearly hysterical. Says she'll sit *shivah* for Sol . . . and for me too."

"I'm sorry, Abe. I still don't understand."

"By proclaiming Jesus as Israel's Messiah—accepting him as my Lord and Savior—I have cut myself off from her, and, she claims, from my people. In her eyes, I'm now as dead as Uncle Sol."

Tears pooled in Toni's eyes, and she reached across the table and touched his hand. "I'm so sorry. I hadn't realized . . . how big a price you'd pay."

He smiled, her touch easing the pain in his heart. "There's always a price, isn't there? Consequences for our choices."

Toni nodded. "I suppose there is."

Abe closed his eyes for a moment, breathed a silent prayer, then looked at the woman he loved and began to confess his past. "It was a long time ago. Almost twelve years, just after my parents died. I was in college, and there was this girl. . . . Amanda and I dated for several months, and being with her seemed to help me get my mind off losing my mom and dad. We got . . . too close. Before I knew it, she was pregnant."

He paused, watching Toni closely. There didn't seem to be any visible reaction to his words, so he continued. "When she told me, I panicked. Amanda was Catholic, so abortion was out of the question for her. The last thing in the world I needed right then was a wife and a baby. I couldn't even support myself. At that point I was only in school because Uncle Sol had picked up where my parents left off paying my tuition. So, naturally, I turned to him for advice. He told me he knew of a lawyer who arranged for private adoptions and that this would definitely be the way to go, the best for everyone involved, including the baby. He said the adoptive parents would be financially comfortable and would pay not only the medical and legal costs for the adoption but a hefty sum of cash for Amanda and me, as well. I have to admit, it sounded pretty good. I was able to talk Amanda into it, and . . . well, the rest is history, as they say."

"You . . . gave your baby up for adoption then."

Abe nodded. "Yes, we did. Never even saw him."

"A boy."

Abe nodded again, a lump forming in his throat.

"Do you . . . think about him?"

"Not often. Maybe it's that I haven't allowed myself to. But lately . . . yes, I have thought of him. I've wondered how he is, where he is, if he knows he's adopted, and if so, what he must think of his parents . . . of me. With the adoption laws changing, I've even wondered if he might . . . someday . . . try to find me. Then I wonder . . . would he ever be able to forgive me?"

Toni's eyes were filled with compassion, her voice soft as she spoke. "I believe he will—someday."

Abe looked down at his uneaten soup, trying to gather the courage to go on with his confession. She hadn't yet heard the worst part. He looked up and stared at her intently as he spoke, watching for any tell-tale reactions. "There's more. After the adoption, Amanda and I drifted apart. Eventually she transferred to another college and we lost touch, which was fine with me. I did my best to ignore the guilt feelings I had over what I felt was 'selling' my baby and even allowed myself to become involved in recruiting other pregnant college students to sell their babies. Someone—I never knew until yesterday that it was Bruce Jensen—called me and asked me to do it. He said I would get a small cut on each pregnant girl I brought in who ended up going through with the adoption. Even though Uncle Sol was paying my tuition, I had no extra spending money of my own beyond what I'd gotten from the people who adopted my . . . my son, so I did it."

Still waiting for Toni's face to register shock and revulsion, he saw neither, so he continued. "I did that for a couple of years until I just couldn't stand it any longer. Finally I went to Uncle Sol and told him what I'd been doing. I told him I knew it was wrong, but I'd needed the money. He got mad and told me I should have come to him if I needed anything, but he also said he'd deal with the lawyer involved and let him know I didn't want any part in it anymore. That was the last I heard about any of it until I graduated from college and was getting established in law enforcement. Uncle Sol, who had just taken an early retirement, put in a good word for me and helped me get into the detectives' division, but he warned me that I should never say anything about the adoption business or it might cause trouble for my career. He also assured me that he'd done some checking and the business had folded. At the time, of course, I believed him, never realizing that he'd been involved in it all along, even when I was bringing in the pregnant college girls. I thought his only contact with that sordid business was the one time he helped me and that he was just looking out for my best interests as he always had. That may have been part of it, but I know now that he was also covering his own trail." His voice cracked, and he fought the wave of emotion that swept over him. "That's . . . probably one of the hardest parts of this whole thing. That . . . and how what I did so long ago has affected you and Melissa. Nothing could be worse than that."

His shoulders slumped as he realized there was nothing more to say. Exhausted but relieved at finally having told Toni everything, he waited. Was this the end of their relationship? Would she walk away from him in disgust and never look back? Or could she somehow find it in her heart to forgive him, at least to the point of maintaining a friendship if nothing else? Each second seemed an eternity as he watched and waited . . . and prayed.

Slowly Toni rose from her seat, and Abe's heart sank. She was leaving, walking out on him without a word. Still, he couldn't blame her. After all, what he had done was reprehensible. . . .

Then she was at his side, sitting down next to him on the cushioned bench. Leaning toward him, she kissed his cheek. "I love you," she whispered.

In a daze he turned toward her. Her lashes were rimmed with tears, her blue eyes more beautiful than ever. He tried to speak, but there were no words. He kissed her, then pulled her close with his good arm. "Forgive me," he said.

"I already have," she answered.

And his heart sang.

~~~

It was Saturday, September 18, and Tyler Johnson was now officially seven years old. As Toni and Melissa wrapped presents and waited for Abe to pick them up to take them to the party, they did so with mixed emotions. It had been almost a week since April had gone back to Colorado, but they still missed her. They knew she would return once the first trial started, but that might be a while yet. In the meantime, April, with a twinkle in her eye, had promised to come back "for any special occasions that might arise, such as a wedding. . . ."

Toni smiled as she remembered seeing her off at the airport. "I'm so glad that you and your handsome detective have finally found each other," April had said, kissing Toni's cheek before boarding the plane. "Now that he's been temporarily suspended from the force until his involvement in all this baby-selling mess can be cleared up, I think you two ought to consider keeping your parents' agency open . . . the two of you, together. Another Matthews and Matthews team, just like your parents." She'd smiled when Toni had started to protest. "Now, my dear, don't dismiss it without some consideration. You never know, but God may have purposed this very thing." She kissed her again, then walked toward her plane, turning for one final wave.

April Lippincott, Toni scolded silently, a smile tugging at her lips as she taped a bow to her package, *you really are quite a lady, even if you do tend to poke your nose into other people's business. I just can't imagine what we'll do around here without you.*

The doorbell rang then, and Melissa sprang to her feet and threw open the door to greet Abe before Toni could even get up from the couch. Toni smiled. She knew Melissa still missed Brad and occasionally even sat with him and his parents at church. Brad, too, still seemed at loose ends when he ran into Toni, particularly when Abe was with her—which seemed to be most of the time these days, but both Brad and Melissa appeared to have accepted the fact that Abe and Toni were now an item, most probably a permanent one if things continued to progress as they had been, and Toni was thrilled to see the growing relationship between Abe and Melissa.

Abe, minus his sling, followed Melissa into the living room. Toni stood and greeted him with a kiss as he slipped his arms around her waist and pulled her close. "Ready to party?" she asked.

His dark eyes smiled down at her. "Why not? A guy only turns seven once, you know."

"Are you talking about Tyler or yourself?"

Abe grinned. "Tyler, of course. I hate to be the one to tell you this, but I'm slightly older than seven."

"I know. Thirty-one to be exact. Quite old when you compare it to my youthful twenty-six. But then, I've always thought older men were attractive."

He kissed her again. "I'm glad to hear that because I've always been partial to twenty-six-year-olds."

"All right, you two," Melissa interjected. "Let's not get carried away here. We've got a party to go to, remember? You guys can get mushy later."

"You're right," Abe agreed, releasing Toni even as his eyes still held hers. "Serious things first, mushy stuff later. Are you two party girls ready?"

Toni tore her eyes away and grabbed her present and her purse. "Ready," she assured him. Melissa was already waiting at the door.

By the time they arrived at the Johnson home, several cars lined the street, and the party was in full swing. The weather had held—a perfect Pacific Northwest early autumn day, sunny and clear and golden—so the guests were all in the backyard, children squealing, running, and playing on the swings, adults sitting in the shade, chatting and sipping punch. As the trio stepped out onto the back porch and laid their gifts on the table next to the food, Tyler spotted Melissa and ran straight toward her.

"Lissa! You're here, you came!"

"Of course I came," Melissa laughed, scooping the excited seven-year-old up into her arms. "You didn't think I'd miss your birthday party, did you?"

"Wait till you see what I got," he announced, his dark eyes shining.

"You mean you already opened one of your presents? I thought you were going to wait until everyone arrived."

"I didn't have to open this one," he said. "Look." He pointed to his mother, who was standing next to the punch bowl. At her side stood a man Toni had never seen before. "That's my dad," Tyler announced proudly. "My very best present. He got here yesterday. He says he wants to stay, but Mom says they have a lot of things to work out first. You want to meet him?"

Melissa looked stunned. "That's your dad? He's . . . here?"

"Sure. Don't you remember? We prayed."

Abe slipped his arm around Toni's waist as she fought tears and watched Melissa's expression change from disbelief to excitement. "Yes," Melissa said, putting Tyler down and taking his hand. "I would love to meet your dad." She turned to Toni and Abe and smiled, as if to say, "Are you getting this?" Then she and Tyler walked over to the punch bowl to meet the man who had come in answer to a little boy's prayers.

Toni looked up at Abe. His smile melted her heart, and she was overcome with joy as she realized the depth of God's faithfulness. "I love you, Mr. Matthews," she said.

"I love you too . . . *Miss* Matthews." He kissed her. "And you know, I think April just might be on to something."

"What do you mean?"

"Didn't you tell me she said we'd make a good team—Matthews and Matthews, like your parents?"

"That's true. She did say that."

"Then maybe we should consider all the advantages of that Matthews and Matthews team concept."

"Name one."

"I'll give you two. If you decide to keep the agency open, you wouldn't have to change the listing in the phonebook—it would still be Matthews and Matthews—and if we make this 'partner' thing permanent, you wouldn't even have to change the name on your driver's license. What do you think?"

"I think maybe both of those advantages are worth discussing further."